"FACE IT, ALLISON.
WE'RE NOWHERE IN THE WORLD
WE KNEW."

They argued it back and forth for hours. The day passed, warm and beautiful—and untouched by any sign of other human life. In the end they agreed to hike down to the coast, and then along it till they found some form of humanity.

It was late afternoon when they heard it: a whistling scream that grew abruptly to a roar.

"Aircraft!" Allison struggled to her feet.

Something dark and arrow-shaped swept over them. "An A-five-eleven, by God," exulted Angus. He hugged her.

There were at least three jets. One was the new Sikorsky troop carrier. Only the Marines flew those. They glimpsed it coming to a hover just three hundred meters away.

They started down the narrow path, Allison's gait a limping jog. Suddenly Angus' hand closed on her arm. He pointed through a large gap in the branches, at the hovering Sikorsky. *"Paisley?"* was all he said.

"What?" Then she saw it. The outer third of the wings was covered with an extravagant paisley pattern. In the middle was set a green phi or theta symbol. It was utterly unlike any military insignia she had ever seen.

Other books by Vernor Vinge

VERNOR VINGE
THE PEACE WAR

science fiction
BAEN BOOKS

I am grateful to:
Chuck Glines and Bil Townsend of the US Forest Service
    for talking to me about Los Padres National Forest;
Jim Concannon and Concannon Winery of Livermore,
    California, for their hospitality and a very interesting
    tour of the Concannon Winery;
Lea Braff, Jim Frenkel, Mike Gannis, Sharon Jarvis, and
    Joan D. Vinge for all their help and ideas.

THE PEACE WAR

A Baen Book

Baen Enterprises
8-10 W. 36th Street
New York, N.Y. 10018

First Baen printing, June 1985

ISBN: 0-671-55965-6

Cover art by Tom Kidd

Printed in the United States of America

Distributed by
SIMON & SCHUSTER
MASS MERCHANDISE SALES COMPANY
1230 Avenue of the Americas
New York, N.Y. 10020

To my parents,
Clarence L. Vinge and Ada Grace Vinge,
with Love.

Flashback

One hundred kilometers below and nearly two hundred away, the shore of the Beaufort Sea didn't look much like the common image of the arctic: Summer was far advanced in the Northern Hemisphere, and a pale green spread across the land, shading here and there to the darker tones of grass. Life had a tenacious hold, leaving only an occasional peninsula or mountain range gray and bone.

Captain Allison Parker, USAF, shifted as far as the restraint harness would permit, trying to get the best view she could over the pilot's shoulder. During the greater part of a mission, she had a much better view than any of the "truck-drivers," but she never tired of looking out, and when the view was the hardest to obtain, it became the most desirable. Angus Quiller, the pilot, leaned forward, all his attention on the retrofire readout. Angus was a nice guy, but he didn't waste time looking out. Like many pilots—and some mission specialists—he had accepted his environment without much continuing wonder.

But Allison had always been the type to look out windows. When she was very young, her father had taken her flying. She could never decide what would be the most fun: to look out the windows at the ground—or to learn to fly. Until she was old enough to get her own license, she had settled for looking at the ground. Later, she discovered that without combat aircraft experience she would never pilot the machines that went as high as she wanted to go. So again she had settled for a job that would let her look out the windows. Sometimes she thought the electronics, the geography, the espionage angles of her job were all unimportant compared to the pleasure that came from simply looking down at the world as it really is.

"My compliments to your autopilot, Fred. That burn puts us right down the slot." Angus never gave Fred Torres, the command pilot, any credit. It was always the autopilot or ground control that was responsible for anything good that happened when Fred was in charge. Torres grunted something similarly insulting, then said to Allison, "Hope you're enjoying this. It's not often we fly this thing around the block just for a pretty girl."

Allison grinned but didn't reply. What Fred said was true. Ordinarily a mission was planned several weeks in advance and carried multiple tasks that kept it up for three or four days. But this one had dragged the two-man crew off a weekend leave and stuck them on the end of a flight that was an unscheduled quick look, just fifteen orbits and back to Vandenberg. This was clearly a deep-range, global reconnaissance—though Fred and Angus probably knew little more. Except that the newspapers had been pretty grim the last few weeks.

The Beaufort Sea slid out of sight to the north. The sortie craft was in an inverted, nose-down attitude that gave some specialists a sick stomach but that just made Allison feel she was looking at the world pass by overhead. She hoped that when the Air Force got its permanent recon platform, she would be stationed there.

Fred Torres—or his autopilot, depending on your point of view—slowly pitched the orbiter through 180 degrees to bring it into entry attitude. For an instant the craft was pointing straight down. Glacial scouring could never be an abstraction to someone who had looked down from this height: the land was clearly scraped and grooved, like ground before a dozer blade. Tiny puddles had been left behind: hundreds of Canadian lakes, so many that Allison could follow the sun in specular glints that shifted from one to another.

They pitched still further. The southern horizon, blue and misty, fell into and then out of view. The ground wouldn't be visible again until they were much lower, at altitudes some normal aircraft could attain. Allison sat back and pulled the restraint more tightly over her shoulders. She patted the optical disk pack tied down beside her. It contained her reason for being here. There were going to be a lot of relieved generals—and some even more relieved politicians—when she got back. The "detonations" the Livermore crew had detected must have been glitches. The Soviets were as innocent as those bastards ever were. She had scanned them with all her "normal" equipment, as well as with deep penetration gear known only to certain military intelligence agencies, and had detected no new offensive preparations. Only . . .

. . . Only the deep probes she had made on her own over Livermore were unsettling. She had been looking forward to her date with Paul Hoehler, if only to enjoy the expression on his face when she told him that the results of her test were secret. He had been so sure his bosses were up to something sinister at Livermore. She now saw that Paul may have been right; there was something going on at Livermore. It might have gone undetected without her deep-probe equipment; there had been an obvious effort at concealment. But one thing Allison Parker knew was her high-intensity reactor profiles, and there was a new one down there that didn't show up on the AFIA listings. And she had detected other things—probe-opaque spheres below ground in the vicinity of the reactor.

That was also as Paul Hoehler had predicted.

NMV specialists like Allison Parker had a lot of freedom to make ad lib additions to their snoop schedules; that had saved more than one mission. She would be in no trouble for the unscheduled probe of a US lab, as long as a thorough report was made. But if Paul was right, then this would cause a major scandal. And if Paul was wrong, then *he* would be in major trouble, perhaps on the road to jail.

Allison felt her body settle gently into the acceleration couch as creaking sounds came through the orbiter's frame. Beyond the forward ports, the black of space was beginning to flicker in pale shades of orange and red. The colors grew stronger and the sensation of weight increased. She knew it was still less than half a gee, though after a day in orbit it felt like more. Quiller said something about transferring to laser comm. Allison tried to imagine the land eighty kilometers below, Taiga forest giving way to farm land and then the Canadian Rockies—but it was not as much fun as actually being able to see it.

Still about four hundred seconds till final pitchover. Her mind drifted idly, wondering what ultimately would happen between Paul and herself. She had gone out with better-looking men, but no one smarter. In fact, that was probably part of the problem. Hoehler was clearly in love with her, but she wasn't allowed to talk technical with him, and what nonclassified work he did made no sense to her. Furthermore, he was obviously something of a troublemaker on the job—a paradox considering his almost clumsy diffidence. A physical attraction can only last for a limited time, and Allison wondered how long it would take him to tire of her—or vice versa. This latest thing about Livermore wasn't going to help.

The fire colors faded from the sky, which now had a faint tinge of blue in it. Fred—who claimed he intended to retire to the airlines—spoke up. "Welcome, lady and gentleman, to the beautiful skies of California . . . or maybe it's still Oregon."

The nose pitched down from reentry attitude. The view was much like that from a commercial flyer, if you could ignore the slight curvature of the horizon and the darkness of the sky. California's Great Valley was a green corridor across their path. To the right, faded in the haze, was San Francisco Bay. They would pass about ninety kilometers east of Livermore. The place seemed to be the center of everything on this flight: it had been incorrect reports from their detec-

tor array which convinced the military and the politicians that Sov treachery was in the offing. And that
detector was part of the same project Hoehler was so
suspicious of—for reasons he would not fully reveal.

Allison Parker's world ended with that thought.

1

The Old California Shopping Center was the Santa Ynez Police Company's biggest account—and one of Miguel Rosas' most enjoyable beats. On this beautiful Sunday afternoon, the Center had hundreds of customers, people who had traveled many kilometers along Old 101 to be there. This Sunday was especially busy: all during the week, produce and quality reports had shown that the stores would have best buys. And it wouldn't rain till late. Mike wandered up and down the malls, stopping every now and then to talk or go into a shop and have a closer look at the merchandise. Most people knew how effective the shoplift-detection gear was, and so far he hadn't had any business whatsoever.

Which was okay with Mike. Rosas had been officially employed by the Santa Ynez Police Company for three years. And before that, all the way back to when he and his sisters had arrived in California, he had been associated with the company. Sheriff Wentz had more or less adopted him, and so he had grown up with police work, and was doing the job of a paid undersheriff by the time he was thirteen. Wentz had encouraged him to look at technical jobs, but somehow police work was always the most attractive. The SYP Company was a popular outfit that did business with most of the families around Vandenberg. The pay was good, the area was peaceful, and Mike had the feeling that he was really doing something to help people.

Mike left the shopping area and climbed the grassy hill that management kept nicely shorn and cleaned. From the top he could look across the Center to see all the shops and the brilliantly dyed fabrics that shaded the arcades.

He tweaked up his caller in case they wanted him to come down for some traffic control. Horses and wagons were not permitted beyond the outer parking area. Normally this was a convenience, but there were so many customers this afternoon that the owners might want to relax the rules.

Near the top of the hill, basking in the double sunlight, Paul Naismith sat in front of his chessboard. Every few months, Paul came down to the coast, sometimes to Santa Ynez, sometimes to towns further north. Naismith and Bill Morales would come in early enough to get a good parking spot, Paul would set up his chessboard, and Bill would go off to shop for him. Come evening, the Tinkers would trot out their specialties and he might do some trading. For now the old man slouched behind his chessboard and munched his lunch.

Mike approached the other diffidently. Naismith was not personally forbidding. He was easy to talk to, in fact. But Mike knew him better than most—

and knew the old man's cordiality was a mask for things as strange and deep as his public reputation implied.

"Game, Mike?" Naismith asked.

"Sorry, Mr. Naismith, I'm on duty." *Besides, I know you never lose except on purpose.*

The older man waved impatiently. He glanced over Mike's shoulder at something among the shops, then lurched to his feet. "Ah, I'm not going to snare anyone this afternoon. Might as well go down and window-shop."

Mike recognized the idiom, though there were no "windows" in the shopping center, unless you counted the glass covers on the jewelry and electronics displays. Naismith's generation was still a majority, so even the most archaic slang remained in use. Mike picked up some litter but couldn't find the miscreants responsible. He stowed the trash and caught up with Naismith on the way down to the shops.

The food vendors were doing well, as predicted. Their tables were overflowing with bananas and cacao and other local produce, as well as things from farther away, such as apples. On the right, the game area was still the province of the kids. That would change when evening came. The curtains and canopies were bright and billowing in the light breeze, but it wasn't till dark that the internal illumination of the displays would glow and dance their magic. For now, all was muted, many of the games powered down. Even chess and the other symbiotic games were doing a slow business. It was almost a matter of custom to wait till the evening for the buying and selling of such frivolous equipment.

The only crowd, five or six youngsters, stood around Gerry Tellman's Celest game. What was going on here? A little black kid was playing—had been playing for fifteen minutes, Mike realized. Tellman had Celest running at a high level of realism, and he was not a generous man. Hmmm.

Ahead of him, Naismith creaked toward the game. Apparently his curiosity was pricked, too.

Inside the shop it was shady and cool. Tellman perched on a scuffed wood table and glared at his small customer. The boy looked to be ten or eleven and was clearly an outlander: his hair was bushy, his clothes filthy. His arms were so thin that he must be a victim of disease or poor diet. He was chewing on something that Mike suspected was tobacco— definitely not the sort of behavior you'd see in a local boy.

The kid clutched a wad of Bank of Santa Ynez gAu notes. From the look on Tellman's face, Rosas could guess where they came from.

"Otra vez," the boy said, returning Tellman's glare. The proprietor hesitated, looked around the circle of faces, and noticed the adults.

"Aw right," agreed Tellman, "but this'll have to be the last time ... *Esta es el final, entiende?"* he repeated in pidgin Spanish. "I, uh, I gotta go to lunch." This remark was probably for the benefit of Naismith and Rosas.

The kid shrugged. "Okay."

Tellman initialized the Celest board—to level nine, Rosas noticed. The kid studied the setup with a calculating look. Tellman's display was a flat one, showing a hypothetical solar system as seen from above the plane of rotation. The three planets were small disks of light moving around the primary. Their size gave a clue to mass; the precise values appeared near the bottom of the display. Departure and arrival planets moved in visibly eccentric orbits, the departure planet at one rev every five seconds—fast enough so precession was clearly occurring. Between it and the destination planet moved a third world, also in an eccentric orbit. Rosas grimaced. No doubt the only reason Tellman left the problem coplanar was that he didn't have a holo display for his Celest. Mike had never seen anyone without a symbiotic processor play the departure/destination version of Celest at level nine. The timer on the display showed that the player—the kid—had ten seconds to launch his rocket and try to make it to the destination. From the fuel display, Rosas was certain that there was not enough energy available to make the flight in a direct orbit. A cushion shot on top of everything else!

The kid laid all his bank notes on the table and squinted at the screen. Six seconds left. He grasped the control handles and twitched them. The tiny golden spark that represented his spacecraft fell away from the green disk of the departure world, *inward* toward the yellow sun about which all revolved. He had used more than nine-tenths of his fuel and had boosted in the wrong direction. The children around him murmured their displeasure, and a smirk came over Tellman's face. The smirk froze.

As the spacecraft came near the sun, the kid gave the controls another twitch, a boost which—together with the gravity of the primary—sent the glowing dot far out into the mock solar system. It edged across the two-meter screen, slowing at the greater remove, heading not for the destination planet but for the intermediary. Rosas gave a low, involuntary whistle. He had played Celest, both alone and with a processor. The game was nearly a century old and almost as popular as chess; it made you remember what the human race had almost attained. Yet he had never seen such a two-cushion shot by an unaided player.

Tellman's smile remained but his face was turning a bit gray. The vehicle drew close to the middle planet, catching up to it as it swung slowly about the primary. The kid made barely perceptible adjustments in the trajectory during the closing period. Fuel status on the display showed 0.001 full. The representation of the planet and the spacecraft merged for an instant, but did not record as a collision, for the tiny dot moved quickly away, going for the far reaches of the screen.

Around them, the other children jostled and hooted. They smelled a winner, and old Tellman was going to lose a little of the money he had been winning off them earlier in the day. Rosas and Naismith and Tellman just watched and held their breaths. With virtually no fuel left, it would be a matter of luck whether contact finally occurred.

The reddish disk of the destination planet swam placidly along while the mock spacecraft arced higher and higher, slower and slower, their paths becoming almost tangent. The craft was accelerating now, falling into the gravity well of the destination, giving the tantalizing impression of success that always comes with a close shot. Closer and closer. And the two lights became one on the board.

"Intercept" the display announced, and the stats streamed across the lower part of the screen. Rosas and Naismith looked at each other. The kid had done it.

Tellman was very pale now. He looked at the bills the boy had wagered. "Sorry, kid, but I don't have that much here right now." He started to repeat the excuse in Spanish, but the kid erupted with an unintelligible flood of Spañolnegro abuse. Rosas looked meaningfully at Tellman. He was hired to protect customers as well as proprietors. If Tellman didn't pay off, he could kiss his lease good-bye. The Shopping Center already got enough flak from parents whose children had lost money here. And if the kid were clever enough to press charges . . .?

The proprietor finally spoke over youthful screaming. "Okay, so I'll pay. *Pago, pago* . . . you little son of a bitch." He pulled a handful of gAu notes out of his cash box and shoved them at the boy. "Now *get* out."

The black kid was out the door before anyone else. Rosas eyed his departure thoughtfully. Tellman went on, plaintively, talking as much to himself as anyone else. "I don't know. I just don't know. The little bastard has been in here all morning. I swear he had never seen a game board before. But he watched and watched. Diego Martinez had to explain it to him. He started playing. Had barely enough money. And he just got better and better. I never seen anything like it. . . . In fact—" he brightened and looked at Mike, "in fact, I think I've been set up. I betcha the kid is carrying a processor and just pretending to be young and dumb. Hey, Rosas, how about that? I should be protected. There's some sorta con here, especially on that last game. He—"

"—really did have a snowball's chance, eh, Telly?" Rosas finished where the proprietor had broken off. "Yeah, I know. You had a sure win. The odds should have been a thousand to one—not the even money you gave him. But I know symbiotic processing, and there's no way he could do it without some really expensive equipment." Out of the corner of his eye, he saw Naismith nod agreement. "Still"—he rubbed his jaw and looked out into the brightness beyond the entrance—"I'd like to know more about him."

Naismith followed him out of the tent, while behind them Tellman sputtered. Most of the children were still visible, standing in clumps along the Tinkers' mall.

The mysterious winner was nowhere to be seen. And yet he should have been. The game area opened onto the central lawn which gave a clear view down all the malls. Mike spun around a couple times, puzzled. Naismith caught up with him. "I think the boy has been about two jumps ahead of us since we started watching him, Mike. Notice how he didn't argue when Tellman gave him the boot. Your uniform must have spooked him."

"Yeah. Bet he ran like hell the second he got outside."

"I don't know. I think he's more subtle than that." Naismith put a finger to his lips and motioned Rosas to follow him around the banners that lined the side of the game shop. There was not much need for stealth. The shoppers were noisy, and the loading of furniture onto several carts behind the refurbishers' pavilion was accompanied by shouting and laughter.

The early afternoon breeze off Vandenberg set the colored fabric billowing. Double sunlight left nothing to shadow. Still, they almost tripped over the boy, curled up under the edge of a tarp. The boy exploded like a bent spring, directly into Mike's arms. If Rosas had been of the older generation, there would have been no contest: ingrained respect for children and an unwillingness to damage them would have let the kid slip from his grasp. But the undersheriff was willing to play fairly rough, and for a moment there was a wild mass of swinging arms and legs. Mike saw something gleam in the boy's hand, and then pain ripped through his arm.

Rosas fell to his knees as the boy, still clutching the knife, pulled loose and sprinted away. He was vaguely conscious of red spreading through the tan fabric of his left sleeve. He narrowed his eyes against the pain and drew his service stunner.

"No!" Naismith's shout was a reflex born of having grown up with slug guns and later having lived through the first era in history when life was truly sacred.

The kid went down and lay twitching in the grass. Mike holstered his pistol and struggled to his feet, his right hand clutching at the wound. It looked superficial, but it hurt like hell. "Call Seymour," Mike grated at the old man. "We're going to have to carry that little bastard to the station."

2

The Santa Ynez Police Company was the largest protection service south of San Jose. After all, Santa Ynez was the first town north of Santa Barbara and the Aztlán border. Sheriff Seymour Wentz had three full-time deputies and contracts with eighty percent of the locals. That amounted to almost four thousand customers.

Wentz's office was perched on a good-sized hill overlooking Old 101. From it one could follow the movements of Peace Authority freighters for several kilometers north and south. Right now, no one but Paul Naismith was admiring the view. Miguel Rosas watched gloomily as Seymour spent half an hour on the phone to Santa Barbara, and then even managed to patch through to the ghetto in Pasadena. As Mike expected, no one south of the border could help. The rulers of Aztlán spent their gold trying to prevent "illegal labor emigration" from Los Angeles but never wasted time tracking the people who made it. The

22

sabio in Pasadena seemed initially excited by the description, then froze up and denied any interest in the boy. The only other lead was with a contract labor gang that had passed though Santa Ynez earlier in the week, heading for the cacao farms near Santa Maria. Sy had some success with that. One Larry Faulk, labor contract agent, was persuaded to talk to them. The nattily dressed agent was not happy to see them.

"Certainly, Sheriff, I recognize the runt. Name is Wili Wáchendon." He spelled it out. The "w"s sounded like a hybird of "w" with "v" and "b." Such was the evolution of Spañolnegro. "He missed my crew's departure yesterday, and I can't say that I or anyone else up here is sorry."

"Look, Mr. Faulk. This child has clearly been mistreated by your people." He waved over his shoulder at where the kid—Wili—lay in his cell. Unconscious, he looked even more starved and pathetic than he had in motion.

"Ha!" came Faulk's reply over the fiber. "I notice you have the punk locked up; and I also see your deputy has his arm bandaged." He pointed at Rosas, who stared back almost sullenly. "I'll bet little Wili has been practicing his people-carving hobby. Sheriff, Wili Wáchendon may have had a hard time someplace; I think he's on the run from the Ndelante Ali. But I never roughed him up. You know how labor contractors work. Maybe it was different in the good old days, but now we are agents, we get ten percent, and our crews can dump on us any time they please. At the wages they get, they're always shifting around, bidding for new contracts, squeezing for money. I have to be damn popular and effective or they would get someone else.

"This kid has been worthless from the beginning. He's always looked half-starved; I think he's a sicker. How he got from LA to the border is ..." His next words were drowned out by a freighter whizzing along the highway beneath the station. Mike glanced out the window at the behemoth diesel as it moved off southward carrying liquified natural gas to the Peace Authority Enclave in Los Angeles. " ... took him because he claimed he could run my books. Now, the little bas—the kid may know something about accounting. But he's a lazy thief, too. And I can prove it. If your company hassles me about this when I come back through Santa Ynez, I'll sue you into oblivion."

There were a couple more verbal go-arounds, and then Sheriff Wentz rang off. He turned in his chair. "You know, Mike, I think he's telling the truth. We don't see it so much in the new generation, but children like your Sally and Arta—"

Mike nodded glumly and hoped Sy wouldn't pursue it. His Sally and Arta, his little sisters. Dead years ago. They had been twins, five years younger than he, born when his parents had lived in Phoenix. They had made it to California with him, but they had always been sick. They both died before they were twenty and never looked to be older than ten. Mike knew who had caused that bit of hell. It was something he never spoke of.

"The generation before that had it worse. But back then it was just another sort of plague and people didn't notice especially." The diseases, the sterility, had brought a kind of world never dreamed of by the bomb makers of the previous century. "If this Wili is like your sisters, I'd estimate he's about fifteen. No wonder he's brighter than he looks."

"It's more than that, Boss. The kid is really smart. You should have seen what he did to Tellman's Celest."

Wentz shrugged. "Whatever. Now we've got to decide what to do with him. I wonder whether Fred Bartlett would take him in." This was gentle racism; the Bartletts were black.

"Boss, he'd eat 'em alive." Rosas patted his bandaged arm.

"Well, hell, you think of something better, Mike. We've got four thousand customers. There must be someone who can help. . . . A lost child with no one to take care of him—it's unheard of!"

Some child! But Mike couldn't forget Sally and Arta. "Yeah."

Through this conversation, Naismith had been silent, almost ignoring the two peace officers. He seemed more interested in the view of Old 101 than what they were talking about. Now he twisted in the wooden chair to face the sheriff and his deputy. "I'll take the kid on, Sy."

Rosas and Wentz looked at him in stupefied silence. Paul Naismith was considered old in a land where two-thirds of the population was past fifty. Wentz licked his lips, apparently unsure how to refuse him. "See here, Paul, you heard what Mike said. The kid practically killed him this afternoon. I know how people your, uh, age feel about children, but . . ."

The old man shook his head, caught Mike with a quick glance that was neither abstracted nor feeble. "You know they've been after me to take on an apprentice for years, Sy. Well, I've decided. Besides trying to kill Mike, he played Celest like a master. The gravity-well maneuver is one I've never seen discovered unaided."

"Mike told me. It's slick, but I see a lot of players do it. We almost all use it. Is it really that clever?"

"Depending on your background, it's more than clever. Isaac Newton didn't do a lot more when he deduced elliptical orbits from the inverse square law."

"Look, Paul . . . I'm truly sorry, but even with Bill and Irma, it's just too dangerous."

Mike thought about the pain in his arm. And then about the twin sisters he had once had. "Uh, Boss, could you and I have a little talk?"

Wentz raised an eyebrow. "So . . . ? Okay.'Scuse us a minute, Paul."

There was a moment of embarrassed silence as the two left the room. Naismith rubbed his cheek with a faintly palsied hand and gazed across Highway 101 at the pale lights just coming on in the Shopping Center. So very much had changed and all the years in between were blurred now. Shopping Center? All of Santa Ynez would have been lost in the crowd at a good high-school basketball game in the 1990s. These days a county with seven thousand people was considered a thriving concern.

It was just past sunset now, and the office was growing steadily darker. The room's displays were vaguely glowing ghosts hovering in the near distance. Cameras from down in the shopping areas drove most of those displays. Paul could see that business was picking up there. The Tinkers and mechanics and 'furbishers had trotted out their wares, and crowds were hanging about the aerial displays. Across the room, other screens showed pale red and green, relaying infrared images from cameras purchased by Wentz's clients.

In the next room the two officers' talk was a faint

murmur. Naismith leaned back and pushed up his hearing aid. For a moment the sound of his lung and heart action was overpoweringly loud in his ears. Then the filters recognized the periodic noises and they were diminished, and he could hear Wentz and Rosas more clearly than any unaided human. Not many people could boast such equipment, but Naismith demanded high pay and Tinkers from Norcross to Beijing were more than happy to supply him with better-than-average prosthetics.

Rosas' voice came clearly: " . . . think Paul Naismith can take care of himself, Boss. He's lived in the mountains for years. And the Moraleses are tough and not more than fifty-five. In the old days there were some nasty bandits and ex-military up there—"

"Still are," Wentz put in.

"Nothing like when there were still a lot of weapons floating around. Naismith was old even when they were going strong, and he survived. I've heard about his place. He has gadgets we won't see for years. He isn't called the Tinker wizard for nothing. I—"

The rest was blotted out by a loud creaking that rose to near painful intensity in Naismith's ear, then faded as the filters damped out the amplification. Naismith looked wildly around, then sheepishly realized it was a microquake. They happened all the time this near Vandenberg. Most were barely noticeable—unless one used special amplification, as Paul was now. The roar had been a slight creaking of wall timbers. It passed . . . and he could hear the two peace officers once more.

" . . . what he said about needing an apprentice is true, Boss. It hasn't been just us in Middle California who've been after him. I know people in Medford and

Norcross who are scared witless he'll die without leaving a successor. He's hands-down the best algorithms man in North America—I'd say in the world except I want to be conservative. You know that comm gear you have back in the control room? I know it's close to your heart, your precious toy and mine. Well, the bandwidth compression that makes possible all those nice color pictures coming over the fiber and the microwave would be plain impossible without the tricks he's sold the Tinkers. And that's not all—"

"All right!" Wentz laughed. "I can tell you took it serious when I told you to specialize on our high tech clients. I know Middle California would be a backwater without him, but—"

"And it will be again, once he's gone, unless he can find an apprentice. They've been trying for years to get him to take on some students, or even to teach classes like before the Crash, but he's refused. And I think he's right. Unless you are terribly creative to begin with, there's no way you can make new algorithms. I think he's been waiting—not taking anyone on—and watching. I think today he found his apprentice. The kid's mean . . . he'd kill. And I don't know what he really wants besides money. But he has one thing that all the good intentions and motivation in the world can't get us, and that's brains. You should have seen him on the Celest, Boss . . . ."

The argument—or lecture—went on for several more minutes, but the outcome was predictable. The wizard of the Tinkers had at long last got himself an apprentice.

3

Night and triple moonlight. Wili lay in the back of the buckboard, heavily bundled in blankets. The soft springs absorbed most of the bumps and lurches as the wagon passed over the tilting, broken concrete. The only sounds Wili heard were the cool wind through the trees, the steady *clapclapclap* of the horse's rubberized shoes, its occasional snort in the darkness. They had not yet reached the great black forest that stretched north to south; it seemed like all Middle California was spread out around him. The sea fog which so often made the nights here dark was absent, and the moonlight gave the air an almost luminous blue tone. Directly west—the direction Wili faced— Santa Ynez lay frozen in the still light. Few lights were visible, but the pattern of the streets was clear, and there was of a hint of orange and violet from the open square of the bazaar.

Wili wriggled deeper in the blankets, the tingling paralysis in his limbs mostly gone now; the warmth in his arms and legs, the cold air on his face, and the vision spread below him was as good as any drug high he'd ever stolen in Pasadena. The land was beautiful, but it had not turned out to be the easy pickings he had hoped for when he had defected from the Ndelante and headed north. There were unpeopled ruins, that was true: he could see what must have been the pre-Crash location of Santa Ynez, rectangular tracings all overgrown and no lights at all.

The ruins were bigger than the modern version of the town, but nothing like the promise of the LA Basin, where kilometer after kilometer of ruins—much of it unlooted—stretched as far as a man could walk in a week. And if one wanted some more exciting, more profitable way of getting rich, there were the Jonque mansions in the hills above the Basin. From those high vantage points, Los Angeles had its own fairyland aspect: horizon to horizon had sparkled with little fires that marked towns in the ruins. Here and there glowed the incandescent lights of Jonque outposts. And at the center, a luminous, crystal growth, stood the towers of the Peace Authority Enclave. Wili sighed. That had all been before his world in the Ndelante Ali had fallen apart, before he discovered Old Ebenezer's con . . . . If ever he returned, it would be a contest between the Ndelante and the Jonques over who'd skin him first.

Wili couldn't go back.

But he had seen one thing on this journey north that made it worth being chased here. That one thing made this landscape forever more spectacular than LA's. He looked over Santa Ynez at the object of his wonder.

The silver dome rose out of the sea, into the moonlight. Even at this remove and altitude, it still seemed to tower. People called it many things, and even in Pasadena he had heard of it, though he'd never believed the stories. Larry Faulk called it Mount Vandenberg. The old man Naismith—the one who even now was whistling aimlessly as his servant drove their wagon into the hills—he had called it the Vandenberg Bobble. But whatever they called it, it transcended the name.

In its size and perfection it seemed to transcend nature itself. From Santa Barbara he had seen it. It was a hemisphere at least twenty kilometers across. Where it fell into the Pacific, Wili could see multiple lines of moon-lit surf breaking soundlessly against its curving arc. On its inland side, the lake they called Lompoc was still and dark.

Perfect, perfect. The shape was an abstraction beyond reality. Its mirror-perfect surface caught the moon and held it in a second image, just as clear as the first. And so the night had two moons, one very high in the sky, the other shining from the dome. Out in the sea, the more normal reflection was a faint silver bar lying straight to the ocean's horizon. Three moons' worth of light in all! During the day, the vast mirror captured the sun in a similar way. Larry Faulk claimed the farmers planted their lands to take advantage of the double sunlight.

Who had made Vandenberg Dome? The One True God? Some Jonque or Anglo god? And if made by man, how? What could be inside? Wili dozed, imagining the burglary of all burglaries—to get inside and steal what treasures would be hidden by a treasure so great as that Dome. . . .

When he woke, they were in the forest, rolling upward still, the trees deep and dark around them.

The taller pines moved and spoke unsettlingly in the wind. This was more of a forest than he had ever seen. The real moon was low now; an occasional splash of silver shouldered past the branches and lay upon further trees, glistening on their needles. Over his head, a band of night, brighter than the trees, was visible. The stars were there.

The Anglo's servant had slowed the horse. The ancient concrete road was gone; the path was scarcely wide enough for the cart. Wili tried to face forward, but the blankets and remaining effects of the cop's stunner prevented this. Now the old man spoke quietly into the darkness. *Password!* Wili doubled forward to see if the cops had discovered his other knife. No. It was still there, strapped to the inside of his calf. Old men running labor camps were something he knew a lot about from LA. He was one slave this old man was not going to own.

After a moment, a *woman's* voice came back, cheerfully telling them to come ahead. The horse took up its former pace. Wili saw no sign of the speaker.

The cart turned through the next switchback, its tires nearly soundless in the carpet of pine needles that layered the road. Another hundred meters, another turn, and—

It was a palace! Trees and vines closed in on all sides of the structure, but it was clearly a palace, though more open than the fortresses of the Jonque *jefes* in Los Angeles. Those lords usually rebuilt pre-Crash mansions, installed electrified fences and machine-gun nests for security. This place was old, too, but in other ways strange. There was no outward sign of defenses—which could only mean that the owner must control the land for kilometers all around. But Wili had seen no guardian forts on their trip up here. These northerners could not be as stupid and defenseless as they seemed.

The cart drove the length of the mansion. The trail broadened into a clearing before the entrance, and Wili had the best view yet. It was smaller than the palaces of LA. If the inner court was a reasonable size, then it couldn't house all the servants and family of a great *jefe*. But the building was massive, the wood and stone expertly joined. What moonlight was left glinted off metal tracery and shone streaming images of the moon's face in the polish of the wood. The roof was darker, barely reflecting. There were gables and a strange turret: dark spheres, in diameters varying from five centimeters to almost two meters, impaled on a glinting needle.

"Wake up. We are here." Hands undid the blankets, and the old man gently shook his shoulder. It took an effort to keep from lashing out. He grunted faintly, pretended he was slowly waking. *"Estamos llegado, chico,"* the servant, Morales, said. Wili let himself be helped from the cart. In truth he was still a little unsteady on his feet, but the less they knew of his capabilities the better. Let them think he was weak, and ignorant of English.

A servant came running out of the main entrance (or could the servants' entrance be so grand?). No one else appeared, but Wili resolved to be docile until he knew more. The woman—like Morales, middle-aged—greeted the two men warmly, then guided Wili across the stone flagging to the entrance. The boy kept his eyes down, pretending to be dopey. Out of the corner of his eye, though, he saw something more—a silver net like some giant spider web stretched between a tree and the side of the mansion.

Past the huge carven doors, a light glowed dimly,

and Wili saw that the place was the equal of anything in Pasadena, though there were no obvious art treasures or golden statuary lying about. They led him up (not down! What sort of *jefe* put his lowest servants on an upper floor?) a wide staircase, and into a room under the eaves. The only light was the moon's, coming through a window more than large enough to escape by.

"*¿Tienes hambre?*" the woman asked him.

Wili shook his head dumbly, surprised at himself. He really wasn't hungry; it must be some residual effect of the stunner. She showed him a toilet in an adjoining room and told him to get some sleep.

And then he was left alone!

Wili lay on the bed and looked out over the forest. He thought he could see a glint from the Vandenberg Dome. His luck was almost past marveling at. He thanked the One God he had not bolted at the entrance to the mansion. Whoever was the master here knew nothing of security and employed fools. A week here and he would know every small thing worth stealing. In a week he would be gone with enough treasure to live for a long, long time!

FLASHFORWARD

Captain Allison Parker's new world began with the sound of tearing metal.

For several seconds she just perceived and reacted, not trying to explain anything to herself: the hull was breached. Quiller was trying to crawl back toward her. There was blood on his face. Through rents in the hull she could see trees and pale sky. *Trees?*

Her mind locked out the wonder, and she struggled from her harness. She snapped the disk pack to her side and pulled down the light helmet with its ten-minute air supply. Without thinking, she was following the hull-breach procedures that had been drilled into all of them so many times. If she had thought about it she might have left off the helmet—there were sounds of birds and wind-rustled trees—and she would have died.

Allison pulled Quiller away from the panel and saw why the harness had not protected him: the front of the shuttle was caved in toward the pilot. Another few centimeters and he would have been crushed. A harsh, crackling sound came clearly through the thin shell of her helmet. She slipped Quiller's in place and turned the oxygen feed. She recognized the smell that still hung in her helmet: the tracer stench that tagged their landing fuel.

Angus Quiller straightened out of her grasp. He looked around dazedly. "Fred?" he shouted.

Outside, the improbable trees were beginning to flare. God only knew how long the forward hull would keep the fire in the nose tanks from breaking into the crew area.

Allison and Quiller pulled themselves forward ... and saw what had happened to Fred Torres. The terrible sound that had begun this nightmare had been the left front of the vehicle coming down into the flight deck. The back of Fred's acceleration couch was intact, but Allison could see that the man was beyond help. Quiller had been very lucky.

They looked through the rent that was almost directly over their heads. It was ragged and long, perhaps wide enough to escape through. Allison glanced across the cabin at the main hatch. It was subtly bowed in; they would never get out that way. Even through their pressure suits, they could now feel the heat. The sky beyond the rent was no longer blue. They were looking up a flue of smoke and flame that climbed the nearby pines.

Quiller made a stirrup with his hands and boosted the NMV specialist though the ragged tear in the hull. Allison's head popped through. Under anything less than these circumstances she would have screamed at what she saw sitting in the flames: an immense dark octopus shape, its limbs afire, cracked and swaying. Allison wriggled her shoulders free of the hole and pulled herself up. Then she reached down for the pilot. At the same time, some part of her mind realized that what she had seen was not an octopus but the mass of roots of a rather large tree which somehow had fallen downward on the nose of the sortie craft. This was what had killed Fred Torres.

Quiller leaped up to grab her hand. For a moment his broader form stuck in the opening, but after a single coordinated push and tug he came through— leaving part of his equipment harness on the jagged metal of the broken hull.

They were at the bottom of a long crater, now filled with heat and reddish smoke. Without their oxygen, they would have had no chance. Even so, the fire was intense. The forward area was well involved, sending rivulets of fire toward the rear, where most of the landing fuel was tanked. She looked wildly around, absorbing what she saw without further surprise, simply trying to find a way out.

Quiller pointed at the right wing section. If they could run along it, a short jump would take them to the cascade of brush and small trees that had fallen into the crater. It wasn't till much later that she wondered how all that brush had come to lie *above* the orbiter when it crashed.

Seconds later they were climbing hand-over-hand up the wall of brush and vines. The fire edged steadily through the soggy mass below them and sent flaming streamers ahead along the pine needles imbedded in the vines. At the top they turned for a moment and looked down. As they watched, the cargo bay broke in half and the sortie craft slumped into the strange emptiness below it. Thus died all Allison's millions of dollars of optical and deep-probe equipment. Her hand tightened on the disk pack that still hung by her side.

The main tank blew, and simultaneously Allison's right leg buckled beneath her. She dropped to the ground, Quiller a second behind her. "Damn stupidity," she heard him say as debris showered down on them, "us standing here gawking at a bomb. Let's move out."

Allison tried to stand, saw the red oozing from the side of her leg. The pilot stooped and carried her through the damp brush, twenty or thirty meters upwind from the crater. He set her down and bent to look at the wound. He pulled a knife from his crash kit and sawed the tough suit fabric from around her wound.

"You're lucky. Whatever it was passed right through the side of your leg. I'd call this a nick, except it goes so deep." He sprayed the area with first-aid glue, and the pain subsided to a throbbing pressure that kept time with her pulse.

The heavy red smoke was drifting steadily away from them. The orbiter itself was hidden by the crater's edge. The explosions were continuing irregularly but without great force. They should be safe here. He helped her out of her pressure suit, then struggled out of his own.

Quiller walked several paces back toward the wreck. He bent and picked up a strange, carven shape. "Looks like it got thrown here by the blast." It was a Christian cross, its base still covered with dirt.

"We crashed in a damn cemetery." Allison tried to laugh, but it made her dizzy. Quiller didn't reply. He studied the cross for some seconds. Finally he set it down and came back to look at Allison's leg. "That stopped the bleeding. I don't see any other punctures. How do you feel?"

Allison glanced down at the red on her gray flight fatigues. Pretty colors, except when it's your own red. "Give me some time to sit here. I bet I'll be able to walk to the rescue choppers when they come."

"Hmm. Okay, I'm going to take a look around . . . . There may be a road nearby." He unclipped the crash kit and set it beside her. "Be back in fifteen minutes."

4

___

They started on Wili the next morning. It was the woman, Irma, who brought him down, fed him breakfast in the tiny alcove off the main dining room. She was a pleasant woman, but young enough to be strong, and she spoke very good Spanish. Wili did not trust her. But no one threatened him, and the food seemed endless; he ate so much that his eternal gnawing hunger was almost satisfied. All this time Irma talked—but without saying a great deal, as though she knew he was concentrating on his enormous breakfast. No other servants were visible. In fact, Wili was beginning to think the mansion was untenanted, that these three must be housekeeping staff holding the mansion for their absent lord. That *jefe* was very powerful or very stupid, because even in the light of day, Wili could see no evidence of defenses. If he could be gone before the *jefe* returned . . .

"—and do you know why you are here, Wili?" Irma

said as she collected the plates from the mosaicked surface of the breakfast table.

Wili nodded, pretending shyness. Sure he knew. Everyone needed workers, and the old and middle-aged often needed whole gangs to keep them living in style. But he said, "To help you?"

"Not me, Wili. Paul. You will be his apprentice. He has looked a long time, and he has chosen you."

That figured. The old gardener—or whatever he was—looked to be eighty if he was a day. Right now Wili was being treated royally. But he suspected that was simply because the old man and his two flunkies were making illegitimate use of their master's house. No doubt there would be hell to pay when the *jefe* returned. "And ... and what am I to do for My Lady?" Wili spoke with his best diffidence.

"Whatever Paul asks."

She led him around to the back of the mansion where a large pool, almost a lake, spread away under the pines. The water looked clear, though here and there floated small clots of pine needles. Toward the center, out from under the trees, it reflected the brilliant blue of the sky. Downslope, through an opening in the trees, Wili could see thunderheads gathering about Vandenberg.

"Now off with your clothes and we'll see about giving you a bath." She moved to undo the buttons on his shirt, an adult helping a child.

Wili recoiled. "No!" To be naked here with the woman!

Irma laughed and pinned his arm, continued to unbutton the shirt. For an instant, Wili forgot his pose—that he was a child, and an obedient one. Of course this treatment would be unthinkable within the Ndelante. And even in Jonque territory, the body was respected. No woman forced baths and naked-ness on males.

But Irma was strong. As she pulled the shirt over his head, he lunged for the knife strapped to his leg, and brought it up toward her face. Irma screamed. Even as she did, Wili was cursing himself.

"No, no! I am going to tell Paul." She backed away, her hands held between them, as if to protect herself. Wili knew he could run away now (and he couldn't imagine these three catching him)—or he could do what was necessary to stay. For now he wanted to stay.

He dropped the knife and groveled. "Please, Lady, I acted without thought." Which was true. "Please forgive me. I will do anything to make it up." Even, even . . . .

The woman stopped, came back, and picked up the knife. She obviously had no experience as a foreman, to trust anything he said. The whole situation was alien and unpredictable. Wili would almost have pre-ferred the lash, the predictability. Irma shook her head, and when she spoke there was still a little fear in her voice. Wili was sure she now knew that he was a good deal older than he looked; she made no move to touch him. "Very well. This is between us, Wili. I will not tell Paul." She smiled, and Wili had the feeling there was something she was not telling him. She reached her arm out full length and handed him the brush and soap. Wili stripped, waded into the chill water, and scrubbed.

"Dress in these," she said after he was out and had dried himself. The new clothes were soft and clean, a minor piece of loot all by themselves. Irma was al-most her old self as they walked back to the mansion, and Wili felt safe in asking the question that had been on his mind all that morning: "My Lady, I notice we are all alone here, the four of us—or at least so it appears. When will the protection of the manor lord be returned to us?"

Irma stopped and after a second, laughed. "What manor lord? Your Spanish is so strange. You seem to think this is a castle that should have serfs and troops all around." She continued, almost to herself, "Though perhaps that is your reality. I have never lived in the South.

"You have already met the lord of the manor, Wili." She saw his uncomprehending stare. "It's Paul Naismith, the man who brought you here from Santa Ynez."

"And . . ." Wili could scarcely trust himself to ask the question, ". . . you all, the three of you, are alone here?"

"Certainly. But don't worry. You are much safer here than you ever were in the South, I am sure."

I am sure, too, My Lady. Safe as a coyote among chickens. If ever he'd made a right decision, it had been his escape to Middle California. To think that Paul Naismith and the others had the manor to themselves—it was a wonder the Jonques had not overrun this land long ago. The thought almost kindled his suspicions. But then the prospects of what he could do here overwhelmed all. There was no reason he should have to leave with his loot. Wili Wáchendon, weak as he was, could probably be ruler here—if he was clever enough during the next few weeks. At the very least he would be rich forever. If Naismith were the *jefe*, and if Wili were to be his apprentice, then in essence he was being adopted by the manor lord. That happened occasionally in Los Angeles. Even the richest families were cursed with sterility. Such families often sought an appropriate heir. The adopted one was usually high-born, an orphan of another family, perhaps the survivor of a vendetta. But there were not many children to go around, especially in the old days. Wili knew of at least one case where the oldsters adopted from the Basin—not a black child, of course, but still, a boy from a peasant family. Such was the stuff of dreams; Wili could scarcely believe that it was being offered to him. If he played his cards right, he would eventually own all of this—and without having to steal a single thing, or risk torture and execution! It was . . . unnatural. But if these people were crazy, he would certainly do what he could to profit by it.

Wili hurried after Irma as she returned to the house.

A week passed, then two. Naismith was nowhere to be seen, and Bill and Irma Morales would only say that he was traveling on "business." Wili began to wonder if "apprenticeship" really meant what he had thought. He was treated well, but not with the fawning courtesy that should be shown the heir-apparent of a manor. Perhaps he was on some sort of probation: Irma woke him at dawn, and after breakfast he spent most of the day—assuming it wasn't raining—in the manor's small fields, weeding, planting, hoeing. It wasn't hard work—in fact, it reminded him of what Larry Faulk's labor company did—but it was deadly boring.

On rainy days, when the weather around Vandenberg blew inland, he stayed indoors and helped Irma with cleaning. He had scarcely more enthusiasm for this, but it did give him a chance to snoop: the mansion had no interior court, but in some ways it was more elaborate than he had first imagined. He

and Irma cleaned some large rooms hidden below
ground level. Irma would say nothing about them,
though they appeared to be for meetings or banquets.
The building's floor space, if not the available food
supply, implied a large household. Perhaps that was
how these innocents protected themselves: they simply hid until their enemies got tired of searching for
them. But it didn't really make sense. If he were a
bandit, he'd burn the place down or else occupy it.
He wouldn't simply go away because he could find
no one to kill. And yet there was no evidence of past
violence in the polished hardwood walls or the deep,
soft carpeting.

In the evenings, the two treated him more as they
should the adopted son of a lord. He was allowed to
sit in the main living room and play Celest or chess.
The Celest was every bit as fascinating as the one in
Santa Ynez. But he never could attain quite the accuracy he'd had that first time. He began to suspect
that part of his win had been luck. It was the precision of his eye and hand that betrayed him, not his
physical intuition. Delays of a thousandth of a second in a cushion shot could cause a miss at the
destination. Bill said there were mechanical aids to
overcome this difficulty, but Wili had little trust for
such. He spent many hours hunched before the glowing volume of the Celest, while on the other side of
the room Bill and Irma watched the holo. (After the
first couple of days, the shows seemed uniformly
dull—either local gossip, or flat television game shows
from the last century.)

Playing chess with Bill was almost as boring as the
holo. After a few games, he could easily beat the
caretaker. The programmed version was much more
fun than playing Bill.

As the days passed, and Naismith did not return, Wili's boredom intensifed. He reconsidered his options. After all this time, no one had offered him the master's rooms, no one had shown him the appropriate deference. (And no tobacco was available, though that by itself was something he could live with.) Perhaps it was all some benign labor contract operation, like Larry Faulk's. If this were the Anglo idea of adoption, he wanted none of it, and his situation became simply a grand opportunity for burglary.

Wili began with small things: jeweled ashtrays from the subterranean rooms, a pocket Celest he found in an empty bedroom. He picked a tree out of sight behind the pond and hid his loot in a waterproof bag there. The burglaries, small as they were, gave him a sense of worth and made life a lot less boring. Even the pain in his gut lessened and the food seemed to taste better.

Wili might have been content to balance indefinitely between the prospect of inheriting the estate and stealing it, but for one thing: the mansion was haunted. It was not the air of mystery or the hidden rooms. There was something alive in the house. Sometimes he heard a woman's voice—not Irma's, but the one he had heard talk to Naismith on the trail. Wili saw the creature once. It was well past midnight. He was sneaking back to the mansion after stashing his latest acquisitions. Wili oozed along the edge of the veranda, moving silently from shadow to shadow. And suddenly there was someone behind him, standing full in the moonlight. It was a woman, tall and Anglo. Her hair, silver in the light, was cut in an alien style. The clothes were like something out of the Moraleses' old-time television: she turned to look straight at him. There was a faint smile on her face. He bolted—and the creature twisted, vanished.

Wili was a fast shadow through the veranda doors, up the stairs, and into his room. He jammed a chair under the doorknob and lay for many minutes, heart pounding. *What had he seen?* How he would like to believe it was a trick of the moonlight: the creature had vanished as if by the flick of a mirror, and large parts of the walls surrounding the veranda were of slick black glass. But tricks of the eye do not have such detail, do not smile faint smiles. What then? Television? Wili had seen plenty of flat video, and since coming to Middle California had used holo tanks. Tonight went beyond all that. Besides, the vision had turned to look *right at him*.

So that left ... a haunting. It made sense. No one—certainly no woman—had dressed like that since before the plagues. Old Naismith would have been young then. Could this be the ghost of a dead love? Such tales were common in the ruins of LA, but until now Wili had been skeptical.

Any thought of inheriting the estate was gone. The question was, could he get out of this alive?—and with how much loot? Wili watched the doorknob with horrified fascination. If he lived through this night, then it was probably safe to stay a few more days. The vision might be just the warning of a jealous spirit. Such a ghost would not begrudge him a few more trinkets, as long as he departed when Naismith returned.

Wili got very little sleep that night.

5

The horsemen—four of them, with a row of five pack mules—arrived the afternoon of a slow, rainy day. It had been thundering and windy earlier, but now the rains off Vandenberg came down in a steady drizzle from a sky so overcast that it already seemed evening.

When Wili saw the four, and saw that none of them was Naismith, he faded around the mansion, toward the pond and his cache. Then he stopped for a foolish moment, wondering if he should run back and warn Irma and Bill.

But the two stupid caretakers were already running down the front steps to greet the intruders: an enormous fat fellow and three rifle-carrying men-at-arms. As he skulked in the bushes, Bill turned and seemed to look directly at his hiding place. "Wili, come help our guests."

Mustering what dignity he could, the boy emerged and walked toward the group. The old fat one dismounted. He looked like a Jonque, but his English was strangely accented. "Ah, so this is his apprentice, *hein*? I have wondered if the master would ever find a successor and what sort of person he might be." He patted the bristling Wili on the head, making the usual error about the boy's age.

The gesture was patronizing, but Wili thought there was a hint of respect, almost awe, in his voice. Perhaps this slob was not a Jonque and had never seen a black before. The fellow stared silently at Wili for a moment and then seemed to notice the rain. He gave an exaggerated shiver and most of the group moved up the steps. Bill and Wili were left to take the animals around to the outbuilding.

Four guests. That was not the end. By twos and threes and fours, all through the afternoon and evening, others drifted in. The horses and mules quickly overflowed the small outbuilding, and Bill showed Wili hidden stables. There were no servants. The guests themselves, or at least the more junior of them, carried the baggage indoors and helped with the animals. Much of the luggage was not taken to their rooms, but disappeared into the halls below ground. The rest turned out to be food and drink—which made sense, since the manor produced only enough to feed three or four people.

Night and more rain. The last of the visitors arrived—and one of these was Naismith. The old man took his apprentice aside. "Ah, Wili, you have remained." His Spanish was as stilted as ever, and he paused frequently as if waiting for some unseen speaker to supply him with a missing word. "After the meetings, when our guests have gone, you and I must talk on your course of study. You are too old to delay. For now, though, help Irma and Bill and do not ... bother ... our guests." He looked at Wili as though suspecting the boy might do what Wili had indeed been considering. There was many a fat purse to be seen among these naive travelers.

"A new apprentice has nothing to tell his elders, and there is little he can learn from them in this short time." With that the old man departed for the halls beneath his small castle, and Wili was left to work with Irma and two of the visitors in the dimly lit kitchen.

Their mysterious guests stayed all that night and through the next day. Most kept to their rooms and the meeting halls. Several helped Bill with repairs on the outbuilding. Even here they behaved strangely: for instance, the roof of the stable badly needed work. But when the sun came out, the men wouldn't touch it. They seemed only willing to work on things where there was shade. And they never worked outside in groups of more than two or three. Bill claimed this was all Naismith's wish.

The next evening, there was a banquet in one of the halls. Wili, Bill, and Irma brought the food in, but that was all they got to see. The heavy doors were locked and the three of them went back up to the living room. After the Moraleses had settled down with the holo, Wili drifted away as if to go to his room.

He cut through the kitchen to the side stairs. The thick carpet made speedy, soundless progress possible, and a moment later he was peeking round at the entrance to the meeting hall. There were no guards, but the oak doors remained closed. A wood tripod carried a sign of gold on black. Wili silently crossed the hall and touched the sign. The velvet was deep but the gold was just painted on. It was cracked here and there and seemed very old. The letters said:

NCC

And below this, hand-lettered on vellum, was:

2047

Wili stepped back, more puzzled than ever. Why? Who was there to read the sign, when the doors were shut and locked? Did these people believe in spirit spells? Wili crept to the door and set his ear against the dark wood. He heard . . .

Nothing. Nothing but the rush of blood in his ear. These doors were thick, but he should at least hear the murmur of voices. He could hear the sound of a century-old game show from all the way up in the living room, but the other side of this door might as well be the inside of a mountain.

Wili fled upstairs, and was a model of propriety until their guests departed the next day.

There was no single leave-taking; they left as they had come. Strange customs indeed, the Anglos had.

But one thing was as in the South. They left gifts. And the gifts were conveniently piled on the wide table in the mansion's entrance way. Wili tried to pretend disinterest, but he felt his eyes must be visibly bugging out of his head whenever he walked by. Till now he had not seen much that was like the portable wealth of Los Angeles, but here were rubies, emeralds, diamonds, gold. There were gadgets, too, in artfully carved boxes of wood and silver. He couldn't tell if they were games or holos or what. There was so much here that a fortune could be taken and not be missed.

The last were gone by midnight. Wili crouched at the window of his attic room and watched them depart. They quickly disappeared down the trail, and the beat of hooves ceased soon after that. Wili suspected that, like the others, these three had left the main trail and were departing along some special path of their own.

Wili did not go back to his bed. The moon's waning crescent slowly rose and the hours passed. Wili tried to see familiar spots along the coast, but the fog had rolled in, and only the Vandenberg Dome rose into sight. He waited till just before morning twilight. There were no sounds from below. Even the horses were quiet. Only the faint buzzing of insects edged the silence. If he was going to have part of that treasure, he would have to act now, moonlight or not.

Wili slipped down the stairs, his hand lightly touching the haft of his knife. (It was not the same one he had flashed at Irma. That he had made a great show of giving up. This was a short carving knife from the kitchen set.) There had been no more ghostly apparitions since that night on the veranda. Wili had almost convinced himself that it had been an illusion, or some holographic scare show. Nevertheless, he had no desire to stay.

There, glinting in the moonlight, was his treasure. It looked even more beautiful than by lamplight. Far away, he heard Bill turn over, begin to snore. Wili silently filled his sack with the smallest, most clearly valuable items on the table. It was hard not to be greedy, but he stopped when the bag was only half-full. Five kilos would have to do! More wealth than

Old Ebenezer passed to the lower Ndelante in a year! And now out the back, around the pond, and to his cache.

Wili crept out onto the veranda, his heart suddenly pounding. This would be the spirit's last chance to get him.

¡Dio! There *was* someone out there. Wili stood absolutely still, not breathing. It was Naismith. The old man sat on a lounge chair, his body bundled against the chill. He seemed to be gazing into the sky—but not at the moon, since he was in the shadows. Naismith was looking away from Wili; this could not be an ambush. Nevertheless, the boy's hand tightened on his knife. After a moment, he moved again, away from the old man and toward the pond.

"Come here to sit," said Naismith, without turning his head. Wili almost bolted, then realized that if the old man could be out here stargazing, there was no reason why the excuse should not also serve him. He set his sack of treasure down in the shadows and moved closer to Naismith.

"That's close enough. Sit. Why are you here so late, young one?"

"The same as you, I think, My Lord. . . . To view the sky." What else could the old man be out here for?

"That's a good reason." The tone was neutral, and Wili could not tell if there was a smile or a scowl on his face; he could barely make out the other's profile. Wili's hand tightened nervously on the haft of his knife. He had never actually killed anyone before, but he knew the penalties for burglary.

"But I don't admire the sky as a whole," Naismith continued, "though it is beautiful. I like the morning and the late evening especially, because then it is possible to see the—" there was one of his characteristic pauses as he seemed to listen for the right word, "satellites. See? There are two visible right now." He pointed first near the zenith and then waved at something close to the horizon. Wili followed his first gesture, and saw a tiny point of light moving slowly, effortlessly across the sky. Too slow to be an aircraft, much too slow to be a meteor: it was a moving star, of course. For a moment, he had thought the old man was going to show him something really magical. Wili shrugged and somehow Naismith seemed to catch the gesture.

"Not impressed, eh? There were men there once, Wili. But no more."

It was hard for Wili to conceal his scorn. How could that be? With aircraft you could see the vehicle. These little lights were like the stars and as meaningless. But he said nothing and a long silence overcame them. "You don't believe me, do you, Wili? But it is true. There were men and women there, so high up you can't see the form of their craft."

Wili relaxed, squatted before the other's chair. He tried to sound humble. "But then, Lord, what keeps them up? Even aircraft must come down for fuel."

Naismith chuckled. "That from the expert Celest player! Think, Wili. The universe is a great game of Celest. Those moving lights are swinging about the Earth, just like planets on a game display.

¡Del Nico Dio! Wili sat on the flags with an audible thump. A wave of dizziness passed over him. The sky would never be the same. Wili's cosmology had—until that moment—been an unexamined flatland image. Now, suddenly, he found the interior cosmos of Celest surrounding him forever and ever, with no up or down, but only the vast central force field that was

the Earth, with the moon and all those moving stars circling about. And he couldn't disguise from himself the distances involved; he was far too familiar with Celest to do that. He felt like an infinitesimal shrinking toward some unknowable zero.

His mind tumbled over and over in the dark, caught between the relationships flashing through his mind and the night sky that swung overhead. So all those objects had their own gravity, and all moved—at least in some small way—at the behest of all the others. An image of the solar system not too different from the reality slowly formed in his mind. When at last he spoke, his voice was very small, and his humility was not pretended, "But then the game, it represents trips that men have actually made? To the moon, to the stars that move? You . . . we . . . can do *that?*"

"We *could* do that, Wili. We could do that and more. But no longer."

"But why *not?*" It was as though the universe had suddenly been taken back from his grasp. His voice was almost a wail.

"In the beginning, it was the War. Fifty years ago there were men alive up there. They starved or they came back to Earth. After the War there were the plagues. Now . . . now we could do it again. It would be different from before, but we could do it . . . if it weren't for the Peace Authority." The last two words were in English. He paused and then said, *"Mundopaz."*

Wili looked into the sky. The Peace Authority. They had always seemed a part of the universe as far away and indifferent as the stars themselves. He saw their jets and occasionally their helicopters. The major highways passed two or three of their freighters every hour. They had their enclave in Los Angeles. The

Ndelante Ali had never considered hitting it; better to burgle the feudal manors of Aztlán. And Wili remembered that even the lords of Aztlán, for all their arrogance, never spoke of the Peace Authority except in neutral tones. It was fitting in a way that something so nearly supernatural should have stolen the stars from mankind. Fitting, yet, now he knew, intolerable.

"They brought us peace, Wili, but the price was very high." A meteor flashed across the sky, and Wili wondered if that had been a piece of man's work, too. Naismith's voice suddenly became businesslike. "I said we must talk, and this is the perfect time for it. I want you for my apprentice. But this is no good unless you want it also. Somehow, I don't think our goals are the same. I think you want wealth: I know what's in the bag yonder. I know what's in the tree behind the pond."

Naismith's voice was dry, cool. Wili's eyes hung on the point where the meteor had swept to nothingness. This was like a dream. In Los Angeles, he would be on his way to the headsman now, an adopted son caught in treachery. "But what will wealth get you, Wili? Minimal security, until someone takes it from you. Even if you could rule here, you would still be nothing more than a petty lord, insecure.

"Beyond wealth, Wili, there is power, and I think you have seen enough so that you can appreciate it, even if you never thought to have any."

Power. Yes. To control others the way he had been controlled. To make others fear as he had feared. Now he saw the power in Naismith. What else could really explain this man's castle? And Wili had thought the spirit a jealous lover. Hah! Spirit or projection, it was this man's servant. An hour ago, this insight alone would have made him stay and return all he had stolen. Somehow, he still couldn't take his eyes off the sky.

"And beyond power, Wili, there is knowledge—which some say is power." He had slipped into his native English, and Wili didn't bother to pretend ignorance. "Whether it is power or not depends on the will and the wisdom of its user. As my apprentice, Wili, I can offer you knowledge, for a surety; power, perhaps; wealth, only what you have already seen."

The crescent moon had cleared the pines now. It was one more thing that would never be the same for Wili.

Naismith looked at the boy and held out his hand. Wili offered his knife hilt-first. The other accepted it with no show of surprise. They stood and walked back to the house.

6

Many things were the same after that night. They were the outward things: Wili worked in the gardens almost as much as before. Even with the gifts of food the visitors had brought, they still needed to work to feed themselves. (Wili's appetite was greater than the others'. It didn't seem to help; he remained as under-nourished and stunted as ever.) But in the afternoons and evenings he worked with Naismith's machines.

It turned out the ghost was one of those machines. Jill, the old man called her, was actually an interface program run on a special processor system. She was good, almost like a person. With the projection equipment Naismith had built into the walls of the veranda, she could even appear in open space. Jill was the perfect tutor, infinitely patient but with enough "humanity" to make Wili want to please her. Hour after hour, she flashed language questions at him. It was like some verbal Celest. In a matter of weeks,

Wili progressed from being barely literate to having a fair command of technical written English.

At the same time, Naismith began teaching him math. At first Wili was contemptuous of these problems. He could do arithmetic as fast as Naismith. But he discovered that there was more to math than the four basic arithmetic operations. There were roots and transcendental functions; there were the relationships that drove both Celest and the planets.

Naismith's machines showed him functions as graphs and related function operations to those pictures. As the days passed, the functions became very specialized and interesting. One night, Naismith sat at the controls and caused a string of rectangles of varying widths to appear on the screen. They looked like irregular crenellations on some battlement. Below the first plot, the old man produced a second and then a third, each somewhat like the first but with more and narrower rectangles. The heights bounced back and forth between 1 and -1.

"Well," he said, turning from the display, "what is the pattern? Can you show me the next three plots in this series?" It was a game they had been playing for several days now. Of course, it was all a matter of opinion what really constituted a pattern, and sometimes there was more than one answer that would satisfy a person's taste, but it was amazing how often Wili felt a certain rightness in some answers and an unesthetic blankness in others. He looked at the screen for several seconds. This was harder than Celest, where he merely cranked on deterministic relationships. Hmmm. The squares got smaller, the heights stayed the same, the minimum rectangle width decreased by a factor of two on every new line. He reached out and slid his finger across the screen, sketching the three graphs of his answer.

"Good," said Naismith. "And I think you see how you could make more plots, until the rectangles became so narrow that you couldn't finger-sketch or even display them properly.

"Now look at this." He drew another row of crenellations, one clearly not in the sequence: the heights were not restricted to 1 and −1. "Write me that as the sum and differences of the functions we've already plotted. Decompose it into the other functions." Wili scowled at the display; worse than "guess the pattern," this was. Then he saw it: three of the first graph minus four copies of the third graph plus . . .

His answer was right, but Wili's pride was short-lived, since the old man followed this problem with similar decomposition questions that took Wili many minutes to solve . . . until Naismith showed him a little trick—something called orthogonal decomposition—that used a peculiar and wonderful property of these graphs, these "walsh waves" he called them. The insight brought a feeling of awe just a little like learning about the moving stars, to know that hidden away in the patterns were realities that might take him days to discover by himself.

Wili spent a week dreaming up other orthogonal families and was disappointed to discover that most of them were already famous—haar waves, trig waves—and that others were special cases of general families known for more than two hundred years. He was ready for Naismith's books now. He dived into them, rushed past the preliminary chapters, pushed himself toward the frontier where any new insights would be beyond the farthest reach of previous explorers.

In the outside world, in the fields and the forest that now were such a small part of his consciousness, summer moved into fall. They worked longer hours, to get what crops remained into storage before the frosts. Even Naismith did his best to help, though the others tried to prevent this. The old man was not weak, but there was an air of physical fragility about him.

From the high end of the bean patch, Wili could see over the pines. The leafy forests had changed color and were a band of orange-red beyond the evergreen. The land along the coast was clouded over, but Wili suspected that the jungle there was still wet and green. Vandenberg Dome seemed to hang in the clouds, as awesome as ever. Wili knew more about it now, and someday he would discover all its secrets. It was simply a matter of asking the right questions— of himself and of Paul Naismith.

Indoors, in his greater universe, Wili had completed his first pass through functional analysis and now undertook a three-pronged expedition that Naismith had set for him: into finite Galois theory, stochastics, and electromagnetics. There was a goal in sight, though (Wili was pleased to see) there was no ultimate end to what could be learned. Naismith had a project, and it would be Wili's if he was clever enough.

Wili saw why Naismith was valued and saw the peculiar service he provided to people all over the continent. Naismith solved problems. Almost every day the old man was on the phone, sometimes talking to people locally—like Miguel Rosas down in Santa Ynez—but just as often to people in Fremont, or in places so far away that it was night on the screen while still day here in Middle California. He talked to people in English and in Spanish, and in languages that Wili had never heard. He talked to people who were neither Jonques nor Anglos nor blacks.

Wili had learned enough now to see that these were not nearly as simple as making local calls. Communication between towns along the coast was trivial over the fiber, where almost any bandwidth could be accommodated. For longer distances, such as from Naismith's palace to the coast, it was still relatively easy to have video communication: the coherent radiators on the roof could put out microwave and infrared beams in any direction. On a clear day, when the IR radiator could be used, it was almost as good as a fiber (even with all the tricks Naismith used to disguise their location). But for talking around the curve of the Earth, across forests and rivers where no fiber had been strung and no line of sight existed, it was a different story: Naismith used what he called "short-waves" (which were really in the one- to ten-meter range). These were quite unsuitable for high-fidelity communication. To transmit video—even the wavery black-and-white flat pictures Naismith used in his transcontinental calls—took incredibly clever coding schemes and some real-time adaptation to changing conditions in the upper atmosphere.

The people at the other end brought Naismith problems, and he came back with answers. Not immediately, of course; it often took him weeks, but he eventually thought of something. At least the people at the other end seemed happy. Though it was still unclear to Wili how gratitude on the other side of the continent could help Naismith, he was begin-

ning to understand what had paid for the palace and
how Naismith could afford full-scale holo projectors.
It was one of these problems that Naismith turned
over to his apprentice. If he succeeded, they might
actually be able to steal pictures off the Authority's
snooper satellites.

It wasn't only people that appeared on the screens.

One evening shortly after the first snowfall of the
season, Wili came in from the stable to find Naismith
watching what appeared to be an empty patch of
snow-covered ground. The picture jerked every few
seconds, as if the camera were held by a drunkard.
Wili sat down beside the old man. His stomach was
more upset than usual and the swinging of the picture did nothing to help the situation—but his curiosity gave him no rest. The camera suddenly swung up
to eye level and looked through the pine trees at a
house, barely visible in the evening gloom. Wili
gasped—it was the building they were sitting in.

Naismith turned from the screen and smiled. "It's
a deer, I think. South of the house. I've been following her for the last couple of nights." It took Wili a
second to realize he was referring to what was holding the camera. Wili tried to imagine how anyone
could catch a deer and strap a camera on it. Naismith
must have noticed his puzzlement. "Just a second."
He rummaged through a nearby drawer and handed
Wili a tiny brown ball. "That's a camera like the one
on the critter. It's wide enough so I have resolution
about as good as the human eye. And I can shift the
decoding parameters so it will 'look' in different directions without the deer's having to move.

"Jill, move the look axis, will you?"

"Right, Paul." The view slid upward till they were
looking into overhanging branches and then down

the other side. Wili and Naismith saw a scrawny back and part of a furry ear.

Wili looked at the object Paul had placed in his hand. The "camera" was only three or four millimeters across. It felt warm and almost sticky in Wili's hand. It was a far cry from the lensed contraptions he had seen in Jonque villas. "So you just stick them to the fur, true?" said Wili.

Naismith shook his head. "Even easier than that. I can get these in hundred lots from the Greens in Norcross. I scatter them through the forest, on branches and such. All sorts of animals pick them up. It provides just a little extra security. The hills are safer than they were years ago, but there are still a few bandits."

"Umm." If Naismith had weapons to match his senses, the manor was better protected than any castle in Los Angeles. "This would be greater protection if you could have people watching all the views all the time."

Naismith smiled, and Wili thought of Jill. He knew enough now to see that the program could be made to do just that.

Wili watched for more than an hour as Naismith showed him scenes from a number of cameras, including one from a bird. That gave the same sweeping view he imagined could be seen from Peace Authority aircraft.

When at last he went to his room, Wili sat for a long while looking out the garret window at the snow-covered trees, looking at what he had just seen with godlike clarity from dozens of other eyes. Finally he stood up, trying to ignore the cramp in his gut that had become so persistent these last few weeks. He removed his clothes from the closet and lay them on the bed, then inspected every square centimeter with his eyes and fingers. His favorite jacket and his usual work pants both had tiny brown balls stuck to cuffs or seams. Wili removed them; they looked so innocuous in the room's pale lamplight.

He put them in a dresser drawer and returned his clothes to the closet.

He lay awake for many minutes, thinking about a place and time he had resolved never to dwell on again. What could a hovel in Glendora have in common with a palace in the mountains? Nothing. Everything. There had been safety there. There had been Uncle Sylvester. He had learned there, too—arithmetic and a little reading. Before the Jonques, before the Ndelante—it had been a child's paradise, a time lost forever.

Wili quietly got up and slipped the cameras back into his clothing. Maybe not lost forever.

7

January passed, an almost uninterrupted snowstorm. The winds coming off Vandenberg brought ever-higher drifts that eventually reached the mansion's second story and would have totally blocked the entrances if not for the heroic efforts of Bill and Irma. The pain in Wili's middle became constant, intense. Winters had always been bad for him, but this one was worse than ever before, and the others eventually became aware of it. He could not suppress the occasional grimace, the faint groan. He was always hungry, always eating—and yet losing weight.

But there was great good, too. He was beyond the frontiers of Naismith's books! Paul claimed that no previous human had insight on the coding problem that he had attacked! Wili didn't need Naismith's machines now; the images in his mind were so much more complete. He sat in the living room for hours—through most of his waking time—almost unaware of the outside world, almost unaware of his pain, dreaming of the problem and his schemes for its defeat. All existence was groups and graphs and endless combinatorical refinements on the decryption scheme he hoped would break the problem.

But when he ate and even when he slept, the pain levered itself back into his soul.

It was Irma, not Wili, who noticed that the paler skin on his palms had a yellow cast beneath the brown. She sat beside him at the dining table, holding his small hands in her large, calloused ones. Wili bristled at her touch. He was here to eat, not to be inspected. But Paul stood behind her.

"And the nails look discolored, too." She reached across to one of Wili's yellowed fingernails and gave it a gentle tug. Without sound or pain, the nail came away at its root. Wili stared stupidly for a second, then jerked his hand back with a shriek. Pain was one thing; this was the nightmare of a body slowly dismembering itself. For an instant terror blotted out his gut pain the way mathematics had done before.

They moved him to a basement room, where he could be warm all the time. Wili found himself in bed most of each day. His only view of the outside, of the cloudswept purity of Vandenberg, was via the holo. The mountain snows were too deep to pass travelers; there would be no doctors. But Naismith moved cameras and high-bandwidth equipment into the room, and once when Wili was not lost in dreaming, he saw that someone from far away was looking on, was being interrogated by Naismith. The old man seemed very angry.

Wili reached out to touch his sleeve. "It will be all right, Uncle Syl—Paul. This problem I have always had and worst in the winters. I will be okay in the spring."

Naismith smiled and nodded, then turned away.

But Wili was not delirious in any normal sense. During the long hours an average patient would have lain staring at the ceiling or watching the holo and trying to ignore his pain, Wili dreamed on and on about the communications problem that had resisted his manifold efforts all these weeks. When the others were absent, there was still Jill, taking notes, ready to call for help; she was more real than any of them. It was hard to imagine that her voice and pretty face had ever seemed threatening.

In a sense, he had already solved the problem, but his scheme was too slow; he needed $n*\log(n)$ time for this application. He was far beyond the tools provided by his brief, intense education. Something new, something clever was needed, and by the One True God he would find it!

And when the solution did come it was like a sun rising on a clear morning, which was appropriate since this was the first clear day in almost a month. Bill brought him up to ground level to sit in the sunlight before the newly cleared windows. The sky was not just clear, but an intense blue. The snow was piled deep, a blinding white. Icicles grew down from every edge and corner, dripping tiny diamonds in the warm light.

Wili had been dictating to Jill for nearly an hour when the old man came down for breakfast. He took one look over Wili's shoulder and then grabbed his reader, saying not a word to Wili or anyone else. Naismith paused many times, his eyes half-closed in concentration. He was about a third of the way through when Wili finished. He looked up when Wili stopped talking. "You got it?"

Wili nodded, grinning. "Sure, and in $n*\log(n)$ time,

too." He glanced at Naismith's reader. "You're still looking at the filter setting up. The real trick isn't for a hundred more lines." He scanned forward. Naismith looked at it for a long time, finally nodded. "I, I think I see. I'll have to study it, but I think ... My little Ramanujan. How do you feel?"

"Great," he said, filled with elation, "but tired. The pain has been less these last days, I think. Who is Ramanujan?"

"Twentieth-century mathematician. An Indian. There are a lot of similarities: you both started out without much formal education. You are both very, very good."

Wili smiled, the warmth of the sun barely matching what he felt. These were the first words of real praise he had heard from Naismith. He resolved to look up everything on file about this Ramanujan. . . . His mind drifted, freed from the fixation of the last weeks. Through the pines, he could see the sun on Vandenberg. There were so many mysteries left to master. . . .

8

Naismith made some phone calls the next day. The first was to Miguel Rosas at the SYP Company. Rosas was undersheriff to Sy Wentz, but the Tinkers around Vandenberg hired him for almost all their police operations.

The cop's dark face seemed a touch pale after he watched Naismith's video replay. "Okay," he finally said, "who *was* Ramanujan?"

Naismith felt the tears coming back to his eyes. "That was a bad slip; now the boy is sure to look him up. Ramanujan was everything I told Wili: a really brilliant fellow, without much college education." This wouldn't impress Mike, Naismith knew. There were no colleges now, just apprenticeships. "He was invited to England to work with some of the best number theorists of the time. He got TB, died young."

" . . . Oh. I get the connection, Paul. But I hope you

70

don't think that bringing Wili into the mountains did anything to hurt him."

"His problem is worse during winters, and our winters are fierce compared to LA's. This has pushed him over the edge."

"Bull! It may have aggravated his problem, but he got better food here and more of it. Face it, Paul. This sort of wasting just gets worse and worse. You've seen it before."

"More than you!" That and the more acute diseases of the plague years had come close to destroying mankind. Then Naismith brought himself up short, remembering Miguel's two little sisters. Three orphans from Arizona they had been, but only one survived. Every winter, the girls had sickened again. When they died, their bodies were near-skeletons. The young cop had seen more of it than most in his generation.

"Listen, Mike, we've got to do something. Two or three years is the most he has. But hell, even before the War a good pharmaceutical lab could have cured this sort of thing. We were on the verge of cracking DNA coding and—"

"Even then, Paul? Where do you think the plagues came from? That's not just Peace Authority jive. We know the Peace is almost as scared of bioresearch as they are that someone might find the secret of their bobbles. They bobbled Yakima a few years ago just because one of their agents found a recombination analyzer in the city hospital. That's ten thousand people asphyxiated because of a silly antique. Face it: the bastards who started the plagues are forty years dead—and good riddance."

Naismith sighed. His conscience was going to hurt him on this—a little matter of protecting your customers. "You're wrong, Mike. I have business with lots of people. I have a good idea what most of them do."

Rosas' head snapped up. "Bioscience labs, even in our time?"

"Yes. At least three, perhaps ten. I can't be sure, since of course they don't admit to it. And there's only one whose location is certain."

"Jesus, Paul, how can you deal with such vermin?"

Naismith shrugged. "The Peace Authority is the real enemy. In spite of what you say, it's only their word that the bioscience people caused the plagues, trying to win back for their governments what all the armies could not. I *know* the Peace." He stopped for a moment, remembering treachery that had been a personal, secret thing for fifty years.

"I've tried to convince you tech people: the Authority can't tolerate you. You follow their laws: you don't make high-density power sources, don't make vehicles or experiment with nucleonics or biology. But if the Authority knew what was going on *within* the rules ... You must have heard about the NCC: I showed conclusively that the Peace is beginning to catch on to us. They are beginnning to understand how far we have gone without big power sources and universities and old-style capital industry. They are beginning to realize how far our electronics is ahead of their best. When they see us clearly, they'll step on us the way they have on all opposition, and we're going to have to *fight*."

"You've been saying that for as long as I can remember, Paul, but—"

"But secretly you Tinkers aren't that unhappy with the status quo. You've read about the wars before the War, and you're afraid of what could happen if suddenly the Authority lost power. Even though you deceive the Peace, you're secretly glad they're there. Well, let me tell you something, Mike." The words came in an uncontrollable rush. "I knew the mob you call the Peace Authority when they were just a bunch of R and D administrators and petty crooks. They were at the right place at the right time to pull the biggest con and rip-off of all history. They have zero interest in humanity or progress. That's the reason they've never invented anything of their own."

He stopped, shocked by his outburst. But he saw from Rosas' face that his revelation had not been understood. The old man sat back, tried to relax. "Sorry, I wandered off. What's important right now is this: a lot of people—from Beijing to Norcross— owe me. If we had a patent system and royalties it would be a lot more gAu than has ever trickled in. I want to call those IOUs due. I want my friends to get Wili to the bioscience underground.

"And if the past isn't enough, think about this: I'm seventy-eight. If it's not Wili, it's no one. I've never been modest: I know I'm the best mathman the Tinkers have. Wili's not merely a replacement for me. He is actually better, or will be with a few years' experience. You know the problem he just cracked? It's the thing the Middle California Tinkers have been bugging me about for three years: eavesdropping on the Authority's recon satellites."

Rosas' eyes widened slightly.

"Yes. That problem. You know what's involved. Wili's come up with a scheme I think will satisfy your friends, one that runs a very small chance of detection. Wili did it in six weeks, with just the technical background he picked up from me last fall.

His technique is radical, and I think it will provide leverage on several other problems. You're going to need someone like him over the next ten years."

"Um." Rosas fiddled with his gold-and-blue sheriff's brassard. "Where is this lab?"

"Just north of San Diego."

"That close? Wow." He looked away. "So the problem is getting him down there. The Aztlán nobility is damned unpleasant about blacks coming in from the north, at least under normal circumstances."

" 'Normal circumstances'?"

"Yes. The North American Chess Federation championships are in La Jolla this April. That means that some of the best high tech people around are going to be down there—legitimately. The Authority has even offered transportation to entrants from the East Coast, and they hardly ever sully their aircraft with us ordinary humans. If I were as paranoid as you, I would be suspicious. But the Peace seems to be playing it just for the propaganda value. Chess is even more popular in Europe than here; I think the Authority is building up to sponsorship of the world championships in Berne next year.

"In any case, it provides a cover and perfect protection from the Aztlán: black or Anglo, they've never touched anyone under Peace Authority protection."

Naismith found himself grinning. Some good luck after all the bad. There were tears in his eyes once more, but now for a different reason. "Thanks, Mike. I needed this more than anything I've ever asked for."

Rosas smiled briefly in return.

FLASHFORWARD

Allison didn't know much about plant identification (from less than one hundred kilometers anyway), but there was something very odd about this forest. In places it was overgrown right down to the ground; in other places, it was nearly clear. Everywhere a dense canopy of leaves and vines prevented anything more than fragmented views of the sky. It reminded her of the scraggly second growth forests of Northern California, except there was such a jumble of types: conifers, eucalyptus, even something that looked like a sickly manzanita. The air was very warm, and muggy. She rolled back the sleeves of her flight fatigues.

The fire was barely audible now. This forest was so wet that it could not spread. Except for the pain in her leg, Allison could almost believe she were in a park on some picnic. In fact, they might be rescued by *real* picnickers before the Air Force arrived.

She heard Quiller's progress back toward her long

before she could see him. When he finally came into view, the pilot's expression was glum. He asked again about her injury.

"I—I think I'm fine. I pinched it shut and resprayed." She paused and returned his somber look. "Only . . ."

"Only what?"

"Only . . . to be honest, Angus, the crash did something to my memory. I don't remember a thing from right after entry till we were on the ground. What went wrong anyway? Where did we end up?"

Angus Quiller's face seemed frozen. Finally he said, "Allison, I think your memory is fine—as good as mine, anyway. You see, I don't have any memory from someplace over Northern California till the hull started busting up on the ground. In fact, I don't think there *was* anything to remember."

"What?"

"I think we were something like forty klicks up and then we were down on a planetary surface—just like that." He snapped his fingers. "I think we've fallen into some damn fantasy." Allison just stared at him, realizing that he was probably the more distressed of the two of them. Quiller must have interpreted the look correctly. "Really, Allison, unless you believe that we could have exactly the same amount of amnesia, then the only explanation is . . . I mean one minute we're on a perfectly ordinary reconnaissance operation, and the next we're . . . we're here, just like in a lot of movies I saw when I was a kid."

"Parallel amnesia is still more believable than that, Angus." *If only I could figure out where we are.*

The pilot nodded. "Yes, but you didn't climb a tree and take a look around, Allison. Plant life aside, this area looks vaguely like the California coast. We're boxed in by hills, but in one direction I could see that the forests go down almost to the sea. And . . ."

"And?"

"There's something out there on the coast, Allison. It's a mountain, a silver mountain sticking kilometers into the sky. There's never been anything on Earth like that."

Now Allison began to feel the bedrock fear that was gnawing at Angus Quiller. For many people, the completely inexplicable is worse than death. Allison was such a person. The crash—even Fred's death—she could cope with. The amnesia explanation had been so convenient. But now, almost half an hour had passed. There was no sign of aircraft, much less of rescue. Allison found herself whispering, reciting all the crazy alternatives. "You think we're in some kind of parallel world, or on the planet of another star—or in the future?" *A future where alien invaders set their silvery castle-mountains down on the California shore?*

Quiller shrugged, started to speak, seemed to think better of it—then finally burst out with, "Allison, you know that . . . cross near the edge of the crater?"

She nodded.

"It was old, the stuff carved on it was badly weathered, but I could see . . . It had your name on it and . . . and today's date."

Just the one cross, and just the one name. For a long while they were both silent.

9

It was April. The three travelers moved through the forest under a clear, clean sky. The wind made the eucs and vines sway above them, sending down misty sprays of water. But at the level of the mud road, the air was warm and still.

Wili slogged along, reveling in the strength he felt returning to his limbs. He been fine these last few weeks. In the past, he always felt good for a couple months after being really sick, but this last winter had been so bad he'd wondered if he would get better. They had left Santa Ynez three hours earlier, right after the morning rain stopped. Yet he was barely tired and cheerfully refused the others' suggestions that he get back into the cart.

Every so often the road climbed above the surrounding trees and they could see a ways. There was still snow in the mountains to the east. In the west there was no snow, only the rolling rain forests, Lake Lompoc spread sky-blue at the base of the Dome—

and the whole landscape appearing again in that vast, towering mirror.

It was strange to leave the home in the mountains. If Paul were not with them, it would have been more unpleasant than Wili could admit.

Wili had known for a week that Naismith intended to take him to the coast, and then travel south to La Jolla—and a possible cure. It was knowledge that made him more anxious than ever to get back in shape. But it wasn't until Jeremy Kaladze met them at Santa Ynez that Wili realized how unusual this first part of the journey might be. Wili eyed the other boy surreptitiously. As usual, Jeremy was talking about everything in sight, now running ahead of them to point out a peculiar rockfall or side path, now falling behind Naismith's cart to study something he had almost missed. After nearly a day's acquaintance, Wili still couldn't decide how old the boy was. Only very small children in the Ndelante Ali displayed his brand of open enthusiasm. On the other hand, Jeremy was nearly two meters tall and played a good game of chess.

"Yes sir, Dr. Naismith," said Jeremy—he was the only person Wili had ever heard call Paul a doctor—"Colonel Kaladze came down along this road. It was a night drop, and they lost a third of the Red Arrow Battalion, but I guess the Russian government thought it must be important. If we went a kilometer down those ravines, we'd see the biggest pile of armored vehicles you can imagine. Their parachutes didn't open right." Wili looked in the direction indicated, saw nothing but green undergrowth and the suggestion of a trail. In LA the oldsters were always talking about the glorious past, but somehow it was strange that in the middle of this utter peace a war was buried, and that this boy talked about ancient history as if it were a living yesterday. His grandfather, Lt. Col. Nikolai Sergeivich Kaladze, had commanded one of the Russian air drops, made before it became clear that the Peace Authority (then a nameless organization of bureaucrats and scientists) had made warfare obsolete.

Red Arrow's mission was to discover the secret of the mysterious force-field weapon the Americans had apparently invented. Of course, they discovered the Americans were just as mystified as everyone else by the strange silvery bubbles, baubles—bobbles?—that were springing up so mysteriously, sometimes preventing bombs from exploding, more often removing critical installations.

In that chaos, when everyone was losing a war that no one had started, the Russian airborne forces and what was left of the American army fought their own war with weapon systems that now had no depot maintenance. The conflict continued for several months, declining in violence until both sides were slugging it out with small arms. Then the Authority had miraculously appeared, announcing itself as the guardian of peace and the maker of the bobbles.

The remnant of the Russian forces retreated into the mountains, hiding as the nation they invaded began to recover. Then the war viruses came, released (the Peace Authority claimed) by the Americans in a last attempt to retain national autonomy. The Russian guerrillas sat on the fringes of the world and watched for some chance to move. None came. Billions died and fertility dropped to near zero in the years following the War. The species called Homo sapiens came very close to extinction. The Russians in the hills became old men, leading ragged tribes.

But Colonel Kaladze had been captured early (through no fault of his own), before the viruses, when the hospitals still functioned. There had been a nurse, and eventually a marriage. Fifty years later, the Kaladze farm covered hundreds of hectares along the south edge of the Vandenberg Dome. That land was one of the few places north of Central America where bananas and cacao could be farmed. Like so much of what had happened to Colonel Kaladze in the last half century, it would have been impossible without the bobbles, in particular the Vandenberg one: the doubled sunlight was as intense as could be found at any latitude, and the high obstacle the Dome created in the atmosphere caused more than 250 centimeters of rain a year in a land that was otherwise quite dry. Nikolai Sergeivich Kaladze had ended up a regular Kentucky colonel—even if he was originally from Georgia.

Most of this Wili learned in the first ninety minutes of Jeremy's unceasing chatter.

In late afternoon they stopped to eat. Belying his gentle exterior, Jeremy was a hunting enthusiast, though apparently not a very expert one. The boy needed several shots to bring down just one bird. Wili would have preferred the food they had brought along, but it seemed only polite to try what Jeremy shot. Six months before, politeness would have been the last consideration to enter his mind.

They trudged on, no longer quite so enthusiastic. This was the shortest route to Red Arrow Farm but it was still a solid ten-hour hike from Santa Ynez. Given their late start, they would probably have to spend the night on this side of the Lompoc ferry crossing. Jeremy's chatter slowed as the sun slanted toward the Pacific and spread double shadows behind them.

In the middle of a long discussion (monologue) on his various girl friends, Jeremy turned to look up at Naismith. Speaking very quietly, he said, "You know, sir, I think we are being followed."

The old man seemed to be half-dozing in his seat, letting Berta, his horse, pull him along without guidance. "I know," he said. "Almost two kilometers back. If I had more gear, I could know precisely, but it looks like five to ten men on foot, moving a little faster than we are. They'll catch up by nightfall."

Wili felt a chill that was not in the afternoon air. Jeremy's stories of Russian bandits were a bit pale compared to what he had seen with the Ndelante Ali, but they were bad enough. "Can you call ahead, Paul?"

Naismith shrugged. "I don't want to broadcast; they might jump on us immediately. Jeremy's people are the nearest folks who could help, and even on a fast horse that's a couple hours. We're going to have to handle most of this ourselves."

Wili glared at Jeremy, whose distant relatives—the ones he had been bragging about all day—were apparently out to ambush them. The boy's wide face was pale. "But I was mostly farking you. No one has actually seen one of the outlaw bands down this far in . . . well, in ages."

"I know," Naismith muttered agreement. "Still, it's a fact we're being crowded from behind." He looked at Berta, as if wondering if there was any way the three of them might outrun ten men on foot. "How good is that cannon you carry, Jeremy?"

The boy raised the weapon. Except for its elaborate telescopic sight and chopped barrel, it looked pretty ordinary to Wili: a typical New Mexico autorifle, heavy and simple. The clip probably carried ten

8-mm rounds. With the barrel cut down, it wouldn't be much more accurate than a pistol. Wili had successfully dodged such fire from a distance of one hundred meters. Jeremy patted the rifle, apparently ignorant of all this, "Really hot stuff, sir. It's smart."

"And the ammunition?"

"That too. One clip anyway."

Naismith smiled a jagged smile. " 'Kolya really coddles you youngsters—but I'm glad of it. Okay." He seemed to reach a decision. "It's going to depend on you, Jeremy. I didn't bring anything that heavy. . . . An hour walk from here is a trail that goes south. We should be able to reach it by twilight. A half hour along that path is a bobble. I know there's a clear line of sight from there to your farm. And the bobble should confuse our 'friends,' assuming they aren't familiar with the land this close to the coast."

New surprise showed on Jeremy's face. "Sure. We know about that bobble, but how did you? It's real small."

"Never you mind. I go for hikes, too. Let's just hope they let us get there."

They proceeded down the road, even Jeremy's tongue momentarily stilled. The sun was straight ahead. It would set behind Vandenberg. Its reflection in the Dome edged higher and higher, as if to touch the true sun at the moment of sunset. The air was warmer and the green of the trees more intense than in any normal sunset. Wili could hear no evidence of the men his friends said were pursuing.

Finally the two suns kissed. The true disk slipped behind the Dome into eclipse. For several minutes, Wili thought he saw a ghostly light hanging over the Dome above the point of the sun's setting.

"I've notified that, too," Naismith replied to Wili's unspoken question. "I think it's the corona, the glow around the sun that's ordinarily invisible. That's the only explanation I can think of, anyway."

The pale light slowly disappeared, leaving a sky that went from orange to green to deepest blue. Naismith urged Berta to a slightly faster walk and the two boys swung onto the back of the cart. Jeremy slipped a new clip into his rifle and settled down to cover the road.

Finally they reached the cutoff. The path was as small as any Jeremy had pointed to during the day, too narrow for the cart. Naismith carefully climbed down and unhitched Berta, then distributed various pieces of equipment to the boys.

"Come on. I've left enough on the cart to satisfy them . . . I hope." They set off southward with Berta. The trail narrowed till Wili wondered if Paul was lost. Far behind them, he heard an occasional branch snap, and now even the sound of voices. He and Jeremy looked at each other. "They're loud enough," the boy muttered. Naismith didn't say anything, just switched Berta to move a bit faster. If the bandits weren't satisfied with the wagon, the three of them would have to make a stand, and evidently he wanted that to be further on.

The sounds of their pursuers were louder now, surely past the wagon. Paul guided Berta to the side. For a moment the horse looked back at them stupidly. Then Naismith seemed to say something in its ear and the animal moved off quickly into the shadows. It was still not really dark. Wili thought he could see green in the treetops, and the sky held only a few bright stars.

They headed into a deep and narrow ravine, an

apparent cul-de-sac. Wili looked ahead and saw—*three figures coming toward them out of a brightly lit tunnel!* He bolted up the side of the ravine, but Jeremy grabbed his jacket and pointed silently toward the strange figures: now one of *them* was holding another and pointing. *Reflections.* That's what he was seeing. Down there at the back of the ravine, a giant curved mirror showed Jeremy and Naismith and himself silhouetted against the evening sky.

Very quietly, they slid down through the underbrush to the base of the mirror, then began climbing around its sides. Wili couldn't resist: here at last was a bobble. It was much smaller than Vandenberg, but a bobble nevertheless. He paused and reached out to touch the silvery surface—then snatched his hand back in shock. Even in the cool evening air, the mirror was warm as blood. He peered closer, saw the dark image of his head swell before him. There was not a nick, not a scratch in that surface. Up close, it was as perfect as Vandenberg appeared from a distance, as transcendentally perfect as mathematics itself. Then Jeremy's hand closed again on his jacket and he was dragged upward around the sphere.

The forest floor was level with the top. A large tree grew at the edge of the soil, its roots almost like tentacles around the top of the sphere. Wili hunkered down between the roots and looked back along the ravine. Naismith watched a dim display while Jeremy slid forward and panned the approaches through his rifle sight. From their vantage Wili could see that the ravine was an elongated crater, with the bobble—which was about thirty meters across—forming the south end. The history seemed obvious: somehow, this bobble had fallen out of the sky, carving a groove in the hills before finally coming to rest. The trees above it had grown in the decades since the War. Given another century, the sphere might be completely buried.

For a moment they sat breathless. A cicada started buzzing, the noise so loud he wondered if they would even hear their pursuers. "They may not fall for this." Naismith spoke almost to himself. "Jeremy, I want you to scatter these around behind us as far as you can in five minutes." He handed the boy something, probably tiny cameras like those around the manor. Jeremy hesitated, and Naismith said, "Don't worry, we won't be needing your rifle for at least that long. If they try to come up behind us, I want to know about it."

The vague shadow that was Jeremy Kaladze nodded and crawled off into the darkness. Naismith turned to Wili and pressed a coherent transmitter into his hands. "Try to get this as far up as you can." He gestured at the conifer among whose roots they crouched.

Wili moved out more quietly than the other boy. This had been Wili's specialty, though in the Los Angeles Basin there were more ruins than forests. The muck of the forest floor quickly soaked his legs and sleeves, but he kept close to the ground. As he oozed up to the base of the tree, he struck his knee against something hard and artificial. He stopped and felt out the obstacle: an ancient stone cross, a Christian cemetery cross really. Something limp and fragrant lay in the needle mulch beside it—flowers?

Then he was climbing swiftly up the tree. The branches were so regularly spaced they might as well have been stair steps. He was soon out of breath. He was just out of condition; at least he hoped that was the explanation.

The tree trunk narrowed and began to sway in response to his movement. He was above the nearby trees, pointed, dark forms all around him. He was really not very high up; almost all the trees in the rain forest were young.

Jupiter and Venus blazed like lanterns, and the stars were out. Only a faint yellow glow showed over Vandenberg and the western horizon. He could see all the way to the base of the Dome; this was high enough. Wili fastened the emitter so it would have a clear line of sight to the west. Then he paused a moment, letting the evening breeze turn his pants and sleeves cold on his skin. There were no lights anywhere. Help was very far away.

They would have to depend on Naismith's gadgets and Jeremy's inexperienced trigger finger.

He almost slid down the tree and was back at Naismith's side soon after that. The old man scarcely seemed to notice his arrival, so intent was he on the little display. "Jeremy?" Wili whispered.

"He's okay. Still laying out the cameras." Paul was looking through first one and then another of the little devices. The pictures were terribly faint, but recognizable. Wili wondered how long his batteries would last. "Fact is, our friends are coming in along the path we left for them." In the display, evidently from some camera Paul had dropped along the way, Wili could see an occasional booted foot.

"How long?"

"Five or ten minutes. Jeremy'll be back in plenty of time." Naismith took something out of his pack—the master for the transmitter Wili had set in the tree. He fiddled with the phase aimer and spoke softly, trying to raise the Strela farm. After long seconds, an insectlike voice answered from the device, and the old man was explaining their situation.

"Got to sign off. Low on juice," he finished. Behind them, Jeremy slid into place and unlimbered his rifle. "Your grandpa's people are coming, Jeremy, but it'll be hours. Everyone's at the house."

They waited. Jeremy looked over Naismith's shoulder for a moment. Finally he said. "Are they sons of the originals? They don't walk like old men."

"I know," said Naismith.

Jeremy crawled to the edge of the crater. He settled into a prone position and rested his rifle on a large root. He scanned back and forth through the sight.

The minutes passed, and Wili's curiosity slowly increased. What was the old man planning? What was there about this bobble that could be a threat to anyone? Not that he wasn't impressed. If they lived through to morning, he would see it by daylight and that would be one of the first joys of survival. There was something almost alive about the warmth he had felt in its surface, though now he realized it was probably just the reflected heat of his own body. He remembered what Naismith once had told him. Bobbles reflected everything; nothing could pass through, in either direction. What was within might as well be in a separate, tiny universe. Somewhere beneath their feet lay the wreckage of an aircraft or missile, embobbled by the Peace Authority when they put down the national armies of the world. Even if the crew of that aircraft could have survived the crash, they would have suffocated in short order. There were worse ways to die: Wili had always sought the ultimate hiding place, the ultimate safety. To his inner heart, the bobbles seemed to be such.

Voices. They were not loud, but there was no attempt at secrecy. There were footsteps, the sounds of branches snapping. In Naismith's fast-dimming display, Wili could see at least five pairs of feet. They walked past a bent and twisted tree he remembered just two hundred meters back. Wili strained his ears to make sense of their words, but it was neither English nor Spanish. Jeremy muttered, "Russian, after all!"

Finally, the enemy came over the ridge that marked the far end of the ravine. Unsurprisingly, they were not in a single file now. Wili counted ten figures strung out against the starry sky. Almost as a man, the group froze, then dove for cover with their guns firing full automatic. The three on the bobble hugged the dirt as rounds whizzed by, thunking into the trees. Ricochets off the bobble sounded like heavy hail on a roof. Wili kept his face stuck firmly in the moist bed of forest needles and wondered how long the three of them could last.

10

"Gentlemen of the Peace Authority, Greater Tucson has been destroyed." The New Mexico Air Force general slapped his riding crop against the topographical map by way of emphasis. A neat red disk had been laid over the downtown district, and paler pink showed the fallout footprint. It all looked very precise, though Hamilton Avery suspected it was more show than fact. The government in Albuquerque had communication equipment nearly on a par with the Peace but it would take aircraft or satellite recon to get a detailed report on one of their western cities this quickly: the detonation had happened less than ten hours earlier.

The general—Avery couldn't see his name tag, and it probably didn't matter anyway—continued. "That's three thousand men, women, and children immediately dead, and God knows how many hundreds to die of radiation poisoning in the months to come." He glared across the conference table at Avery and the assistants he'd brought to give his delegation the properly important image.

For a moment it seemed as though the officer had finished speaking, but in fact he was just catching his breath. Hamilton Avery settled back and let the blast roll over him. "You of the Peace Authority deny us aircraft, tanks. You have weakened what is left of the nation that spawned you until we must use force simply to protect our borders from states that were once friendly. But what have you given us in return?" The man's face was getting red. The implication had been there, but the fool insisted on spelling it out: if the Peace Authority couldn't protect the Republic from nuclear weapons, then it could scarcely be the organization it advertised itself to be. And the general claimed the Tucson blast was incontrovertible proof that some nation possessed nukes and was using them, despite the Authority and all its satellites and aircraft and bobble generators.

On the Republic's side of the table, a few heads nodded agreement, but those individuals were far too cautious to say aloud what their scapegoat was shouting to the four walls. Hamilton pretended to listen; best to let this fellow hang himself. Avery's subordinates followed his lead, though for some it was an effort. After three generations of undisputed rule, many Authority people took their power to be God-given. *Hamilton knew better.*

He studied those seated around the general. Several were Army generals, one just back from the Colorado. The others were civilians. Hamilton knew this group. In the early years, he had thought the Republic of New Mexico was the greatest threat to the Peace in North America, and he had watched them accordingly. This was the Strategic Studies

Committee. It ranked higher in the New Mexico government than the Group of Forty or the National Security Council—and, of course, higher than the cabinet. Every generation, governments seemed to breed a new inner circle out of the older, which was then used as a sop to satisfy larger numbers of less influential people. These men, together with the President, were the real power in the Republic. Their "strategic studies" extended from the Colorado to the Mississippi. New Mexico was a powerful nation. They could invent the bobble and nuclear weapons all over again if they were allowed.

They were easy to frighten nonetheless. This Air Force general couldn't be a full-fledged member of the group. The NMAF manned a few hot-air balloons and dreamed of the good old days. The closest they ever got to modern aircraft was a courtesy flight on an Authority plane. He was here to say things their government wanted said but did not have the courage to spit out directly.

The old officer finally ran down, and sat down. Hamilton gathered his papers and moved to the podium. He looked mildly across at the New Mexico officials and let the silence lengthen to significance.

It was probably a mistake to come here in person. Talking to national governments was normally done by officers two levels below him in the Peace Authority. Appearing in person could easily give these people an idea of the true importance of the incident. Nevertheless, he had wanted to see these men close up. There was an outside chance they were involved in the menace to the Peace he had discovered the last few months.

Finally he began. "Thank you, General, uh, Halberstamm. We understand your anxiety, but wish to emphasize the Peace Authority's long-standing promise. No nuclear weapon has exploded in nearly fifty years and none exploded yesterday in Greater Tucson."

The general spluttered. "Sir! The radiation! The blast! How can you say—

Avery raised his hand and smiled for silence. There was a sense of noblesse oblige and faint menace in the action. "In a moment, General. Bear with me. It is true: there was an explosion and some radiation. But I assure you no one besides the Authority has nuclear weapons. If some existed, we would deal with them by methods you all know.

"In fact, if you consult your records, you will find that the center of the blast area coincides with the site of a ten-meter confinement sphere generated"—he pretended to consult his notes—"5 July 1997."

He saw various degrees of shock, but no questions broke the silence. He wondered how surprised they really were. From the beginnning, he'd known there was no point in trying to cover up the source of the blast. Old Alex Schelling, the President's science adviser, would have put two and two together correctly.

"I know that several of you have studied the open literature on confinement," *and you, Schelling, have spent a good many thousand cautious man-hours out in the Sandia ruins, trying to duplicate the effect,* "but a review is in order.

"Confinement spheres—bobbles—are not so much force fields as they are partitions, separating the in- and outside of their surfaces into distinct universes. Gravity alone can penetrate. The Tucson bobble was orginally generated around an ICBM over the arctic. It fell to earth near its target, the missile fields at

Tucson. The hell bomb inside exploded harmlessly, in the universe on the far side of the bobble's surface.

"As you know, it takes the enormous energy output of the Authority's generator in Livermore to create even the smallest confinement sphere. In fact, that is why the Peace Authority has banned all energy-intensive usages, to safeguard this secret of keeping the Peace. But, once established, you know that a bobble is stable and requires no further inputs to maintain itself."

"Lasting forever," put in old Schelling. It was not quite a question.

"That's what we all thought, sir. But nothing lasts forever. Even black holes undergo quantum decay. Even normal matter must eventually do so, though on a time-scale beyond imagination. A decay analysis has not been done for confinement spheres until quite recently." He nodded to an assistant who passed three heavy manuscripts across the table to the NM officials. Schelling scarcely concealed his eagerness as he flipped past the Peace Authority Secret seal—the highest classification a government official ever saw—and began reading.

"So, gentlemen, it appears that—like all things—bobbles do decay. The time constant depends on the sphere's radius and the mass enclosed. The Tucson blast was a tragic, fluke accident."

"And you're telling us that every time one of the damn things goes, it's going to make a bang as bad as the bombs you're supposed to be protecting us from?"

Avery permitted himself to glare at the general. "No, I am not. I thought my description of the Tucson incident was clear: there was an exploded nuclear weapon inside that confinement."

"Fifty years ago, Mr. Avery, *fifty* years ago."

Hamilton stepped back from the podium. "General. Halberstamm, can you imagine what it's like inside a ten-meter bobble? Nothing comes in or goes out. If you explode a nuke in such a place, there is nowhere to cool off. In a matter of milliseconds, thermodynamic equilibrium is reached, but at a temperature of several million degrees. The innocent-seeming bobble, buried in Tucson all these decades, contained the heart of a fireball. When the bobble decayed, the explosion was finally released."

There was an uneasy stirring among the Strategic Studies Committee as those worthies considered the thousands of bobbles that littered North America. Geraldo Alvarez, a presidential confidant of such power that he had no formal position whatsoever, raised his hand and asked diffidently, "How frequently does the Authority expect this to happen?"

"Dr. Schelling can describe the statistics in detail, but in principle the decay is exactly like that of other quantum processes: we can only speak of what will happen to large numbers of objects. We could go for a century or two and not have a single incident. On the other hand, it is conceivable that three or four might decay in a single year. But even for the smallest bobbles, we estimate a time constant of decay greater than ten million years."

"So they go off like atoms with a given half-life, rather than chicken eggs hatching all at once?"

"Exactly, sir. A good analogy. And in one regard, I can be more specific and encouraging: most bobbles do not contain nuclear explosions. And large bobbles— even if they contain 'fossil' explosions—will be harmless. For instance, we estimate the equilibrium temperature produced by a nuke inside the Vandenberg or Langley bobbles to be less than one hundred degrees. There would be some property damage around the perimeter, but nothing like in Tucson.

"And now, gentlemen, I'm going to give our side of the meeting over to Liaison Officers Rankin and Nakamura." He nodded at his third-level people. "In particular, you must decide with them how much public attention to give this incident." *And it better not be much!* "I must fly to Los Angeles. Aztlán detected the explosion, and they deserve an explanation, too."

He gestured his top Albuquerque man, the usual Peace rep to the highest levels of the Republic, to leave with him. They walked out, ignoring the tightened lips and red faces across the table. It was necessary to keep these people in their place, and one of the best ways of doing that was to emphasize that New Mexico was just one fish among many.

Minutes later they were out of the nondescript building and on the street. Fortunately, there were no reporters. The NM press was under fair control; besides, the existence of the Stategic Studies Committee was itself a secret.

He and Brent, the chief liaison officer here, climbed into the limo, and the horses pulled them into the afternoon traffic. Since Avery's visit was unofficial, he used local vehicles, and there was no escort; he had an excellent view. The layout was similar to that of the capitol of the old United States, if you could ignore the bare mountains that jaggedly edged the sky. He could see at least a dozen other vehicles on the wide boulevard. Albuquerque was almost as busy and cosmopolitan as an Authority Enclave. But that made sense: the Republic of New Mexico was one of the most powerful and populous nations on Earth.

He glanced at Brent. "Are we clean?"

The younger man looked briefly puzzled, then said, "Yessir. We went over the limo with those new procedures."

"Okay. I want to take the detail reports with me, but summarize. Are Schelling and Alvarez and company as innocently surprised as they claim?"

"I'd stake the Peace on it, sir." From the look on Brent's face, the fellow understood that was exactly what he was doing. "They don't have anything like the equipment you warned us of. You've always supported a strong counter-intel department here. We haven't let you down; we'd know if they were anywhere near being a threat."

"Hmm." The assessment agreed with Avery's every intuition. The Republic government would do whatever they could get away with. But that was why he'd kept watch on them all these years: he knew they didn't have the tech power to be behind what he was seeing.

He sat back in the padded leather seat. So Schelling was "innocent." Well then, would he buy the story Avery was peddling? Was it really a story at all? Every word Hamilton spoke in that meeting was the absolute truth, reviewed and rereviewed by the science teams at Livermore. . . . But the whole truth it was not. The NM officials did not know about the ten-meter bobble burst in Central Asia. The theory could explain that incident, too, but who could believe that two decays would happen within a year after fifty years of stability?

Like chicken eggs hatching all at once. That was the image Alvarez had used. The science team was certain it was simple, half-life decay, but they hadn't seen the big picture, the evidence that had been trick-

ling in for better than a year. *Like eggs hatching* . . . .
When it comes to survival, the rules of evidence become an art, and Avery felt with dread certainty that someone, somewhere, had figured how to cancel bobbles.

11

___

The bandits' rifle fire lit the trees. There came another volley and another. Wili heard Jeremy move, as if getting ready to jump up and return fire. He realized the Russians must be shooting at themselves. The reflection that had fooled him had taken them in, too. What would happen when they realized it was only a bobble that faced them? A bobble and one rifle in the hands of an incompetent marksman?

The gunfire came to a ragged stop. "Now, Jeremy!" Naismith said. The larger boy jumped into the open and swung his weapon wildly across the ravine. He fired the whole clip. The rifle stuttered in an irregular way, as though on the verge of jamming. Its muzzle flash lit the ravine. The enemy was invisible, except for one fellow vaguely seen against the light-colored rock at the side of the cleft. That one had bad luck: he was almost lifted off his feet by the impact of bullet on chest, and slammed back against the rock.

Cries of pain rose from all along the ravine. How had Jeremy done it? Even one hit was fantastic luck. And Jeremy Kaladze was the fellow who in daylight could miss the broad side of a barn.

Jeremy slammed down beside him. "Did I g-get them all?" There was an edge of horror in his voice. But he slipped another clip into his sawed-off weapon.

There was no return fire. But wait. The bandit lying by the outcrop—he was up and running! The hit should have left him dead or crawling. Through the bushes below, he could hear the others picking themselves up and running for the far end of the ravine. One by one, they appeared in silhouette, still running.

Jeremy rose to his knees, but Naismith pulled him down.

"You're right, son. There's something strange with them. Let's not press our luck."

They lay for a long time in the ringing silence, till at last the animal sounds resumed and the starlight seemed bright. There was no sign of humans inside of five hundred meters.

Projections? Jeremy wondered aloud. *Zombies?* Wili thought silently to himself. But they could be neither. They had been hit; they had gone down. Then they had gotten up and run in a panic—and that was unlike the zombies of Ndelante legend. Naismith had no speculations he was willing to share.

It was raining again by the time their rescuers arrived.

Only nine o'clock on an April morning and already the air was a hot, humid thirty degrees. Thunderheads hung high on the arch of the Dome. It would rain in the afternoon. Wili Wáchendon and Jeremy

Sergeivich Kaladze walked down the wide, graveled road that led from the main farmhouse toward outbuildings by the Dome. They made a strange sight: one boy near two meters tall, white and lanky; the other short, thin, and black, apparently subadolescent. But Wili was beginning to realize that there were similarities, too. It turned out they were the same age—fifteen. And the other boy was sharp, though not in the same class as Wili. He had never tried to intimidate with his size. If anything, he seemed slightly in awe of Wili (if that were possible in one as rambunctious and outspoken as Jeremy Sergeivich).

"The Colonel says"—Jeremy and the others never called Old Kaladze "grandfather," though there seemed to be no fear in their attitude, and a lot of affection—"the Colonel says the farm is being watched, has been since the three of us got here."

"Oh? The bandits?"

"Don't know. We can't afford the equipment Dr. Naismith can buy—those micro-cameras and such. But we have a telescope and twenty-four-hour camera on top of the barn. The processor attached to it detected several flashes from the trees"—he swept his hand toward the ridgeline where the rain forest came down almost to the farm's banana plants—"that are probably reflections from old-style optics."

Wili shivered in the warm sunlight. There were lots of people here compared to Naismith's mansion in the wilderness, but it was not a properly fortified site: there were no walls, watchtowers, observation balloons. There were many very young children, and most of the adults were over fifty. That was a typical age distribution, but one unsuitable for defense. Wili wondered what secret resources the Kaladzes might have.

"So what are you going to do?"

"Nothing much. There can't be too many of 'em; they're awful shy. We'd go out after them if *we* had more people. As it is, we've got four smart rifles and men who can use them. And Sheriff Wentz knows about the situation.... C'mon, don't worry." He didn't notice Wili bristle. The smaller boy hid it well. He was beginning to realize that there was scarcely a mean bone in Jeremy's body. "I want to show you the stuff we have here."

He turned off the gravel road and walked toward a large, one-story building. It could scarcely be a barn; the entire roof was covered with solar batteries. "If it weren't for the Vandenberg Bobble, I think Middle California would be most famous for Red Arrow Products—that's our trade name. We're not as sophisticated as the Greens in Norcross, or as big as the Qens in Beijing, but the things we do are the best."

Wili pretended indifference. "This place is just a big farm, it looks like to me."

"Sure, and Dr. Naismith is just a hermit. It is big and it's terrific farmland. But where do you think my family got the money to buy it? We've been real lucky: Grandmother and the Colonel had four children after the War, and each of them had at least two. We're practically a clan, and we've adopted other folk, people who can figure out things we can't. The Colonel believes in diversification; between the farm and our software, we're unsinkable."

Jeremy pounded on the heavy white door. There was no answer, but it swung slowly inward and the boys entered. Down each side of the long building, windows let in morning light and enough breeze to make it relatively comfortable. He had an impression of elegant chaos. Ornamental plants surrounded scattered desks. There was more than one aquarium. Most of the desks were unoccupied: some sort of conference was going on at the far end of the room. The men waved to Jeremy but continued with what sounded perilously close to being an argument.

"Lots more people here than usual. Most guys like to work from home. Look." He pointed to one of the few seated workers. The man seemed unaware of them. In the holo above his desk floated colored shapes, shapes that shifted and turned. The man watched intently. He nodded to himself, and suddenly the pattern was tripled and sheared. Somehow he was in control of the display. Wili recognized the composition of linear and nonlinear transformations: inside his head, Wili had played with those through most of the winter.

"What's he doing?"

Jeremy's normal loudness was muted. "Who do you think implements those algorithms you and Dr. Naismith invent?" He swept his hand across the room. "We've done some of the most complicated implementations in the world."

Wili just stared at him. "Look, Wili. I know you have all sorts of wonderful machines up in the mountains. Where do you think they come from?"

Wili pondered. He had never really thought about it! His education had moved very fast along the paths Naismith laid out. One price for this progress was that in most respects Wili's opinions about what made things work were a combination of mathematical abstraction and Ndelante myth. "I guess I thought Paul made most of them."

"Dr. Naismith is an amazing man, but it takes hundreds of people all over the world to make all the things he needs. Mike Rosas says it's like a pyramid:

at the top there are just a few men—say Naismith in algorithms or Masaryk in surface physics—guys who can invent really new things. With the Peace Authority Bans on big organizations, these people got to work alone, and there probably aren't more than five or ten of them in the whole world. Next down in the pyramid are software houses like ours. We take algorithms and implement them so that machines can run them."

Wili watched the programmatic phantoms shift and turn above the desk. Those shapes were at once familiar and alien. It was as if his own ideas had been transformed into some strange form of Celest. "But these people don't *make* anything. Where do the machines come from?"

"You're right; without hardware to run our programs, we're just daydreamers. That's the next level of the pyramid. Standard processors are cheap. Before the plagues, several families from Sunnyvale settled in Santa Maria. They brought a truckload of gamma-ray etching gear. It's been improved a lot since. We import purified base materials from Oregon. And special-purpose stuff comes from even further: for instance, the Greens make the best synthetic optics."

Jeremy started for the door. "I'd show you more here except they seem awfully busy today. That's probably your fault. The Colonel seems real excited about whatever you and Dr. Naismith invented this winter." He stopped and looked at Wili, as though hoping for some inside information. And Wili wondered to himself, *How can I explain?* He could hardly describe the algorithm in a few words. It was a delicate matter of coding schemes, of packing and unpacking certain objects very cleverly and very quickly.

Then he realized that the other was interested in its *effects*, in the ability it could give the Tinkers to listen to the Authority satellites.

His uncertainty was misinterpreted, for the taller boy laughed. "Never mind, I won't push you. Fact is, I probably shouldn't know. C'mon, there's one thing more I want to show you—though maybe it should be a secret, too. The Colonel thinks the Peace Authority might issue a Ban if they knew about it."

They continued down the farm's main road, which ran directly into the side of the Vandenberg Dome some thousand meters further on. It made Wili dizzy just to look in that direction. This close, there was no feeling of the overall shape of the Dome. In a sense, it was invisible, a vast vertical mirror. In it he saw the rolling hills of the farm, the landscape that spread away behind them: there were a couple of small sailboats making for the north shore of Lake Lompoc, and he could see the ferry docked on the near side of the Salsipuedes fiord.

As they walked closer to the bobble, he saw that the ground right at the edge was torn, twisted. Rain off the Dome had gouged a deep river around the base, runoff to Lake Lompoc. The ground shook faintly but constantly with tiny earthquakes. Wili tried to imagine the other half of the bobble, extending kilometers into the earth. No wonder the world trembled around this obstruction. He looked up and swayed.

"Gets you, doesn't it?" Jeremy grabbed his arm and steadied him. "I grew up close to it, and I still fall flat on my behind when I stand here and imagine trying to climb the thing." They scrambled up the embanked mud and looked down at the river. Even though it hadn't rained for hours, the waters moved fast and muddy, gouging at the land. Across the river, a phantom Jeremy and Wili stared back. "It's dangerous to get much closer. The water channel extends a ways underground. We've had some pretty big landslides.

"That's not why I brought you here, anyway." He led Wili down the embankment toward a small building. "There's another level in Mike's pyramid: the folks who make things like carts and houses and plows. The refurbishers still do a lot of that, but they're running out of ruins, at least around here. The new stuff is made just like it was hundreds of years ago. It's expensive and takes a lot of work—the type of thing the Republic of New Mexico or Aztlán is good at. Well, we can program processors to control moving-parts machines. I don't see why we can't make a moving-parts machine to *make* all those other things. That's my own special project."

"Yes, but that's Banned. Are you telling me—"

"Moving-parts machines aren't Banned. Not directly. It's high-energy, high-speed stuff the Authority is death on. They don't want anyone making bombs or bobbles and starting another War." The building looked like the one they had left up the road, but with fewer windows.

An ancient metal pylon stuck out of the ground near the entrance. Wili looked at it curiously, and Jeremy said, "It doesn't have anything to do with my project. When I was little, you could still see numbers painted on it. It's off the wing of a pre-Authority airplane. The Colonel thinks it must have been taking off from Vandenberg Air Force Base at the instant they were bobbled: half of it fell out here, and the rest crashed inside the Dome."

He followed Jeremy into the building. It was much dimmer than inside the software house. Something moved; something made high-pitched humming noises. It took Wili a second to realize that he and Jeremy were the only living things present. Jeremy led him down an aisle toward the sounds. A small conveyer belt stretched into the darkness. Five tiny arms that ended in mechanical hands were making a . . . what? It was barely two meters long and one high. It had wheels, though smaller than those on a cart. There was no room for passengers or cargo. Beyond this machine aborning, Wili saw at least four completed copies.

"This is my fabricator." Jeremy touched one of the mechanical arms. The machine immediately stopped its precise movements, as though in respect to a master. "It can't do the whole job, only the motor windings and the wiring. But I'm going to improve it."

Wili was more interested in what was being fabricated. "What . . . are they?" He pointed to the vehicles.

"Farm tractors, of course! They're not big. They can't carry passengers; you have to walk behind them. But they can draw a plow, and do planting. They can be charged off the roof batteries. It's a dangerous first project, I know. But I wanted to make something nice. The tractors aren't really vehicles; I don't think the Authority will even notice. If they do, we'll just make something else. My fabricators are flexible."

They'll Ban your fabricators, too. Not surprisingly, Wili had absorbed Paul's opinion of the Peace Authority. They had Banned the research that could cure his own problems. They were like all the other tyrannies, only more powerful.

But Wili said none of this aloud. He walked to the nearest completed "tractor" and put his hand on the motor shell, half expecting to feel some electric power.

This was, after all, a machine that could move under its own power. How many times had he dreamed of driving an automobile. He knew it was the fondest wish of some minor Jonque aristocrats that one of their sons might be accepted as an Authority truck driver.

"You know, Jeremy, this thing *can* carry a passenger. I bet I could sit here on its back and still reach the controls."

A grin slowly spread across Jeremy's face. "By golly, I see what you mean. If only I weren't so big, I could, too. Why, you could be an automobilist! C'mon, let's move this one outside. There's smooth ground behind the building where we can—"

A faint *beep* came from the phone at Jeremy's waist. He frowned and raised the device to his ear. "Okay. Sorry.

"Wili, the Colonel and Dr. Naismith want to see us—and they mean right now. I guess we were expected to hang around the main house and wait on their pleasure." It was closest Wili ever heard Jeremy come to disrespect for his elders. They started toward the door. "We'll come back before the afternoon rain and try to ride."

But there was sadness in his voice, and Wili looked back into the shadowed room. Somehow he doubted he would return any time soon.

12

It might have been a council of war. Colonel Kaladze certainly looked the part. In some ways Kaladze reminded Wili of the bosses in the Ndelante Ali: he was almost eighty, yet ramrod straight. His hair was cut as theirs, about five millimeters long everywhere, even on the face. The silvery stubble was stark against his tan. His gray-green work clothes were unremarkable except for their starched and shiny neatness. His blue eyes were capable of great good humor—Wili remembered from the welcoming dinner—but this morning they were set and hard. Next to him Miguel Rosas—even armed and wearing his sheriff's brassard—looked like a loose civilian.

Paul looked the same as always, but he avoided Wili's eyes. And that was the most ominous sign of all.

"Be seated, gentlemen," the old Russian spoke to the boys. All his sons—except Jeremy's father, who was on a sales expedition to Corvallis—were present.

"Wili, Jeremy, you'll be leaving for San Diego earlier than we had planned. The Authority desires to sponsor the North American Chess Tourney, much as they've sponsored the Olympics these last few years: they are providing special transportation, and have moved up the semifinals correspondingly."

This was like a burglar who finds his victim passing out engraved invitations, thought Wili.

Even Jeremy seemed a little worried by it: "What will this do to Wili's plan to, uh, get some help down there? Can he do this right under their noses?"

"I think so. Mike thinks so." He glanced at Miguel Rosas, who gave a brief nod. "At worst, the Authority is suspicious of us Tinkers as a group. They don't have any special reason to be watching Wili. In any case, if we are to participate, our group must be ready for their truck convoy. It will pass the farm in less than fifteen hours."

Truck convoy. The boys stared at each other. For an instant, any danger seemed small. The Authority was going to let them ride like kings down the coast of California all the way to La Jolla! "All who go must leave the farm in two or three hours to reach Highway One-oh-one before the convoy passes through." He grinned at Ivan, his eldest son. "Even if the Authority is watching, even if Wili didn't need help, Kaladzes would still be going. You boys can't fool me. I know you've been looking forward to this for a long time. I know all the time you've wasted on programs you think are unbeatable."

Ivan Nikolayevich seemed startled, then smiled back. "Besides, there are people there we've known for years and never met in person. It would be even more suspicious if we pulled out now."

Wili looked across the table at Naismith. "Is it okay, Paul?"

Suddenly Naismith seemed much older even than the Colonel. He lowered his head and spoke softly. "Yes, Wili. It's our best chance to get you some help. . . . But we've hired Mike to go instead of me. I can't come along. You see—"

Paul's voice continued, but Wili heard no more. *Paul will not come. This one chance to find a cure and Paul will not come.* For a moment that lasted long inside his head, the room whirled down to a tiny point and was replaced by Wili's earliest memories:

Claremont Street, seen through an unglazed window, seen from a small bed. The first five years of his life, he had spent most of every day in that bed, staring out into the empty street. Even in that he had been lucky. At that time Glendora had been an outland, beyond the reach of the Jonque lords and the milder tyranny of the Ndelante Ali. Wili, those first few years, was so weak he could scarcely eat even when food was right at hand. Survival had depended on his Uncle Sly. If he still lived, Sylvester would be older than Naismith himself. When Wili's parents wanted to give their sickly newborn to the coyotes and the hawks, it had been Uncle Sly who argued and pleaded and finally persuaded them to abandon Wili's worthless body to him instead. Wili would never forget the old man's face—so black and gnarled, fringed with silver hair. Outside he was so different from Naismith, inside so like him.

For Sylvester Washington (he insisted on the Anglo pronunciation of his last name) had been over thirty when the War came. He had been a schoolteacher, and he would not give up his last child easily. He made a bed for Wili, and made sure it faced on to the street so that the invalid boy could see and hear as much as possible. Sylvester Washington talked to him hours every day. Where similar children wasted and starved, Wili slowly grew. His earliest memories, after the view of Claremont Street through the window hole, were of Uncle Sly playing number games with him, forcing him to work with his mind when he could do nothing with his body.

Later the old man helped the boy exercise his body, too. But that was after dark, in the dusty yard behind the ruin he called their "ranch house." Night after night, Wili crawled across the warm earth, till finally his legs were strong enough to stand on. Sly would not let him stop till he could walk..

But he never took him out during the day, saying that it was too dangerous. The boy didn't see why. The street beyond his window was always quiet and empty.

Wili was almost six years old when he found the answer to that mystery, and his world ended. Sylvester had already left for work at the secret pond his friends had build above the Ndelante irrigation project. He had promised to come home early with something special, a reward for all the walking.

Wili was tired of the terrible daytime heat within the hovel. He peered through the crooked doorway and then walked slowly out onto the street, reveling in his freedom. He walked down the empty street and suddenly realized that a few more steps would take him to the intersection of Claremont and Catalina—and beyond the furthest reach of his previous explorations. He wandered down Catalina for fifteen or twenty minutes. What a wonderland: vacant ruins desiccating in the sun. They were all sizes, and of subtly different colors depending on the original paint.

Rusted metal hulks sat like giant insects along one side of the street.

More than one house in twenty was occupied. The area had been looted and relooted. But—as Wili learned in later adventures—parts of the Basin were still untouched. Even fifty years after the War there were treasure hoards in the farthest suburbs. Aztlán did not claim a recovery tax for nothing.

Wili was not yet six, but he did not lose his way; he avoided houses that might be occupied and kept to the shadows. After a time he tired and started back. He stopped now and then to watch some lizard scurry from one hole to another. Gaining confidence, he cut across a grocery store parking lot, walked under a sign proclaiming bargains fifty years dead, and turned back onto Claremont. Then everything seemed to happen at once.

There was Uncle Sly, home early from the pond, struggling to carry a bag slung over his back. He saw Wili and his jaw fell. He dropped the bag and started running toward the boy. At the same time the sound of hooves came from a side alley. Five young Jonques burst into the sunlight—labor raiders. One swept the boy up while the rest held off old Sly with their whips. Lying on his belly across the saddle, Wili twisted about and got one last look. There was Sylvester Washington, already far down the street. He was wringing his hands, making no sound, making no effort to save him from the strange men who were taking Wili away.

Wili survived. Five years later he was sold to the Ndelante Ali. Two more years and he had some reputation for his burgling. Eventually, Wili returned to that intersection on Claremont Street. The house was still there; things don't change suddenly in the Basin. But the house was empty. Uncle Sly was gone.

And now he would lose Paul Naismith, too.

The boy's walleyed stare must have been taken for attentiveness. Naismith was talking, still not looking directly at Wili. "You are really to be thanked for the discovery, Wili. What we've seen is ... well, it's strange and wonderful and maybe ominous. I *have* to stay. Do you understand?"

Wili didn't really mean the words, but they came anyway. "I understand you won't come along. I understand some silly piece of math is more important."

Worse, the words didn't anger Paul. His head bowed slightly. "Yes. There are some things more important to me than any person. Let me tell you what we saw—"

"Paul, if Mike and Jeremy and Wili are to be in the mouth of the lion, there is no sense in their knowing more right now."

"As you say, 'Kolya." Naismith rose and walked slowly to the door. "Please excuse me."

There was a short silence, broken by the Colonel. "We'll have to work fast to get you three on the way in time. Ivan, show me just what your chess fans want to send with Jeremy. If the Authority is providing transport, maybe Mike and the boys can take a more elaborate processor." He departed with his sons and Jeremy.

That left Wili and Mike. The boy stood and turned to the door.

"Just a minute, you." Mike's voice had the hard edge Wili remembered from their first encounter months before. The undersheriff came around the table and pushed Wili back into his chair. "You think Paul has deserted you. Maybe he has, but from what

I can tell, they've discovered something more important than the lot of us. I don't know exactly what it is, or I couldn't go with you and Jeremy either. Get it? We can't afford to let Naismith fall into Authority hands.

"Consider yourself damn lucky we're going through with Paul's hare-brained scheme to get you cured. He's the only man on Earth who could've convinced Kaladze to deal even indirectly with the bioscience swine." He glared down at Wili, as if expecting some counterattack. The boy was silent and avoided his eyes.

"Okay. I'll be waiting for you in the dining house." Rosas stalked out of the room.

Wili was motionless for a long time. There were no tears; there had been none since that afternoon very long ago on Claremont Street. He didn't bame Sylvester Washington and he didn't blame Paul Naismith. They had done as much as one man can do for another. But ultimately there is only one person who can't run away from your problems.

13

Still five meters up, the twin-rotor chopper sent a shower of grit across the Tradetower helipad. From her place in the main cabin, Della Lu watched the bystanders grab their hats and squint into the wash. Old Hamilton Avery was the only fellow who kept his aplomb.

As the chopper touched down, one of her crew slid open the front hatch and waved at the standing VIPs. Through her silvered window, she saw Director Avery nod and turn to shake hands with Smythe, the LA franchise owner. Then Avery walked alone toward the crewman, who had not stepped down from the doorway.

Smythe was probably the most powerful Peacer in Southern California. She wondered what he thought when his boss submitted to such a cavalier pickup. She smiled lopsidedly. Hell, she was in charge of the operation, and she didn't know what was coming off either.

The rotors spun up even as she heard the hatch slam. Her crew had their orders: the helipad dropped away as the chopper rose like some magic elevator from the top of the Tradetower. They slid out from the roof and she looked down eighty stories at the street.

As the helicopter turned toward LAX and Santa Monica, Della came to her feet. An instant later Avery entered her cabin. He looked completely relaxed yet completely formal, his dress both casual and expensive. In theory, the Board of Directors of the Peace Authority was a committee of equals. In fact, Hamilton Avery had been the driving force behind it for as long as Della Lu had been following inner politics. Though not a famous man, he was the most powerful one in the world.

"My dear! So good to see you." Avery walked quickly to her, shook her hand as if she were an equal and not an officer three levels below him. She let the silver-haired Director take her elbow and lead her to a seat. One might think she was his guest.

They sat down, and the director looked quickly about the cabin. It was a solid, mobile command room. There was no bar, no carpets. With her priority, she could have had such, but Della had not gotten to her present job by sucking up to her bosses.

The aircraft hummed steadily westward, the chop of the blades muted by the office's heavy insulation. Below, Della could see Peace Authority housing. The Enclave was really a corridor that extended from Santa Monica and LAX on the coast, inland to what had once been the center of Los Angeles. It was the largest Enclave in the world. More than fifty thousand people lived down there, mostly near the News

Service studios. And they lived well. She saw swimming pools and tennis courts on the three-acre suburban lots that passed below.

In the north glowered the castles and fortified roads of the Aztlán aristocrats. They had governmental responsibility for the region, but without Banned technology their "palaces" were medieval dumps. Like the Republic of New Mexico, Aztlán watched the Authority with impotent jealousy and dreamed of the good old days.

Avery looked up from the view. "I noticed you had the Beijing insignia painted over."

"Yes, sir. It was clear from your message that you didn't want people to guess you were using people from off North America." That was one of the few things that was crystal clear. Three days before she had been at the Beijing Enclave, just returned from her final survey of the Central Asian situation. Then a megabyte of detailed instructions came over the satellite from Livermore—and not to the Beijing franchise owner, but to one Della Lu, third-level counterguerrilla cop and general hatchetman. She was assigned a cargo jet—its freight being this chopper—and told to fly across the Pacific to LAX. No one was to emerge at any intermediate stop. At LAX, the freighter crew was to disgorge the chopper with her people, and return immediately.

Avery nodded approvingly. "Good. I need someone who doesn't need everything spelled out. Have you had a chance to read the New Mexico report?"

"Yes, sir." She had spent the flight studying the report and boning up on North American politics. She had been gone three years; there'd have been a lot of catching up to do—even without the Tucson crisis.

"Do you think the Republic bought our story?"

She thought back on the meeting tape and the dossiers. "Yes. Ironically, the most suspicious of them were also the most ignorant. Schelling bought it hook, line, and sinker. He knows enough theory to see that it's reasonable."

Avery nodded.

"But they'll continue to believe only if no more bobbles burst. And I understand it's happened at least twice more during the last few weeks. I don't believe the quantum decay explanation. The old USA missile fields are littered with thousands of bobbles. If decays continue to happen, they won't be missed."

Avery nodded again, didn't seem especially upset by her analysis.

The chopper did a gentle bank over Santa Monica, giving her a close-up view of the largest mansions in the Enclave. She had a glimpse of the Authority beach and the ruined Aztlán shoreline further south, and then they were over the ocean. They flew south several kilometers before turning inland. They would fly in vast circles until the meeting was over. Even the Tucson event could not explain this mission. Della almost frowned.

Avery raised a well-manicured hand. "What you say is correct, but may be irrelevant. It depends on what the true explanation turns out to be. Have you considered the possibility that someone has discovered how to destroy bobbles, that we are seeing their experiments?"

"The choice of 'experiment sites' is very strange, sir: the Ross Iceshelf, Tucson, Ulan Ude. And I don't see how such an organization could escape direct detection."

Fifty-five years ago, before the War, what had become the Peace Authority had been a contract laboratory, a corporation run under federal grants to do certain esoteric—and militarily productive—research. That research had produced the bobbles, force fields whose generation took a minimum of thirty minutes of power from the largest nuclear plant in the lab. The old US government had not been told of the discovery; Avery's father had seen to that. Instead, the lab directors played their own version of geopolitics. Even at the rarefied bureaucratic heights Della inhabited, there was no solid evidence that the Avery lab had started the War, but she had her suspicions.

In the years following the great collapse, the Authority had stripped the rest of the world of high-energy technology. The most dangerous governments—such as that of the United States—were destroyed, and their territories left in a state that ranged from the village anarchy of Middle California, to the medievalism of Aztlán, to the fascism of New Mexico. Where governments did exist, they were just strong enough to collect the Authority Impost. These little countries were in some ways sovereign. They even fought their little wars—but without the capital industry and high-energy weapons that made war a threat to the race.

Della doubted that, outside the Enclaves, there existed the technical expertise to reproduce the old inventions, much less improve on them. And if someone did discover the secret of the bobble, Authority satellites would detect the construction of the power plants and factories needed to implement the invention.

"I know, I may sound paranoid. But one thing you youngsters don't understand is how technologically stultified the Authority is." He glanced at her, as though expecting debate. "We have all the universities and all the big labs. We control most degreed persons on Earth. Nevertheless, we do very little research. I should know, since I can remember my father's lab right before the War—and even more, because I've made sure no really imaginative projects got funded since.

"Our factories can produce most any product that existed before the War." He slapped his hand against the bulkhead. "This is a good, reliable craft, probably built in the last five years. But the design is almost sixty years old."

He paused and his tone became less casual. "During the last six months, I've concluded we've made a serious mistake in this. There are people operating under our very noses who have technology substantially in advance of pre-War levels."

"I hope you're not thinking of the Mongolian nationalists, sir. I tried to make it clear in my reports that their nuclear weapons were from old Soviet stockpiles. Most weren't usable. And without those bombs they were just pony sol—"

"No, my dear Della, that's not what I am thinking of." He slid a plastic box across the table. "Look inside."

Five small objects sat in the velvet lining. Lu held one in the sunlight. "A bullet?" It looked like an 8-mm. She couldn't tell if it had been fired; there was some damage, but no rifling marks. Something dark and glossy stained the nose.

"That's right. But a bullet with a brain. Let me tell you how we came across that little gem.

"Since I became suspicious of these backyard scientists, these Tinkers, I've been trying to infiltrate. It hasn't been easy. In most of North America, we have tolerated no governments. Even though it's cost us on the Impost, the risk of nationalism seemed too high. Now I see that was a mistake. Somehow they've gone further than any of the governed areas—and we have no easy way to watch them, except from orbit.

"Anyway, I sent teams into the ungoverned lands, using whatever cover was appropriate. In Middle California, for instance, it was easiest to pretend they were descendents of the old Soviet invasion force. Their instructions were to hang around in the mountains and ambush likely-looking travelers. I figured we would gradually accumulate information without any official raids. Last week, one crew ambushed three locals in the forests east of Vandenberg. The quarry had only one gun, a New Mexico eight-millimeter. It was nearly dark, but from a distance of forty meters the enemy hit every one of the ten-man crew—with one burst from the eight-millimeter."

"The New Mexico eight-millimeter only has a ten-round clip. That's—"

"A perfect target score, my dear. And my men swear the weapon was fired on full automatic. If they hadn't been wearing body armor, or if the rounds had had normal velocity, not one of them would have lived to tell the story. Ten armed men killed by one man and a handmade gun. Magic. And you're holding a piece of that magic. Others have been through every test and dissection that Livermore labs could come up with. You've heard of smart bombs? Sure, your air units in Mongolia used them. Well, Miss Lu, these are smart bullets.

"The round has a video eye up front, connected to a processor as powerful as anything we can pack in a suitcase—and our suitcase version would cost a hundred thousand monets. Evidently the gun barrel isn't rifled; the round can change attitude in flight to close with its target."

Della rolled the metal marble in her palm. "So it's under the control of the gunman?"

"Only indirectly, and only at 'launch' time. There must be a processor on the gun that queues the targets, and chooses the firing instant. The processor on the bullet is more than powerful enough to latch the assigned target. Rather interesting, eh?"

Della nodded. She remembered how delicate the attack gear on the A5ll's had been—and how expensive. They'd needed a steady supply of replacement boards from Beijing. If these things could be made cheaply enough to throw away . . . ?

Hamilton Avery gave a small smile, apparently satisfied with her reaction. "That's not all. Take a look at the other things in the box."

Della dropped the bullet onto the velvet padding and picked up a brownish ball. It was slightly sticky on her fingers. There were no markings, no variations in its surface. She raised her eyebrows.

"That is a bug, Della. Not one of your ordinary, audio bugs, but full video—we expect in all directions, at that. Something to do with Fourier optics, my experts tell me. It can record, or transmit a very short distance. We've guessed all this from x-ray micrographs of the interior. We don't even have equipment that can interface with it!"

"You're sure it's not recording right now?"

"Oh yes. They fried its guts before I took it. The microscopists claim there's not a working junction in there.

"Now I think you see the reason for all the precautions."

Della nodded slowly. The bobble bursts were not

the reason; he expected their true enemies already knew all about those. Yes, Avery was being clever—and he was as frightened as his cool personality would ever allow.

They sat silently for about thirty seconds. The chopper made another turn, and the sunlight swept across Della's face. They were flying east over Long Beach toward Anaheim—those were the names in the history books anyway. The street pattern stretched off into gray-orange haze. It gave a false sense of order. The reality was kilometer on kilometer of abandoned, burned-out wilderness. It was hard to believe that this threat could grow in North America. But, after the fact, it made sense. If you deny big industry and big research to people, they will look for other ways of getting what they need.

. . . And if they could make these things, maybe they were clever enough to go beyond all the beautiful quantum-mechanical theories and figure a way to burst bobbles.

"You think they've infiltrated the Authority?"

"I'm sure of it. We swept our labs and conference rooms. We found seventeen bugs on the West Coast, two in China, and a few more in Europe. There were no repeaters near the overseas finds, so we think they were unintentional exports. The plague appears to spread from California."

"So they know we're on to them."

"Yes, but little more. They've made some big mistakes and we've had a bit of good luck: we have an informer in the California group. He came to us less than two weeks ago, out of the blue. I think he's legitimate. What he's told us matches our discoveries but goes a good deal further. We're going to run these people to ground. And do it officially. We haven't made an example of anyone in a long time, not since the Yakima incident.

"Your role in this will be crucial, Della. You are a woman, and outside the Authority the frailer sex is disregarded nowadays."

Not only outside the Authority, thought Della.

"You'll be invisible to the enemy, until it's too late."

"You mean a *field* job?"

"Why, yes, my dear. You've certainly had rougher assignments."

"Yes, but—" *but I was a field director in Mongolia.*

Avery put his hand on Della's. "This is no demotion. You'll be responsible only to me. As communications permit, you'll control the California operation. But we need our very best out there on the ground, someone who knows the land and can be given a credible cover." Della had been born and raised in San Francisco. For three generations, her family had been furbishers—and Authority plants.

"And there is a very special thing I want done. This may be more important than all the rest of the operation." Avery laid a color picture on the table. The photo was grainy, blown up to near the resolution limit. She saw a group of men standing in front of a barn: northern farmers—except for the black child talking to a tall boy who carried an NM 8-mm. She could guess who these were.

"See the guy in the middle—by the one with the soldier frizz."

His face was scarcely more than a blotch, but he looked perfectly ordinary, seventy or eighty years old. Della could walk through a crowd in any North American enclave and see a dozen such.

"We think that's Paul Hoehler." He glanced at his

agent. "The name doesn't mean anything to you, does it? Well, you won't find it in the history books, but I remember him. Back in Livermore, right before the War. I was just a kid. He was in my father's lab and . . . he's the man who invented the bobble."

Della's attention snapped back to the photo. She knew she had just been let in on one of those secrets which was kept from everyone, which would otherwise die with the last of the old Directors. She tried to see something remarkable in the fuzzy features.

"Oh, Schmidt, Kashihara, Bhadra, they got the thing into projectable form. But it was one of Hoehler's bright ideas. The hell of it is, the man wasn't—isn't— even a physicist.

"Anyway, he disappeared right after the War started. Very clever. He didn't wait to do any moral posturing, to give us a chance to put him away. Next to eliminating the national armies, catching him was one of our highest priorities. We never got him. After ten or fifteen years, when we had control of all the remaining labs and reactors, the search for Dr. Hoehler died. But now, after all these years, when we see bobbles being burst, we have rediscovered him . . . . You can see why I'm convinced the 'bobble decay' is not natural."

Avery tapped the picture. "This is the man, Della. In the next weeks, we'll take Peace action against hundreds of people. But it will all be for nothing if you can't nail this one man."

FLASHFORWARD

Allison's wound showed no sign of reopening, and she didn't think there was much internal bleeding. It hurt, but she could walk. She and Quiller set up camp—more a hiding place than a camp, really— about twenty minutes from the crash site.

The fire had put a long plume of reddish smoke into the sky. If there was a sane explanation for all this, that plume would attract Air Force rescue. And if it attracted unfriendlies first, then they were far enough away from the crash to escape. She hoped.

The day passed, warm and beautiful—and untouched by any sign of other human life. Allison found herself impatient and talkative. She had theories: a cabin leak on their last revolution could almost explain things. Hypoxia can sneak up on you before you know it—hadn't something like that killed three Sov pilots in the early days of space? Hell, it could probably account for all sorts of jumbled memories. Somehow their reentry sequence had been delayed.

They'd ended up in the Australian jungles.... No that wasn't right, not if the problem had really happened on the last rev. Perhaps Madagascar was a possibility. That People's Republic would not exactly welcome them. They would have to stay undercover till Air Force tracking and reconnaissance spotted the crash site.... A strike-rescue could come any time now, say with the Air Force covering a VTOL Marine landing.

Angus didn't buy it. "There's the dome, Allison. No country on Earth could build something like that without us knowing about it. I swear it's kilometers high." He waved at the second sun that stood in the west. The two suns were difficult to see through the forest cover. But during their hike from the crash site they'd had better views. When Allison looked directly at the false sun with narrowed eyes, she could see that the disk was a distorted oval—clearly a reflection off some vast curved surface. "I know it's huge, Angus. But it doesn't have to be a physical structure. Maybe it's some sort of inversion layer effect."

"You're only seeing the part that's way off the ground, where there's nothing to reflect except sky. If you climb one of the taller trees, you'd see the coastline reflected in the dome's base."

"Hmm." She didn't have to climb any trees to believe him. What she couldn't believe was his explanation.

"Face it, Allison. We're nowhere in the world we knew. Yet the tombstone shows we're still on Earth."

The tombstone. So much smaller than the dome, yet so much harder to explain. "You still think it's the future?"

Angus nodded. "Nothing else fits. I don't know how fast something like stone carving wears: I sup-

pose we can't be more than a thousand years ahead."
He grinned. "An ordinary, Buck Rogers-like interval."

She smiled back. "Better Buck Rogers than *The Last Remake* or *Planet of the Apes.*"

"Yeah. I never like it where they kill off all the 'extra' time-travelers."

Allison gazed through the forest canopy at the second sun. There had to be some other explanation.

They argued it back and forth for hours, in the end agreeing to give the "rescued from Madagascar" theory twenty-four hours to show success. After that they would hike down to the coast, and then along it till they found some form of humanity.

It was late afternoon when they heard it: a whistling scream that grew abruptly to a roar.

"Aircraft!" Allison struggled to her feet.

Angus shook himself, and looked into the sky. Then he was standing, too, all but dancing from one foot to the other.

Something dark and arrow-shaped swept over them. "An A-five-eleven, by God," exulted Angus. "Somehow you were right, Allison!" He hugged her.

There were at least three jets. The air was filled with their sound. And it was a joint operation. They glimpsed the third coming to a hover just three hundred meters away. It was one of the new Sikorsky troop carriers. Only the Marines flew those.

They started down the narrow path toward the nearest of the ships, Allison's gait a limping jog. Suddenly Angus' hand closed on her arm. She spun around, off balance. The pilot was pointing through a large gap in the branches, at the hovering Sikorsky. *"Paisley?"* was all he said.

"What?" Then she saw it. The outer third of the

wings was covered with an extravagant paisley pattern. In the middle was set a green phi or theta symbol. It was utterly unlike any military insignia she had ever seen.

14

The atmosphere of an open chess tournament hadn't changed much in the last hundred years. A visitor from 1948 might wonder at the plush, handmade clothing and the strange haircuts. But the important things—the informality mixed with intense concentration, the wide range of ages, the silence on the floor, the long tables and rows of players—all would be instantly recognizable.

Only one important thing had changed, and that might take the hypothetical time-traveler a while to notice: the contestants did not play alone. Teams were not allowed, but virtually all serious players had assistance, usually in the form of a gray box sitting by the board or on the floor near their feet. The more conservative players used small keyboards to communicate with their programs. Others seemed unconnected to any aid but every so often would look off into the distance, lost in concentration. A few of

131

these were players in the old sense, disdaining all programmatic magic.

Wili was the most successful of these atavists. His eyes flickered down the row of boards, trying to decide who were the truly human players and who were the fakes. Beyond the end of the table, the Pacific Ocean was a blue band shining through the open windows of the pavilion.

Wili pulled his attention back to his own game, trying to ignore the crowd of spectators and trying even less successfully to ignore his opponent. Though barely out of a Ruy Lopez opening—that's what Jeremy had called it the other night, anyway—Wili had a good feeling about the game. A strong kingside attack should now be possible, unless his opponent had a complete surprise up her sleeve. This would be his fifth straight win. That accounted for the crowd. He was the only purely human player still undefeated. Wili smiled to himself. This was a totally unexpected by-product of the expedition, but a very pleasant one. He had never been admired for anything (unless his reputation within the Ndelante counted as admirable). It would be a pleasure to show these people how useless their machines really were. For the moment he forgot that every added attention would make it harder for him to fade away when the time came.

Wili considered the board a second longer, then pushed his bishop pawn, starting a sequence of events that ought to be unstoppable. He punched his clock, and finally raised his eyes to look at his opponent.

Dark brown eyes looked back at him. The girl— woman, she must be in her twenties—smiled at Wili as she acknowledged his move. She leaned forward, and raised an input/output band to her temple. Soft black hair spilled across that hand.

Almost ten minutes passed. Some of the spectators began drifting off. Wili just sat and tried to pretend he was not looking at the girl. She was just over one meter fifty, scarcely taller than he. And she was the most beautiful creature he had ever seen. He could sit this close to her and not have to say anything, not have to make conversation. . . . Wili rather wished the game might last forever.

When she finally moved, it was another pawn push. Very strange, very risky. She was definitely a soft player: in the last three days, Wili had played more chess than in the last three months. Almost all of it had been against assisted players. Some were mere servants to their machines. You could trust them never to make a simple mistake, and to take advantage of any you made. Playing them was like fighting a bull, impossible if you attack head on, easy once you identify the weak points. Other players, like Jeremy, were soft, more fallible, but full of intricate surprises. Jeremy said his program interacted with his own creativity. He claimed it made him better than either machine or human alone. Wili would only agree that it was better than being the slave of a processor.

This Della Lu, her play was as soft as her skin. Her last move was full of risk and—he saw now—full of potential. A machine alone could never have proposed it.

Rosas and Jeremy drifted into view behind her. Rosas was not entered in the tournament. Jeremy and his Red Arrow special were doing well, but he had a bye on this round. Jeremy caught his eye; they wanted him outside. Wili felt a flash of irritation.

Finally he decided on the best attack. His knight came out from the third rank, brazen ahead of the pawns. He pushed the clock; several minutes passed. The girl reached for her king . . . and turned it over! She stood, extended her hand across the table to Wili. "A nice game. Thank you very much." She spoke in English, with a faint Bay Area twang.

Wili tried to cover his surprise. She had lost, he was sure of that. But for her to see it this early. . . . She must be almost as clever as he. Wili held her cool hand a moment, then remembered to shake it. He stood and gargled something unintelligible, but it was too late. The spectators closed in with their congratulations. Wili found himself shaking hands all around, and some of those hands were jeweled, belonged to Jonque aristocrats. This was, he was told, the first time in five years an unaided player had made it to the final rounds. Some thought he had a chance of winning it all, and how long had it been since a plain human had been North American champion?

By the time he was out of his circle of admirers, Della Lu had retired in graceful defeat. Anyway, Miguel Rosas and Jeremy Sergeivich were waiting to grab him. "A good win," Mike said, setting his arm across the boy's shoulder. "I'll bet you'd like to get some fresh air after all that concentration."

Wili agreed ungraciously and allowed himself to be guided out. At least they managed to avoid the two Peace reporters who were covering the event.

The Fonda la Jolla pavilions were built over one of the most beautiful beaches in Aztlán. Across the bay, two thousand meters away, graygreen vineyards topped the tan-and-orange cliffs. Wili could follow those cliffs and the surf north and north till they vanished in the haze somewhere near Los Angeles.

They started up the lawn toward the resort's restaurant. Beyond it were the ruins of old La Jolla: there was more stonework than in Pasadena. It was dry and pale, without the hidden life of the Basin. No wonder the Jonque lords had chosen La Jolla for their resort. The place was far from both slums and estates. The lords could meet here in truce, their rivalries ignored. Wili wondered what the Authority had done to persuade them to allow the tournament here, though it was possible that the popularity of the game alone explained it.

"I found Paul's friends, Wili," said Rosas.

"Huh?" He came back to their real problems with an unpleasant lurch. "When do we go?"

"This evening. After your next game. You've got to lose it."

"What? Why?"

"Look," Mike spoke intensely, "we're risking a lot for you. Give us an excuse to drop this project and *we will.*"

Wili bit his lip. Jeremy followed in silence, and Wili realized that Rosas was right for once. Both of them had put their freedom, maybe even their lives, on the line for him—or was it really for Paul? No matter. Next to bobble research, bioscience was the blackest crime in the Authority's book. And they were mixing in it to get him cured.

Rosas took Wili's silence for the acquiescence it was. "Okay. I said you'll have to lose the next one. Make a big scene about it, something that will give us the excuse to get you outside and away from everyone else." He gave the boy a sidelong glance. "You won't find it too hard to do that, will you?"

"Where is . . . it . . . anyway?" asked Jeremy.

But Rosas just shook his head, and once inside the restaurant there was no chance for further conversation.

Roberto Richardson, the tournament roster said. That was his next opponent, the one he must lose to. *This is going to be even harder than I thought*. Wili watched his fat opponent walk across the pavilion toward the game table. Richardson was the most obnoxious of Jonque types, the Anglo. And worse, the pattern of his jacket showed he was from the estates above Pasadena. There were very few Anglos in the nobility of Aztlán. Richardson was as pale as Jeremy Sergeivich, and Wili shuddered to think of the compensating nastiness the man must contain. He probably had the worst-treated labor gangs in Pasadena. His type always took it out on the serfs, trying to convince his peers that he was just as much a lord as they.

Most Jonques kept only a single bodyguard in the pavilion. Richardson was surrounded by four.

The big man smiled down at Wili as he put his equipment on the table and attached a scalp connector. He extended a fat white hand, and Wili shook it. "I am told you are a former countryman of mine, from Pasadena, no less." He used the formal "you."

Wili nodded. There was nothing but good fellowship on the other's face, as though their social differences were some historical oddity. "But now I live in Middle California."

"Ah, yes. Well, you could scarcely have developed your talents in Los Angeles, could you, son?" He sat down, and the clock was started. Appropriately, Richardson had white.

The game went fast at first, but Wili felt badgered by the other's chatter. The Jonque was all quite friendly, asking him if he liked Middle California, saying how nice it must be to get away from his "disadvantaged condition" in the Basin. Under other circumstances, Wili would have told the Jonque off— there was probably no danger doing so in the truce area. But Rosas had told him to let the game go at least an hour before making an argument.

It was ten moves into the game before Wili realized how far astray his anger was taking him. He looked at Richardson's queen side opening and saw that the advantage of position was firmly in his fat opponent's hands. The conversation had not distracted Richardson in the least. Wili looked over his opponent's shoulder at the pale ocean. On the horizon, undisturbed and far away, an Authority tanker moved slowly north. Nearer, two Aztlán sail freighters headed the other way. He concentrated on their silent, peaceful motion till Richardson's comments were reduced to unintelligible mumbling. Then he looked down at the board and put all his concentration into recovery.

Richardson's talk continued for several moments, then faded away completely. The pale aristocrat eyed Wili with a faintly nonplussed expression, but did not become angry. Wili did not notice. For him, the only evidence of his opponent was in the moves of the game. Even when Mike and Jeremy came in, even when his previous opponent, Della Lu, stopped by the table, Wili did not notice.

For Wili was in trouble. This was his weakest opening of the tournament, and—psychological warfare aside—this was his strongest opponent. Richardson's play was both hard and soft: he didn't make mistakes and there was imagination in everything he did. Jeremy had said something about Richardson's being a strong opponent, one who had a fast machine, superb interactive programs, and the intelligence to use them. That had been several days ago, and Wili had forgotten. He was finding out firsthand now.

The attack matured over the next five moves, a tightening noose about Wili's playing space. The enemy—Wili no longer thought of him by name, or even as a person—could see many moves into the future, could pursue broad strategy even beyond that. Wili had almost met his match.

Each move took longer and longer as the players lapsed into catatonic evaluation of their fate. Finally, with the endgame in sight, Wili pulled the sharpest finesse of his short career. His enemy was left with two rooks—against Wili's knight, bishop, and three well-placed pawns. To win he needed some combinatoric jewel, something as clever as his invention of the previous winter. Only now he had twenty minutes, not twenty weeks.

With every move, the pressure in his head increased. He felt like a runner racing an automobile, or like the John Henry of Naismith's story disks. His naked intelligence was fighting an artificial monster, a machine that analyzed a million combinations in the time he could look at one.

The pain shifted from his temples to his nose and eyes. It was a stinging sensation that brought him out of the depths, into the real world.

Smoke! Richardson had lit an enormous cigar. The tarry smoke drifted across the table into Wili's face.

"Put that out." Wili's voice was flat, the rage barely controlled.

Richardson's eyes widened in innocent surprise. He stubbed out his expensive light. "I'm sorry. I knew Northerners might not be comfortable with this, but you blacks get enough smoke in your eyes." He smiled. Wili half rose, his hands making fists. Someone pushed him back into his chair. Richardson eyed him with tolerant contempt, as if to say "race will out."

Wili tried to ignore the look and the crowd around the table. He had to win now!

He stared and stared at the board. Done right, he was sure those pawns could march through the enemy's fire. But his time was running out and he couldn't recapture his previous mental state.

His enemy was making no mistakes; *his* play was as infernally deep as ever.

Three more moves. Willi's pawns were going to die. All of them. The spectators might not see it yet, but Wili did, and so did Richardson.

Wili swallowed, fighting nausea. He reached for his king, to turn it on its side and so resign. Unwillingly, his eyes slid across the board and met Richardson's. "You played a good game, son. The best I've ever seen from an unaided player."

There was no overt mockery in the other's voice, but by now Wili knew better. He lunged across the table, grabbing for Richardson's throat. The guards were fast. Wili found himself suspended above the table, held by a half-dozen not-too-gentle hands. He screamed at Richardson, the Spañolnegro curses expert and obscene.

The Jonque stepped back from the table and motioned his guards to lower Wili to the floor. He caught Rosas' eye and said mildly, "Why don't you take your little Alekhine outside to cool off?"

Rosas nodded. He and Jeremy frog-marched the

still-struggling loser toward the door. Behind them,
Wili heard Richardson trying to convince the tourna-
ment directors—with all apparent sincerity—to let
Wili continue in the tournament.

15

Moments later, they were outside and shed of gawkers. Wili's feet settled back on the turf and he walked more or less willingly between Rosas and Jeremy.

For the first time in years, for the first time since he lost Uncle Sly, Wili found himself crying. He covered his face with his hands, trying to separate himself from the outside world. There could be no keener humiliation than this.

"Let's take him down past the buses, Jeremy. A little walk will do him good."

"It really was a good game, Wili," said Jeremy. "I told you Richardson's rated Expert. You came close to beating him."

Wili barely heard. "I had that Jonque bastard. *I had him!* When he lit that cigar, I lost my concentration. I tell you, if he did not cheat, I would have killed him."

They walked thirty meters, and Wili gradually quieted. Then he realized there had been no encouraging reply. He dopped his hands and glared at Jeremy. "Well, don't you think so?"

Jeremy was stricken, honesty fighting with friendship. "Richardson is a Mouth, you're right. He goes after everyone like that; he seems to think it's part of the game. You notice how it hardly affected his concentration? He just checkpoints his program when he gets talking, so he can dump back into his original mental set any time. He never loses a beat."

"And so I should have won." Wili was not going to let the other wriggle out of the question.

"Well, uh, Wili, look. You're the best unaided player I've ever seen. You lasted more rounds than any other purely-human. But be honest: didn't you feel something different when you played him? I mean apart from his lip? Wasn't he a little more tricky than the earlier players . . . a little more deadly?"

Wili thought back to the image of John Henry and the steam drill. And he suddenly remembered that Expert was the low end of champion class. He began to see Jeremy's point. "So you really think the machines and the scalp connects make a difference?"

Jeremy nodded. It was no more than bookkeeping and memory enhancement, but if it could turn Roberto Richardson into a genius, what would it do for . . . ? Wili remembered Paul's faint smile at Wili's disdain of mechanical aids. He remembered the hours Paul himself spent in processor connect. "Can you show me how to use such things, Jeremy? Not just for chess?"

"Sure. It will take a while. We have to tailor the program to the user, and it takes time to learn to interpret a scalp connect. But come next year, you'll beat anything—animal, vegetable, or mineral." He laughed.

"Okay," Rosas said suddenly. "We can talk now."

Wili looked up. They had walked far past the parking lots. They were moving down a dusty road that went north around the bay, to the vineyards. The hotel was lost to sight. It was like waking from a dream suddenly to realize that the game and argument were mere camouflage.

"You did a real good job, Wili. That was exactly the incident we needed, and it happened at just the right time." The sun was about twenty minutes above the horizon, its light already misted. Orange twilight was growing. A puffy fog gathered along the beach like some silent army, preparing for its assault inland.

Wili wiped his face with the back of his arm. "No act."

"Nevertheless, it couldn't have worked out better. I don't think anybody will be surprised if you don't show till morning."

"Great."

The road descended. The only vegetation was aromatic brush bearing tiny purple flowers; it grew, scraggly, around the foundations and the ruined walls.

The fog moved over the coast, scruffy clots of haze, quite different from an inland fog; these were more like real clouds brought close to earth. The sun shone through the mists. The cliffsides were still visible, turning steadily more gold—a dry color that contrasted with the damp of the air.

As they reached beach level, the sun went behind the dense cloud deck at the horizon and spread into an orange band. The colors faded and the fog became more substantial. Only a single star, almost overhead, could penetrate the murk.

The road narrowed. The ocean side was lined with eucalyptus, their branches rattling in the breeze. They passed a large sign that proclaimed that the State's

Highway—this dirt road—was now passing through Viñas Scripps. Beyond the trees, Wili could see regular rows of vertical stakes. The vines were dim gargoyles on the stakes. They walked steadily higher, but the invading fog kept pace, became even thicker. The surf was loud, even sixty meters above the beach.

"I think we're all alone up here," Jeremy said in a low voice.

"Of course, without this fog, we'd be clear as Vandenberg to anyone at the hotel."

"That's one reason for doing it tonight."

They passed an occasional wagon, no doubt used to carry grapes up the grade to the winery. The way widened to the left and split into a separate road. They followed the turnoff and saw an orange glow floating in the darkness. It was an oil lamp hung at the entrance to a wide adobe building. A sign—probably grand and colorful in the day—announced in Spanish and English that this was the central winery of Viñas Scripps and that tours for gentlemen and their ladies could be scheduled for the daylight hours. Only empty winery carts were parked in the lot fronting the building.

The three walked almost shyly to the entrance. Rosas tapped on the door. It was opened by a thirtyish Anglo woman. They stepped inside, but she said immediately, "Tours during daylight hours only, gentlemen." The last word had a downward inflection; it was clear they were not even minor aristocrats. Wili wondered that she opened the door at all.

Mike replied that they had left the tournament at Fonda la Jolla while it was still day and hadn't realized the walk was so long. "We've come all the way from Santa Ynez, in part to see your famous winery and its equipment. . . ."

"From Santa Ynez," the woman repeated and appeared to commiserate. She seemed younger in the light, but not nearly as pretty as Della Lu. Wili's attention wandered to the posters that covered the foyer walls. They illustrated the various stages of the grape-growing and winemaking processes. "Let me check with my supervisor. He may still be up; in which case, perhaps." She shrugged.

She left them alone. Rosas nodded to Jeremy and Wili. So this was the secret laboratory Paul had discovered. Wili had suspected from the moment the buses pulled into La Jolla. This part of the country was so empty that there hadn't been many possibilities.

Finally a man (the supervisor?) appeared at the door. "Mr. Rosas?" he said in English. "Please come this way." Jeremy and Wili looked at each other. *Mr. Rosas.* Apparently they had passed inspection.

Beyond the door was a wide stairway. By the light of their guide's electric flash, Wili saw that the walls were of natural rock. This was the cave system the winery signs boasted of. They reached the floor and walked across a room filled with enormous wooden casks. An overpowering but not unpleasant yeasty smell filled the cavern. Three young workers nodded to them but did not speak. The supervisor walked behind one of the casks. The back of the wooden cylinder came silently open, revealing a spiral stair. There was barely enough room on it for Jeremy to stand sideways.

"Sorry about the tight fit," the supervisor said. "We can actually pull the stairs downward, out of the cask, so even a thorough search won't find the entrance." He pushed a button on the wall, and a green glow spread down the shaft. Jeremy gave a start of surprise. "Tailored biolight," the man explained. "The stuff uses the carbon dioxide we exhale. Can you imagine what it would do to indoor lighting if we were allowed to market it?" He continued in this vein as they descended, talking about the harmless bioscience inventions that could make so much difference to today's world if only they weren't Banned.

At the bottom, there was another cavern. This one's ceiling was covered with glowing green. It was bright enough to read by, at least where it clumped up, over tables and instrument boards. Everyone looked five weeks dead in the fungal glow. It was very quiet; not even surfsound penetrated the rock. There was no one else in the room.

He led them to a table covered with worn linen sheeting. He patted the table and glanced at Wili. "You're the fellow we've been, uh, hired to help?"

"That's right," said Rosas when Wili gave only a shrug.

"Well, sit up here and I'll take a look at you."

Wili did so, cautiously. There was no antiseptic smell, no needles. He expected the man to tell him to strip, but no such command was given. The supervisor had neither the arrogant indifference of a slave gang vet, nor the solicitous manner of the doctor Paul had called during the winter.

"First off, I want to know if there are any structural problems. . . . Let me see, I've got my scope around here somewhere." He rummaged in an ancient metal cabinet.

Rosas scowled. "You don't have any assistants?"

"Oh, dear me, no." The other did not look up from his search. "There are only five of us here at a time. Before the War, there were dozens of bioscientists in La Jolla. But when we went underground, things changed. For a while, we planned to start a pharmaceutical house as a cover. The Authority hasn't Banned those, you know. But it was just too risky. They would naturally suspect anyone in the drug business.

"So we set up Scripps Vineyards. It's nearly ideal. We can openly ship and receive biologically active materials. And some of our development activities can take place right in our own fields. The location is good, too. We're only five kilometers from Old Five. The beach caves were used for smuggling even before the War, even before the United States ... Aha, here it is." He pulled a plastic cylinder into the light. He walked to another cabinet and returned with a metal hoop nearly 150 centimeters across. There was a click as he slid it into the base of the cylinder. It looked a little foolish, like a butterfly hoop without a net.

"Anyway," he continued as he approached Wili, "the disadvantage is that we can only support a very few 'vineyard technicians' at a time. It's a shame. There's so much to learn. There's so much good we could do for the world." He passed the loop around the table and Wili's body. At the same time he watched the display at the foot of the table.

Rosas said, "I'm sure. Just like the good you did with the plag—" He broke off as the screen came to life. The colors were vivid, glowing with their own light. They seemed more alive than anything else in the green-tinted lab. For a moment it looked like the sort of abstract design that's so easy to generate. Then Wili noticed movement and asymmetries. As the supervisor slid the hoop back over Willi's chest, the elliptical shape shrank dramatically, then grew again as the hoop moved by his head. Wili rose to his elbows in surprise, and the image broadened.

"Lie back down. You don't have to be motionless, but let me choose the view angle."

Wili lay back and felt almost violated. They were seeing a cross section of his own guts, taken in the plane of the hoop! The supervisor brought it back to Willi's chest. They watched his heart squeezing, *thuddub thuddub*. The bioscientist made an adjustment, and the view swelled until the heart filled the display. They could see the blood surge in and out of each chamber. A second display blinked on beside the first, this new one filled with numbers of unknown meaning.

The supervisor continued for ten or fifteen minutes, examining all of Wili's torso. Finally, he removed the hoop and studied the summary data on the displays. "So much for the floor show.

I won't even have to do a genopsy on you, my boy. It's clear that your problem is one we've cured before." He looked at Rosas, finally responding to the other's hostility. "You object to our price, Mr. Rosas?"

The undersheriff started to answer, but the supervisor waved him quiet. "The price is high. We always need the latest electronic equipment. During the last fifty years, the Authority has allowed you Tinkers to flourish. I daresay, you're far ahead of the Authority's own technology. On the other hand, we few poor people in bioresearch have lived in fear, have had to hide in caves to continue our work. And since the Authority has convinced you that we're monsters, most of you won't even sell to us.

"Nevertheless, we've worked miracles these fifty years, Mr. Rosas. If we'd had your freedom, we'd have worked more than miracles. Earth would be Eden now."

"Or a charnel house," Rosas muttered.

The supervisor nodded, seemed only slightly angered. "You say that even when you need us. The plagues warped both you and the Authority. If it hadn't been for those strange accidents, how different things would be. In fact, given a free hand, we could have saved people like this boy from ever having been diseased."

"How?" asked Wili.

"Why, with another plague," the other replied lightly, reminding Wili of the "mad scientists" in the old TV shows Irma and Bill watched. To suggest a plague after all the plagues had done. "Yes, another. You see, your problem was caused by genetic damage to your parents. The most elegant countermeasure would be to tailor a virus that moves through the population, correcting just those genotypes that cause the problem."

Fascination with experiment was clear in his voice. Wili didn't know what to think of his savior, this man of goodwill who might be more dangerous than the Peace Authority and all the Jonque aristocrats put together.

The supervisor sighed and turned off the display. "And yes, I suppose we are crazier than before, maybe even less responsible. After all, we've pinned our whole lives on our beliefs, while the rest of you could drift in the open light without fearing the Authority. . . .

"In any case, there are other ways of curing your disease, and we've known them for decades." He glanced at Rosas. "Safer ways." He walked part way down the corridor to a locker and glanced at a display by the door. "Looks like we have enough on hand." He filled an ordinary looking glass bottle from the locker and returned. "Don't worry, no plague stuff. This is simply a parasite—I should say a symbiont." He laughed shortly. "In fact, it's a type of yeast. If you take five tablets every day till the bottle's empty, you'll establish a stable culture in your gut. You should notice some improvement within ten days."

He put the jar in Wili's hand. The boy stared. Just "—here, take this and all your problems will be gone by morning—" or in ten days, or whatever. Where was the sacrifice, the pain? Salvation came this fast in dreams alone.

Rosas did not seem impressed. "Very well. Red Arrow and the others will pay as promised: programs and hardware to your specifications for three years." The words were spoken with some effort, and Wili realized just how reluctant a guide Miguel Rosas had been—and how important Paul Naismith's wishes were to the Tinkers.

The supervisor nodded, for the first time cowed by Rosas' hostility, for the first time realizing that the trade would produce no general gratitude or friendship.

Wili jumped down from the table and they started back to the stairs. They had not gone ten steps when Jeremy said, "Sir, you said Eden?" His voice sounded diffident, almost frightened. But still curious. After all, Jeremy was the one who dared the Authority with his self-powered vehicles. Jeremy was the one who always talked of science remaking the world. "You said Eden. What could you do besides cure a few diseases?"

The supervisor seemed to realize there was no mockery in the question. He stopped under a bright patch of ceiling and gestured Jeremy Sergeivich closer. "There are many things, son. But here is one. . . . How old do you think I am? How old do you think the others at the winery are?"

Discounting the greenish light that made everyone look dead, Wili tried to guess. The skin was smooth and firm, with just a hint of wrinkles around the eyes. The hair looked natural and full. He had thought forty before. Now he would say even younger.

And the others they had seen? About the same. Yet in any normal group of adults, more than half were past fifty. And then Wili remembered that when the supervisor spoke of the War, he talked like an oldster, of time in personal memory. "We" decided this, and "we" did that.

He had been adult at the time of the War. He was as old as Naismith or Kaladze.

Jeremy's jaw sagged, and after a moment he nodded shyly. His question had been answered. The supervisor smiled at the boy. "So you see, Mr. Rosas talks of risks—and they may be as great as he claims. But what's to gain is very great, too." He turned and walked the short distance to the stairs door—

—which opened in his face. It was one of the workers from the cask room. "Juan," the man began, talking fast, "the place is being deep-probed. There are helicopters circling the fields. Lights everywhere."

16

The supervisor stepped back, and the man came off the spiral stair.

"What! Why didn't you call down? Never mind, I know. Have you powered down all Banned equipment?" The man nodded. "Where is the boss?"

"She's sticking at the front desk. So are the others. She's going to try to brazen it out."

"Hmm." The supervisor hesitated only a second. "It's really the only thing to do. Our shielding should hold up. They can inspect the cask room all they want." He looked at the three Northerners. "We two are going up and say hello to the forces of worldwide law and order. If they ask, we'll tell them you've already departed along the beach route."

Wili's cure might still be safe.

The supervisor made some quick adjustment at a wall panel. The fungus gradually dimmed, leaving a single streak that wobbled off into the dark. "Follow the glow and you'll eventually reach the beach. Mr.

Rosas, I hope you understand the risk we take in letting you go. If we survive, I expect you to make good on our bargain."

Rosas nodded, then awkwardly accepted the other's flashlight. He turned and hustled Jeremy and Wili off into the dark. Behind them, Wili heard the two bioscientists climbing the stairs to their own fate.

The dim band turned twice, and the corridor became barely shoulder wide. The stone was moist and irregular under Wili's hand. The tunnel went downhill now and was deathly dark. Mike flicked on his light and urged them to a near run. "Do you know what the Authority would do to a lab?"

Jeremy was hot on Wili's heels, occasionally bumping into the smaller boy, though never quite hard enough to make them lose their balance. What would the Authority do? Wili's answer was half a pant. "Bobble it?"

Of course. Why risk a conventional raid? If they even had strong suspicions, the safest action would be to embobble the whole place, killing the scientists and isolating whatever death seed might be stored here. Even without the Authority's reputation of harsh punishment for Banned research, it made complete sense. Any second now, they might find themselves inside a vast silver sphere. Inside.

Dio, perhaps it had happened already. Wili half stumbled at the thought, nearly losing his grip on the glass jar that was the reason for the whole adventure. They would not know till they ran headlong into the wall. They would live for hours, maybe days, but when the air gave out they would die as all the thousands before them must have died, at Vandenberg and Point Loma and Huachuca and . . . .

The ceiling came lower, till it was barely centimeters above Wili's head. Jeremy and Mike pounded clumsily along, bent over yet trying to run at full speed. Light and shadow danced jaggedly about them.

Wili watched ahead for three figures running toward them: the first sign of embobblement would be their own reflections ahead of them. And there *was* something moving up there. Close.

"Wait! Wait!" he screamed. The three came to an untidy stop before—a door, an almost ordinary door. Its surface was metallic, and that accounted for the reflection. He pushed the opener. The door swung outward, and they could hear the surf. Mike doused the light.

They started down a stairway, but too fast. Wili heard someone trip and an instant later he was hit from behind. The three tumbled down the steps. Stone bit savagely into his arms and back. Wili's fingers spasmed open and the jar flew into space, its landing marked by the sound of breaking glass.

Life's blood spattering down unseen steps.

He felt Jeremy scramble past him. "Your flashlight, Mike, quick."

After a second, light filled the stairs. If any Peace cops were on the beach looking inland . . . ?

It was a risk they took for him.

Wili and Jeremy scrabbled back and forth across the stairs, unmindful of the glass shards. In seconds they had recovered the tablets—along with considerable dirt and glass. They dumped it in Jeremy's waterproof hiking bag. The boy dropped a piece of paper into the bag. "Directions, I bet." He zipped it shut and handed it to Wili.

Rosas kept the light on a second longer, and the three memorized the path they must follow. The steps were scarcely more than water-worn corrugations. The cave was free of any other human touch.

Darkness again, and the three started carefully downward, still moving faster than was really comfortable. If only they had a night scope. Such equipment wasn't Banned, but the Tinkers didn't flaunt it. The only high tech equipment they'd brought to La Jolla was the Red Arrow chess processor.

Wili thought he saw light ahead. Over the surf drone he heard a *thupthupthup* that grew first louder and then faded. A helicopter.

They made a final turn and saw the outside world through the vertical crack that was the entrance to the cave. The evening mist curled in, not as thick as earlier. A horizontal band of pale gray hung at eye level. After a moment, he realized the glow was thirty or forty meters away—the surf line. Every few seconds, something bright reflected off the surf and waters beyond.

Behind him Rosas whispered, "Light splash from their search beams on top of the bluff. We may be in luck." He pushed past Jeremy and led them to the opening. They hid there a few seconds and looked as far as they could up and down the beach. No one was visible, though there were a number of aircraft circling the area. Below the entrance spread a rubble of large boulders, big enough to hide their progress.

It happened just as they stepped away from the entrance: a deep, bell-like tone was followed by the cracking and crashing of rock now free of its parent strata. The avalanche proceeded all around them, thousands of tons of rock adding itself to the natural debris of the coastline. They cowered beneath the noise, waiting to be crushed.

But nothing fell close by, and when Wili finally

looked up, he saw why. Silhouetted against the mist and occasional stars was the perfect curve of a sphere. The bobble had to be two or three hundred meters across, extending from the lowest of the winery's caves to well over the top of the bluff and from the inland vineyards to just beyond the edge of the cliffs.

"They did it. They really did it," Rosas muttered to himself.

Wili almost shouted with relief. A few centimeters the other way and they would have been entombed.

Jeremy!

Wili ran to the edge of the sphere. The other boy had been standing right behind them, surely close enough to be safe. Then where was he? Wili beat his fists against the blood warm surface. Rosas' hand closed over his mouth and he felt himself lifted off the ground. Wili struggled for a moment in enforced silence, then went limp. Rosas set him down.

"I know." Mike's voice was a strangled whisper. "He must be on the other side. But let's make sure." He flicked on his light—almost as brightly as he had risked in the cave—and they walked several meters back and forth along the line where the bobble passed into the rocks. They did not find Jeremy, but—

Rosas' flash stopped for a moment, freezing one tiny patch of ground in its light. Then the light winked out, but not before Wili saw two tiny spots of red, two . . . fingertips . . . lying in the dirt.

Just centimeters away, Jeremy must lie writhing in pain, staring into the darkness, feeling the blood on his hands. The wound could not be fatal. Instead, the boy would have hours still to die. Perhaps he would return to the labs, and sit with the others—waiting for the air to run out. The ultimate excommunication.

"You have the bag?" Rosas' voice quavered.

The question caught Wili as he was reaching for the mangled fingers. He stopped, straightened. "Yes."

"Well then, let's go." The words were curt. The tone was clamped-down hysteria.

The undersheriff grabbed Wili's shoulder and urged him down the jumble of half-seen rocks. The air was filled with dust and the cold moistness of the fog. The fresh broken rock was already wet and slippery. They clung close to the largest boulders, fearing both land-slides and detection from the air. The bobble and bluffs cut a black edge into the hazy aura of the lights that swept the ground above. They could hear both trucks and aircraft up there.

But no one was down on the beach. As they crawled and climbed across the rocks, Wili wondered at this. Could it be the Authority did not know about the caves?

They didn't speak for a long time. Rosas was leading them slowly back toward the hotel. It might work. They could finish the tournament, get on the buses, and return to Middle California as though nothing had happened. As though Jeremy had never existed.

It took nearly two hours to reach the beach below the hotel. The fog was much thinner now. The tide had advanced; phosphorescent surf pounded close by, pushing surging tendrils of foam near their feet.

The hotel was brightly lit, more than he remembered on previous evenings. There were lots of lights in the parking areas, too. They hunkered down between two large rocks and inspected the scene. There were far too many lights. The parking lots were swarming with vehicles and men in Peacer green. To one side stood a ragged formation of civilians—

prisoners? They stood in the glare of the trucks' lights, with their hands clasped on top of their heads. A steady procession of soldiers brought boxes and displays—the chess-assist equipment—from the hotel. It was much too far away to see faces, but Wili thought he recognized Roberto Richardson's fat form and flashy jacket there among the prisoners. He felt a quick thrill to see the Jonque standing like some recaptured slave.

"They raided everybody. . . . Just like Paul said, they finally decided to clean us all out." Anger was back in Mike's voice.

Where was the girl, Della Lu? He looked back and forth over the forlorn group of prisoners. She was so short. Either she was standing in back, or she was not there. Some of the buses were leaving. Maybe she had already been taken.

They had had amazing luck avoiding the bobble, avoiding detection, and avoiding the hotel raid. That luck must end now: they had lost Jeremy. They had lost the equipment at the hotel. Aztlán territory extended northward three hundred kilometers. They would have to walk more than a hundred klicks through wilderness just to reach the Basin. Even if the Authority was not looking for them, they could not avoid the Jonque barons, who would take Wili for a runaway slave—and Rosas for a peasant till they heard him talk, and then for a spy.

And if by some miracle they could reach Middle California, what then? This last was the most depressing thought of all. Paul Naismith had often talked of what would happen when the Authority finally saw the Tinkers as enemies. Apparently that time had come. All across the continent (all across the world? Wili remembered that some of the best chip engrav-

Revenge had waited, impotent, these fifty years, but its time might now come.

Naismith geed the horse. The cart and horse were not what he had come to the farm with. 'Kolya had supplied everything—including a silly, old-lady disguise which he suspected was more embarrassing than effective.

Nikolai had not stinted, but neither had he been happy about the departure. Naismith slouched back on the padded seat and thought ruefully of that last argument. They had been sitting on the porch of the main house. The blinds were drawn, and a tiny singing vibration in the air told Naismith that the window panes were incapable of responding to a laser-driven audio probe. The Peace Authority "bandits" —what an appropriate cover—had made no move. Except for what was coming over the radio, and what Paul had seen, there was no sign that the world was turning upside down.

Kaladze understood the situation—or thought he did—and wanted no part of Naismith's project. "I tell you honestly, Paul, I do not understand you. We are relatively safe here. No matter what the Peacers say, they can't act against us all at once; that's why they grabbed our friends at the tournament. For hostages." He paused, probably thinking of a certain three hostages. Just now, they had no way of knowing if Jeremy and Wili and Mike were dead or alive, captive or free. Taking hostages might turn out to be an effective strategy indeed. "If we keep our heads down, there's no special reason to believe they'll invade Red Arrow Farm. You'll be as safe here as anywhere. *But*," Nikolai rushed on as if to forestall an immediate response, "if you leave now, you'll be alone and in the open. You want to head for one of the few spots in North America where the Peacers are guaranteed to swarm. For which risk, you get *nothing*."

"You are three times wrong, old friend," Paul answered quietly, barely able to suppress his frantic impatience to be gone. He ticked off the points. "First, your second claim: if I leave right now, I can probably get there before the Authority. They have much else to worry about. Since we got Wili's invention working, I and my programs have spent every second monitoring the Peacer recon satellites for evidence of bobble decay. I'll bet the Authority itself doesn't have the monitor capability I do. It's possible they don't yet realize that a bobble burst up there in the hills this morning.

"As to your third claim: the risk *is* worth the candle. I stand to win the greatest prize of all, the means to destroy the Authority. Something or someone is causing bobbles to burst. So there is some defense against the bobbles. If I can discover that secret—"

Kaladze shrugged. "So? You'd still need a nuclear power generator to do anything with the knowledge."

"Maybe . . . Finally, my response to your first claim: you—we—are not at all safe lying low on the farm. For years, I tried to convince you the Authority is deadly once it sees you as a danger. You're right, they can't attack everywhere at once. But they'll use the La Jolla hostages to identify you, and to draw you out. Even if they don't have Mike and the boys, Red Arrow Farm will be high on their hit-list. And if they suspect I'm here, they'll raid you just as soon as they have enough force in the area. They have some reason to fear me."

"They want *you*?" Kaladze's jaw sagged. "Then why haven't they simply bobbled us?"

Paul grinned. "Most likely, their 'bandit' reconnaissance didn't recognize me—or maybe they want to be sure I'm inside their cage when they lock it." *Avery missed me once before. He can't stand uncertainty.*

"Bottom line, 'Kolya: the Peace Authority is out to get us. We must give them the best fight we can. Finding out what's bursting the bobbles might give us the whole game." No need to tell 'Kolya that he would be doing it even if the Peacers hadn't raided the tournament. Like most Tinkers, Nikolai Kaladze had never been in direct conflict with the Authority. Though he was as old as Naismith, he had not seen firsthand the betrayal that had brought the Authority to power. Even the denial of bioproducts to children like Wili was not seen by today's people as real tyranny. But now at last there was the technical and—if the Authority was foolish enough to keep up its pressure on the likes of Kaladze—the political opportunity to overturn the Peacers.

The argument continued for thirty minutes, with Naismith slowly prevailing. The real problem in getting 'Kolya's help was to convince him that Paul had a chance of discovering anything from a simple inspection of this latest bobble burst. In the end, Naismith was successful, though he had to reveal a few secrets out of his past that might later cause him considerable trouble.

The path Naismith followed leveled briefly as it passed over a ridgeline. If it weren't for the forest, he could see the crater from here. He had to stop daydreaming and decide just how to make his approach. There was still no sign of Peacers, but if he were picked up near the site, the old-lady disguise would be no protection.

He guided his horse off the path some thousand meters inland of the crater. Fifty meters into the brush, he got down from the cart. Under ordinary circumstances there was more than enough cover to hide horse and vehicle. Today, and here, he couldn't be so confident.

It was a chance he must take. For fifty years, bobbles—and the one up ahead, in particular—had haunted him. For fifty years he had tried to convince himself that all this was not his fault. For fifty years he had hoped for some way to undo what his old bosses had made of his invention.

He took his pack off the cart and awkwardly slipped it on. The rest of the way would be on foot. Naismith trudged grimly back up the forested hillside, wondering how long it would be before the pack harness began to cut, wondering if he would run out of breath first. What was a casual walk for a sixty-year-old might be life-threatening for someone his age. He tried to ignore the creaking of his trick knee and the rasping of his breath.

Aircraft. The sound passed over but did not fade into the distance. Another and another. Damn it.

Naismith took out some gear and began monitoring the remotes that Jeremy had scattered the night of the ambush. He was still three thousand meters from the crater, but some of the pellets might be in enough sun to be charged up and transmitting.

He searched methodically through the entire packet space his probes could transmit on. The ones nearest the crater were gone or so deeply embedded in the forest floor that all he could see was the sky above them. There had been a fire, maybe even a small explosion, when this bobble burst. But no ordinary fire could have burned within the bobble for fifty years. If a nuclear explosion had been trapped inside, there would have been something much more spectacular than a fire when it burst. (And Naismith knew this one: there had been no nuke in it.) That was the unique thing about this bobble burst; it might explain the whole mystery.

He had fragmentary views of uniforms. Peacer troops. They had left their aircraft and were spreading around the crater. Naismith piped the audio to his hearing aid. He was so close. But it would be crazy to go any nearer now. Maybe if they didn't leave too many troops, he could sneak in tomorrow morning. He had arrived too late to scoop them and too early to avoid them. Naismith swore softly to himself and unwrapped the lightweight camping bag Kaladze had given him. All the time he watched the tiny screen he had propped against a nearby tree trunk. The controlling program shifted the scene between the five best views he had discovered in his initial survey. It would also alert him if anyone started moving in his direction.

Naismith settled back and tried to relax. He could hear lots of activity, but it must be right down in the crater, since he could see none of it.

The sun slowly drifted west. Another time, Naismith would have admired the beautiful day: temperatures in the high twenties, birds singing. The strange forests around Vandenberg might be unique: dry climate vegetation suddenly plunged into something resembling the rainy tropics. God only knew what the climax forms would be like.

Today, all he could think of was getting at that crater just a few thousand meters to the north.

Even so, he was almost dozing when a distant rifle shot brought him to full alertness. He diddled the display a moment and had some good luck: he saw a man in gray and silver, running almost directly away from the camera. Naismith strained close to the screen, his jaw sagging. More shots. He zoomed on the figure. Gray and silver. He hadn't seen an outfit like that since before the War. For a moment his mind offered no interpretation, just cranked on as a stunned observer. Three troopers rushed past the camera. They must have been shooting over the fellow's head, but he wasn't stopping and now the trio fired again. The man in gray spun and dropped. For a moment, the three soldiers seemed as stricken as their target. Then they ran forward, shouting recriminations at each other.

The screen was alive with uniforms. There was a sudden silence at the arrival of a tweedy civilian. The man in charge. From his high-pitched expostulations, Naismith guessed he was unhappy with events. A stretcher was brought up and the still form was carted off. Naismith changed the phase of his camera and followed the victim down the path that led northward from the crater.

Minutes later the shriek of turbines splashed off the hills, and a needle-nosed form rose into the sky north of Naismith. The craft vectored into horizontal flight and sprinted southward, passing low over Naismith's hiding place.

The birds and insects were deathly silent the next several minutes, almost as silent and awestruck as Paul's own imagination. *He knew now.* The bursting bobbles were not caused by quantum decay. The bursting bobbles were not the work of some anti-Peacer underground. He fought down hysterical laughter. He had invented the damn things, provided his bosses with fifty years of empire, but he and they had never realized that—though his invention worked superbly—his theory was a crock of sewage from beginning to end.

He knew that now. The Peacers would know it in a matter of hours, if they had not already guessed. They would fly in a whole division with their science teams. He would likely die with his secret if he didn't slip out now and head eastward for his mountain home.

. . . But when Naismith finally moved, it was not back to his horse. He went north. Carefully, quietly, he moved toward the crater: for there was a corollary to his discovery, and it was more important than his life, perhaps even more important than his hatred of the Peace Authority.

18

Naismith stopped often, both to rest and to consult the screen that he had strapped to his forearm. The scattered cameras showed fewer than thirty troopers. If he had guessed their locations correctly, he might be able to crawl in quite close. He made a two-hundred-meter detour just to avoid one of them; the fellow was well concealed and was quietly listening and watching. Naismith suffered the rocks and brambles with equal silence. He carefully inspected the ground just ahead of him for branches and other noise-makers. Every move must be a considered one. This was something he had very little practice at, but he had to do it right the first time.

He was very close to his goal now: Naismith looked up from the display and peered into a small ravine. This was the place! Her suddenly still form was huddled deep within the brush. If he hadn't known from the scanners exactly where to look, he would not have noticed the flecks of silver beyond the leaves and branches. During the last half hour he had watched her move slowly south, trying to edge away from the troopers at the crater rim. Another fifteen minutes, and she would blunder into the soldier Naismith had noticed.

He slid down the cleft, through clouds of midges that swirled in the musty dampness. He was sure she could see him now. But he was obviously no soldier, and he was crawling along just as cautiously as she. Paul lost sight of her the last three or four meters of his approach. He didn't look for her, instead eased into the depths of shadow that drowned her hiding place.

Suddenly a hand slammed over his mouth and he found himself spun onto his back and forced to the ground. He looked up into a pair of startlingly blue eyes.

The young woman waited to see if Naismith would struggle, then released his shoulder and placed her finger to her lips. Naismith nodded, and after a second she removed her hand from his mouth. She lowered her head to his ear and whispered, "Who are you? Do you know how to get away from them?"

Naismith realized with wry bleakness that she had not seen through his disguise: she thought she'd landed some dazed crone. Perhaps that was best. He had no idea what she imagined was going on, but it could hardly be any approximation to reality. There was no truthful answer she would understand, much less believe. Naismith licked his lips in apparent nervousness and whispered back, "They're after me, too. If they catch us they'll kill us, just like your friend." *Oops.* "We've got to turn from the way you're going. I saw one of 'em hiding just ahead."

The young woman frowned, her suspicion clear.

Naismith's omniscience was showing. "So you know a way out?"

He nodded. "My horse and wagon are southeast of all this ruckus. I know ways we can sneak past these folks. I have a little farm up in—"

His words were lost in a steadily increasing roar that passed almost overhead. They looked up and had a quick impression of something large and winged, fire glowing from ports at wings and tail. Another troop carrier. He could hear others following. This was the beginning of the real invasion. The only place they could land would be on the main road north of the crater. But given another half hour, there would be wall-to-wall troopers here and not even a mouse could escape.

Naismith rolled to his knees and pulled at her hand. She had no choice now. They stood and walked quickly back the way he had come. The sound of the jets was a continuous rumble; they could have shouted and still not been heard. They had perhaps fifteen minutes to move as fast as they were able.

Greenish twilight had fallen on the forest floor. In his mottled brown dress, Naismith would be hard to spot, but the girl's flight fatigues made her a perfect target. He held her hand, urging her to paths he thought safe. He glanced at his wrist again and again, trying to see where the invaders were posted. The girl was busy looking in all directions and didn't notice his display.

The sounds fell behind them. The jets were still loud, but the soldiers' voices were fading in the distance. A dove lilted nearby.

They were trotting now, where the undergrowth thinned. Naismith's lungs burned and a steady pain pushed in his chest. The woman had a limp, but her breath came effortlessly. No doubt she was slowing her pace to his.

Finally he was forced to a stumbling walk. She put her arm around his shoulder to keep him steady. Naismith grimaced but did not complain. He should be grateful that he could even walk, he supposed. But somehow it seemed a great injustice that a short run could be nearly fatal to someone who still felt young inside. He croaked directions, telling the girl where the horse and cart were hidden.

Ten minutes more, and he heard a faint nickering. There was no sign of an ambush. From here, he knew dozens of trails into the mountains, trails that guerrillas of bygone years had worked hard to conceal. With even a small amount of further luck, they could escape. Paul sagged against the side of the cart. The forest rippled and darkened before him. Not now, Lord, *not now!*

His vision cleared, but he didn't have the strength to hoist himself onto the cart. The young woman's arm slipped to his waist, while her other went under his legs. Paul was a little taller than she, but he didn't weigh much anymore, and she was strong. She lifted him easily into the back, then almost dropped him in surprise. "You're not a—"

Naismith gave her a weak grin. "A woman? You're right. In fact, there's scarcely a thing you've seen today that is what it seems." Her eyes widened even further.

Paul was almost beyond speech now. He pointed her at one of the hidden paths. It should get them safely away, if she could follow it.

And then the world darkened and fell away from him.

19

The ocean was placid today, but the fishing boat was small. Della Lu stood at the railing and looked down into the sun-sparkled water with a sick fascination. In all the Peace, she had as much countersubversive experience as anyone. In a sense her experience had begun as soon as she was old enough to understand her parents' true job. And as an adult, she had planned and participated in airborne assaults, had directed the embobbling of three Mongolian strongholds, had been as tough as her vision of the Peace demanded ... but until now she had never been in a watercraft bigger than a canoe.

Was it possible she could be seasick? Every three seconds, the swell rose to within a couple meters of her face, then sank back to reveal scum-covered timbers below the waterline. It had been vaguely pleasant at first, but one thing she'd learned during the last thirty-six hours was that it *never ended*. She had no doubt she would feel fine just knowing the motion could be stopped at her whim. But short of calling off this charade, there was no way to get away from it.

Della ordered her guts to sleep and her nose to ignore the stench of sardines. She looked up from the waterline to the horizon. She really had a lot to be proud of. In North America—and in Middle California, especially—the Authority's espionage service was an abomination. There had been no threats from this region in many, many years. The Peace kept most of the continent in a state of anarchy. Satellite reconnaissance could spot the smallest agglomeration of power there. Only in the nation states, like Aztlán and New Mexico, did the Directors see any need for spies. Things were very different in the great land-ocean that was Central Asia.

But Della was managing. In a matter of days, she had improvised from her Asian experience to come up with something that might work against the threat Avery saw here. She had not simply copied her Mongolian procedures. In North America, the subversives had penetrated—at least in an electronic sense—some of the Authority secrets. Communications, for instance: Della's eyes caught on the Authority freighter near the horizon. She could not report directly from her little fishing boat without risking her cover. So she had a laser installed near the waterline, and with it talked to the freighter—which surcrypted the messages and sent them through normal Authority channels to Hamilton Avery and the operations Della was directing for him.

Laughter. One of the fisherman said something in Spanish, something about "persons much inclined to sleep." Miguel Rosas had climbed out of the boat's tiny cabin. He smiled wanly at their jokes as he picked his way past the nets. (Those fishermen were a weak point in her cover. They were real, hired for the job. Given time, they would likely figure out whom they were working for. The Authority should have a whole cadre of professionals for jobs like this. Hell, that had been the original purpose in planting her grandparents in San Francisco: the Authority had been worried about the large port so close to the most important enclave. They reasoned that 'furbishers would be the most likely to notice any buildup of military material. If only they had chosen to plant them among Tinkers instead. As it was, the years passed and no threat developed, and the Authority never expanded their counter-underground.)

Della smiled at him, but didn't speak till the Californian was standing beside her. "How is the boy?"

Rosas frowned. "Still sleeping. I hope he's okay. He's not in good health, you know."

Della was not worried. She had doctored the black kid's bread, what the fishermen fed him last night. It wouldn't do the boy any harm, but he should sleep for several more hours. It was important that she and Rosas have a private conversation, and this might be the last natural opportunity for it.

She looked up at him, keeping her expression innocent and friendly. *He doesn't look weak. He doesn't look like a man who would betray his people. . . .* And yet he had. So his motives were very important if they were to manipulate him further. Finally she said, "We want to thank you for uncovering the lab in La Jolla."

The undersheriff's face became rigid, and he straightened.

Lu cocked her head quizzically. "You mean you didn't guess who I am?"

Rosas slumped back against the railing, looked dully over the side. "I suspected. It was all too pat: our escape, these fellows picking us up. I didn't think you'd be a woman, though. That's so old-fashioned." His dark hands clenched the wood till the knuckles shone pale. "Damn it, lady, you and your men killed Jere—killed one of the two I was here to protect. And then you grabbed all those innocent people at the tournament. *Why?* Have you gone crazy?"

The man hadn't guessed that the tournament raid was the heart of Avery's operation: the biolab had been secondary, important mainly because it had brought Miguel Rosas to them. They needed hostages, information.

"I'm sorry our attack on the lab killed one of your people, Mr. Rosas. That wasn't our intent." This was true, though it might give her a welcome leverage of guilt. "You could have simply told us its location, not insisted on a 'Judas kiss' identification. You must realize, we couldn't take any chance that what was in the lab might get out. . . ."

Rosas was nodding, almost to himself. *That must be it*, Lu thought. The man had a pathological hatred of bioscience, far beyond the average person's simple fear. That was what had driven him to betrayal. "As for the raid on the tournament, we had very good reasons for that, reasons which you will someday understand and support. For now you must trust us, just as the whole world has trusted us these last fifty years, and follow our direction."

"Direction? The hell you say. I did what I had to do, but that's the end to my cooperation. You can lock me up like the rest."

"I think not. Your safe return to Middle California is a high priority with us. You and I and Wili will put ashore at Santa Barbara. From there we should be able to get to Red Arrow Farm. We'll be heroes, the only survivors of the infamous La Jolla raid.'' She saw the defiance on his face. "You really have no choice, Miguel Rosas. You have betrayed your friends, your employers, and all the people we arrested at the tournament. If you don't go along, we will let it be known you were behind the raids, that you have been our agent for years.''

"That's a damn lie!" His outburst was clipped short as he realized its irrelevance.

"Oh the other hand, if you do help us . . . well, then you will be serving a great good"—Rosas did not sneer, but clearly he did not believe it either—"and when all this is over you will be very rich, and if necessary, protected by the Peace for the rest of your life." It was a strategy that had worked on many, and not just during the history of the Peace: take a weak person, encourage him to betrayal (for whatever reason), and then use the stick of exposure and the carrot of wealth to force him to do far more than he'd ever have had the courage or motive for in the beginning. Hamilton Avery was confident it would work here and had refused her the time for anything more subtle. Miguel Rosas might get them a line on the Hoehler fellow.

Della watched him carefully, trying to pierce his tense expression and see whether he was strong enough to sacrifice himself.

The undersheriff stared at the gulls that circled the boat and called raucously to their brethren as the first catch was drawn aboard. For a moment he seemed lost in the swirl of wings, and his jaw muscles slowly relaxed.

Finally he looked back at her. "You must be very

good at chess. I can't believe the Authority has chess programs that could play the way you did Wili."

Della almost laughed at the irrelevance of the statement, but she answered honestly. "You're right; they don't. But I scarcely know the moves. What you all thought was my computer was actually a phone link to Livermore. We had our hottest players up there going over my game, figuring out the best moves and then sending them down to me."

Now Rosas did laugh. His hand came down on her shoulder. She almost struck before she realized this was a pat and not a blow. "I had wondered. I had really wondered.

"Lady, I hate your guts, and after today I hate everything you stand for. But you have my soul now." The laughter was gone from his voice. "What are you going to make me do?"

No, Miguel, I don't have your soul, and I see that I never will. Della was suddenly afraid—for no reason that could ever convince Hamilton Avery—that Miguel Rosas was not their tool. Certainly, he was naive; outside Aztlán and New Mexico, most North Americans were. But whatever weakness caused him to betray the Scripps lab ended there. And somehow she knew that whatever decision he had just made could not be changed by gradually forcing him to more and more treacherous acts. There was something very strong in Rosas. Even after his act of betrayal, those who counted him friend might still be lucky to know him.

"To do? Not a great deal. Sometime tonight we reach Santa Barbara. I want you to take me along when we put ashore. When we reach Middle California, you'll back up my story. I want to see the Tinkers firsthand." She paused. "There is one thing. Of all the subversives, there is one most dangerous to world peace. A man named Paul Hoehler." Rosas did not react. "We've seen him at Red Arrow Farm. We want to know what he's doing. We want to know where he is."

That had become the whole point of the operation for Hamilton Avery. The Director had an abiding paranoia about Hoehler. He was convinced that the bursting bobbles were not a natural phenomenon, that someone in Middle California was responsible. Up till yesterday, she had considered it all dangerous fantasy, distorting their strategy, obscuring the long-term threat of Tinker science. Now she was not so sure. Last night, Avery called to tell her about the spacecraft the Peace had discovered in the hills east of Vandenberg. The crash was only hours old and reports were still fragmentary, but it was clear that the enemy had a manned space operation. If they could do that in secret, then almost anything was possible. This was a time for greater ruthlessness than ever she had needed in Mongolia.

Above and around, the gulls swooped through the chill blue glare, circling closer and closer as the fish piled up at the rear of the boat. Rosas' gaze was lost among the scavengers. Della, for all her skill, could not tell whether she had a forced ally or a double traitor. For both their sakes she hoped he was the former.

20

Parties and fairs were common among the West Coast Tinkers.

Sometimes it was difficult to tell one from the other, so large were the parties and so informal the fairs. When he was a child, the high points of Rosas' existence had been such events: tables laden with food, kids and oldsters come from kilometers around to enjoy each other's company in the bright outdoors of sunny days or crowded into warm and happy dining rooms while rain swept by outside.

The La Jolla crackdown had changed much of that. Rosas strained to appear attentive as he listened to a Kaladze niece marvel at their escape and long trek back to Middle California. His mind roamed grim and nervous across the scene of their welcome-home party. Only Kaladze's family attended. There was no one from other farms or from Santa Ynez; even Seymour Wentz had not come. The Peacers were not to suspect that anything special was happening at Red Arrow Farm.

But Sy was not totally missing. He and some of the neighbors had shown up on line of sight from their homes inland. Sometime this evening they would have a council of war.

I wonder if I can face Sy and not give away what really happened in La Jolla?

Wilma Wentz—Kaladze's niece and Sy's sister-in-law, a woman in her late forties—was struggling to be heard over music that came from a speaker hidden in a nearby tree. "But I still don't understand how you managed once you reached Santa Barbara. You and a black boy and an Asian woman traveling together. We know the Authority had asked Aztlán to stop you. How did you get past the border?"

Rosas wished his face were in shadows, not lit by the pale glow-bulbs that were strung between the trees. Wilma was only a woman, but she was clever and more than once had caught him out when he was a child. He must be as careful with her as anyone. He laughed. "It was simple, Wilma—once Della suggested it: we stuck our heads right back into the lion's mouth. We found a Peacer fuel station and climbed into the undercarriage of one of the tankers. No Aztlán cop stops one of those. We had a nonstop ride from there to the station south of Santa Ynez." Even so, it had not been fun. There had been kilometer after kilometer of noise and diesel fumes. More than once during the two-hour trip they had nearly fainted, fallen past the spinning axles onto the concrete of Old 101. But Lu had been adamant: their return must be realistically difficult. No one, including Wili, must suspect.

Wilma's eyes grew slightly round. "Oh, that Della Lu. She is so wonderful. Don't you think?"

Rosas looked over Wilma's head to where Della was making herself popular with the womenfolk. "Yes, she is wonderful." She had them all agog with her tales of life in San Francisco. No matter how much (and how suicidally) he might wish it, she never slipped up. She was a supernaturally good liar. How he hated that small Asian face, those clean good looks. He had never known anyone—man, woman or animal—who was so attractive and yet so evil. He forced his eyes away from her, trying to forget the slim shoulders, the ready smile, the power to destroy him and all the good he had ever done. . . .

"It's marvelous to have you back, Mikey." Wilma's voice was suddenly very soft. "But I'm sorry for those poor people down at La Jolla and in that secret lab."

And Jeremy. Jeremy who was left behind forever. She was too kind to say it, too kind to remind him that he had not brought back one of those he had been hired to protect. The kindness rubbed unknowingly on deeper guilt. Rosas could not conceal the harshness in his voice. "Don't you worry about the biosci people, Wilma. They were an evil we had to use to cure Wili. As for the others—I promise you we'll get them back." He reached out to squeeze her hand. *All but Jeremy.*

"*Da,*" said a voice behind him. "We will get all the rest back indeed." It was Nikolai Kaladze, who had snuck up on them with his usual lack of warning. "But now that is what we are ready to discuss, Wilma, my dear."

"Oh." She accepted the implied dismissal, a thoroughly modern woman. She turned to gather up the women and younger men, to leave the important matters to the seniors.

Della looked momentarily surprised at this turn of events. She smiled and waved to Mike just as she left. He would like to think he'd seen anger in her face, but she was too good an actress for that. He could only imagine her rage at being kicked out of the meeting. He hoped she'd been counting on attending it.

In minutes, the party was over, the women and children gone. The music from the trees softened, and insect sounds grew louder. Seymour Wentz's holo remained. His image could almost be mistaken for that of someone sitting at the far end of the picnic table. Thirty seconds passed, and several more electronic visitors appeared. One was on a flat, black-and-white display—someone from very far indeed. Rosas wondered how well his transmission was shielded. Then he recognized the sender, one of the Greens from Norcross. With them, it was probably safe.

Wili drifted in, nodded silently to Mike. The boy had been very quiet since that night in La Jolla.

"All present?" Colonel Kaladze sat down at the head of the table. Images far outnumbered the flesh-and-blood now. Only Mike, Wili, and Kaladze and his sons were truly here. The rest were images in holo tanks. The still night air, the pale glow of bulbs, the aged faces, and Wili—dark, small, yet somehow powerful. The scene struck Rosas like something out of a fantasy: a dark elfin prince, holding his council of war at midnight in a faerie-lit forest.

The participants looked at each other for a moment, perhaps feeling the strangeness themselves. Finally, Ivan Nikolayevich said to his father, "Colonel, with all due respect, is it proper that someone so young and unknown as Mr. Wáchendon should sit at this meeting?"

Before the eldest could speak, Rosas interrupted, a further breach of decorum. "I asked that he stay. He shared our trip south, and he knows more about some of the technical problems we face than any of us." Mike nodded apologetically to Kaladze.

Sy Wentz grinned crookedly at him. "As long as we're ignoring all the rules of propriety, I want to ask about our communications security."

Kaladze sounded only faintly irritated by the usurpations. "Rest assured, Sheriff. This part of the woods is in a little valley, blocked from the inland. And I think we have more confusion gear in these trees than there are leaves." He glanced at a display. "No leaks from this end. If you line-of-sighters take even minimum precautions, we're safe." He glanced at the man from Norcross.

"Don't worry about me. I'm using knife-edges, convergent corridors—all sorts of good stuff. The Peacers could monitor forever and not even realize they were hearing a transmission. Gentlemen, you may not realize how primitive the enemy is. Since the La Jolla kidnappings, we've planted some of our bugs in their labs. The great Peace Authority's electronic expertise is fifty years obsolete. We found researchers ecstatic at achieving component densities of ten million per square millimeter." There were surprised chuckles from around the table. The Green smiled, baring bad teeth. "In field operations, they are much worse."

"So all they have are the bombs, the jets, the tanks, the armies, and the bobbles."

"Correct. We are very much like Stone age hunters fighting a mammoth: we have the numbers and the brains, and the other side has the physical power. I predict our fate will be similar to the hunters'. We'll suffer casualties, but the enemy will eventually be defeated."

"What an encouraging point of view," Sy put in dryly.

"One thing I would like to know," said a hardware man from San Louis Obispo. "Who put this bee in their drawers? The last ten years we've been careful not to flaunt our best products; we agreed not to bug the Peacers. That's history now, but I get the feeling that *somebody* deliberately scared them. The bugs we've just planted report they were all upset about high tech stuff they found in their labs earlier this year. . . . Anybody want to fess up?"

He looked around the table; no one replied. But Mike felt a sudden certainty. There was at least one man who might wish to rub the Authority's nose in the Tinkers' superiority, one man who always wanted a scrap. Two weeks ago, he would have felt betrayed by the action. Mike smiled sadly to himself; he was not the only person who could risk his friends' lives for a Cause.

The Green shrugged. "If that's all there were to it, they'd do something more subtle than take hostages. The Peacers think we've discovered something that's an immediate threat. Their internal communications are full of demands that someone named Paul Hoehler be found. They think he's in Middle California. That's why there are so many Peacer units in your area, 'Kolya."

"Yes, you're quite right," said Kaladze. "In fact that's the real reason I asked for this meeting. Paul wanted it. Paul Hoehler, Paul Naismith—whatever we call him—has been the center of their fears for a long time. Only now, he may be as deadly as they believe. He may have something that can kill the 'mammoth' you speak of, Zeke. You see, Paul thinks he can generate bobbles without a nuclear power plant. He wants us to prepare—"

Wili's voice broke through the ripple of consternation that spread around the table. "No! Don't say more. You mean Paul will not be here tonight, even as a picture?" He sounded panicked.

Kaladze's eyebrows rose. "No. He intends to stay thoroughly . . . submerged . . . until he can broadcast his technique. You're the only person he—"

Wili was on his feet now, almost shaking. "But he has to see. He has to listen. He is maybe the only one who will believe me!"

The old soldier sat back. "Believe you about what?"

Rosas felt a chill crawl up his back. Wili was glaring down the table at him.

"Believe me when I tell you that Miguel Rosas is a traitor!" He looked from one visitor to the next but found no response. "It's true, I tell you. He knew about La Jolla from the beginning. He told the Peacers about the lab. He got J-J-Jeremy killed in that hole in the cliffs! And now he sits here while you say everything, while you tell him Paul's plan."

Wili's voice rose steadily to become childish and hysterical. Ivan and Sergei, big men in their late forties, started toward him. The Colonel motioned them back, and when Wili had finished, he responded mildly, "What's your evidence, son?"

"On the boat. You know, the 'lucky rescue' Mike is so happy to tell you of?" Wili spat. "Some rescue. It was a Peacer fake."

"Your proof, young man!" It was Sy Wentz, sticking up for his undersheriff of ten years.

"They thought they had me drugged, dead asleep. But I was some awake. I crawled up the cabin stairs.

I saw him talking to that *puta de la Paz*, that monster Lu. She *thanked* him for betraying us! They know about Paul; you are right. And these two are up here sniffing around for him. They killed Jeremy. They—"

Wili stopped short, seemed to realize that the rush of words was carrying his cause backward.

Kaladze asked, "Could you really hear all they were saying?"

"N-no. There was the wind, and I was very dizzy. But—"

"That's enough, boy." Sy Wentz's voice boomed across the clearing. "We've known Mike since he was younger than you. Me and the Kaladzes shared his upbringing. He grew up *here*"—not in some Basin ghetto—"and we know where his loyalties are. He's risked his life more than once for customers. Hell, he even saved Paul's neck a couple of years ago."

"I'm sorry, Wili." Kaladze's voice was mild, quite unlike Sy's. "We do know Mike. And after this morning, I'm sure Miss Lu is what she appears. I called some friends in San Francisco: her folks have been heavy-wagon 'furbishers for years up there. They recognized her picture. She and her brother went to La Jolla, just as she says."

Has she no limits? thought Rosas.

"*Caray.* I knew you'd not believe. If Paul was here—" The boy glared at Kaladze's sons. "Don't worry. I'll remain a gentleman." He turned and walked stiffly out of the clearing.

Rosas struggled to keep his expression one of simple surprise. If the boy had been a bit cooler, or Della a bit less superhuman, it would have been the end of Miguel Rosas. At that moment, he came terribly close to confessing what all the boy's accusations could not prove. But he said nothing. Mike wanted his revenge to precede his own destruction.

21

Nikolai Sergeivich and Sergei Nikolayevich were pale mauve sitting on the driver's bench ahead of Wili. The late night rain was a steady hushing all around them. For the last four kilometers, the old Russian's "secret tunnel" had been aboveground: when the cart got too near the walls, Wili could feel wet leaves and coarse netting brush against him. Through his night glasses, the wood glowed faintly warmer than the leaves or the netting, which must be some sort of camouflage. The walls were thickly woven, probably looked like heavy forest from the outside. Now that the roof of the passage was soaked, a retarded drizzle fell upon the four of them. Wili shifted his slicker against the trickle that was most persistent.

Without the night glasses the world was absolutely black. But his other senses had things to tell him about this camouflaged path that was taking them inland, past the watchers the Authority had strung around the farm. His nose told him they were far beyond the groves of banana trees that marked the eastern edge of the farm. On top of the smell of wet wood and roping, he thought he smelled lilacs, and that meant they must be about halfway to Highway 101. He wondered if Kaladze intended to accompany him that far.

Over the creaking of the cart's wheels, he could hear Miguel Rosas up ahead, leading the horses.

Wili's lips twisted, a voiceless snarl. No one had believed him. Here he was, a virtual prisoner of the people who should be his allies, and the whole lot of them were being led through the dark by the Jonque traitor! Wili slipped the heavy glasses back on and glared at the mauve blob that was the back of Rosas' head. Funny how Jonque skin was the same color as his own in the never-never world of the night glasses.

Where would their little trip end? He knew that Kaladze and son thought they were simply going to the end of the tunnel, to let Wili return to Naismith in the mountains. And the fools thought that Rosas would let them get away with it. For twenty minutes he had been almost twitchy, expecting a flash of real light ahead of them, sharp commands backed up by men in Authority green with rifles and stunners, the La Jolla betrayal all over again. But the minutes stretched on and on with nothing but the rain and the creaking of the cart's high wheels. The tunnel bent around the hills, occasionally descending underground, occasionally passing across timbers built over washouts. Considering how much it rained around Vandenberg, it must have taken a tremendous effort to keep this pathway functioning yet concealed. Too bad the old man was throwing it all away, thought Wili.

"Looks like we're near the end, sir." Rosas' whisper came back softly—ominously?—over the quiet drone of the rain. Wili rose to his knees to look over the Kaladzes' shoulders: the Jonque was pushing against a door, a door of webbed branches and leaves which nevertheless swung smoothly and silently. Brilliant light glowed through the opening. Wili almost bolted off the cart before his glasses adjusted and he realized that they were still undiscovered.

Wili slipped his glasses off for a second and saw that the night was still as dark as the back of his hand. He almost smiled; to the glasses, there were shades of absolute black. In the tunnel, the glasses had only their body heat to see by. Outside, even under a thick cloud deck, even in the middle of a rainy night, there must be enough ordinary light for them. This gear was far better than the night scope on Jeremy's rifle.

Rosas led the extra horse into the light. "Come ahead." Sergei Nikolayevich slapped the reins, and the cart squeezed slowly through the opening.

Rosas stood in a strange, shadowless landscape, but now the colors in his slicker and face didn't glow, and Wili could see his features clearly. The bulky glasses made his face unreadable. Wili shinnied down and walked to the center of the open space. All around them the trees hung close. Clouds glowed through occasional openings in the branches. Beyond Rosas, he could see an ordinary-looking path. He turned and looked at the doorway. Living shrubs grew from the cover.

The cart pulled forward until the elder Kaladze was even with the boy. Rosas came back to help the old man down, but the Russian shook his head. "We'll only be here a few minutes," he whispered.

His son looked up from some instrument in his lap. "We're the only man-sized animals nearby, Colonel."

"Good. Nevertheless, we still have much to do tonight back at home." For a moment, he sounded tired. "Wili, do you know why we three came the way out here with you?"

"No, sir." The "sir" came naturally when he talked to the Colonel. Next to Naismith himself, Wili had found more to respect in this man than anyone else. Jonque leaders—and the bosses of the Ndelante Ali— all demanded a respectful manner from their stooges, but old Kaladze actually gave his people something in return.

"Well, son, I wanted to convince you that you are important, and that what you must do is even more important. We didn't mean insult at the meeting last night; we just know that you are wrong about Mike." He lifted his hand a couple of centimeters, and Wili stifled the fresh pleading that rose to his lips. "I'm not going to try to convince you that you're wrong. I know you believe all you say. But even with such disagreement, we still need you desperately. You know that Paul Naismith is the key to all of this. He may be able to crack the secret of the bobbles. He may be able to get us out from under the Authority."

Wili nodded.

"Paul has told us that he needs you, that without your help his success will be delayed. They're looking for him, Wili. If they get him before he can help us—well, I don't think we'll have a chance. They'll treat us all like the Tinkers in La Jolla. So. We brought Elmir with us." He gestured at the mare Rosas had been leading. "Mike says you learned how to ride in LA."

Wili nodded again. That was an exaggeration; he

knew how not to fall off. With the Ndelante Ali, getaways had occasionally been on horseback.

"We want you to return to Paul. We think you can make it from here. The path ahead crosses under Old One-oh-one. You shouldn't see anyone else unless you stray too far south. There's a trucker camp down that way."

For the first time Rosas spoke. "He must really need your help, Wili. The only thing that protects him is his hiding place. If you were captured and forced to talk—"

"*I* won't talk," Wili said and tried not to think of things he had seen happen to uncooperative prisoners in Pasadena.

"With the Authority there would be no choice."

"So? Is that what happened to you, Jonque Señor? Somehow, I don't think you planned from the beginning to betray us. What was it? I know you have fallen for the Chinese bitch. Is that what it was?" Wili heard his voice steadily rising. "Your price is so low?"

"Enough!" Kaladze's voice was not loud but its sharpness cut Wili short. The Colonel struggled off the driving bench to the ground, then bent till his face—eyes still obscured by the night glasses—was even with Wili's. Somehow, Wili could feel those eyes glaring through the dark plastic lenses.

"If anyone is to be bitter, it should be Sergei Nikolayevich and I, should it not? It is *I*, not you, who lost a grandson to the Authority bobble. If anyone is to be suspicious, it should be *I*, not you. Mike Rosas saved your life. And I don't mean simply that he got you back here alive. He got you in and out of those secret labs; seconds either way and it would be all of you left trapped inside. And what you got in there was life itself. I saw you when you left for La Jolla: if you were so sick now, you would be too *weak* to afford the luxury of this anger."

That stopped Wili. Kaladze was right, though not about Rosas' innocence. These last eight days had been so busy, so full of fury and frustration, that he hadn't fully noticed: in previous summers his condition had always improved. But since he started eating that *stuff*, the pain had begun leaching away—faster than ever before. Since getting back to the farm, he had been eating with more pleasure than he had at any time in the last five years.

"Okay. I will help. On a condition."

Nikolai Sergeivich straightened but said nothing. Wili continued, "The game is lost if the Authority finds Naismith. Mike Rosas and the Lu woman maybe know where he is. If you promise—*on your honor*—to keep them for ten days away from all outside communication, then it will be worth it to me to do as you say."

Kaladze didn't answer immediately. It would be such an easy promise to give, to humor him in his "fantasies," but Wili knew that if the Russian agreed to this, it would be a promise kept. Finally, "What you ask is very difficult, very inconvenient. It would almost mean locking them up." He glanced at Rosas.

"Sure. I'm willing." The traitor spoke quickly, almost eagerly, and Wili wondered what angle he was missing.

"Very well, sir, you have my word." Kaladze extended a thin, strong hand to shake Wili's. "Now let us be gone, before twilight herself joins our cozy discussions."

Sergei and Rosas turned the horse and cart around and carefully erased the marks of their presence. The traitor avoided Wili's look even as he swung the camouflaged door shut.

And Wili was alone with one small mare in darkest night. All around him the rain splattered just audibly. Despite the slicker, a small ribbon of wet was starting down his back.

Wili hadn't realized how difficult it was to lead a horse in such absolute dark; Rosas had made it look easy. Of course, Rosas didn't have to contend with odd branches which—if not bent carefully out of the way—would swipe the animal across the face. He almost lost control of poor Elmir the first time that happened. The path wound around the hills, disappeared entirely at places where the constant rains had enlarged last season's gullies. Only his visualization of Kaladze's maps saved him then.

It was at least fifteen kilometers to Old 101, a long, wet walk. Still, he was not really tired, and the pain in his muscles was the healthy feeling of exercise. Even at his best, he had never felt quite so bouncy. He patted the thin satchel nestled against his skin and said a short prayer to the One True God for continued good fortune.

There was plenty of time to think. Again and again, Wili came back to Rosas' apparent eagerness to accept house arrest for himself and the Lu woman. They must have something planned. Lu was so clever . . . so beautiful. He didn't know what had turned Rosas rotten, but he could almost believe that he did it simply for her. Were all *chicas chinas* like her? He had never seen a lady, black, Anglo, or Jonque, like Della Lu. Wili's mind wandered, imagining several final, victorious confrontations, until—night glasses and all—he almost walked over the edge of a wash-

out half-full of racing water. It took him and Elmir
fifteen minutes to get down and back up the mud-
slicked sides of the gully, and he almost lost the
glasses in the process.

It brought him back to reality. Lu was beautiful
like oleander—or better—like a Glendora cat. She
and Rosas had thought of something, and if he could
not guess what it was, it could kill him.

Hours later he still hadn't figured it out. Twilight
couldn't be far off now, and the rain had ceased. Wili
stopped where a break in the forest gave him a view
eastward. Parts of the sky were clear. They burned
with tiny spots of flame. The trees cast multiple shadows (each a slightly different color). A long section of
101 was visible between the shoulders of the hills.
There was no traffic, though to the south he saw
shifting swaths of light that must be Authority road
freighters. There was also a steady glow that might
be the truckers' camp Kaladze had mentioned.

Directly below his viewpoint, a forested marsh extended right up to Old 101. The highway had been
washed out and rebuilt many times, till it was little
more than a timber bridge over the marshlands. He
would have his choice of any of a hundred places to
cross under.

It was farther away than it looked. By the time
they were halfway there, the eastern sky was brightly
lit, and Elmir seemed to have more faith in what he
was doing.

He chose a lightly traveled path through the wet
and started under the highway. Still he wondered
what Lu and Rosas had planned. If they couldn't get
a message out, then who could? Who knew where to
look for Naismith and was also outside of Red Arrow

Farm? Sudden understanding froze him in his tracks; Elmir's soft nose knocked him to his knees, but he scarcely noticed. *Of course!* Poor stupid little Wili, always ready to give his enemies a helping hand.

Wili got to his feet and walked back along Elmir, looking carefully for unwanted baggage. He ran his hand along the underside of her belly, and on the cinch found what he was looking for: the transmitter was large, almost two centimeters across. No doubt it had some sort of timer so it hadn't begun radiating back where the Kaladzes would have been sure to notice. He weighed the device with his hand. It was awfully big, probably an Authority bug. *But Rosas could have supplied something more subtle.* He went back to the horse and inspected her and her gear again, much more carefully. Then he took off his own clothes and did the same for them. The early morning air was chill, and muck oozed up between his toes. It felt great.

He looked very carefully, but found nothing more, which left him with nagging doubts. If it had just been Lu, he could understand. . . .

And there was still the question of what to do with the bug he had found. He got dressed and started to lead Elmir out from under the roadway. In the distance a rumbling grew louder and louder. The timbers began shaking, showering them with little globs of mud. Finally the land freighter passed directly overhead, and Wili wondered how the wooden trestle could take it.

It gave him an idea, though. There was that truckers' camp to the south, maybe just a couple of kilometers away. If he tied Elmir up here, he could probably make it in less than an hour. Not just Authority freighters used the stop. Ordinary truckers, with their big wagons and horse teams, would be there, too. It should be easy to sneak up early in the twilight and give one of those wagons a fifty-gram hitchhiker.

Wili chuckled out loud. So much for Missy Lu and Rosas. With a little luck, he'd have the Authority thinking Naismith was hiding in Seattle!

22

She was trapped in some sort of gothic novel. And that was the least of her problems.

Allison Parker sat on an outcropping and looked off to the north. This far from the Dome the weather was as before, with maybe a bit more rain. If she looked neither right nor left, she could imagine that she was simply on a camping trip, taking her ease in the late morning coolness. Here she could imagine that Angus Quiller and Fred Torres were still alive, and that when she got back to Vandenberg, Paul Hoehler might be down from Livermore for a date.

But a glance to the left and she would see her rescuer's mansion, buried dark and deep in the trees. Even by day, there seemed something gloomy and alien about the building. Perhaps it was the owner. The old man, Naismith, seemed so furtive, so apparently gentle, yet still hiding some terrible secret or desire. And as in any gothic, his servants—themselves in their fifties—were equally furtive and closemouthed.

Of course, a lot of mysteries had been solved these last days, the greatest the first night. When she had brought the old man in, the servants had been very surprised. All they would say was that the "master will explain all that needs explaining." "The master" was nearly unconscious at the time, so that was little help. Otherwise they had treated her well, feeding her and giving her clean, though ill-fitting clothes. Her bedroom was almost a dormer, its windows half in and half out of the roof. The furniture was simple but elegant; the oiled burl dresser alone would have been worth thousands back . . . where she came from. She had sat on the bright patchwork quilt and thought darkly that there better be some explanations coming in the morning, or she was going to leg it back to the coast, unfriendly armies or no.

The huge house had been still and dead as the twilight deepened. Faint but clear against the silence, Allison could hear the sounds of applause and an audience laughing. It took her a second to realize that someone had turned on a television—though she hadn't seen a set during the day. *Ha!* Fifteen minutes of programming would tell her as much about this new universe as a month of talking to "Bill" and "Irma." She slid open her bedroom door and listened to the tiny, bright sounds.

The program was weirdly familiar, conjuring up memories of a time when she was barely tall enough to reach the on switch of her mother's TV. "Saturday Night"? It was either that or something very similar. She listened a few moments more, heard references to actors, politicians who had died before she ever entered college. She walked down the stairs, and sat with the Moraleses through an evening of old TV shows.

They hadn't objected, and as the days passed they'd opened up about some things. This was the future, about a half-century forward of her present. They told her of the war and the plagues that ended her world, and the force fields, the "bobbles," that birthed the new one.

But while some things were explained, others became mysteries in themselves. The old man didn't socialize, though the Moraleses said that he was recovered. The house was big and there were many rooms whose doors stayed closed. He—and whoever else was in the house besides the servants—was avoiding her. Eerie. She wasn't welcome here. The Morales were not unfriendly and had let her take a good share of the chores, but behind them she sensed the old man wishing she would go away. At the same time, they couldn't afford to have her go. They feared the occupying armies, the "Peace Authority," as much as she did; if she were captured, their hiding place would be found. So they continued to be her uneasy hosts.

She had seen the old man scarcely a handful of times since the first afternoon, and never to talk to. He was in the mansion though. She heard his voice behind closed doors, sometimes talking with a woman—not Irma Morales. That female voice was strangely familiar.

God, what I wouldn't give for a friendly face right now. Someone to talk to. Angus, Fred, Paul Hoehler.

Allison slid down from her rocky vantage point and paced angrily into the sunlight. On the coast, morning clouds still hung over the lowlands. The silver arch of the force field that enclosed Vandenberg and Lompoc seemed to float halfway up the sky. No structure could possibly be so big. Even mountains had the decency to introduce themselves with foothills and highlands. The Vandenberg Bobble simply rose, sheer and insubstantial as a dream. So that glistening hemisphere contained much of her old world, her old friends. They were trapped in timelessness in there, just as she and Angus and Fred had been trapped in the bobble projected around the sortie craft. And one day the Vandenberg Bobble would burst. . . .

Somewhere in the trees beyond her vision there was a cawing; a crow ascended above the pines, circled down at another point. Over the whine of insects, Allison heard padded clopping. A horse was coming up the narrow trail that went past her rock pile. Allison moved back into the shadows and watched.

Three minutes passed and a lone horseman came into view: it was a black male, so spindly it was hard to guess his age, except to say that he was young. He was dressed in dark greens, almost a camouflage outfit, and his hair was short and unbraided. He looked tired, but his eyes swept attentively back and forth across the trail ahead of him. The brown eyes flickered across her.

"Jill! How did you get so far from the veranda?" The words were spoken with a heavy Spanish accent; at this point it was an incongruity beneath Allison's notice. A broad grin split the boy's face as he slid off the horse and scrambled across the rocks toward her. "Naismith says that—" The words came to an abrupt halt along with the boy himself. He stood an arm's-length away, his jaw sagging in disbelief. "Jill? Is that really you?" He swung his hand in a flat arc toward Allison's midsection. The gesture was too slow to be a blow, but she wasn't taking any chances. She grabbed his wrist.

The boy actually squeaked—but with surprise, not pain. It was as if he could not believe she had actually touched him. She marched him back to the trail, and they started toward the house. She had his arm behind his back now. The boy did not struggle, though he didn't seem intimidated either. There was more shock and surprise in his eyes than fear.

Now that it was the other guy who was at a disadvantage, maybe she could get some answers. "You, Naismith, none of you have ever seen me before, yet you all seem to know me. I want to know why." She bent his arm a bit more, though not enough to hurt. The violence was in her voice.

"But, but I *have* seen you." He paused an instant, then rushed on. "In pictures, I mean."

It might not be the whole truth, but . . . . Perhaps it was like those fantasies Angus used to read. Perhaps she was somehow important, and the world had been waiting for them to come out of stasis. In that case their pictures might be widely distributed.

They walked a dozen steps along the soft, needle-covered path. No, there was something more. These people acted as if they had known her as a person. Was that possible? Not for the boy, but Bill and Irma and certainly Naismith were old enough that she might have known them . . . before. She tried to imagine those faces fifty years younger. The servants couldn't have been more than children. The old man, he would have been around her own age.

She let the boy lead the way. She was more holding his hand than twisting his arm now; her mind was far away, thinking of the single tombstone with her name, thinking how much someone must have cared. They walked past the front of the house, descended the grade that led to a below-ground-level entrance. The door there was open, perhaps to let in the cool smells of morning. Naismith sat with his back to them, his attention all focused on the equipment he was playing with. Still holding his horse's reins, the boy leaned past the doorway and said, "Paul?"

Allison looked past the old man's shoulder at the screen he was watching: a horse and a boy and a woman stood looking through a doorway at an old man watching a screen that ... Allison echoed the boy, but in a tone softer, sadder, more questioning. "Paul?"

The old man, who just last month had been young, turned at last to meet her.

23

There were few places on Earth that were busier or more populous than they had been before the War. Livermore was such a place.

At its pre-War zenith, there had been the city and the clusters of commercial and federal labs scattered through the rolling hills. Those had been boom times, with the old Livermore Energy Laboratories managing dozens of major enterprises and a dozen-dozen contract operations from their square-mile reservation just outside of town. And one of those operations, unknown to the rest, had been the key to the future. Its manager, Hamilton Avery's father, had been clever enough to see what could be done with a certain staff scientist's invention, and had changed the course of history.

And so when the old world had disappeared behind silver bobbles, and burned beneath nuclear fireballs, and later withered in the warplagues— Livermore had grown. First from all over the conti-

nent and then from all over the planet, the new
rulers had brought their best and brightest here. Except for a brief lapse during the worst of the plague
years, that growth had been near-exponential. And
Peace had ruled the new world.

The heart of Authority power covered a thousand
square kilometers, along a band that stretched westward toward the tiny Bay towns of Berkeley and
Oakland. Even the Beijing and the Paris Enclaves
had nothing to compare with Livermore. Hamilton
Avery had wanted an Eden here. He had had forty
years and the wealth and genius of the planet to
make one.

But still at the heart of the heart there was the
Square Mile, the original federal labs, their century-
old University of California architecture preserved
amidst the sweep of one-thousand-meter bobbles,
obsidian towers, and forested parks.

If the three of us are to meet, thought Avery, *what
more appropriate place than here?* He had left his
usual retinue on the greensward which edged the
Square Mile. He and a single aide walked down the
aged concrete sidewalk toward the gray building with
the high narrow windows that had once held central
offices.

Away from the carefully irrigated lawns and ornamental forests, the air was hot, more like the natural
summer weather of the Livermore Valley. Already
Avery's plain white shirt was sticking to his back.

Inside, the air-conditioning was loud and old-
fashioned, but effective enough. He walked down ancient linoleum flooring, his footsteps echoing in the
past. His aide opened the conference room's doors
before him and Hamilton Avery stepped forward to
meet—or confront—his peers.

*   *   *

"Gentlemen." He reached across the conference table to shake first Kim Tioulang's hand, then Christian Gerrault's. The two were not happy; Avery had kept them waiting. *And the hell of it is, I didn't mean to.* Crisis had piled on top of crisis these last few hours, to the point that even a lifetime of political and diplomatic savvy was doing him no good.

Christian Gerrault, on the other hand, never had had much time for diplomacy. His piggish eyes were even more recessed in his fat face than they had seemed on the video. Or perhaps it was simply that he was angry: "You have a very great deal of explaining to do, monsieur. We are not your servants, to be summoned from halfway around the world."

Then why are you here, you fat fool? But out loud he said, "Christian—Monsieur le Directeur—it is precisely because we are the men who count that we must meet here today."

Gerrault threw up a meaty arm. "Pah! The television was always good enough before."

"The 'television,' monsieur, no longer works." The Central African looked disbelieving, but Avery knew Gerrault's people in Paris were clever enough to verify that the Atlantic comsat had been out of action for more than twenty-four hours. It had not been a gradual or partial failure, but an abrupt, total cessation of relayed communication.

But Gerrault simply shrugged, and his three bodyguards moved uneasily behind him. Avery shifted his gaze to Tioulang. The elderly Cambodian, Director for Asia, was not nearly so upset. K.T. was one of the originals: he had been a graduate student at Livermore before the War. He and Hamilton and some hundred others picked by Avery's father had been the founders of the new world. There were very few of them left now. Every year they must select a few more successors. Gerrault was the first director from outside the original group. *Is this the future?* He saw the same question in Tioulang's eyes. Christian was much more capable than he acted, but every year his jewels, his harems, his . . . excesses, became harder to ignore. After the old ones were gone, would he proclaim himself an emperor—or simply a god?

"K.T., Christian, you've been getting my reports. You know we have what amounts to an insurrection here. Even so, I haven't told you everything. Things have happened that you simply won't believe."

"*That* is entirely possible," said Gerrault.

Avery ignored the interruption. "Gentlemen, our enemy has space-flight."

For a long moment there was only the sighing of the air-conditioning. Gerrault's sarcasm had evaporated, and it was Tioulang who raised protest. "But, Hamilton, the industrial base that requires! The Peace itself has only a small, unmanned program. We saw to it that all the big launch complexes were lost during the War." He realized he was rattling on with the obvious and waited for Avery to continue.

Avery motioned his aide to lay the pictures on the table. "I know, K.T. This should be impossible. But look: a fully functional sortie craft—the type the old USAF was flying just before the War—has crashed near the California-Aztlán border. This isn't a model or a mockup. It was totally destroyed in a fire subsequent to its landing, but my people assure me that it had just returned from orbit."

The two directors leaned forward to look at the holos. Tioulang said, "I take your word for this, Hamilton, but it could still be a hoax. I thought all those vehicles were accounted for, but perhaps there has been one in storage all these years. Granted, it is intimidating even as a hoax, but . . ."

"As you say. But there is no evidence of the vehicle's being dragged into the area—and that's heavy forest around the crash site. We are bringing as much of the wreck as we can back here for a close look. We should be able to discover if it was made since the War or if it is a refurbished model from before. We are also putting pressure on Albuquerque to search the old archives for evidence of a secret US launch site."

Gerrault tipped his massive form back to look at his bodyguards. Avery could imagine his suspicion. Finally the African seemed to reach a decision. He leaned forward and said quietly, "Survivors. Did you find anyone to question?"

Avery shook his head. "There were at least two aboard. One was killed on impact. The other was killed by . . . one of our investigating teams. An accident." The other's face twisted, and Avery imagined the slow death Christian would have given those responsible for any such accident. Avery had dealt quickly and harshly with the incompetents involved, but he had gotten no pleasure from it. "There was no identification on the crewman, beyond an embroidered name tag. His flightsuit was old US Air Force issue."

Tioulang steepled his fingers. "Granting the impossible, what were they up to?"

"It looks like a reconnaissance mission. We've brought parts of the wreck back to the labs, but there is still equipment we can't identify."

Tioulang studied one of the aerial photos. "It probably came in from the north, maybe even overflew

Livermore." He gave a wan smile. "History repeats. Remember that Air Force orbiter we bobbled? If they had reported what we were up to right at that critical moment . . . what a different world it would be today."

Days later Avery would wonder why Tioulang's comment didn't make him guess the truth. Perhaps it was Gerrault's interruption; the younger man was not interested in reminiscence. "This then explains why our communication satellites have failed!"

"We think so. We're trying to bring up the old radar watch we maintained through the twenties. It would help if both of you would do this, too.

"However you cut it, it seems we have our first effective opposition in nearly thirty years. Personally, I think they have been with us a long, long time. We've always ignored these 'Tinkers,' assuming that without big energy sources their technology could be no threat to us. 'Cottage industry,' we called it. When I showed you how far their electronics was ahead of ours, you seemed to think they were at most a threat to my West Coast holdings.

"Now it's clear that they have a worldwide operation in some ways equal to our own. I know there are Tinkers in Europe and China. They exist most places where there was a big electronics industry before the War. You should regard them as much a threat as I do mine."

"Yes, and we must flush out the important ones and . . ." Gerrault was in his element now. Visions of torture danced in his eyes.

"And," said Tioulang, "at the same time convince the rest of the world that the Tinkers are a direct threat to their safety. Remember that we all need goodwill. I have direct military control over most of

China, but I could never keep India, Indonesia, and Japan in line if the people at the bottom didn't trust me more than their governments. There are more than twenty million people in those holdings."

"Ah, that is your problem. You are like the grasshopper, lounging in the summer of public approval. I am the industrious ant"—Gerrault looked down at his enormous torso and chuckled at the metaphor—"who has diligently worked to maintain garrisons from Oslo to Capetown. If this is 'winter' coming, I'll need no public approval." His eyes narrowed. "But I do need to know more about this new enemy of ours."

He glanced at Avery. "And I think Avery has cleverly provided us with a lever against them. I wondered why you supported their silly chess tournament in Aztlán, why you used your aircraft to transport their teams from all over the continent. Now I know: when you raided that tournament, you arrested some of the best Tinkers in the world. Oh, no doubt, just a few of them have knowledge of the conspiracy against us, but at the same time they must have many loved ones—and some of those will know more. If, one at a time, we try the prisoners for treason against Peace . . . why, I think we'll find someone who is willing to talk."

Avery nodded. He would get none of the pleasure out of the operation that Christian might. He would do only what was necessary to preserve the Peace. "And don't worry, K.T., we can do it without antagonizing the rest of our people.

"You see, the Tinkers use a lot of x- and gamma-ray lithography; they need it for microcircuit fabrication. Now, my public affairs people have put together a story that we've discovered the Tinkers are secretly upgrading these etching lasers for use as weapons lasers like the governments had before the War."

Tioulang smiled. "Ah. That's the sort of direct threat that should get us a lot of support. It's almost as effective as claiming they're involved in bioscience research."

"There." Gerrault raised his hands beneficently to his fellow directors. "We are all happy then. Your people are pacified, and we can go after the enemy with all vigor. You were right to call us, Avery; this is a matter that deserves our immediate and personal attention."

Avery felt grim pleasure in replying, "There is another matter, Christian, at least as important. Paul Hoehler is alive."

"The old-time mathematician you have such a fixation on? Yes, I know. You reported that in hushed and terrified tones several weeks ago."

"One of my best agents has infiltrated the Middle California Tinkers. She reports that Hoehler has succeeded—or is near to succeeding—in building a bobble generator."

It was the second bombshell he had laid on them, and in a way the greater. Spaceflight was one thing; several ordinary governments had had it before the War. But the bobble: for an enemy to have that was as unwelcome and incredible as hell opening a chapel. Gerrault was emphatic: "Absurd. How could one old man fall on a secret we have kept so carefully all these years?"

"You forget, Christian, that *one old man* invented the bobble in the first place! For ten years after the War, he moved from laboratory to laboratory always just ahead of us, always working on ways to bring us down. Then he disappeared so thoroughly that only I of all the originals believed he was out there somewhere plotting against us. And I was right; he has an incredible ability to survive.''

"I'm sorry, Hamilton, but I have trouble believing, too. There is no hard evidence here, apparently just the word of a woman. I think you always have been overly distressed by Hoehler. He may have had some of the original ideas, but it was the rest of your father's team that really made the invention possible. Besides, it takes a fusion plant and some huge capacitors to power a generator. The Tinkers could never . . .'' Tioulang's voice trailed off as he realized that if you could hide space-launch facilities, you could certainly do the same for a fusion reactor.

"You see?" said Avery. Tioulang hadn't been in Father's research group, couldn't realize Hoehler's polymath talent. There had been others in the project, but it had been Hoehler on all the really theoretical fronts. Of course, history was not written that way. But stark after all the years, Avery remembered the rage on Hoehler's face when he realized that in addition to inventing "the monster" (as he called it), the development could never have been kept secret if he had not done the work of a lab full of specialists. It had been obvious the fellow was going to report them to LEL, and Father had trusted only Hamilton Avery to silence the mathematician. Avery had not succeeded in that assignment. It had been his first— and last—failure of resolve in all these years, but it was a failure that refused to be buried.

"He's out there, K.T., he really is. And my agent is Della Lu, who did the job in Mongolia that none of your people could. What she says you can believe. . . . Don't you see where we are if we fail to act? If they have spaceflight and the bobble, too, then they are our *superiors*. They can sweep us aside as easily as we did the old-time governments."

24

The *sabios* of the Ndelante Ali claimed the One True God knows all and sees all.

Those powers seemed Wili's, now that he had learned to use the scalp connect. He blushed to think of all the months he had dismissed symbiotic programs as crutches for weak minds. If only Jeremy—who had finally convinced him to try—could be here to see. If only Roberto Jonque Richardson were here to be crushed.

Jeremy had thought it would take months to learn. But for Wili, it was like suddenly remembering a skill he'd always had. Even Paul was surprised. It had taken a couple of days to calibrate the connector. At first, the sensations coming over the line had been subtle things, unrelated to their real significance. The mapping problem—the relating of sensation to meaning—was what took most people months. Jill had been a big help with that. Wili could talk to her at the same time he experimented with the signal parameters, telling her what he was seeing. Jill would then alter the output to match what Wili most expected. In a week he could communicate through the interface without opening his mouth or touching the keyboard. Another couple of days and he was transferring visual information over the channel.

The feeling of power was born. It was like being able to add extra rooms to his imagination. When a line of reasoning became too complex, he could simply expand into the machine's space. The low point of every day was when he had to disconnect. He was so stupid then. Typing and vocal communication with Jill made him feel like a deafmute spelling out letters.

And every day he learned more tricks. Most he discovered himself, though some things—like concentration enhancement and Jill-programming—Paul showed him. Jill could proceed with projects during the time when Wili was disconnected and store results in a form that read like personal memories when Wili was able to reconnect. Using the interface that way was almost as good as being connected all the time. At least, once he reconnected, it seemed he'd been "awake" all the time.

Paul had already asked Jill to monitor the spy cameras that laced the hills around the mansion. When Wili was connected, he could watch them all himself. One hundred extra eyes.

And Wili/Jill monitored local Tinker transmissions and the Authority's recon satellites the same way. That was where the feeling of omniscience came strongest.

Both Tinkers and Peacers were waiting—and preparing in their own ways—for the secret of generating bobbles that Paul had promised. From Julian in the South to Seattle in the North and Norcross in the East, the Tinkers were withdrawing from view, trying to get their gear undercover and ready for whatever construction Paul might tell them was necessary. In the high tech areas of Europe and China, something similar was going on—though the Peace cops were so thick in Europe it was difficult to get away with anything there. Four of that continent's self-producing design machines had already been captured or destroyed.

It was harder to tell what was happening in the world's great outback. There were few Tinkers there—in all Australia, for instance, there were less than ten thousand humans—but the Authority was spread correspondingly thin. The people in those regions had radios and knew of the world situation, knew that with enough trouble elsewhere they might overthrow the local garrisons.

Except for Europe, the Authority was taking little direct action. They seemed to realize their enemy was too numerous to root out with a frontal assault. Instead the Peacers were engaged in an all-out search to find one Paul Naismith before Paul Naismith could make good on his promises to the rest of the world.

Jill?

Yes, Wili? Nothing was spoken aloud and no keys were tapped. Input/output was like imagination itself. And when Jill responded, he had a fleeting impression of the face and the smile that he would have seen in the holo if he'd been talking to her the old way. Wili could have bypassed Jill; most symbiotic programs didn't have an intermediate surrogate. But Jill was a friend. And though she occupied lots of program space, she reduced the confusion Wili still felt in dealing with the flood of input. So Wili frequently had Jill work in parallel with him, and called her when he wanted updates on the processes she supervised.

Show me the status of the search for Paul.

Wili's viewpoint was suddenly suspended over California. Silvery traces marked the flight paths of hundreds of aircraft. He sensed the altitude and speed of every craft. The picture was a summary of all Jill had learned monitoring the Authority's recon satellites and Tinker reports over the last twenty-four hours. The rectangular crisscross pattern was still centered over Northern California, though it was more diffuse and indecisive than on earlier days.

Wili smiled. Sending Della Lu's bug north had worked better than he'd hoped. The Peacers had been chasing their tails up there for more than a week. The satellites weren't doing them any good. One of the first fruits of Wili's new power was discovering how to disable the comm and recon satellites. At least, they appeared disabled to the Authority. Actually, the recon satellites were still broadcasting but according to an encryption scheme that must seem pure noise to the enemy. It had seemed an easy trick to Wili; once he conceived the possibility, he and Jill had implemented it in less than a day. But looking back—after having disconnected—Wili realized that it was deeper and trickier than his original method of tapping the satellites. What had taken him a winter of mind-busting effort was an afternoon's triviality now.

Of course, none of these tricks would have helped if Paul had not been very cautious all these years; he and Bill Morales had traveled great distances to shop at towns farther up the coast. Many Tinkers thought his hideout was in Northern California or even Oregon. As long as the Peacers didn't pick up any of the few people who had actually visited here—say at the NCC meeting—they might be safe.

Wili frowned. There was still the greatest threat. Miguel Rosas probably did not know the location, though he must suspect it was in Middle California. But Wili was sure Colonel Kaladze knew. It could only be a matter of time before Mike and the Lu woman ferreted out the secret. If subtlety were unsuccessful, then Lu would no doubt call in the Peace goons and try to beat it out of him. *Are they still on the farm?*

Yes. And there have been no outgoing calls from them. However, the Colonel's ten-day promise lapses tomorrow. Then Kaladze would no doubt let Lu call her "family" in San Francisco. But if she hadn't called in the Army already, she must not have anything critical to report to her bosses.

Wili had not told Paul what he knew of Mike and Lu. Perhaps he should. But after trying to tell Kaladze . . . Instead he'd been trying to identify Della Lu with independent evidence. More than ten percent of Jill's time was spent in the effort. So far she had nothing definite. The story about relatives in the Bay Area appeared to be true. If he had some way of tapping Peacer communication or records, things would be different. He saw now he should have disabled their recon satellites alone. If their comsats were usable, it would give them some advantage—but perhaps he could eventually break into their high crypto channels. As it was, he knew very little about what went on inside the Authority.

. . . and sometimes, he really wondered if Colonel Kaladze might be right. Wili had been half-delirious that morning on the boat; Mike and Della had been several meters away. Was it possible he'd misinterpreted what he heard? Was it possible they were innocent after all? *No!* By the One True God, he had heard what he had heard. Kaladze hadn't been there.

25

Sunlight still lay on the hills, but the lowlands and Lake Lompoc were shrouded in blue shadows. Paul sat on his veranda and listened to the news that Wili's electronic spies brought in from all over the world.

There was a small cough and Naismith looked up. For an instant he thought it was Allison standing there. Then he noticed how carefully she stood between him and the holo surface built into the wall. If he moved more than a few centimeters, parts of the image would be cut off. This was only Jill.

"Hi." He motioned for her to come and sit. She stepped forward, careful to generate those little moving sounds that made her projection seem more real, and sat in the image of a chair. Paul watched her face as she approached. There really were differences, he realized. Allison was very pretty, but he had made Jill's face beautiful. And of course the personalities were subtly different, too. It could not have been otherwise considering that he had done his design from memories forty-five years stale (or embellished), and considering that the design had grown by itself in response to his reactions. The real Allison was more outgoing, more impatient. And Allison's mere presence seemed to be changing Jill. The interface program had been much quieter these last days.

He smiled at her. "You've got the new bobble theory all worked out?"

She grinned back and was more like Allison than ever. "Your theory. I do nothing but crunch away—"

"I set up the theory. It would take a hundred lifetimes for me to do the symbolic math and see the theory's significance." It was a game they—he—had played many times before. The back-and-forth had always made Jill seem so real. "What have you got?"

"Everything seems consistent. There are a lot of things that were barred under your old theory, that are still impossible: it's still impossible to burst a bobble before its time. It's impossible to generate a bobble around an existing one. On the other hand—in theory at least—it should be possible to balk an enemy bobbler."

"Hmm . . ." Simply carrying a small bobble was a kind of defense against bobble attack—a very risky defense, once noticed: it would force the attacker to project smaller bobbles, or off-center ones, trying to find a volume that wasn't "banned." A device that could prevent bobbles from being formed nearby would be a tremendous improvement, and Naismith had guessed the new theory might allow such, but . . .

"Betcha that last will be an *engineering* impossibility for a long time. We should concentrate on making a low-power bobbler. That looks hard enough."

"Yes. Wili's right on schedule with that."

Jill's image suddenly froze, then flicked out of existence. Naismith heard the veranda door slide open. "Hi, Paul," came Allison's voice. She walked up the steps. "You out here by yourself?"

". . . Yes. Just thinking."

She walked to the edge of the veranda and looked westward. These last weeks, every day had brought more change in Paul's life and in the world beyond the mountains than a normal year. Yet for Allison, it was different. Her world had turned inside out in the space of an hour. He knew the present rate of change was agonizingly slow for her. She paced the stone flags, stopping occasionally to glare off into the sunset at the Vandenberg Bobble.

Allison. Allison. Few old men had dreams come quite so stunningly true. She was so young; her energy seemed to flash about her in every stride, in every quick movement of her arms. In some ways the memories of Allison lost were less hurtful than the present reality. Still, he was glad he had not succeeded in disguising what became of Paul Hoehler.

Allison suddenly looked back at him, and smiled. "Sorry about the pacing."

"No problem. I . . ."

She waved toward the west. The air was so clear that—except for the lake and the coastline reflected in its base—the Dome was almost invisible. "When will it burst, Paul? There were three thousand of us there the day I left. They had guns, aircraft. When will they come out?"

A month ago he would not have thought of the question. Two weeks ago he couldn't have answered. In those weeks a theory had been trashed and his new theory born. It was totally untested, but soon, soon that would change. "Uh. My answer's still guessing Allison: the Authority technique, the only way I could think of then, is a brute force method. With it, the lifetime is about fifty years. So now I can represent radius or mass as a perturbation series about a fifty-year decay time. The smallest bobbles the Authority made were about ten meters across. They burst first. Your sortie craft was trapped in a thirty-meter bobble; it decayed a little later." Paul realized he was wandering and tried to force his answer into the mold she must want. He thought a moment. "Vandenberg ought to last fifty-five years."

"Five more years. Damn it." She walked back across the veranda. "I guess you'll have to win without them. I was wondering why you hadn't told your friends about me—you haven't even told them that time stops inside the bobbles. I thought maybe you expected to surprise the Peacers with their long-dead victims suddenly alive."

"You're close. You, me, Wili, and the Morales are the only ones who know. The Authority hasn't guessed—Wili says they've carted your orbiter up to Livermore as if it were full of clues. No doubt the fools think they've stumbled on some new conspiracy. . . . But then, I guess it's not so stupid. I'll bet you didn't have any paper records aboard the orbiter."

"Right. Even our notepads were display flats. We could trash everything in seconds if we fell among unfriendlies. The fire would leave them with nothing but slagged optical memory. And if they don't have the old fingerprint archives, they're not going to identify Fred or Angus."

"Anyway, I've told the Tinkers to be ready, that I'm going to tell them how to make bobble generators. Even then, I may not say anything about the stasis effect. That's something that could give us a real edge, but only if we use the knowledge at the right time. I don't want some leak to blow it."

Allison turned as if to pace back to the edge of the veranda, then noticed the display that Paul had been studying. Her hand rested lightly on his shoulder as she leaned over to look at the displays. "Looks like a recon pattern," she said.

"Yes. Wili and Jill synthesized it from the satellites we're tapping. This shows where Authority aircraft have been searching."

"For you."

"Probably." He touched the keyboard at the margin of the flat, and the last few days' activity were displayed.

"Those bums." There was no lightness in her voice. "They destroyed our country and then stole our own procedures. Those search patterns look SOP 1997 for medium-level air recon. I bet your damn Peacers never had an original thought in their lives. . . . Hmm. Run that by again." She knelt to look closely at the daily.summaries. "I think today's sorties were the last for that area, Paul. Don't be surprised if they move the search several hundred klicks in the next day or two." In some ways, Allison's knowledge was fifty years dead and useless—in other ways, it could be just what they needed.

Paul gave a silent prayer of thanks to Hamilton Avery for having kept the heat on all these years, for having forced Paul Hoehler to disguise his identity and his location through decades when there would have otherwise been no reason to. "If they shift further north, fine. If they come all the way south. Hmm. We're well hidden, but we wouldn't last more than a couple days under that sort of scrutiny. Then . . ." He drew a finger across his throat and made a croaking noise.

"No way you could put this show on the road, huh?"

"Eventually we could. Have to start planning for it. I have an enclosed wagon. It may be big enough for the essential equipment. But right now, Allison ... Look, we don't yet have anything but a lot of theories. I'm translating the physics into problems Wili can handle. With Jill, he's putting them into software as fast as he can."

"He seems to spend his time daydreaming, Paul."

Naismith shook his head. "Wili's the best." The boy had picked up symbiotic programming faster than Paul had ever seen, faster than he'd thought possible. The technique improved almost any programmer, but in Wili's case, it had turned a first-rank genius into something Naismith could no longer completely understand. Even when he was linked with Wili and Jill, the details of their algorithms were beyond him. It was curious, because off the symbiosis Wili was not that much brighter than the old man. Paul wondered if he could have been that good, too, if he had started young. "I think we're nearly there, Allison. Based on what we understand now, it ought to be possible to make bobbles with virtually no energy input. The actual hardware should be something Jill can prototype here."

Allison didn't come off her knees. Her face was just centimeters from his. "That Jill program is something. Just the motion holo for the face would have swamped our best array processors. . . . But why make it look like me, Paul? After all those years, did I really mean so much?"

Naismith tried to think of something flippant and

diversionary, but no words came. She looked at him a second longer, and he wondered if she could see the young man trapped within.

"Oh, *Paul.*" Then her arms were around him, her cheek next to his.

She held him as one would hold something very fragile, very old.

Two days later, Wili was ready.

They waited till after dark to make the test. In spite of Paul's claims, Wili wasn't sure how big the bobble would be, and even if it did not turn out to be a monster, its mirrorlike surface would be visible for hundreds of kilometers to anyone looking in the right direction in the daytime.

The three of them walked to the pond north of the house. Wili carried the bulky transmitter for his symb link. Near the pond's edge he set his equipment down and slipped on the scalp connector. Then he lit a candle and placed it on a large tree stump. It was a tiny spot of yellow, bright only because all else was so dark. A gray thread of smoke rose from the glow.

"We think the bobble, it will be small, but we don't want to take chances. Jill is going to make its lower edge to snip the top of this candle. Then if we're wrong, and it is huge—"

"Then as the night cools, the bobble will rise and be just another floater. By morning it could be many kilometers from here." Paul nodded. "Clever . . ."

He and Allison backed further away, Wili following. From thirty meters, the candle was a flickering yellow star on the stump. Wili motioned them to sit; even if the bobble was super-large, its lower surface would still clear them.

"You don't need any power source at all?" said

Allison. "The Peace Authority uses fusion generators and you can do it for free?"

"In principle, it isn't difficult—once you have the right insight, once you know what really goes on inside the bobbles. And the new process is not quite free. We're using about a thousand joules here—compared to the gigajoules of the Authority generators. The trade-off is in complexity. If you have a fusion generator backing you up, you can bobble practically anything you can locate. But if you're like us, with solar cells and small capacitors, then you must finesse it.

"The projection needs to be supervised, and it's no ordinary process control problem. This test is about the easiest case: the target is motionless, close by, and we only want a one-meter field. Even so, it will involve—how much crunching do we need, Wili?"

"She needs thirty seconds initial at about ten billion flops, and then maybe one microsecond for 'assembly'—at something like a trillion."

Paul whistled. A *trillion* floating-point operations per second! Wili had said he could implement the discovery, but Paul hadn't realized just how expensive it might be. The gear would not be very portable. And long distance or very large bobbles might not be feasible.

Wili seemed to sense his disappointment. "We think we can do it with a slower processor. It maybe takes many minutes for the setup, but you could still bobble things that don't move or are real close."

"Yeah, we'll optimize later. Let's make a bobble, Wili."

The boy nodded.

Seconds passed. Something—an owl—thuttered over the clearing, and the candle went out. Nuts. He had hoped it would stay lit. It would have been a nice demonstration of the stasis effect to have the candle still burning later on when the bobble burst.

"Well?" Wili said. "What do you think?"

"You did it!" said Paul. The words were somewhere between a question and an exclamation.

"Jill did, anyway. I better grab it before it floats away."

Wili slipped off the scalp connector and sprinted across the clearing. He was already coming back before Naismith had walked halfway to the tree stump. The boy was holding something in front of him, something light on top and dark underneath. Paul and Allison moved close. It was about the size of a large beach ball, and in its upper hemisphere he could see reflected stars, even the Milky Way, all the way down to the dark of the tree line surrounding the pond. Three silhouettes marked the reflections of their own heads. Naismith extended his hand, felt it slide silkily off the bobble, felt the characteristic bloodwarm heat—the reflection of his hand's thermal radiation.

Wili had his arms extended around its girth and his chin pushed down on the top. He looked like a comedian doing a mock weight lift. "It feels like it will shoot from my hands if I don't hold it every way."

"Probably could. There's no friction."

Allison slipped her hand across the surface. "So that's a bobble. Will this one last fifty years, like the one . . . Angus and I were in?"

Paul shook his head. "No. That's for big ones done the old way. Eventually, I expect to have very flexible control, with duration only loosely related to size. How long does Jill estimate this one will last, Wili?"

Before the boy could reply, Jill's voice interrupted from the interface box. "There's a PANS bulletin coming over the high-speed channels. It puffs out to a thirty-minute program. I'm summarizing:

"Big story about threat to the Peace. Biggest since Huachuca plaguetime. Says the Tinkers are the villains. Their leaders were captured in La Jolla raids last month. . . . The broadcast has video of Tinker 'weapons labs,' pictures of sinister-looking prisoners. . . .

"Prisoners to be tried for Treason against the Peace, starting immediately, in Los Angeles.

" . . . all government and corporate stations must rebroadcast this at normal speed every six hours for the next two days."

There was a long silence after she finished. Wili held up the bobble. "They picked the wrong time to put the squeeze on *us*!"

Naismith shook his head. "It's the worst possible time for us. We're being forced to use this"—he patted the bobble—"when we've barely got a proof of principle. It puts us right where that punk Avery wants us."

26

The rain was heavy and very, very warm. High in the clouds, lightning chased itself around and around the Vandenberg Dome, never coming to earth. Thunder followed the arching, cloud-smeared glows.

Della Lu had seen more rain the last two weeks than would fall in a normal year in Beijing. It was a fitting backdrop for the dull routine of life here. If Avery hadn't finally gone for the spy trials, she would be seriously planning to escape Red Arrow hospitality—blown cover or not.

"Hey, you tired already? Or just daydreaming?" Mike had stopped and was looking back at her. He stood, arms akimbo, apparently disgusted. The transparent rain jacket made his tan shirt and pants glint metallic even in the gray light.

Della walked a little faster to catch up. They continued in silence for a hundred meters. No doubt they made an amusing pair: two figures shrouded in rain gear, one tall, one so short. Since Wili's ten-day "probation period" had lapsed, the two of them had taken a walk every day. It was something she had insisted on, and—for a change—Rosas hadn't resisted. So far she had snooped as far north as Lake Lompoc and east to the ferry crossing.

Without Mike, her walks would've had to have been with the womenfolk. That would have been tricky. The women were *protected*, and had little freedom or responsibility. She spent most of every day with them, doing the light manual labor that was considered appropriate to her sex. She had been careful to be popular, and she had learned a lot, but all local intelligence. Just as with families in San Francisco, the women were not privy to what went on in the wider world. They were valued, but second-class, citizens. Even so, they were clever; it would be difficult to look in the places that really interested her without raising their suspicions.

Today was her longest walk, up to the highlands that overlooked Red Arrow's tiny sea landing. Despite Mike's passive deceptions, she had put together a pretty good picture of Old Kaladze's escape system. At least she knew its magnitude and technique. It was a small payoff for the boredom and the feeling that she was being held offstage from events she should be directing.

All that could change with the spy trials. If she could just light a fire under the right people . . . .

The timbered path went back and forth across the hill they climbed. There were many repairs, and several looked quite recent, yet there were also washouts. It was like most things among the Tinkers. Their electronic gadgets were superlative (though it was clear now that the surveillance devices Avery had discovered were rare and expensive items amongst the Tinkers; they didn't normally spy on each other). But they were labor poor, and without power equipment, things like road maintenance and laundry were distinctly nineteenth century. And Della had the calluses to prove it.

Finally they reached the overlook point. A steady breeze swept across the hill, blowing the rain into their faces. There was only one tree at the top, though it was a fine, large conifer growing from the highest point. There was some kind of platform about halfway up.

Rosas put his arm across her shoulder, urging her toward the tree. "They had a tree house up here when I was a kid. There ought to be a good view."

Wood steps were built into the tree trunk. She noticed a heavy metallic cable that followed the steps upward. Electronics even here? Then she realized that it was a lightning guide. The Tinkers were very careful with their children.

Seconds later they were on the platform. The cabin was clean and dry with soft padding on the floor. There was a view south and west, somehow contrived to keep out the wind and rain. They shrugged out of their rain jackets and sat for a moment enjoying the sound of wet that surrounded this pocket of dry comfort. Mike crawled to the south-facing window. "A lot of good it will do you, but there it is."

The forested hills dropped away from the overlook. The coast was about four kilometers away, but the rain was so heavy that she had only a vague impression of sand dunes and marching surf. It looked like there was a small breakwater, but no boats at anchor. The landing was not actually on Red Arrow property, but they used it more than anyone else. Mike claimed that more people came to the farm from the ocean than overland. Della doubted that. It sounded like another little deception.

The undersheriff backed away from the opening and leaned against the wall beside her. "Has it really been worth it, Della?" There was a faint edge in his voice. It was clear by now that he had no intention of denouncing her—and implicating himself at the same time. But he was not hers. She had dealt with traitors before, men whose self-interest made them simple, reliable tools. Rosas was not such. He was waiting for the moment when the damage he could do her would be greatest. Till then he played the role of reluctant ally.

Indeed, had it been worth the trouble? He smiled, almost triumphantly. "You've been stuck here for more than two weeks. You've learned a little bit about one small corner of the ungoverned lands, and one group of Tinkers. I think you're more important to the Peacers than that. You're like a high-value piece voluntarily taken out of the game."

Della smiled back. He was saying aloud her own angry thoughts. The only thing that had kept her going was the thought that just a little more snooping might ferret out the location of Paul Hoehler/Naismith. It had seemed such an easy thing. But she gradually realized that Mike—and almost everyone else—didn't know where the old man lived. Maybe Kaladze did, but she'd need an interrogation lab to pry it out of him. Her only progress along that line had been right at the beginning, when she tagged the black boy's horse with a tracer.

Hallelujah, all that had changed. There was a chance now that she was in the best of strategic positions.

Mike's eyes narrowed, and Della realized he sensed some of her triumph. *Damn.* They had spent too much time together, had too many conversations that were not superficial. His hand closed on her upper arm and she was pulled close to his face. "Okay. What is it? What are you going to spring on us?" Her arm suddenly felt as though trapped in a vice.

Della suppressed reflexes that would have left him gargling on a crushed windpipe. Best that he think he had the age-old macho edge. She pretended shocked speechlessness. How much to say? When they were alone, Mike often spoke of her real purpose at Red Arrow. She knew he wasn't trying to compromise her to hidden listeners—he could do that directly whenever chose. And he knew Red Arrow so well, it was unlikely they would be bugged without his knowledge. So the only danger was in telling him too much, in giving him the motive to blow the whole game. But maybe she should tell him a little; if it all came as a surprise, he might be harder to control. She tried to shrug. "I've got a couple maybes going for me. Your friend Hoehler—Naismith—says he has a prototype bobble generator. Maybe he does. In any case, it will be a while before the rest of you can build such. In the meantime, if the Peace can throw you off balance, can get you and Naismith to overextend yourselves. . . ."

"The trials."

"Right." She wondered what Mike's reaction would be if he knew that she had recommended immediate treason trials for the La Jolla hostages. He'd made sure there were Kaladzes in earshot when she was allowed to call her family in San Francisco. She had sounded completely innocent, just telling her parents that she was safe among the Middle California Tinkers, though she mustn't say just where. No doubt Rosas guessed that some sort of prearranged signal scheme was being used, but he could never have known how elaborate it was. Tone codes were something that went right by native speakers of English. "The trials. If they could be used to panic Kaladze and his friends, we might get a look at Naismith's best stuff before it can do the Peace any real harm."

Mike laughed, his grip relaxing slightly. "*Panic* Nikolai Sergeivich? You might as well think to panic a charging bear."

Della did not fully plan what she did next, and that was very unusual for her. Her free hand moved up behind his neck, caressing the short cut hair. She raised herself to kiss him. Rosas jerked back for an instant, then responded. After a moment, she felt his weight on her and they slid to the soft padding that covered the floor of the tree house. Her arms roamed across his neck and wide shoulders and the kiss continued.

She had never before used her body to ensure loyalty. It had never been necessary. It certainly had never before been an attractive prospect. And it was doubtful it could do any good here. Mike had fallen to them out of honor; he could not rationalize the deaths he had caused. In his way, he was as unchangeable as she.

One of his arms wrapped around her back while his free hand pulled at her blouse. His hand slid under the fabric, across her smooth skin, to her breasts. The caresses were eager, rough. There was rage . . . and something else. Della stretched out against him, forcing one of her legs between his. For a long while the world went away and they let their passion speak for them.

. . . Lightning played its ring dance along the Dome that towered so high above them. When the thunder paused in its following march, they could hear the *shish* of warm rain continue all around.

Rosas held her gently now, his fingers slowly tracing the curve of her hip and waist. "What do you get out of being a Peace cop, Della? If you were one of the button-pushers, sitting safe and cozy up in Livermore, I could understand. But you've risked your life stooging for a tyranny, and turning me into something I never thought I'd be. Why?"

Della watched the lightning glow in the rain. She sighed. "Mike, I am for the Peace. Wait. I don't mean that as rote Authority mumbo jumbo. We *do* have something like peace all over the world now. The price is a tyranny, though milder than any in history. The price is twentieth-century types like me, who would sell their own grandmothers for an ideal. Last century produced nukes and bobbles and warplagues. You have been brushed by the plagues—that alone is what turned you into 'something you never thought you'd be.' But the others are just as bad. By the end of the century, those weapons were becoming cheaper and cheaper. Small nations were getting them. If the War hadn't come, I'll bet subnational groups and criminals would have had them. The human race could not survive mass-death technology so widely spread. The Peace has meant the end of sovereign nations and their control of technologies that could kill us all. Our only mistake was in not going far enough. We didn't regulate high tech electronics—and we're paying for that now."

The other was silent, but the anger was gone from his face. Della came to her knees and looked around. She almost laughed. It looked as if a small bomb had gone off in the tree house; their clothes were thrown all across the floor pads. She began dressing. After a moment, so did Mike. He didn't speak until they had on their rain slickers and had raised the trapdoor.

He grinned lopsidedly and stuck his hand out to Della. "Enemies?" he said.

"For sure." She grinned back, and they shook on it.

And even as they climbed out of the tree, she was wondering what it would take to move old Kaladze. Not panic; Mike was right about that. What about shame? Or anger?

Della's chance came the next day. The Kaladze clan had gathered for lunch, the big meal of the day. As was expected of a woman, Lu had helped with the cooking and laying out of the dinnerware, and the serving of the meal. Even after she was seated at the long, heavily laden table, there were constant interruptions to go out and get more food or replace this or that item.

The Authority channels were full of the "Treason against Peace" trials that Avery was staging in LA. Already there had been some death sentences. She knew Tinkers all across the continent were in frantic communication, and there was an increasing sense of dread. Even the women felt it. Naismith had announced his prototype bobble generator. A design had also been transmitted. Unfortunately, the only working model depended on processor networks and programs that would take the rest of the world weeks to grow. And even then, there were problems with the design that would cost still more time to overcome.

The menfolk took these two pieces of news and turned lunch into a debate. It was the first time she had seen them talk policy at a meal; it showed how critical the situation was. In principle the Tinkers now had the same ultimate weapon as the Authority.

But the weapon was no good to them yet. In fact, if the Authority learned about it before the Tinkers had generators in production, it might precipitate the military attack they all feared. So what should be done about the prisoners in Los Angeles?

Lu sat quietly through fifteen minutes of this, until it became clear that caution was winning and the Kaladzes were going to keep a low profile until they could safely take advantage of Naismith/Hoehler's invention. Then she stood up with a shrill, inarticulate shout. The dining hall was instantly silent. The Kaladzes looked at her with shocked surprise. The woman sitting next to her made fluttering motions for her to sit down. Instead, Della shouted down the long table, "You cowardly fools! You would sit here and dither while they execute our people one by one in Los Angeles. You have a weapon now, this bobble generator. And even if you are not willing to risk your own necks, there are plenty of noble houses in Aztlán that are; at least a dozen of their senior sons were taken in La Jolla."

At the far end of the table, Nikolai Sergeivich came slowly to his feet. Even at that distance, he seemed to tower over her diminutive 155 centimeters. "Miss Lu. It is not we who have the bobble generator, but Paul Naismith. You know that he has only one, and that it is not completely practical. He won't give us—"

Della slammed the flat of her hand on the table, the pistol-shot noise cutting the other off and dragging everyone's attention back to her. "Then *make him!* He can't exist without you. He must be made to understand that our own flesh and blood are at stake here—" She stepped back from the table and looked them all up and down, then put surprise and scorn on her face. "But that's not true of you, is it? *My own brother is one of the hostages.* But to you, they are merely fellow Tinkers."

Under his stubbly beard, Kaladze's face became very pale. Della was taking a chance. Publicly disrespectful women were rare here, and when they surfaced—even as guests—they could expect immediate expulsion. But Della had gone a calculated distance *beyond* disrespect. She had attacked their courage, their manhood. She had spoken aloud of the guilt which—she hoped—was lying just below their caution.

Kaladze found his voice and said, "You are wrong, madam. They are not *merely* fellow Tinkers, but our brothers, too." And Della knew she had won. The Authority would get a crack at that bobble generator while it was still easy pickings.

She sat meekly down, her eyes cast shyly at the table. Two large tears started down her cheeks. But she said nothing more. Inside, a Cheshire cat smile spread from ear to ear: for the victory, and for the chance to get back at them for all the days of dumb servility. From the corner of her eye, she saw the stricken look on Mike's face. She had guessed right there, too. He would say nothing. He knew she lied, but those lies *were* a valid appeal to honor. He was caught, even knowing, in the trap with the others.

27

Aztlán encompassed most of what had been Southern and Baja California. It also claimed much of Arizona, though this was sharply disputed by the Republic of New Mexico. In fact, Aztlán was a loose confederation of local rulers, each with an immense estate.

Perhaps it was the challenge of the Authority Enclave in old Downtown, but nowhere in Aztlán were the castles grander than in North Los Angeles. And of those castles, that of the Alcalde del Norte was a giant among giants.

The carriage and its honor guard moved quickly up the well-maintained old-world road that led to El Norte's main entrance. In the darkened interior, a single passenger—one Wili Wáchendon—sat on velvet cushions and listened to the *clopclop* of the carriage team and outriders. He was being treated like a lord. Well, not quite. He couldn't get over the look of stunned surprise on the faces of the Aztlán troops when they saw the travel-grimed black kid they were to escort from Ojai to LA. He looked through tinted bulletproof glass at things he had never expected to see—not by daylight anyway. On the right, the hill rose sheer, pocked every fifty meters by machine-gun nests; on the left, he saw a pike fence half-hidden in the palms. He remembered such pikes, and what happened to unlucky burglars.

Beyond the palms, Wili could see much of the Basin. It was as big as some countries, and—not even counting the Authority personnel in the Enclave—there were more than eighty thousand people out there, making it one of the largest cities on Earth. By now, midafternoon, the wood and petroleum cooking stoves of that population had raised a pall of darkish smoke that hung just under the temperature inversion and made it impossible to see the far hills.

They reached the southern ramparts and crossed the flagstone perimeter that surrounded the Alcalde's mansion. They rolled by a long building fronted with incredible sweeps of perfectly matched plate glass. There was not a bullet hole or shatter star to be seen. No enemy had reached this level in many years. The Alcalde had firm control of the land for kilometers on every side.

The carriage turned inward, and retainers rushed to slide open the glass walls. Wagon, horses, and guard continued inward, past more solid walls; this meeting would take place beyond sight of spying eyes. Wili gathered his equipment. He slipped on the scalp connector, but it was scant comfort. His processor was programmed for one task, and the interface gave him none of the omniscience he felt when working with Jill.

*   *   *

Wili felt like a chicken at a coyote convention. But there was a difference, he kept telling himself. He smiled at the collected coyotes and set his dusty gear on the glistening floor: *this* chicken laid bobbles.

He stood in the middle of the Alcalde's hall of audience, alone there except for the two stewards who had brought him the last hundred meters from the carriage. Four Jonques sat on a dais five meters away. They were not the most titled nobles in Aztlán—though one of them was the Alcalde—but he recognized the embroidery on their jackets. These were men the Ndelante Ali had never dared to burgle.

To the side, subordinate but not cringing, stood three very old blacks. Wili recognized Ebenezer, Pasadena Sabio of the Ndelante, a man so old and set in his ways that he had never even learned Spanish. He needed interpreters to convey his wishes to his own people. Of course, this increased his appearance of wisdom. As near as could be over such a large area, these seven men ruled the Basin and the lands to the east—ruled all but the Downtown and the Authority Enclave.

Wili's impudence was not lost on the coyotes. The youngest of the Jonque lords leaned forward to look down upon him. "*This* is Naismith's emissary? With *this* we are to bobble the Downtown, and rescue our brothers? It's a joke."

The youngest of the blacks—a man in his seventies—whispered in Ebenezer's ear, probably translating the Jonque's comments into English. The Old One's glance was cold and penetrating, and Wili wondered if Ebenezer remembered all the trouble a certain scrawny burglar had caused the Ndelante.

Wili bowed low to the seated noblemen. When he spoke it was in standard Spanish with what he hoped was a Middle California accent. It would be best to convince these people that he was not a native of Aztlán. "My Lords and Wise Ones, it is true that I am a mere messenger, a mere technician. But I have Naismith's invention here with me, I know how to operate it, and I know how it can be used to free the Authority's prisoners."

The Alcalde, a pleasant-looking man in his fifties, raised an eyebrow and said mildly, "You mean your companions are carrying it—disassembled perhaps?"

Companions? Wili reached down and opened his pack. "No, My Lord," he said, withdrawing the generator and processor, "this is the bobbler. Given the plans that Paul Naismith has broadcast, the Tinkers should be able to make these by the hundreds within six weeks. For now, this is the only working model." He showed the ordinary-looking processor box around. Few things could look less like a weapon, and Wili could see the disbelief growing on their faces. A demonstration was in order. He concentrated briefly to let the interface know the parameters.

Five seconds passed and a perfect silver sphere just ... appeared in the air before Wili's face. The bobble wasn't more than ten centimeters across, but it might have been ten kilometers for the reaction of his audience. He gave it the lightest of pushes, and the sphere—weighing exactly as much as an equivalent volume of air—drifted across the hall toward the nobles. Before it had traveled a meter, air currents had deflected it. The youngest of the Jonques, the loudmouthed one, shed his dignity and jumped off the dais to grab at the bobble.

"By God, it's real!" he said as he felt its surface.

Wili just smiled and imaged another command sequence. A second and a third sphere floated across the room. For bobbles this size, where the target was close by and homogeneous, the computations were so simple he could generate an almost continuous stream. For a few moments his audience lost some of its dignity.

Finally old Ebenezer raised a hand and said to Wili in English, "So, boy, you have all the Authority has. You can bobble all Downtown, and we go in and pick up the pieces. All their armies won't stand up to this."

Jonque heads jerked around, and Wili knew they understood the question. Most of them understood English and Spañolnegro—though they often pretended otherwise. He could see the processors humming away in their scheming minds: with this weapon, they could do a good deal more than rescue the hostages and boot the Authority out of Aztlán. If the Peacers were to be replaced, why shouldn't it be by them? And—as Wili had admitted—they had a six weeks' head start on the rest of the world.

Wili shook his head. "No, Wise One. You'd need more power—though still nothing like the fusion power the Authority uses. But even more important, this little generator isn't fast enough. The biggest it can make is about four hundred meters across, and to do that takes special conditions and several minutes setup time."

"Bah. So it's a toy. You could decapitate a few Authority troopers with it maybe, but when they bring out their machine guns and their aircraft you are dead." Señor Loudmouth was back in form. He reminded Wili of Roberto Richardson. Too bad this was going to help the likes of them.

"*It's no toy*, My Lord. If you follow the plan Paul Naismith has devised, it can rescue all the hostages."

Actually it was a plan that Wili had thought of after the first test, when he had felt Jill's test bobble sliding around in his arms. But it would not do to say the scheme came from anyone less than Paul. "There are things about bobbles that you don't know yet, that no one, not even the Authority, knows yet."

"And what are those things, sir?" There was courtesy without sarcasm in the Alcalde's voice.

Across the hall, a couple entered the room. For an instant all Wili could see was their silhouettes against the piped sky light. But that was enough. "You two!" Mike looked almost as shocked as Wili felt, but Lu just smiled.

"Kaladze's representatives," the Alcalde supplied.

"By the One God, no! These are the Authority's representatives!"

"See here." It was Loudmouth. "These two have been vouched for by Kaladze, and he's the fellow who got this all organized."

"I'm not saying anything with them around."

Dead silence greeted this refusal, and Wili felt sudden, physical fear. The Jonque lords had very interesting rooms beneath their castles, places with ... effective ... equipment for persuading people to talk. This was going to be like the confrontation with the Kaladzes, only bloodier.

The Alcalde said, "I don't believe you. We've checked the Kaladzes carefully. We've even dismissed our own court so that this meeting would involve just those with the need to know. But"—he sighed, and Wili saw that in some ways he was more flexible (or less trusting, anyway) than Nikolai Sergeivich—"perhaps it would be safer if you only spoke of what must be done, rather than the secrets behind it all. Then we will judge the risks, and decide if we must have more information just now."

Wili looked at Rosas and Lu. Was it possible to do this without giving away the secret—at least until it was too late for the Authority to counter it? Perhaps. "Are the hostages still being held on the top floor of the Tradetower?"

"The top two floors. Even with aircraft, an assault would be suicide."

"Yes, My Lord. But there is another way. I will need forty Julian-thirty-three storage cells"—other brands would do, but he was sure the Aztlán make was available—"and access to your weather service. Here is what you have to do. . . ." It wasn't until several hours later that Wili looked back and realized that the cripple from Glendora had been giving orders to the rulers of Aztlán and the wise men of the Ndelante Ali. If only Uncle Sly could have seen it.

Early afternoon the next day:

Wili crouched in the tenement ruins just east of the Downtown and studied the display. It was driven by a telescope the Ndelante had planted on the roof. The day was so clear that the view might have been that of a hawk hovering on the outskirts of the Enclave. Looking into the canyons between those buildings, Wili could see dozens of automobiles whisking Authority employees through the streets. Hundreds of bicycles—property of lower-ranking people—moved more slowly along the margins of the streets. And the pedestrians: there were actually crushes of people on the sidewalks by the larger buildings. An occasional helicopter buzzed through the spaces above. It was like some vision off an old video disk, but this was *real* and happening right now, one of the few places on Earth where the bustling past still lived.

Wili shut down the display and looked up at the faces—both Jonque and black—that surrounded him. "That's not too much help for this job. Winning is going to depend on how good your spies are."

"They're good enough." It was Ebenezer's sour-faced aide. The Ndelante Ali was a big organization, but Wili had a dark suspicion that the fellow recognized him from before. Getting home to Paul would depend on keeping his "friends" here intimidated by Naismith's reputation and gadgets. "The Peacers like to be served by people as well as machines. The Faithful have been in the Tradetower as late as this morning. The hostages are all on the top two floors. The next two floors are empty and alarm-ridden, and below that is at least one floor full of Peace Troopers. The utility core is also occupied, and you notice there is a helicopter and fixed-wing patrol. You'd almost think they're expecting a twentieth century armored assault and not. . . ."

And not one scrawny teenager and his miniature bobble blower. Wili silently completed the other's dour implication. He glanced at his hands: skinny maybe, but if he kept gaining weight as he had been these last weeks, he would soon be far from scrawny. And he felt like he could take on the Authority and the Jonques and the Ndelante Ali all at once. Wili grinned at the *sabio*. "What I've got is more effective than tanks and bombs. If you're sure exactly where they are, I'll have them out by nightfall." He turned to the Alcalde's man, a mild-looking old fellow who rarely spoke but got unnervingly crisp obedience from his men. "Were you able to get my equipment upstairs?"

"Yes, sir." *Sir!*

"Let's go, then." They walked back into the main part of the ruin, carefully staying in the shadows and out of sight of the aircraft that droned overhead. The tenement had once been thirty meters high, with row on row of external balconies looking west. Most of the facing had long ago collapsed, and the stairwells were exposed to the sky. The Alcalde's man was devious, though. Two of the younger Jonques had climbed an interior elevator shaft and rigged a sling to hoist the gear and their elders to the fourth-story vantage point that Wili required.

One by one, Ndelante and Jonques ascended. Wili knew such cooperation between the blood enemies would have been a total shock to most of the Faithful. These groups fought and killed under other circumstances—and used each other to justify all sorts of sacrifices from their own peoples. Those struggles were real and deadly, but the secret cooperation was real, too. Two years earlier, Wili had chanced on that secret; it was what finally turned him against the Ndelante.

The fourth-floor hallway creaked ominously under their feet. Outside it had been hot; in here it was like a dark oven. Through holes in the ancient linoleum, Wili could see into the wrecks of rooms and hallways below. Similar holes in the ceiling provided the hallway's only light. One of the Jonques opened a side door and stood carefully apart as Wili and the Ndelante people entered.

More than a half-tonne of Julian-thirty-three storage cells were racked against an interior wall. The balcony side of the room sagged precariously. Wili unpacked the processor and the bobble generator and set about connecting them to the Julians. The others squatted by the wall or in the hallway beyond.

Rosas and Lu were there; Kaladze's representatives could not be denied, though Wili had managed to persuade the Alcalde's man to keep them—especially Della—away from the equipment, and away from the window.

Della looked up at him and smiled a strange, friendly smile; strange because no one else was looking to be taken in by the lie. *When will she make her move?* Would she try to signal to her bosses, or somehow steal the equipment herself? Last night, Wili had thought long and hard about how to defeat her. He had the self-bobbling parameters all ready. Bobbling himself and the equipment would be a last resort, since the current model didn't have much flexibility— he would be taken out of the game for about a year. More likely, one of them was going to end up very dead this day, and no wistful smile could change that.

He dragged the generator and its power cables and camouflage bag close to the ragged edge of the balcony. Under him the decaying concrete swayed like a tiny boat. It felt as if there was only a single support spar left. *Great.* He centered his equipment over the imagined spar and calibrated the mass- and ranging-sensors. The next minutes would be critical. In order that the computation be feasibly simple, the generator had to be clear of obstacles. But this made their operation relatively exposed. If the Authority had had anything like Paul's surveillance equipment, the plan would not have stood a chance.

Wili wet his finger and held it into the air. Even here, almost out of doors, the day was stifling. The westerly breeze barely cooled his finger. "How hot is it?" he asked unnecessarily; it was obviously hot enough.

"Outside air temperature is almost thirty-seven. That's about as hot as it ever gets in LA, and it's the high for today."

Wili nodded. *Perfect.* He rechecked the center and radius coordinates, started the generator's processor, and then crawled back to the others by the inner wall. "It takes about five minutes. Generating a large bobble from two thousand meters is almost too much for this processor."

"So"—Ebenezer's man gave him a sour smile—"you are going to bobble something. Are you ready to share the secret of just what? Or are we simply to watch and learn?"

On the far side of the room, the Alcalde's man was silent, but Wili sensed his attention. Neither they nor their bosses could imagine the bobble's being used as anything but an offensive weapon. They were lacking one critical fact, a fact that would become known to all—including the Authority—very soon.

Wili glanced at his watch: two minutes to go. There was no way he could imagine Della preventing the rescue now. And he had some quick explaining to do, or else—when his allies saw what he had done—he might have deadly problems. "Okay," he said finally. "In ninety seconds, my gadget is going to throw a bobble around the top floors of the Tradetower."

"What?" The question came from four mouths, in two languages. The Alcalde's man, so mild and respectful, was suddenly at his throat. He held up his hand briefly as his men started toward the equipment on the balcony. His other hand pressed against Wili's windpipe, just short of pain, and Wili realized that he had seconds to convince him not to topple the generator into the street. "The bobble will . . . pop . . . later. . . . Time . . . stops inside," choked

Wili. The pressure on his throat eased; the goons edged back from the balcony. Wili saw Jonque and *sabio* trade glances. There would have to be a lot more explanations later, but for now they would cooperate.

A sudden, loud *click* marked the discharge of the Julians. All eyes looked westward through the opening that once held a sliding glass door. Faint "ah"s escaped from several pairs of lips.

The top of the Tradetower was in shadow, surmounted and dwarfed by a four-hundred-meter sphere.

"The building, it must collapse," someone said. But it didn't. The bobble was only as massive as what it enclosed, and that was mostly empty air. There was a long moment of complete silence, broken only by the far, tiny wailing of sirens. Wili had known what to expect, but even so it took an effort to tear his attention from the sky and surreptitiously survey the others.

Lu was staring wide-eyed as any; even her schemes were momentarily submerged. But Rosas: the under-sheriff looked back into Wili's gaze, a different kind of wonder on his face, the wonder of a man who suddenly discovers that some of his guilt is just a bad dream. Wili nodded faintly at him. *Yes, Jeremy is still alive, or at least will someday live again. You did not murder him, Mike.*

In the sky around the Tradetower, the helicopters swept in close to the silver curve of the bobble. From further up they could hear the whine of the fixed-wing patrol spreading in greater and greater circles around the Enclave. They had stepped on a hornets' nest and now those hornets were doing their best to decide what had happened and to deal with the enemy.

Finally, the Jonque chief turned to the Ndelante *sabio*. "Can your people get us out from under all this?"

The black cocked his head, listening to his earphone, then replied, "Not till dark. We've got a tunnel head about two hundred meters from here, but the way they're patrolling, we probably couldn't make it. Right after sunset, before things cool off enough for their heat eyes to work good, that'll be the best time to sneak back. Till then we should stay away from windows and keep quiet. The last few months they've improved. Their snooper gear is almost as good as ours now."

The lot of them—blacks, Jonques, and Lu—moved carefully back into the hallway. Wili left his equipment sitting near the edge of the balcony; it was too risky to retrieve it just now. Fortunately, its camouflage bag resembled the nondescript rubble that surrounded it.

Wili sat with his back against the door. No one was going to get to the generator without his knowing it.

From in here, the sounds of the Enclave were fainter, but soon he heard something ominous and new: the rattle and growl of tracked vehicles.

After they were settled and lookouts were posted at the nearest peepholes, the *sabio* sat beside Wili and smiled. "And now, young friend, we have hours to sit, time for you to tell us just what you meant when you said that the bobble will burst, and that time stops inside." He spoke quietly, and—considering the present situation—it was a reasonable question. But Wili recognized the tone. On the other side of the hallway, the Alcalde's man leaned forward to listen. There was just enough light in the musty hallway for Wili to see the faint smile on Lu's face.

He must mix truth and lies just right. It would be a long afternoon.

28

The hallway was brighter now. As the sun set, its light came nearly horizontally through the rips near the ceiling and splashed bloody light down upon them. The air patrols had spread over a vast area, and the nearest tanks were several thousand meters away; Ebenezer's man had coordinated a series of clever decoy operations—the sort of thing Wili had seen done several times against the Jonques.

"¡Del Nico Dio!" It was almost a shriek. The lookout at the end of the hall jumped down from his perch. "It's happening. Just as he said. It's *flying!*"

Ebenezer's *sabio* made angry shushing motions, but the group moved quickly to the opening, the *sabio* and chief Jonque forcing their way to the front. Wili crawled between them and looked through one of the smaller chinks in the plaster and concrete: the evening haze was red. The sun sat half-dissolved in the deeper red beyond the Enclave towers.

And hanging just above the skyline was a vast new

moon, a dark sphere edged by a crescent of red: the bobble had risen off the top of the Tradetower and was slowly drifting with the evening breeze toward the west.

"Mother of God," the Alcalde's man whispered to himself. Even with understanding, this was hard to grasp. The bobble, with its cargo of afternoon air, was lighter than the evening air around it, the largest hot-air balloon in history. And sailing into the sunset with it went the Tinker hostages. The noise of aircraft came louder, as the hornets returned to their nest and buzzed around this latest development. One of the insects strayed too close to the vast smooth arc. Its rotor shattered; the helicopter fell away, turning and turning.

The *sabio* glanced down at Wili. "You're sure it will come inland?"

"Yes. Uh, Naismith studied the wind patterns very carefully. It's just a matter of time—weeks at most— before it grounds in the mountains. The Authority will know soon enough—along with the rest of the world—the secret of the bobbles, but they won't know just when this one will burst. If the bobble ends up far enough away, the other problems we are going to cause them will be so big they won't post a permanent force around it. Then, when it finally bursts...."

"I know, I know. When it finally bursts we're there to rescue them. But ten years is long to sleep."

It would actually be one year. That had been one of Wili's little lies. If Lu and the Peacers didn't know the potential for short-lived bobbles, then—

It suddenly occurred to him that Della Lu was no longer in his sight. He turned quickly from the wall and looked down the hallway. But she and Rosas were still there, sitting next to a couple of Jonque goons who had not joined the crush at the peephole. "Look, I think we should try to make it back to the tunnel now. The Peacers have plenty of new problems, and it's pretty dark down in the street."

Ebenezer's man smiled. "Now, what would you know about evading armed men in the Basin?" More than ever Wili was sure the *sabio* recognized him, but for now the other was not going to make anything of it. He turned to the Jonque chief. "The boy's probably right."

Wili retrieved the generator, and one by one they descended via the rope sling to the ruined garages below the apartment house. The last man slipped the rope from its mooring. The blacks spent several minutes removing all ground-level signs of their presence. The Ndelante were careful and skilled. There were ways of covering tracks in the ruins, even of restoring the patina of dust in ancient rooms. For forty years the depths of the LA Basin had been the ultimate fortress of the Ndelante; they knew their own turf.

Outside, the evening cool had begun. Two of the *sabio's* men moved out ahead, and another two or three brought up the rear. Several carried night scopes. It was still light enough to read by; the sky above the street was soft red with occasional patches of pastel blue. But it was darkening quickly, and the others were barely more than shadows. Wili could sense the Jonques' uneasiness. Being caught at nightfall deep in the ruins would normally be the death of them. The high-level conniving between the Ndelante and the bosses of Aztlán did not ordinarily extend down to these streets.

Their point men led them through piles of fallen concrete; they never actually stepped out into the open street. Wili hitched up his pack and fell back slightly, keeping Rosas and Lu ahead of him. Behind him, he could hear the Jonque chief and—much quieter—Ebenezer's *sabio*.

Out of the buzzing of aircraft, the sound of a single helicopter came louder and louder. Wili and the others froze, then crouched down in silence. The craft was closer, closer. The *thwupthwupthwup* of its rotors was loud enough so that they could almost feel the overpressures. It was going to pass directly over them. This sort of thing had happened every twenty minutes or so during the afternoon, and should be nothing to worry about. Wili doubted if even observers on the rooftops could have spotted them here below. But this time . . .

As the copter passed over the roofline a flash of brilliant white appeared ahead of Wili. *Lu!* He had been worried she was smuggling some sophisticated homer, and here she was betraying them with a simple handflash!

The helicopter passed quickly across the street. But even before its rotor tones changed and it began to circle back, Wili and most of the Ndelante were already heading for deeper hidey-holes. Seconds later, when the aircraft passed back over the street, it really was empty. Wili couldn't see any of the others, but it sounded as if the Jonques were still rushing madly about, trying to find some way out of the jagged concrete jungle. A monstrously bright light swept back and forth along the street, throwing everything into stark blacks and whites.

As Wili had hoped, the searchlight was followed seconds later by rocket fire. The ground rose and fell under him. Faint behind the explosions, Wili could hear shards of metal and stone snicking back and forth between concrete piles. There were screams.

Heavy dust rose from the ruins. This was his best chance: Wili scuttled back a nearby alley, ignoring the haze and the falling rocks. Another half minute and the enemy would be able to see clearly again, but by then Wili (and probably the rest of the Ndelante) would be a hundred meters away, and moving under much greater cover than he had right here.

An observer might think he ran in mindless panic, but in fact Wili was very careful, was watching for any sign of a Ndelante trail. For more than forty years the Ndelante had been the de facto rulers of these ruins. They used little of it for living space, but they mined most of the vast Basin, and everywhere they went they left subtle improvements—escape hatches, tunnels, food caches—that weren't apparent unless one knew their marking codes. After less than twenty meters, Wili had found a marked path, and now ran at top speed through terrain that would have seemed impassable to anyone standing more than a few meters away. Some of the others were escaping along the same path: Wili could hear at least two pairs of feet some distance behind him, one heavy Jonque feet, the others barely audible. He did not slow down; better that they catch up.

The chopper pilot had lifted out of the space between the buildings and fired no more. No doubt the initial attack had not been to kill, but to jar his prey into the open. It was a decent strategy against any but the Ndelante.

The pilot flew back and forth now, lobbing stun bombs. They were so far away that Wili could barely feel them. In the distance, he heard the approach of more aircraft. Some of them sounded big. Troop carriers. Wili kept running. Till the enemy actually landed, it was better to run than to search for a good hiding place. He might even be able to get out of the drop area.

Five minutes later, Wili was nearly a kilometer away. He moved through a burned-out retail area, from cellar to cellar, each connected to the next by subtle breaks in the walls. His equipment pack had come loose and the whole thing banged painfully against him when he tried to move really fast. He stopped briefly to tighten the harness, but that only made the straps cut into his shoulders.

In one sense he was lost: he had no idea where he was, or how to get to the pickup point the Ndelante and the Jonques had established. On the other hand, he knew which direction he should run *from*, and—if he saw them—he could recognize the clues that would lead to some really safe hole that the Ndelante would look into after all the fuss died down.

Two kilometers run, Wili stopped to adjust the straps again. Maybe he should wait for the others to catch up. If there was a safety hole around here, they might know where it was. And then he noticed it, almost in front of him: an innocent pattern of scratches and breaks in the cornerstone of a bank building. Somewhere in the basement of that bank—in the old vault no doubt—were provisions and water and probably a hand comm. No wonder the Ndelante behind him had stayed so close to his trail. Wili left the dark of the alley and moved across the street in a broken run, flitting from one hiding place to the next. It was just like the old days—after Uncle Sly but before Paul and math and Jeremy—except that in those old days, he had more often than not been carried by his fellow burglars, since he was too weak for sustained running. Now he was as tough as any.

He started down the darkened stairs, his hands fishing outward in almost ritual motions to disarm the boobytraps the Ndelante were fond of leaving. Outside sounds came very faint down here, but he thought he heard the others, the surviving Jonque and however many Ndelante were with him. Just a few more steps and he would be in the—

After so much dark, the light from behind him was blinding. For an instant, Wili stared stupidly at his own shadow. Then he dropped and whirled, but there was no place to go, and the handflash followed him easily. He stared into the darkness around the point of light. He did not have to guess who was holding it.

"Keep your hands in view, Wili." Her voice was soft and reasonable. "I really do have a gun."

"You're doing your own dirty work now?"

"I figured if I called in the helicopters before catching up, you might bobble yourself." The direction of her voice changed. "Go outside and signal the choppers down."

"Okay." Rosas' voice had just the mixture of resentment and cowardice that Wili remembered from the fishing boat. His footsteps retreated up the stairs.

"Now take off the pack—slowly—and set it on the stairs."

Wili slipped off the straps and advanced up the stairs a pace or two. He stopped when she made a warning sound and set the generator down amidst fallen plaster and rat droppings. Then Wili sat, pretending to take the weight off his legs. If she were just a couple of meters closer. . . . "How could you follow me? No Jonque ever could; they don't know the signs." His curiosity was only half pretense. If he hadn't been so scared and angry, he would have been humiliated: it had taken him years to learn the

Ndelante signs, and here a woman—not even an Ndelante—had come for the first time into the Basin, and equaled him.

Lu advanced, waving him back from the stairs. She set her flash on the steps and began to undo the ties on his pack with her right hand. She did have a gun, an *Hacha* 15-mm, probably taken off one of the Jonques. The muzzle never wavered.

"Signs?" There was honest puzzlement in her voice. "No, Wili, I simply have excellent hearing and good legs. It was too dark for serious tracking." She glanced into the pack, then slipped the straps over one shoulder, retrieved her handflash, and stood up. She had everything now. *Through me, she even has Paul*, he suddenly realized. Wili thought of the holes the *Hacha* could make, and he knew what he must do.

Rosas came back down. "I swung my flash all around, but there's so much light and noise over there already, I don't think anyone noticed."

Lu made an irritated noise. "Those featherbrains. What they know about surveillance could be—"

And several things happened at once: Wili rushed her. Her light swerved and shadows leaped like monsters. There was a ripping, cracking sound. An instant later, Lu crashed into the wall and slid down the steps. Rosas stood over her crumpled form, a metal bar clutched in his hand. Something glistened dark and wet along the side of that bar. Wili took one hesitant step up the stairs, then another. Lu lay facedown. She was so small, scarcely taller than he. And so still now.

"Did . . . did you kill her?" He was vaguely surprised at the note of horror, almost accusation, in his voice.

Rosas' eyes were wide, staring. "I don't know; I

t-tried to. S-sooner or later I had to do this. I'm *not* a traitor, Wili. But at Scripps—" He stopped, seemed to realize that this was not the time for long confessions. "Hell, let's get this thing off her." He picked up the gun that lay just beyond Lu's now limp hand. That action probably saved them.

As he rolled her on her side, Lu exploded, her legs striking at Rosas' midsection, knocking him backward onto Wili. The larger man was almost dead weight on the boy. By the time Wili pushed him aside, Della Lu was racing up the stairs. She ran with a slight stagger, and one arm hung at an awkward angle. She still had her handflash. "The gun, Mike, quick!"

But Rosas was doubled in a paroxysm of pain and near paralysis, faint *"unh, unh"* sounds escaping from his lips. Wili snatched the metal bar, and flew up the steps, diving low and to one side as he came onto the street.

The precaution was unnecessary: she had not waited in ambush. Amidst the wailing of faraway sirens, Wili could hear her departing footsteps. Wili looked vainly down the street in the direction of the sounds. She was out of sight, but he could track her down; this was country he knew.

There was a scrabbling noise from the entrance to the bank. "Wait." It was Rosas, half bent over, clutching his middle. "She won, Wili. She won." The words were choked, almost voiceless.

The interruption was enough to make Wili pause and realize that Lu had indeed won. She was hurt and unarmed, that was true. And with any luck he could track her down in minutes. But by then she would have signaled gun and troop copters; they were much nearer than Mike had claimed.

She had won the Authority their own portable bobble generator.

And if Wili couldn't get far away in the next few minutes, the Authority would win much more. For a long second, he stared at the Jonque. The undersheriff was standing a bit straighter now, breathing at last, in great tormented gasps. He really should leave Rosas here. It would divert the troopers for valuable minutes, might even insure Wili's escape.

Mike looked back and seemed to realize what was going on his head. Finally Wili stepped toward him. "C'mon. We'll get away from them yet."

In ten seconds the street was as empty as it had been all the years before.

29

The Jonque nobles believed him when Wili vouched
for Mike. That was the second big risk he took to get
them home. The first had been in evading the Ndelante
Ali; they had walked out of the Basin on their own,
had contacted the Alcalde's men directly. Not many
Jonques had made it out of the operation, and their
reports were confused. But the rescue was obviously
a great success, so it wasn't hard to convince them
that there had been no betrayal. Such explanations
might not have washed with the Ndelante; they already distrusted Wili. And it was likely there were
black survivors who had seen what really happened.

In any case, Naismith wanted Wili back immediately, and the Jonques knew where their hopes for
continued survival lay. The two were on their way
northward in a matter of hours. It was not nearly so
luxurious a trip as coming down. They traveled back
roads in camouflaged wagons, and balanced speed

with caution. The Aztlán convoy knew it was prey to a vigilant enemy.

It was night when they were deposited on a barely marked trail north of Ojai. Wili listened to the sounds of the wagon and outriders fade into the lesser noises of the night. They stood unspeaking for a minute after, the same silence that had been between them through most of the last hours. Finally Wili shrugged and started up the dusty trail. It would get them to the cabin of a Tinker sympathizer on the other side of the border. At least one horse should be ready for them there.

He heard Mike close behind, but there was no talk. This was the first time they had really been alone since the walk out of the Basin—and then it had been necessary to keep very quiet. Yet even now, Rosas had nothing to say. "I'm not angry anymore, Mike." Wili spoke in Spanish; he wanted to say exactly what he meant. "You didn't kill Jeremy; I don't think you ever meant to hurt him. And you saved my life and probably Paul's when you jumped Lu."

The other made a noncommittal grunt. Otherwise there was just the sound of his steps in the dirt and the keening of insects in the dry underbrush. They went on another ten meters before Wili abruptly stopped and turned on the other. "Damnation! Why won't you talk? There is no one to hear but the hills and me. You have all the time in the world."

"Okay, Wili, I'll talk." There was little expression in the voice, and Mike's face was scarcely more than a shadow against the sky. "I don't know that it matters, but I'll talk." They continued the winding path upward. "I did everything you thought, though it wasn't for the Peacers and it wasn't for Della Lu

.... Have you heard of the Huachuca plaguetime, Wili?"

He didn't wait for an answer but rambled on with a loose mixture of history—his own and the world's. The Huachuca had been the last of the warplagues. It hadn't killed that many in absolute numbers, perhaps a hundred million worldwide. But in 2015, that had been one human being in five. "I was born at Fort Huachuca, Wili. I don't remember it. We left when I was little. But before he died, my father told me a lot. He *knew* who caused the plagues, and that's why he left." The Rosas family had not left Huachuca because of the plague that bore its name. Death lapped all around the town, but that and the earlier plagues seemed scarcely to affect it.

Mike's sisters were born *after* they left; they had sickened and slowly died. The family had moved slowly north and west, from one dying town to the next. As in all the plagues, there was great material wealth for the survivors—but in the desert, when a town died, so did services that made further life possible. "My father left because he discovered the secret of Huachuca, Wili. They were like the La Jolla group, only more arrogant. Father was an orderly in their research hospital. He didn't have real technical training. Hell, he was just a kid when the War and the early plagues hit." By that time, government warfare—and the governments themselves—were nearly dead. The old military machinery was too expensive to maintain. Any further state assaults on the Peace had to be with cheaper technologies. This was the story the Peacer histories told, but Mike's father had seen its truth. He had seen shipments going to the places that were first to report the plague, shipments that were postdated and later listed as medical supplies for the victims.

He even overheard a conversation, orders explicitly given. It was then he decided to leave. "He was a good man, Wili, but maybe a coward, too. He should have tried to expose the operation. He should have tried to convince the Peacers to kill those monsters. And they *were* monsters, Wili. By the teens, everyone knew the governments were finished. What Huachuca did was pure vengeance. . . . I remember when the Authority finally figured out where that plague came from. Father was still alive then, very sick though. I was only six, but he had told me the story over and over. I couldn't understand why he cried when I told him Huachuca had been bobbled; then I saw he was laughing, too. People really do cry for joy, Wili. They really do."

To their left, the ground fell almost vertically. Wili could not see if the drop was two meters or fifty. The Jonques had given him a night scope, but they'd told him its batteries would run down in less than an hour. He was saving it for later. In any case, the path was wide enough so that there was no real danger of falling. It followed the side of the hills, winding back and forth, reaching higher and higher. From his memory of the maps, he guessed they should soon reach the crest. Soon after that, they would be able to see the cabin.

Mike was silent for a long time, and Wili did not immediately reply. Six years old. Wili remembered when he was six. If coincidence and foolhardy determination had not thrust him into the truth, he would have gone through life convinced that Jonques had kidnapped him from Uncle Sly, and that—with Sly gone—the Ndelante were his only friends and defenders. Two years ago, he had learned better. The raid—yes, it had been Jonque, but done at the secret request of the Ndelante. Ebenezer had been angered by the unFaithful like Uncle Sly who used the water upstream from the Ndelante reservoir. Besides, the Faithful were ready to move into Glendora, and they needed an outside enemy to make their takeover easier. It worked the other way, too: Jonque commoners without lords protector lived in constant fear of Ndelante raids.

Wili shrugged. It was not something he would say to Mike. Huachuca was probably everything he thought. Still, Wili had infinite cynicism when it came to the alleged motives of organizations.

Wili had seen treacheries big and small, organizational and personal. He knew Mike believed all he said, that he'd done in La Jolla what he thought right, that he'd done it and still tried to do the job of protecting Wili and Jeremy that he had been hired for.

The trail dipped, moved steadily downward. They were past the crest. Several hundred meters further on, the scrub forest opened up a little, and they could look into a small valley. Wili motioned Mike down. He pulled the Jonque night scope from his pack and looked across the valley. It was heavier than the glasses Red Arrow had loaned him, but it had a magnifier, and it was easy to pick out the house and the trails that led in and out of the valley.

There were no lights in the farmhouse. It might have been abandoned except that he could see two horses in the corral. "These people aren't Tinkers, but they are friends, Mike. I think it's safe. With those horses, we can get back to Paul in just a few days."

"What do you mean 'we,' Wili? Haven't you been

listening? I did betray you. I'm the last person you should trust to know where Paul is."

"I listened. I know what you did, and why. That's more than I know about most people. And there's nothing there about betraying Paul or the Tinkers. True?"

"Yes. The Peacers aren't the monsters the plaguemakers were, but they are an enemy. I'll do most anything to stop them ... only, I guess I couldn't kill Della. I almost came apart when I thought she was dead back in the ruins; I couldn't try again."

Wili was silent a moment. "Okay. Maybe I couldn't either."

"It's still a crazy risk for you to take. I should be going to Santa Ynez."

"They'll likely know, Mike. We got out of LA just ahead of the news that you ran with Della. Your sheriff might still accept you, but none of the others, I'll bet. Paul though, he needs another pair of strong hands; he may have to move fast. Bringing you in is safer than calling the Tinkers and telling them where to send help."

More silence. Wili raised the scope and took one more look up and down the valley. He felt Mike's hand on his shoulder. "Okay. But we tell Paul straight out about me, so he can decide what to do with me."

The boy nodded. "And, Wili ... thanks."

They stood and started into the valley. Wili suddenly found himself grinning. He felt so proud. Not smug, just proud. For the first time in his life, he had been the strong shoulder for someone else.

30

What Wili had missed most, even more than Paul and the Moraleses, was the processor hookup. Now that he was back, he spent several hours every day in deep connect. Most of the rest of the time he wore the connector. In discussions with Paul and Allison, it was comforting to have those extra resources available, to feel the background programs proceeding.

Even more, it brought him a feeling of safety.

And safety was something that had drained away, day by day. Six months ago, he had thought the mansion perfectly hidden, so far away in the mountains, so artfully concealed in the trees. That was before the Peacers started looking for them, and before Allison Parker talked to him about aerial reconnaissance. For precious weeks the search had centered in Northern California and Oregon, but now it had been expanded and spread both south and east. Before, the only aircraft they ever saw was the LA/Livermore shuttle—and that was so far to the east, you had to know exactly where and when to look to see a faint glint of silver.

Now they saw aircraft several times a week. The patterns sketched across the sky formed a vast net—and they were the fish.

"All the camouflage in the world won't help, if they decide you're hiding in Middle California." Mike's voice was tight with urgency. He walked across the veranda and tugged at the green-and-brown shroud he and Bill Morales had hung over all the exposed stonework and hard corners of the mansion. Gone were the days when they could sit out by the pond and admire the far view.

Paul protested. "It's no ordinary camouflage, it—"

"I know it was a lot of work. You've told me Allison and the Moraleses spent two weeks putting it together. I know she and Wili added a few electronic twists that make it even better than it looks. But, Paul"—he sat down and glared at Paul, as if to persuade by the force of his own conviction—"they have other ways. They can interrogate del Norte—or at least his subordinates. That will get them to Ojai. They've raided Red Arrow and Santa Ynez and the market towns further north. Apparently the few people— like Kaladze—who really know your location have escaped. But no matter how many red herrings you've dropped over the years, they're eventually going to narrow things down to this part of the country."

"And there's Della Lu," said Allison.

Mike's eyes widened, and Wili could see that the comment had almost unhorsed him. Then he seemed to realize that it was not a jibe. "Yes, there's Lu. I've always thought this place must be closer to Santa Ynez than the other trading towns: I laid my share of red herrings on Della. But she's very clever. She may figure it out. The point is this: in the near future, they'll put the whole hunt on this part of California. It won't be just a plane every other day. If they can spare the people, they might actually do ground sweeps."

"What are you suggesting, Mike?" Allison again.

"That we move. Take the big wagon, stuff it with all the equipment we need, and move. If we study the search patterns and time it right, I think we could get out of Middle California, maybe to someplace in Nevada. We have to pick a place we can reach without running into people on the way, and it has to be some ways from here; once they find the mansion, they'll try to trace us. . . . I know, it'll be risky, but it's our only chance if we want to last more than another month."

Now it was Paul's turn to be upset. "Damn it, we can't move. Not now. Even if we could bring all the important equipment—which we can't—it would still be impossible. I can't afford the time, Mike. The Tinkers need the improvements I'm sending out; they need those bobble generators if they're going to fight back. If we take a month's vacation now, the revolution will be lost. We'll be safe in some hole in Nevada—safe to watch everything we've worked for go down the tubes." He thought a moment and came up with another objection. "Hell, I bet we couldn't even keep in touch with the Tinkers afterwards. I've spent years putting together untraceable communication links from here. A lot of it depends on precise knowledge of local terrain and climate. Our comm would make us sitting ducks if we moved."

Throughout the discussion, Wili sat quietly at the edge of the veranda, where the sunlight came through the camouflage mesh most strongly. In the back of his mind, Jill was providing constant updates on the Authority broadcasts she monitored. From the recon satellites, he knew the location of all aircraft within a thousand kilometers. They might be captured, but they could never be surprised.

This omniscience was little use in the present debate. At one extreme, he "knew" millions of little facts that together formed their situation; at the other, he knew mathematical theories that governed those facts. In between, in matters of judgment, he sensed his incompetence. He looked at Allison. "What do you think? Who is right?"

She hesitated just a moment. "It's the reconnaissance angle I know." It was eerie watching Allison. She was Jill granted real-world existence. "If the Peacers are competent, then I don't see how Mike could be wrong." She looked at Naismith. "Paul, you say the Tinkers' revolt will be completely suppressed if we take time out to move. I don't know; that seems a much iffier contention. Of course, if you're both right, then we've had the course. . . ." She gazed up at the dappled sunlight coming through the green-brown mesh. "You know, Paul, I almost wish you and Wili hadn't trashed the Authority's satellite system."

"What?" Wili said abruptly. That sabotage was his big contribution. Besides, he hadn't "trashed" the system, only made it inaccessible to the Authority. "They would have found us long ago with their satellites, if I had not done that."

Allison held up her hand. "I believe it. From what I've seen, they don't have the resources or the admin structure for wide-air recon. I just meant that given time we could have sabotaged their old comm and recon system—in such a way that the Peacers would think it was still working." She smiled at the astonishment on their faces. "These last weeks, I've been studying what you know about their old system. It's really the automated USAF comm and recon scheme. We had it fully in place right before . . . everything blew up. In theory, it could handle all our command and control functions. All you needed was the satellite system, the ground receivers and computers, and maybe a hundred specialists. In theory, it meant we didn't need air recon or land lines. In theory. OMBP was always twisting our arm to junk our other systems and rely on the automated one instead. They could cut our budget in half that way."

She grinned. "Of course we never went along. We needed the other systems. Besides, we knew how fragile the automated system was. It was slick, it was thorough, but one or two rotten apples on the maintenance staff could pervert it, generate false interpretations, fake communications. We demanded the budget for the other systems that would keep it honest.

"Now it's obvious that the Peacers just took it over. They either didn't know or didn't care about the dangers; in any case, I bet they didn't have the resources to run the other systems the Air Force could. If we could have infiltrated a couple people into their technical staff, we could be making them see whatever we wanted. They'd never find us out here." She shrugged. "But you're right; at this point it's just wishful thinking. It might have taken months or years to do something like that. You had to get results right away."

"Damn," said Paul. "All those years of clever planning, and I never. . . . "

"Oh, Paul," she said softly. "You are a genius. But

you couldn't know everything about everything. You couldn't be a one-man revolution."

"Yeah," said Mike. "And he couldn't convince the rest of us that there was anything worth revolting against."

Wili just stared, his eyes wide, his jaw slack. It would be harder than anything he had done before but . . . "Maybe you do not need spies, Allison. Maybe we can. . . . I've got to think about this. We've still got days. True, Mike?"

"Unless we have real bad luck. With good luck we might have weeks."

"Good. Let me think. I must think. . . ." He stood up and walked slowly indoors. Already the veranda, the sunlight, the others were forgotten.

It was not easy. In the months before he learned to use the mind connect, it would have been impossible; even a lifetime of effort would not have brought the necessary insights. Now creativity was in harness with his processors. He knew what he wanted to do. In a matter of hours he could test his ideas, separate false starts from true.

The recon problem was the most important—and probably the easiest. Now he didn't want to block Peacer reception. He wanted them to receive . . . lies. A lot of preprocessing was done aboard the satellites; just a few bytes altered here and there might be enough to create false perceptions on the ground. Somehow he had to break into those programs, but not in the heavy-handed way he had before. Afterward, the truth would be received by them alone. The enemy would see what Paul wanted them to see. Why, they could protect not just themselves, but many of the Tinkers as well!

Days passed. The answers came miraculously fast, and perilously slow. At the edge of his consciousness, Wili knew Paul was helping with the physics, and Allison was entering what she knew about the old USAF comm/recon system. It all helped, but the hard inner problem—how to subvert a system without seeming to and without any physical contact—remained his alone.

They finally tested it. Wili took his normal video off a satellite over Middle California, analyzed it quickly, and sent back subtle sabotage. On the next orbit, he simulated Peacer reception: a small puff of synthetic cloud appeared in the picture, just where he had asked. The satellite processors could keep up the illusion until they received coded instructions to do otherwise. It was a simple change. Once operational, they could make more complicated alterations: certain vehicles might not be reported on the roads, certain houses might become invisible. But the hard part had been done.

"Now all we have to do is let the Peacers know their recon birds are 'working' again," said Allison when he showed them his tests. She was grinning from ear to ear. At first Wili had wondered why she was so committed to the Tinker cause; everything she was loyal to had been dead fifty years. The Tinkers didn't even exist when her orbiter was bobbled. But it hadn't taken him long to understand: she was like Paul. She blamed the Peacers for taking away the old world. And in her case, that was a world fresh in memory. She might not know anything about the Tinkers, but her hate for the Authority was as deep as Paul's.

"Yeah," said Paul. "Wili could just return the comm protocols to their original state. All of a sudden the

Peacers would have a live system again. But even as stupid as they are, they'd suspect something. We have to do this so they think that somehow *they* have solved the problem. Hmm. I'll bet Avery still has people working on this even now."

"Okay," said Wili. "I'll fix things so the satellites will not start sending to them until they do a complete recompile of their ground programs."

Paul nodded. "That sounds perfect. We might have to wait a few more days, but—"

Allison laughed. "—But I know programmers. They'll be happy to believe their latest changes have fixed the problem."

Wili smiled back. He was already imagining how similar things could be done to the Peacer communication system.

31

War had returned to the planet. Hamilton Avery read the Peace Authority News Service article and nodded to himself. The headline and the following story hit just the right note: for decades, the world had been at peace, thanks to the Authority and the cooperation of peace-loving individuals around the world. But now—as in the early days, when the bioscience clique had attempted its takeover—the power lust of an evil minority had thrown the lives of humankind into jeopardy. One could only pray that the ultimate losses would not be as great as those of the War and the plagues.

The news service story didn't say all this explicitly. It was targeted for high tech regions in the Americas and China and concentrated on "objective" reporting of Tinker atrocities and the evidence that the Tinkers were building energy weapons—and bobble generators. The Peace hadn't tried to cover up that last development: a four-hundred-meter bobble floating through the skies of LA is a bit difficult to explain, much less cover up.

Of course, these stories wouldn't convince the Tinkers themselves, but they were a minority in the population. The important thing was to keep other citizens—and the national militias—from joining the enemy.

The comm chimed softly. "Yes?"

"Sir, Director Gerrault is on the line again. He sounds very . . . upset."

Avery stifled a smile. The comm was voice-only, but even when alone, Avery tried to disguise his true feelings. "Director" Gerrault indeed! There might still be a place for that pupal Bonaparte in the organization, but hardly as a Director. Best to let him hang a few hours more. "Please report to Monsieur Gerrault—again—that the emergency situation here prevents my immediate response. I'll get to him as soon as humanly possible."

"Uh, yes, sir. . . . Agent Lu is down here. She also wishes to see you.

"That's different. Send her right up."

Avery leaned back in his chair and steepled his fingers. Beyond the clear glass of the window wall, the lands around Livermore spread away in peace and silence. In the near distance—yet a hundred meters beneath his tower—were the black-and-ivory buildings of the modern centrum, each one separated from the others by green parkland. Farther away, near the horizon, the golden grasses of summer were broken here and there by clusters of oaks. It was hard to imagine such peace disrupted by the pitiful guerrilla efforts of the world's Tinkers.

Poor Gerrault. Avery remembered his boast of being the industrious ant who built armies and secret police while the American and Chinese Directors depended on the people's good will and trust. Gerrault had spread garrisons from Oslo to Capetown, from Dublin to Szczecin. He had enough troopers to convince the common folk that he was just another tyrant. When the Tinkers finally got Paul Hoehler's toy working, the people and the governments had not hesitated to throw in with them. And then . . . and then Gerrault had discovered that his garrisons were not nearly enough. Most were now overrun, not so much by the enemy's puny bobble generators, as by all the ordinary people who no longer believed in the Authority. At the same time, the Tinkers had moved against the heart of Gerrault's operation in Paris. Where the European Director's headquarters once stood, there was now a simple monument: a three-hundred-meter silver sphere. Gerrault had gotten out just before the debacle, and was now skulking about in the East European deserts, trying to avoid the Teuton militia, trying to arrange transportation to California or China. It was a fitting end to his tyranny, but it was going to be one hell of a problem retaking Europe after the rest of the Tinkers were put down.

There was a muted knock at the door, and Avery pressed "open," then stood with studied courtesy as Della Lu stepped into the room. He gestured to a comfortable chair near the end of his desk, and they both sat.

Week by week his show of courtesy toward this woman was less an act. He had come to realize that there was no one he trusted more than her. She was as competent as any man in his top departments, and there was a loyalty about her—not a loyalty to Avery personally, he realized, but to the whole concept of the Peace. Outside of the old-time Directors, he had never seen this sort of dedication. Nowadays, Authority middle-management was cynical, seemed to think that idealism was the affliction of fools and low-level flunkies. And if Della Lu was faking her dedication, even in that she was a world champion; Avery had forty years of demonstrated success in estimating others' characters.

"How is your arm?"

Lu clicked the light plastic cast with a fingernail. "Getting well slowly. But I can't complain. It was a compound fracture. I was lucky I didn't bleed to death. . . . You wanted my estimate of enemy potential in the Americas?"

Always business. "Yes. What can we expect?"

"I don't know this area the way I did Mongolia, but I've talked with your section chiefs and the franchise owners."

Avery grinned to himself. Between staff optimism and franchise-owner gloom, she thought to find the truth. Clever.

"The Authority has plenty of good will in Old Mexico and Americacentral. Those people never had it so good, they don't trust what's left of their governments, and they have no large Tinker communities. Chile and Argentina we are probably going to lose: they have plenty of people capable of building generators from the plans that Hoehler broadcast. Without our satellite net we can't give our people down there the comm and recon support they need to win. If the locals want to kick us out badly enough, they'll be able—"

Avery held up a hand. "Our satellite problems have been cleared up."

"What? Since when?"

"Three days. I've kept it a secret within our technical branch, until we were sure it was not just a temporary fix."

"Hmm. I don't trust machines that choose their own time and place to work."

"Yes. We know now the Tinkers must have infiltrated some of our software departments and slipped tailor-made bugs into our controller codes. Over the last few weeks, the techs ran a bunch of tests, and they've finally spotted the changes. We've also increased physical security in the programming areas; it was criminally lax before. I don't think we'll lose satellite communications again."

She nodded. "This should make our counter-work a lot easier. I don't know whether it will be enough to prevent the temporary loss of the Far South, but it should be a big help in North America."

She leaned forward. "Sir, I have several recommendations about our local operations. First, I think we should stop wasting our time hunting for Hoehler. If we pick him up along with the other ringleaders, fine. But he's done about all the harm he—"

"No!" The word broke sharply from his lips. Avery looked over Lu's head at the portrait of Jackson Avery on the wall. The painting had been done from photos, several years after his father's death. The man's dress and haircut were archaic and severe. The gaze from those eyes was the uncompromising, unforgiving one he had seen so many times. Hamilton Avery had forbidden the cult of personality, and nowhere else in Livermore were there portraits of leaders. Yet he, a leader, was the follower of such a cult. For three decades he had lived beneath that picture. And every time he looked at it, he remembered his failure—so many years ago. "No," he said again, this time in a softer voice. "Second only to protecting Livermore itself, destroying Paul Hoehler must remain your highest priority.

"Don't you see, Miss Lu? People have said before, 'That Paul Hoehler, he has caused us a lot of harm, but there is nothing more he can do.' And yet Hoehler has always done more harm. He is a genius, Miss Lu, a mad genius who has hated us for fifty years. Personally, I think he's always known that bobbles don't last forever, and that time stops inside. I think he has chosen now to cause the Tinker revolt because he knew when the old bobbles would burst. Even if we are quick to rebobble the big places like Vandenberg and Langley, there are still thousands of smaller installations that will fall back into normal time during the next few years. Somehow he intends to use the old armies against us." Avery guessed that Lu's blank expression was hiding skepticism. Like the other Directors, she just could not *believe* in Paul Hoehler. He tried a different tack.

"There is objective evidence." He described the orbiter crash that had so panicked the Directors ten weeks earlier. After the attack on the LA Enclave, it was obvious that the orbiter was not from outer space, but from the past. In fact, it must have been the Air Force snooper Jackson Avery bobbled in those critical hours just before he won the world for Peace. Livermore technical teams had been over the wreck again and again, and one thing was certain: there had been a third crewman. One had died as the bobble burst, one had been shot by incompetent troopers, and one had . . . disappeared. That missing crewman, suddenly waking in an unimagined future, could not have escaped on his own. The Tinkers must have known that this bobble was about to burst, must have known what was inside it.

Lu was no toady; clearly she was unconvinced. "But what use would they have for such a crewman? Anything he could tell them would be fifty years out of date."

What could he say? It all had the stench of Hoehler's work: devious, incomprehensible, yet leading inexorably to some terrible conclusion that would not be fully recognized until it was too late. But there was no way he could convince even Lu. All he could do was give orders. Pray God that was enough. Avery sat back and tried to reassume the air of dignity he normally projected. "Forgive the lecture, Miss Lu. This is really a policy issue. Suffice it to say that Paul Hoehler must remain one of our prime targets. Please continue with your recommendations."

"Yes, sir." She was all respect again. "I'm sure you know that the technical people have stripped down the Hoehler generator. The projector itself is well understood now. At least the scientists have come up with theories that can explain what they previously thought impossible." Was there a faintly sarcastic edge to that comment? "The part we can't reproduce is the computer support. If you want the power supply to be portable, you need very complex, high-speed processing to get the bobble on target. It's a trade-off we can't manage.

"But the techs have figured how to calibrate our generators. We can now project bobbles lasting anywhere from ten to two hundred years. They see theoretical limits on doing much better."

Avery nodded; he had been following those developments closely. "Sir, this has political significance."

"How so?"

"We can turn what the Tinkers did to us in LA around. They bobbled their friends off the Tradetower to protect them. They know precisely how long it will last, and we don't. It's very clever: we'd look foolish putting a garrison at Big Bear to wait for our prisoners to 'return.' But it works the other way: everyone knows now that bobbling is not permanent, is not fatal. This makes it the perfect way to take suspected enemies out of circulation. Some high Aztlán nobles were involved with this rescue. In the past we couldn't afford vengeance against such persons. If we went around shooting everyone we suspect of treason, we'd end up like the European Directorate. But now ...

"I recommend we raid those we suspect of serious Tinkering, stage brief 'hearings'—don't even call them 'trials'—and then embobble everyone who might be a threat. Our news service can make this very reasonable and nonthreatening: We have already established that the Tinkers are involved with high-energy weapons research, and quite possibly with bioscience. Most people fear the second far more than the first, by the way. I infiltrated the Tinkers by taking advantage of that fear.

"These facts should be enough to keep the rest of the population from questioning the economic impact of taking out the Tinkers. At the same time, they will not fear us enough to band together. Even if we occasionally bobble popular or powerful persons, the public will know that this is being done without harm to the prisoners, and for a limited period of time—which we can announce in advance. The idea is that we are handling a temporary emergency with humanity, greater humanity than they could expect from mere governments."

Avery nodded, concealing his admiration. After reading of her performance in Mongolia, he had half expected Lu to be a female version of Christian Gerrault. But her ideas were sensible, subtle. When necessary she did not shrink from force, yet she also realized that the Authority was not all-powerful, that a balancing act was sometimes necessary to maintain the Peace. There really were people in this new generation who could carry on. If only this one were not a woman.

"I agree. Miss Lu, I want you to continue to report directly to me. I will inform the North American section that you have temporary authority for all operations in California and Aztlán—if things go well, I will push for more. In the meantime, let me know if any of the 'old hands' are not cooperating with you. This is not the time for jealousy."

Avery hesitated, unsure whether to end the meeting or bring Lu into the innermost circle. Finally he keyed a command to his display flat and handed it to Lu. Besides himself—and perhaps Tioulang—she was the only person really qualified to handle Operation Renaissance. "This is a summary. I'll want you to learn the details later; I could use your advice on how to split the operation into uncoupled subprojects that we can run at lower classifications."

Lu picked up the flat and saw the Special Material classification glowing at the top of the display. Not more than ten people now living had seen Special Materials; only top agents knew of the classification— and then only as a theoretical possibility. Special Materials were never committed to paper or transmitted; communication of such information was by courier with encrypted, booby-trapped ROMs that self-destructed after being read.

Lu's eyes flickered down the Renaissance summary. She nodded agreement as she read the description of

Redoubt 001 and the bobble generator to be installed there. She pushed the page key and her eyes suddenly widened; she had reached the discussion that gave Renaissance its name. Her face paled as she read the page.

She finished and silently handed him the flat. "It's a terrifying possibility, is it not, Miss Lu?"

"Yes sir."

And even more than before, Avery knew he had made the right decision; Renaissance was a responsibility that *should* frighten. "Winning with Renaissance would in many ways be as bad as the destruction of the Peace. It is there as the ultimate contingency, and, *by God, we must win without it.*"

Avery was silent for a moment and then abruptly smiled. "But don't worry; think of it as caution to the point of paranoia. If we do a competent job, there's not a chance that we'll lose." He stood and came around his desk to show her to the door.

Lu stood, but did not move toward the door. Instead, she stepped toward the wide glass wall and looked at the golden hills along the horizon.

"Quite a view, isn't it?" Avery said, a bit nonplussed. She had been so purposeful, so militarily precise—yet now she tarried over a bit of landscape. "I can never decide whether I like it more when the hills are summer gold or spring green."

She nodded, but didn't seem to be listening to the chitchat. "There's one other thing, sir. One other thing I wanted to bring up. We have the power to crush the Tinkers in North America; the situation is not like Europe. But craft has won against power before. If I were on the other side . . ."

"Yes?"

"If I were making their strategy, I would attack Livermore and try to bobble our generator."

"Without high-energy sources they can't attack us from a distance."

She shrugged. "That's our scientists' solemn word. And six months ago they would have argued volumes that bobbles can't be generated without nuclear power . . . . But let's assume that they're right. Even then I would try to come up with some attack plan, some way of getting in close enough to bobble the Authority generator."

Avery looked out his window, seeing the beautiful land with Lu's vision: as a possible battlefield, to be analyzed for fields of fire and interdiction zones. At first glance it was impossible to imagine any group getting in undetected, but from camping trips long ago he remembered all the ravines out there. Thank God the recon satellites were back in operation.

That would protect against only part of the danger. There was still the possibility that the enemy might use traitors to smuggle a Tinker bobble generator into the area. Avery's attention turned inward, calculating. He smiled to himself. Either way it wouldn't do them any good. It was common knowledge that one of the Authority's bobble generators was at Livermore (the other being at Beijing). And there were thousands of Authority personnel who routinely entered the Livermore Enclave. But that was a big area, almost fifty kilometers in its longest dimension. Somewhere in there was the generator and its power supply, but out of all the millions on Earth, only five knew exactly where that generator was housed, and scarcely fifty had access. The bobbler had been built under the cover of projects Jackson Avery contracted for the old LEL. Those projects had been the usual combination of military and energy research. The LEL and the US military had been only too happy to have them proceed in secret and had made it possible for the elder Avery to build his gadgets underground and well away from his official headquarters. Avery had seen to it that not even the military liaison had really known where everything was. After the War, that secrecy had been maintained: in the early days, the remnants of the US government still had had enough power to destroy the bobbler if they had known its location.

And now that secrecy was paying off. The only way Hoehler could accomplish what Lu predicted was if he found some way of making Vandenberg-sized bobbles.... The old fear welled up: that was just the sort of thing the monster was capable of.

He looked at Lu with a feeling that surpassed respect and bordered on awe: she was not merely competent—she could actually think like Hoehler. He took her by the arm and led her to the door. "You've helped more than you can know, Miss Lu."

32

Allison had been in the new world more than ten weeks.

Sometimes it was the small things that were the hardest to get used to. You could forget for hours at a time that nearly everyone you ever knew was dead, and that those deaths had been mostly murder. But when night came, and indoors became nearly as dark as outside—that was strangeness she could not ignore. Paul had plenty of electronic equipment, most of it more sophisticated than anything in the twentieth century, yet his power supply was measured in watts, not kilowatts. So they sat in darkness illuminated by the flatscreen displays and tiny holos that were their eyes on the outer world. Here they were, conspirators plotting the overthrow of a world dictatorship—a dictatorship which possessed missiles and nukes—and they sat timidly in the dark.

Their quixotic conspiracy wasn't winning, but, by God, the enemy knew it was in a fight. Take the TV:

the first couple of weeks it seemed that there were hardly any stations, and those were mostly run by families. The Moraleses spent most of their viewing time with old recordings. Then, after the LA rescue, the Authority had begun around-the-clock saturation broadcasting similar to twentieth-century Soviet feeds, and as little watched: it was all news, all stories about the heinous Tinkers and the courageous measures being taken by "your Peace Authority" to make the world safe from the Tinker threat.

Paul called those "measures" the Silvery Pogrom. Every day there were more pictures of convicted Tinkers and fellow-travelers disappearing into the bobble farm the Authority had established at Chico. Ten years, the announcers said, and those bobbles would burst and the felons would have their cases reviewed. Meantime, their property would also be held in stasis. Never in history, the audience was assured, had criminals and monsters been treated with more firmness or more fairness. Allison knew bullshit when she heard it; if she hadn't been bobbled herself, she would have assumed that it was a cover for extermination.

It was a strange feeling to have been present at the founding of the present order, and to be alive now, fifty years later. This great Authority, ruling the entire world—except now Europe and Africa—had grown from nothing more than that third-rate company Paul worked for in Livermore. What would have happened if she and Angus and Fred had made their flight a couple of days earlier, in time to return safely with the evidence?

Allison looked out the mansion's wide windows, into the twilight. Tears didn't come to her eyes anymore when she thought about it, but the pain was still there. If they had gotten back in time, her CO might have listened to Hoehler. They just might have been able to raid the Livermore labs before the brazen takeover that was called the "War" nowadays. And apparently the "War" had been just the beginning of decades of war and plague, now blamed on the losers. Just a couple of days' difference, and the world would not be a near-lifeless tomb, the United States a fading memory. To think that some lousy contractors could have brought down the greatest nation in history!

She turned back into the room, trying to see the three other conspirators in the dimness. An old man, a skinny kid, and Miguel Rosas. This was the heart of the conspiracy? Tonight, at least, Rosas sounded as pessimistic as she felt.

"Sure, Paul, your invention will bring them down eventually, but I'm telling you the Tinkers are all going to be dead or bobbled before that happens. The Peacers are moving *fast*."

The old man shrugged. "Mike, I think you just need something to panic over. A few weeks back it was the Peacers' recon operation. Wili fixed that—more than fixed it—so now you have to worry about something else." Allison agreed with Mike, but there was truth in Paul's complaint. Mike seemed both haunted and trapped: haunted by what he had done in the past, trapped by his inability to do something to make up for that past. "The Tinkers have simply got to hide out long enough to make more bobblers and improve on 'em. Then we can fight back." Paul's voice was almost petulant, as though he thought that he had done all the hard work and now the Tinkers were incompetent to carry through with what remained. Sometimes Paul seemed exactly as she remembered him. But other times—like tonight—he just seemed old, and faintly befuddled.

"I'm sorry, Paul, but I think that Mike is right." The black kid spoke up, his Spanish accent incongruous yet pleasant. The boy had a sharp tongue and a temper to go with it, but when he spoke to Paul—even in contradiction—he sounded respectful and diffident. "The Authority will not give us the time to succeed. They have bobbled the Alcalde del Norte himself. Red Arrow Farm is gone; if Colonel Kaladze was hiding there, then he is gone, too." On a clear day, dozens of tiny bobbles could be seen about the skirts of the Vandenberg Dome.

"But our control of Peacer recon. We should be able to protect large numbers of—" He noticed Wili shaking his head. "What? You don't have the processing power? I thought you—"

"That's not the big problem, Paul. Jill and I have tried to cover for many of the Tinkers that survived the first bobblings. But see: the first time the Peacers fall on to one of these groups, they will have a contradiction. They will see the satellites telling them something different than what is on the ground. Then our trick is worthless. Already we must remove protection from a couple of the groups we agreed on—They were going to be captured very soon no matter what, Paul." He spoke the last words quickly as he saw the old man straighten in his chair.

Allison put in, "I agree with Wili. We three may be able to hold out forever, but the Tinkers in California will be all gone in another couple of weeks. Controlling the enemy's comm and recon is an enormous advantage, but it's something they will learn about sooner or later. It's worthless except for short-term goals."

Paul was silent for a long moment. When he spoke again, it sounded like the Paul she had known so long ago, the fellow who never let a problem defeat him. "Okay. Then victory must be our *short-term* goal. . . . We'll attack Livermore, and bobble *their* generator."

"Paul, you can do that? You can cast a bobble hundreds of kilometers away, just like the Peacers?" From the corner of her eye, Allison saw Wili shake his head.

"No, but I can do better than in LA. If we could get Wili and enough equipment to within four thousand meters of the target, he could bobble it."

"Four thousand meters?" Rosas walked to the open windows. He looked out over the forest, seeming to enjoy the cool air that was beginning to sweep into the room. "Paul, Paul. I know you specialize in the impossible, but . . . In Los Angeles we needed a gang of porters just to carry the storage cells. A few weeks ago you wouldn't hear of taking a wagon off into the eastern wilderness. Now you want to haul a wagonful of equipment through some of the most open and well-populated country on Earth.

"And then, if you do get there, *all* you have to do is get those several tonnes of equipment within four thousand meters of the Peacer generator. Paul, I've been up to the Livermore Enclave. Three years ago. I was police service liaison with the Peacers. They've got enough firepower there to defeat an old-time army, enough aircraft that they don't need satellite pickups. You couldn't get within forty kilometers without an engraved invitation. Four thousand meters range is probably right inside their central compound."

"There is another problem, Paul." Wili spoke shyly. "I had thought about their generator, too. Someday, I know we must destroy it—and the one in Beijing.

But Paul, I can't find it. I mean, the Authority publicity, it gives nice pictures of the generator building at Livermore, but they are fake. I know. Since I took over their communication system, I know everything they say to each other over the satellites. The generator in Beijing is very close to its official place, but the Livermore one is hidden. They never say its place, even in the most secret transmissions."

Paul slumped in his chair, defeat very obvious. "You're right, of course. The bastards built it in secret. They certainly kept the location secret while the governments were still powerful."

Allison stared from one to the other and felt crazy laughter creeping up her throat. They really didn't know. After all these years they didn't know. And just minutes before, she had been hurting herself with might-have-beens. The laughter burbled out, and she didn't try to stop it. The others looked at her with growing surprise. Her last mission, perhaps the last recon sortie the USAF ever flew, might yet serve its purpose.

Finally, she choked down the laughter and told them the cause for joy. ". . . so if you have a reader, I think we can find it."

There followed frantic calls for Irma, then even more frantic searches through attic storage for the old disk reader. An hour later, the reader sat on the living room table. It was bulky, gray, the Motorola insignia almost scratched away. Irma plugged it in and coaxed it to life. "It worked fine years ago. We used it to copy all our old disks onto solid storage. It uses a lot of power though; that's one reason we gave it up."

The reader's screen came to life, a brilliant glow that lit the whole room. This was the honest light

Allison remembered. She had brought her disk pack down, and undone the combination lock. The disk was milspec, but it was commercial format; it should run on the Motorola. She slipped it into the reader. Her fingers danced across the keyboard, customizing off routines on the disk. Everything was so familiar; it was like suddenly being transported back to the before.

The screen turned white. Three mottled gray disks sat near the middle of the field. She pressed a key and the picture was overlaid with grids and legends.

Allison looked at the picture and almost started laughing again. She was about to reveal what was probably the most highly classified surveillance technique in the American arsenal. Twelve weeks "before," such an act would have been unthinkable. Now, it was a wonderful opportunity, an opportunity for the murdered past to win some small revenge. "Doesn't look like much, does it?" she said into the silence. "We're looking down at—I should say 'through' —Livermore." The date on the legend was 01JUL97.

She looked at Paul. "This is what you asked me to look for, Paul. Remember? I don't think you ever guessed just how good our gear really was."

"You mean, those gray things are old Avery's test projections?"

She nodded. "Of course, I didn't know what to make of them at the time. They're about five hundred meters down. Your employers were very cautious."

Wili looked from Allison to Paul and back, bewilderment growing. "But what is it that we are seeing?"

"We are seeing straight through the Earth. There's a type of light that shines from some parts of the sky. It can pass through almost anything."

"Like x-rays?" Mike said doubtfully.

"Something like x-rays." There was no point in talking about massy neutrinos and sticky detectors. They were just words to her, anyway. She could use the gear, and she understood the front-end engineering, but that was all. "The white background is a 'bright' region of the sky—seen straight through the Earth. Those three gray things are the *silhouettes* of bobbles far underground."

"So they're the only things that are opaque to this magic light," Mike said. "It looks like a good bobble hunter, Allison, but what good was it for anything else?" If you could see through literally everything, then you could see nothing.

"Oh, there is a very small amount of attenuation. This picture is from a single 'exposure,' without any preprocessing. I was astounded to see anything on it. Normally, we'd take a continuous stream of exposures, through varying chords of the Earth's crust, then compute a picture of the target area. The math is pretty much like medical tomography." She keyed another command string. "Here's a sixty-meter map I built from all our observations."

Now the display showed intricate detail: a pink surface map of 1997 Livermore lay over the green, blue, and red representation of subsurface densities. Tunnels and other underground installations were obvious lines and rectangles in the picture.

Wili made an involuntary *ah*ing sound.

"So if we can figure out which of those things is the secret generator . . ." said Mike.

"I think I can narrow it down quite a bit." Paul stared intently at the display, already trying to identify function in the shapes.

"No need," said Allison. "We did a lot of analysis right on the sortie craft. I've got a database on the disk; I can subtract out everything the Air Force knew about." She typed the commands.

"And now the moment we've all been waiting for." There was an edge of triumph in the flippancy. The rectangles dimmed—all but one on the southwest side of the Livermore Valley.

"You did it, Allison!" Paul stood back from the display and grabbed her hands. For an instant she thought he would dance her around the room. But after an awkward moment, he just squeezed her hands.

As he turned back to the display, she asked, "But can we be sure it's still there? If the Peacers know about this scanning technique—"

"They don't. I'm sure of it," said Wili.

Paul laughed. "We can do it, Mike! We can do it. Lord, I'm glad you all had the sense to push. I'd have sat here and let the whole thing die."

Suddenly the other three were all talking at once.

"Look. I see answers to your objections, and I have a feeling that once we start to take it seriously we can find even better answers. First off, it's not impossible to get ourselves and some equipment up there. One horse-drawn wagon is probably enough. Using back roads, and our 'invisibility,' we should be able to get at least to Fremont."

"And then?" said Allison.

"There are surviving Tinkers in the Bay Area. We all attack, throw in everything we have. If we do it right, they won't guess we control their comm and recon until we have our bobbler right on top of them."

Mike was grinning now, talking across the conversation at Wili. Allison raised her voice over the others'. "Paul, this has more holes than—"

"Sure, sure. But it's a start." The old man waved his hand airily, as if only trivial details remained. It was a typical Paulish gesture, something she remembered from the first day she met him. The "details" were usually nontrivial, but it was surprising how often his harebrained schemes worked anyway.

33

"Eat Vandenberg Bananas. They Can't Be Beat."
The banner was painted in yellow on a purple
background. The letters were shaped as though built
out of little bananas. Allison said it was the most
asinine thing she had ever seen. Below the slogan,
smaller letters spelled, "Andrews Farms, Santa Maria."

The signs were draped along the sides of their
wagons. A light plastic shell was mounted above the
green cargo. At every stop Allison and Paul carefully
refilled the evap coolers that hung between the shell
and the bananas. The two banana wagons were among
the largest horsedrawn vehicles on the highway.

Mike and the Santa Maria Tinkers had rigged a
hidden chamber in the middle of each wagon. The
front wagon carried the bobbler and the storage cells;
the other contained Wili, Mike, and most of the
electronics.

Wili sat at the front of the cramped chamber and
tried to see through the gap in the false cargo. No air

was ducted from the coolers while they were stopped. Without it, the heat of the ripening bananas and the summer days could be a killer. Behind him, he felt Mike stir restlessly. They both spent the hottest part of the afternoons trying to nap. They weren't very successful; it was just too hot. Wili suspected they must stink so bad by now that the Peacers would *smell* them inside.

Paul's stooped figure passed through Wili's narrow field of view. His disguise was pretty good; he didn't look anything like the blurred pictures the Peacers were circulating. A second later he saw Allison—in farmer's-daughter costume—walk by. There was a slight shifting of the load and the monotonous *clop-clopclop* of the team resumed. They pulled out of the rest stop, past a weigh station moldering toward total ruin.

Wili pressed his face against the opening, both for the air and the view. They were hundreds of kilometers from Los Angeles; he had expected something more exciting. After all, the area around Vandenberg was almost a jungle. But no. Except for a misty stretch just after Salinas, everything stayed dry and hot. Through the hole in the bananas, he could see the ground rising gently ahead of them, sometimes golden grass, sometimes covered with chaparral. It looked just like the Basin, except that the ruins were sparse and only occasional. Mike said there were other differences, but he had a better eye for plants.

Just then a Peace Authority freighter zipped by in the fast lane. Its roar was surmounted by an arrogant horn blast. The banana wagon rocked in the wash and Wili got a faceful of dust. He sighed and lay back. Five days they had been on the road now. The worst of it was that, inside the wagon, he was out of touch; they couldn't disguise the antennas well enough to permit a link to the satellite net. And they didn't have enough to power for Jill to run all the time. The only processors he could use were very primitive.

Every afternoon was like this: hotter and hotter till they couldn't even pretend to sleep, till they started grumping at each other. He almost wished they would have some problems.

This afternoon he might get that almost-wish. This afternoon they would reach Mission Pass and Livermore Valley.

The nights were very different. At twilight Paul and Allison would turn the wagons off Old 101 and drive the tired teams at least five kilometers into the hills. Wili and Mike came out of their hole, and Wili established communication with the satellite net. It was like suddenly coming awake to be back in connection with Jill and the net. They never had trouble finding the local Tinkers' cache. There were always food and fodder and freshly charged storage cells hidden near a spring or well. He and Paul used those power cells to survey the world through satellite eyes, to coordinate with the Tinkers in the Bay Area and China. They must all be ready at the same time.

The previous night the four of them had held their last council of war.

Some things that Allison and Mike had worried about turned out to be no problems at all. For instance, the Peacers could have set checkpoints hundreds of kilometers out along all highways leading to Livermore. They hadn't done so. The Authority obviously suspected an attack on their main base, but they were concentrating their firepower closer in. And their reserve force was chasing Wili's phantoms in the Great Valley. Now that the Authority had wiped away all public Tinkering, there was nothing obvious for them to look for. They couldn't harass every produce wagon or labor convoy on the coast.

But there were other problems that wouldn't go away. The previous night had been their last chance to look at those from a distance. "Anything after tonight, we're going to have to play by ear," Mike had said, stretching luxuriously in the open freedom of the evening.

Paul grunted at this. The old man sat facing them, his back to the valley. His wide farmer hat drooped down at the sides. "Easy for you to say, Mike. You're an action type. I've never been able to ad lib. I get everything worked out in advance. If something really unexpected happens, I'm just no good at real-time flexibility." It made Wili sad to hear him say this. Paul was becoming indecisive again. Every night, he seemed a little more tired.

Allison Parker returned from settling the horses and sat down at the fourth corner of their little circle. She took off her bonnet. Her pale hair glinted in the light of their tiny campfire. "Well then, what are the problems we have to solve? You have the Bay Area Tinkers, what's left of them, all prepared to stage a diversion. You know exactly where the Peacer bobble generator is hidden. You have control of the enemy's communication and intelligence net—that alone is a greater advantage than most generals ever have."

Her voice was firm, matter-of-fact. It gave support by making concrete points rather than comforting noises, Wili thought.

There was a long silence. A few meters away they could hear the horses munching. Something fluttered through the darkness over their heads. Finally Allison continued. "Or is there doubt that you do control their communications? Do they really trust their satellite system?"

"Oh, they do. The Authority is spread very thin. About the only innovative thing they've ever done was to restablish the old Chinese launch site at Shuangcheng. They have close and far reconnaissance from their satellites, as well as communications—both voice and computer." Wili nodded in agreement. He followed the discussion with only a fraction of his mind. The rest was off managing and updating the hundreds of ruses that must fit together to maintain their great deception. In particular, the faked Tinker movements in the Great Valley had to be wound down, but carefully so that the enemy would not realize they had put thousands of men there for no reason.

"And Wili says they don't seem to trust anything that comes over ground links," Paul continued. "Somehow they have the idea that if a machine is thousands of kilometers off in space, then it should be immune to meddling." He laughed shortly. "In their own way, those old bastards are as inflexible as I. Oh, they'll follow the ring in their nose, until the contradictions get too thick. *By then we must have won.*

". . . But there are so many, many things we have to get straight before that can happen." The sound of helplessness was back in his voice.

Mike sat up. "Okay. Let's take the hardest: how to get from their front door to the bobble generator."

"Front door? Oh, you mean the garrison on Mission Pass. Yes, that's the hardest question. They've strengthened that garrison enormously during the last week."

"Ha. If they're like most organizations, that'll just

make them more confused—at least for a while. Look, Paul. By the time we arrive there, the Bay Area Tinkers should be attacking. You told me that some of them have maneuvered north and east of Livermore. They have bobble generators. In that sort of confusion there ought to be lots of ways to get our heavy-duty bobbler in close."

Wili smiled in the dark. Just a few days ago, it had been Rosas who'd been down on the plan. Now that they were close, though . . .

"Then name a few."

"Hell, we could go in just like we are—as banana vendors. We know they import the things."

Paul snorted. "Not in the middle of a war."

"Maybe. But *we* can control the moment the real fighting begins. Going in as we are would be a long shot, I admit, but if you don't want to improvise completely, you should be thinking about various ways things could happen. For instance, we might bobble the Pass and have our people grab the armor that's left and come down into the Livermore Valley on it with Wili covering for us. I know you've thought about that—all day I have to sit on those adapter cables you brought.

"Paul," he continued more quietly, "you've been the inspiration of several thousand people these last two weeks. These guys have their necks stuck way out. We're all willing to risk everything. But we need you more than ever now."

"Or put less diplomatically—I got us all into this pickle, so I can't give up on it now."

"Something like that."

". . . Okay." Paul was silent for a moment. "Maybe we could arrange it so that . . ." He was quiet again and Wili realized that the old Paul had reasserted himself—was trying to, anyway. "Mike, do you have any idea where this Lu person is now?"

"No." The undersheriff's voice was suddenly tight. "But she's important to them, Paul. I know that much. I wouldn't be surprised if she were at Livermore."

"Maybe you could talk to her. You know, pretend you're interested in betraying the Tinker forces we've lined up here."

"No! What I did had nothing to do with hurting . . ." His voice scaled down, and he continued more calmly. "I mean, I don't see what good it would do. She's too smart to believe anything like that."

Wili looked up through the branches of the dry oak that spread over their campsite. The stars should have been beautiful through those branches. Somehow they were more like tiny gleams in a dark-socketed skull. Even if he were never denounced, could poor Mike ever silence his internal inquisitor?

"Still, as you said about the other, it's something to think about." Paul shook his head sharply and rubbed his temples. "I am so tired. Look. I've got to talk to Jill about this. I'll think things out. I promise. But let's continue in the morning. Okay?"

Allison reached across as though to touch his shoulder, but Paul was already coming to his feet. He walked slowly away from the campfire. Allison started to get up, then sat down and looked at the other two. "There's something wrong. . . . There's something so wrong about Paul making a person out of a thing," she said softly. Wili didn't know what to say, and after a moment the three of them spread out their sleeping bags and crawled in.

Wili's lay between the cache of storage cells and the wagon with the processors. There should be enough juice for several hours' operation. He adjusted the scalp connect and wriggled into a comfortable position. He stared up at the half-sinister arches of the oaks and let his mind mesh with the system. He was going into deep connect now, something he avoided when he was with the others. It made his physical self dopey and uncoordinated.

Wili sensed Paul talking to Jill but did not try to participate.

His attention drifted to the tiny cameras they had scattered beyond the edges of the camp, then snapped onto a high-resolution picture from above. From there, their oaks were just one of many tiny clumps of darkness on a rolling map of paler grassland. The only light for kilometers around came from the embers that still glowed at the center of their camp. Wili smiled in his mind; that was the true view. The tiny light flicked out, and he looked down on the scene that was being reported to the Peace Authority. Nobody here but us coyotes.

This was the easiest part of the "high watch." He did it only for amusement; it was the sort of thing Jill and the satellite processors could manage without his conscious attention.

Wili drifted out from the individual viewpoints, his attention expanding to the whole West Coast and beyond, to the Tinkers near Beijing. There was much to do; a good deal more than Mike or Allison—or even Paul—might suspect. He talked to dozens of conspirators. These men had come to expect Paul's voice coming off Peacer satellites in the middle of the West Coast night. Wili must protect them as he did the banana wagons. They were a weak link. If any of them were captured, or turned traitor, the enemy would immediately know of Wili's electronic fraud.

From them, "Paul's" instructions and recommendations were spread to hundreds.

In this state, Wili found it hard to imagine failure. All the details were there before him. As long as he was on hand to watch and supervise, there was nothing that could take him by surprise. It was a false optimism perhaps. He knew that Paul didn't feel it when he was linked up and helping. But Wili had gradually realized that Paul used the system without becoming part of it. To Paul it was like another programming tool, not like a part of his own mind. It was sad that someone so smart should miss this.

This real dream of power continued for several hours. As the cells slowly drained, operations were necessarily curtailed. The slow retreat from omniscience matched his own increasing drowsiness. Last thing before losing consciousness and power, he ferreted through Peacer archives and discovered the secret of Della Lu's family. Now that their cover was blown, they had moved to the Livermore Enclave, but Wili found two other spy families among the 'furbishers and warned the conspirators to avoid them.

Heat, sweat, dust on his face. Something was clanking and screaming in the distance. Wili lurched out of his daydreaming recollection of the previous evening. Beside him Rosas leaned close to the peephole. A splotch of light danced across his face as he tried to follow what was outside in spite of the swaying progress of the banana wagon.

"God. Look at all those Peacers," he said quietly. "We must be right at the Pass, Wili."

"Lemme see," the boy said groggily. Wili suppressed his own surprised exclamation. The wagons were still ascending the same gentle grade they'd been on for the last hour. Ahead he could see the wagon that contained Jill. What was new was the cause of all the clanking. Peacer armor. The vehicles were still on the horizon, coming off an interchange ahead. They were turning north toward the garrison at Mission Pass. "Must be the reinforcements from Medford." Wili had never seen so many vehicles with his own eyes. The line stretched from the interchange for as far as they could see. They were painted in dark green colors— quite an uncamouflage in this landscape. Many of them looked like tanks he had seen in old movies. Others were more like bricks on treads.

As they approached the interchange the clanking got louder and combined with the overtones of turbines. Soon the banana wagons caught up with the military. Civilian traffic was forced over to the rightmost lane. Powered freighters and horse-drawn wagons alike were slowed to the same crawl.

It was late afternoon. There was something big and loud behind them that cast a long shadow across the two banana wagons, and brought a small amount of coolness. But the tanks to the right raised a dust storm that more than made up for the lowered temperatures.

They drove like this for more than an hour. Where were the checkpoints? The road ahead still rose. They passed dozens of parked tanks, their crews working at mysterious tasks. Someone was fueling up. The smell of diesel oil came into the cramped hole along with the dust and the noise.

All was in shadow now. But finally Wili thought he could see part of the garrison. At least there was a building on the crest they were approaching. He remembered what things looked like from above. Most of the garrison's buildings were on the far side of the crest. Only a few positions—for observation and direct fire—were on this side.

Wili wondered what sort of armor they had back there now, considering what he was seeing on this side.

Wili and Mike traded time at the peephole as the spot on the horizon grew larger. The outpost sat like a huge boulder mostly submerged in the earth. There were slots cut in the armor, and he could see guns or lasers within. Wili was reminded of some of the twentieth-century fantasies Bill Morales liked to watch. These last few days—and hopefully the next few as well—were like Lucas' *Lord of the Rings*. Mike had even called Mission Pass the "front door" last night. Beyond these mountains (actually low hills) lay the "Great Enemy's" ultimate redoubt. The mountains hid enemy underlings that watched for the hobbits or elves (or Tinkers) who must sneak through to the plains beyond, who must go right into the heart of evil and perform some simple act that would bring victory.

The similarity went further. This enemy had a supreme weapon (the big bobbler hidden in the Valley), but instead depended on earthly servants (the tanks and the troops) to do the dirty work. The Peacers hadn't bobbled anything for the last three days. That was a mystery, though Wili and Paul suspected the Authority was building up power reserves for the battle they saw coming.

Ahead of them, civilian traffic stopped at a checkpoint. Wili couldn't see exactly what was happening, but one by one—some slowly, some quickly—the wagons and freighters passed through. Finally their turn came. He heard Paul climb down from the driver's seat. A couple of Peacers approached. Both were armed, but they didn't seem especially tense. Twilight was deep now, and he could barely make out the color in their uniforms. The sky came down to the near horizon that was the crest of the Pass. The Earth's shadow, projected into the sky, made a dark wall beyond them. One carried a long metal pole. Some kind of weapon?

Paul hurried up from the back wagon. For a moment all three stood in his field of view. The troopers glanced at Paul and then up at where Allison was sitting. They obviously realized the two wagons were together. "Watcha got here, uncle?" asked the older of them.

"Bananas," Naismith replied unnecessarily. "You want some? My granddaughter and I've got to get them to Livermore before they spoil."

"I have bad news for you, then. Nothing's getting through here for a while." The three walked out of sight, back along the wagon.

"What?" Paul's voice rose, cracked. He was a better actor than Wili would have guessed. "B-but what's going on here? I'll lose business."

The younger soldier sounded sincerely apologetic. "We can't help it, sir. If you had followed the news, you'd know the enemies of Peace are on the move again. We're expecting an attack almost any time. Those damn Tinkers are going to bring back the bad old days."

"Oh no!" The anguish in the old man's voice seemed a compound of his personal problems and this new forecast of doom.

There was the sound of side curtains being dragged off the wagon. "Hey, Sarge, these things aren't even ripe."

"That's right," said Naismith. "I have to time things

so when I arrive they'll be just ready to sell. . . .
Here. Take a couple, officer."

"Um, thanks." Wili could imagine the Peacer holding a clump of bananas, trying to figure what to do
with them. "Okay, Hanson, do your stuff." There was
a rasping and a probing. So *that's* what the metal
pole was. Both Wili and Miguel Rosas held their
breath. Their hiding space was small, and it was
covered with webbed padding. It could probably deceive a sonic probe. What about this more primitive
search?

"It's clean"

"Okay. Let's look at your other wagon."

They walked to the forward wagon, the one that
contained the bobbler and most of the storage cells.
Their conversation faded into the general din of the
checkpoint. Allison climbed down from her driver's
seat and stood where Wili could see her.

Minutes passed. The band of shadow across the
eastern sky climbed, became diffuse. Twilight moved
toward night.

Electric lamps flashed on. Wili gasped. He had
seen miraculous electronics these last months, but
the sudden sheer power of those floodlights was as
impressive as any of it. Every second they must eat
as much electricity as Naismith's house did in a
week.

Then he heard Paul's voice again. The old man had
taken on a whining tone, and the trooper was a bit
more curt than before. "Look, mister, *I* didn't decide
to bring war here. You should count yourself lucky
that you have any sort of protection from these
monsters. Maybe things will blow over in time for
you to save the load. For now, you're stuck. There's a
parking area up ahead, near the crest. We have some

latrines fixed there. You and your granddaughter can stay overnight, then decide if you want to stick it out or turn back. . . . Maybe you could sell part of the load in Fremont."

Paul sounded defeated, almost dazed. "Yes sir. Thanks for your help. Do as he says, Allison dear."

The wagons creaked forward, blue-white light splashing all around them like magic rain. From across the tiny hiding place, Wili heard the whisper of chuckle.

"Paul is really good. Now I wonder if all his whining last night was some sort of reverse whammy to get *our* spirits up."

Horse-drawn wagons and Authority freighters alike had parked in the big lot near the crest of the Pass. There were some electric lamps, but compared to the checkpoint it was almost dark. A good many people were stuck here overnight. Most of them milled around cooking fires at the middle of the lot. The far end was dominated by the squat dome they had seen from far down the highway. Several armored vehicles were parked in front of it; they faced into the civilians.

The armored traffic on the highway had virtually ceased. For the first time in hours there was an absence of clank and turbines.

Paul came back around the side of the wagon. He and Allison adjusted the side curtains. Paul complained loudly to Allison about the disaster that had befallen them, and she was dutifully quiet. A trio of freighter drivers walked by. As they passed out of earshot, Naismith said quietly. "Wili, we're going to have to risk a hookup. I've connected you with the gear in the front wagon. Allison has pulled the narrow-beam antenna out of the bananas. I want contact with our . . . friends. We're going to need help to get any closer."

Wili grinned in the dark. It was a risk—but one he'd been aching to take. Sitting in this hole without processors was like being deaf, dumb, and blind. He attached the scalp connector and powered up.

There was a moment of disorientation as Jill and he meshed with the satellite net. Then he was looking out a dozen new eyes, listening on hundreds of Peacer comm channels. It would take him a little longer to contact the Tinkers. After all, they were humans.

A bit of his awareness still hung in their dark hiding place. With his true ears, Wili heard a car roar off the highway and park at the Peacer dome. The armor at the far end of the lot came to life. Something important was happening right here. Wili found a camera aboard the armor that could transmit to the satellite net. He looked out: the car's driver had jumped out and come to attention. Far across the lot, he could see civilians—somewhere among them Paul and Allison—turn to watch. He felt Mike crawl across him to look out the peephole. Wili juggled the viewpoints, at the same time continuing his efforts to reach the Tinkers, at the same time searching Authority RAM for the cause of the current commotion.

A door opened at the base of the Peacer station. White light spread from it across the asphalt. A Peacer was outlined in the doorway. A second followed him. And between them . . . a child? Someone small and slender, anyway. The figure stepped out of the larger shadows and looked across the parking lot. Light glinted off the black helmet of short hair. He heard Mike suck in a breath.

It was Della Lu.

34

Staff seemed satisfied with the preparations; even Avery accepted the plans.

Della Lu was not so happy. She looked speculatively at the stars on the shoulder of the perimeter commander. The officer looked back with barely concealed truculence. He thought he was tough. He thought she was more nonprofessional interference.

But she knew he was soft. All these troops were. They hadn't ever been in a real fight.

Lu considered the map he had displayed for her. As she, through Avery, had required, the armored units were being dispersed into the hills. Except for a few necessary and transient concentrations, the Tinkers would have to take them out a vehicle at a time. And satellite intelligence assured them that the enemy attack was many hours away, that the infiltrators weren't anywhere near the net of armor.

She pointed to the Mission Pass command post. "I see you stopped all incoming traffic. Why have them park so close to your command point here? A few of those people must be Tinker agents."

The general shrugged. "We inspected the vehicles four thousand meters down the road. That's beyond the range the intelligence people give for the enemy's homemade bobbler. Where we have them now, we can keep them under close watch and interrogate them more conveniently."

Della didn't like it. If even a single generator slipped through, this command post would be lost. Still, with the main attack at least twenty-four hours away, it might be safe to sit here a bit longer. There was time perhaps to go Tinker hunting in that parking area. Anybody they caught would probably be important to the enemy cause. She stepped back from the map display. "Very well, General, let's take a look at these civilians. Get your intelligence teams together. It's going to be a long night for them.

"In the meantime, I want you to move your command and control elements over the ridgeline. When things start happening, they'll be much safer in mobiles."

The officer looked at her for a moment, probably wondering just who she was sleeping with to give such orders. Finally he turned and spoke to a subordinate.

He glanced back at Della. "You want to be present at the interrogations?"

She nodded. "The first few, anyway. I'll pick them for you."

The parking-lot detention area was several hundred meters on a side. It looked almost like a fairground. Diesel freighters loomed over small horse-drawn carts and wagons. The truckers had already started fires. Some of their voices were almost cheerful. The delay by itself didn't worry them; their businesses were internal to the Authority and they stood to be reimbursed.

Lu walked past the staff car the general had ordered for them. The officer and his aides tagged along, uncertain what she would do next. She wasn't sure yet either, but once she got the feel of the crowd. . . .

If she were Miguel Rosas, she'd figure out some way to hijack one of the Peace Authority freighters. There was enough volume in a freighter to hide almost anything the Tinkers might make. Hmm. But the drivers generally knew each other and could probably recognize each other's rigs. The Tinkers would have to park their freighter away from the others, and avoid socializing. She and her entourage drifted through the shadows beyond the fires.

The freighters were clumped together; none was parked apart. That left the non-Peacer civilians. She turned away from the freighters and walked down a row of wagons. The people were ordinary enough: more than half in their fifties and sixties, the rest young apprentices. They did look uneasy—they stood to lose a lot of money if they had to stay here long—but there was little fear. They still believed the Authority's propaganda. And most of them were food shippers. None of their own people had been bobbled in the purges she had supervised the last few weeks. From somewhere over the hill she heard choppers. The intelligence crews would be here shortly.

Then she saw the banana wagons. They could only be from the Vandenberg area. No matter what intelligence was saying nowadays, she still thought Middle California was the center of the infestation. An old man and a woman about Lu's own age stood near the wagons. She felt tiny alarm bells going off.

Behind Della, the helicopters were landing. Dust blew cool and glowing around her. The choppers' lights cast her group's shadow toward the pair by the banana wagons. The old man raised his hand to shade his eyes; the woman just looked at them. There was something strange about her, a straightness in her posture, almost a soldier's bearing. For all that the other was tall and Caucasian, Della felt she was seeing someone very like herself.

Della clapped the general's arm, and when he turned to her she shouted over the sounds of blades and turbines, "There are your prime suspects—"

"The bitch! Is she some kind of mind reader?" Mike watched Lu's progress across the wide field. She still wasn't coming directly toward them, but edged slowly closer, like some cautious huntress. Mike cursed quietly. They seemed doomed at every step to face her and be bested by her.

The field grew bright; shadows shifted and lengthened. Choppers. Three of them. Each craft carried twin lamps hung below the cockpit. Lu's wolves, eyes glowing, settled down behind their mistress.

"Mike, listen." Wili's voice was tense, but the words were slurred, the cadence irregular. He must be in deep connect. He sounded like one talking from a dream. "I'm running at full power; we'll be out of power in seconds—but that is all we have."

Mike looked out at the helicopters; Wili was right about that. "But what can we *do*?" he said.

"Our friends . . . going to distract her . . . no time to explain everything. Just do what I say."

Mike stared into the darkness. He could imagine

the dazed look in Wili's eyes, the slack features. He had seen it often enough the last few evenings. The boy was managing their own problems and coordinating the rest of the revolution, all at the same time. Rosas had played symbiotic games, but this was beyond his imagination. There was only one thing he could say. "Sure."

"You're going to take those two armored equipment carriers at . . . far side of the field. Do you see them?"

Mike had, earlier. They were two hundred meters off. There were guards posted next to them.

"When?"

"A minute. Kick loose the side of the wagon . . . now. When I say go . . . you jump, grab Allison, and run for them. Ignore everything else you see and hear. Everything."

Mike hesitated. He could guess what Wili intended, but—

"Move. Move. *Move!*" Wili's voice was abruptly urgent, angry—the dreamer frustrated. It was as unnerving as a scream. Mike turned and crashed his heels into the specially weakened wall. It had been intended as an emergency escape route. As the tacked nails gave way, Mike reflected that this was certainly an emergency—but they would be getting out in full view of Peacer guns.

Lu's general heard her order and turned to shout to his men. He was below his usual element here, directing operations firsthand. Della had to remind him, "Don't point. Have your people pick up others at the same time. We don't want to spook those two."

He nodded.

The rotors were winding down. Something like quiet should return to the field now, she thought . . .

. . . and was wrong. "Sir!" It was a driver in the field car. "We're losing armor to enemy action."

Lu whipped around the brass before they could do more than swear. She hopped into the car and looked at the display that glowed in front of the soldier. Her fingers danced over the command board as she brought up views and interpretation. The man stared at her for a horrified instant, then realized that she must be somebody very special.

Satellite photos showed eight silvery balls embedded in the hills north of them, eight silvery balls gleaming in starlight. Now there were nine. Patrols in the hills reported the same thing. One transmission ended in midsentence. Ten bobbles. The infiltration was twenty-four hours ahead of the schedule Avery's precious satellites and intelligence computers had predicted. The Tinkers must have dozens of manpack generators out there. If they were like the one Wili Wáchendon had carried, they were very short range. The enemy must be sneaking right up on their targets.

Della looked across the detention area at the banana wagons. Remarkably timed, this attack.

She slipped out of the car and walked back to the general and his staff. *Cool. Cool. They may hold off as long as we don't move on the wagons.*

"Looks bad, General. They're way ahead of our estimates. Some of them are already operating north of us." That much was true.

"My God. I've got to get back to command, lady. These interrogations will have to wait."

Lu smiled crookedly. The other still didn't get the point. "You do that. Might as well leave these people alone anyway." But the other was already walking away from her. He waved acknowledgment and got into the field car.

To the north she heard tac air, scrambled up from the Livermore Valley. Something flashed white, and far hills stood in momentary silhouette. That was one bobbler that wouldn't get them this night.

Della looked over the civilian encampment as though pondering what to do next. She was careful to give no special attention to the banana wagons. Apparently, they thought their diversion successful—at least she remained unbobbled.

She walked back to her personal chopper, which had come in with the interrogation teams. Lu's aircraft was smaller, only big enough for pilot, commander, and gunner. It bristled with sensor equipment and rocket pods. The tail boom might be painted with LA paisley, but these were her own people on this machine, veterans of the Mongolian campaign. She pulled herself onto the command seat and gave the pilot an emphatic up-and-away sign. They were off the ground immediately.

Della ignored this efficiency; she was already trying to get her priority call through to Avery. The little monochrome display in front of her pulsed red as her call stayed in the queue. She could imagine the madhouse Livermore Central had become the last few minutes. *But, damn you, Avery, this is not the time to forget I come first!*

Red. Red. Red. The call pattern disappeared, and the display was filled with a pale blob that might have been someone's face. "Make it quick." It was Hamilton Avery's voice. Other voices, some almost shouting, came from behind him.

She was ready. "No proof, but I know they've infiltrated right up to the Mission Pass Gate. I want you to lay a thousand-meter bobble just south of the CP—"

"No! We're still charging. If we start using it now, there won't be juice for rapid fire when we really need it, when they get over the ridgeline."

"Don't you see? The rest is diversion. Whatever I've found here must be *important*."

But the link was broken; the screen glowed a faint, uniform red. Damn Avery and his caution! He was so afraid of Paul Hoehler, so certain the other would figure out a way to get into Livermore Valley, that he was actually making it possible for the enemy to do so.

She looked past the instrument displays. They were about four hundred meters up. Splashes of blue-white light from the pole lamps lit the detention area; the camp looked like some perfect model. There was little apparent motion, though the pilot's thermal scanner showed that some of the armor was alive, awaiting orders. The civilian camp was still and bluish white, little tents sitting by scarcely larger wagons. The darker clumps around the fires were crowds of people.

Della swallowed. If Avery wouldn't bobble the camp . . . .

She knew, without looking, what her ship carried. She had stun bombs, but if those wagons were what she thought, they would be shielded. She touched her throat mike and spoke to her gunner. "Fire mission. Rockets on the civilian wagons. No napalm." The people around the campfires would survive. Most of them.

The gunner's "Roger" sounded in her ear. The air around the chopper glowed as if a small sun had suddenly risen behind them, and a roar blotted out the rotor thupping. Looking almost into the exhaust of the rocket stream dimmed all other lights to nothing.

Or almost nothing. For an instant, she glimpsed rockets coming *up* from below. . . .

Then their barrage exploded. In the air. Not halfway to the target. The fireballs seemed to *splash* across some unseen surface. The chopper staggered as shrapnel ripped through it. Someone screamed.

The aircraft tipped into an increasing bank that would soon turn them upside down. Della didn't think, didn't really notice the pilot slumped against his controls. She grabbed her copy of the stick, pulled, and jabbed at the throttle. *Ahead she saw another copter, on a collision path with theirs.* Then the pilot fell back, the stick came free, and her aircraft shot upward, escaping both ground and the mysterious other. The gunner crawled up between them and looked at the pilot. "He's dead, ma'am."

Della listened, and also listened to the rotors. There was something ragged in their rhythm. She had heard worse. "Okay. Tie him down." Then she ignored them and flew the helicopter slowly around what had been the Mission Pass Gate.

The phantom missiles from below, the mysterious helicopter—all were explained now. Near the instant her gunner fired his rockets, someone had bobbled the Pass. She circled that great dark sphere, a perfect reflection of her lights following her. The bobble was a thousand meters across. But this hadn't been Avery relenting: along with the civilian and freighter encampment, the bobble also contained the Gate's command post. Far below, Authority armor moved around the base, like ants suddenly cut off from the nest.

So. Perfect timing, once again. They had known she was going to attack, and known precisely when. Tinker communication and intelligence must be the equal of the Peace's. And whoever was down there had been important. The generator they carried must have been one of the most powerful the Tinkers had. When they had seen the alternative was death, they had opted out of the whole war.

She looked across at her chopper's reflection, seemingly a hundred meters off. The fact that they had bobbled themselves instead of her aircraft was evidence that the Hoehler technique—at least with small power sources—was not very good for moving targets. Something to remember.

At least now, instead of a hundred new deaths on her soul, the enemy had burdened her with just one, her pilot. And when this bobble burst—the minimum ten years from now or fifty—the war would be history. A flick of the eye to them, and there would be no more killing. She suddenly envied these losers very much.

She banked away and headed for Livermore Central.

35

"Now!" Wili's command came abruptly, just seconds after Rosas had loosened the false wall. Mike crashed his heels one last time into the wood. It gave way, bananas and timber falling with it.

And suddenly there was light all around them. Not the blue-point lights the Authority had strung around the campground, but an all-enveloping white glare, brighter than any of the electrics.

"Run now. Run!" Wili's voice was faint from within the compartment. The undersheriff grabbed Allison and urged her across the field. Paul started to follow them, then turned back at Wili's call.

An Authority tank swiveled on its treads, its turret turning even faster. Behind him an unfamiliar voice shouted for him to stop. Mike and Allison only ran faster. And the tank disappeared in a ten-meter-wide silver sphere.

They ran past civilians cowering in the nebulous glare, past troopers and Authority equipment that one after another were bobbled before they could come into action.

Two hundred meters is a long way to sprint. It is more than long enough to think, and understand.

The glare all around them was only bright by comparison with night. This was simply morning light, masked and diffused by fog. Wili had bobbled the campground through to the next morning, or the morning after that—to some later time when the mass of the Authority's forces would have moved away from the Gate they now thought blocked. Now he was mopping up the Peacers that had been in the bobble. If they moved fast, they could be gone before the Peace discovered what had happened.

When Mike and Allison reached the armored carriers, they were unguarded—except for a pair of three-meter bobbles that gleamed on either side of them. Wili must have chosen these just because their crews were standing outside.

Mike clambered up over the treads and paused, panting. He turned and pulled Allison onto the vehicle. "Wili wants us to drive these to the wagons." He threw the open hatch and shrugged helplessly. "Can you do it?"

"Sure." She caught the edge of the hatch and swung down into the darkness. "C'mon."

Mike followed awkwardly, feeling a little stupid at his question. Allison was from the age of such machines, when everyone knew how to drive.

The smell of lubricants and diesel oil was faint perfume in the air. There was seating for three. Allison was already in the forward position, her hands moving tentatively over the controls. There were no windows and no displays—unless the pale-painted walls were screens. Wait. The third crew position faced to the rear, into formidable racks of electronic equipment. There were displays there.

"See here," said Allison. He turned and looked over her shoulder. She turned a handle, firing up the crawler's turbine. The whine ascended the scale, till Mike felt it through the metal walls and floor as much as through his ears.

Allison pointed. There *was* a display system on the panel in front of her. The letters and digits were bar-formed, but legible. "That's fuel. It's not full. Should be able to go at least fifty kilometers, though. These others, engine temperature, engine speed—as long as you have autodriver set you'd best ignore them.

"Hold tight." She grabbed the driving sticks and demonstrated how to control the tracks. The vehicle slewed back and forth and around.

"How can you see out?"

Allison laughed. "A nineteenth-century solution. Bend down a little further." She tapped the hull above her head. Now he saw the shallow depression that ringed the driver's head, just above the level of her temples. "Three hundred and sixty degrees of periscopes. The position can be adjusted to suit." She demonstrated.

"Okay. You say Wili wants both the crawlers over to the banana wagons? I'll bring the other one." She slipped out of the driver's seat and disappeared through the hatch.

Mike stared at the controls. She had not turned off the engine. All he had to do was sit down and *drive*. He slid into the seat and stuck his head through the ring of periscope viewers. It was almost as if he had stood up through the hatch; he really could see all around.

Straight ahead, Naismith stood by the wagons. The old man was tearing at the side panels, sending his "precious bananas" cascading across the ground. To the left a puff of vapor came from the other armored carrier, and Mike heard Allison start its engine.

He looked past the lower edge of the periscope ring at the drive sticks. He touched the left tread control, and the carrier jerked incrementally till it was lined up on the wagons. Then he pressed both sticks, and he was moving forward! Mike accelerated to what must have been six or seven meters per second, as fast as a man could run. It was just like in the games. The trip was over in seconds. He cautiously slowed the carrier to a crawl the last few meters, and turned in the direction Paul motioned. Then he was stopped. The turbine's keening went on.

Allison had already opened the rear of the other vehicle and was sliding the bulky electronics gear out onto the dirt. Mike wondered at the mass of equipment the Peacers seemed to need in these vehicles. All of Sy Wentz's police electronics would fit in one of the carriers with room to spare. "Leave the comm and sense equipment aboard, Allison. Wili may be able to interface it." While Allison concentrated on the equipment she knew, Mike and Paul worked to move Wili's processor and the Tinker communications gear out of the banana wagons.

The boy came out of the gutted wagon. He was off the system now, but still seemed dazed, his efforts to help ineffectual. "I have used almost all, Paul. I can't even talk to the net anymore. If we can't use the generators on the these"—he waved at the carriers—"we are dead."

That was the big question. Without foreplanning there wasn't a chance, but Paul had brought power interfaces and connector cables. They were based on Allison's specs. If, as with many things, the Peacers had not changed the old standards, then they had a chance.

They could almost fool themselves that the morning was quiet and still. Even the insects were silent. The air around them got steadily brighter, yet the morning fog was still so thick that the sun's disk was not visible. Far away, much farther than the ridgeline, they heard aircraft. Once or twice a minute there was a muffled explosion. Wili had started the Tinker forces on their invasion of the Livermore Valley, but from the north edge, where he had told them to mass through the night. Hopefully the diversion would be some help.

From the corner of his eyes, Mike had the constant impression of motion half-seen, of figures all across the campground working at projects similar to their own. He glanced across the field and saw the reason for the illusion: Wili had cast dozens of bobbles of varying sizes, all in a few seconds' time after the big, overnight bobble had burst. Some must hold just one or two men. Others, like the ones he had put around the main civilian campsite and the Peacer outpost, were more than fifty meters across. And in every one of them he could see the reflections of the four of them, working frantically to finish the transfer before the Peacers down in the Valley realized that the one big bobble had already burst.

It seemed longer, but the work took only minutes. Leaving most of the power cells behind, they didn't have more than fifty kilos of hardware. The processor and the larger bobble generator went into one carrier, while their own satellite comm equipment and a smaller bobbler went into the other. It was an incon-

gruous sight, the Tinker gear sitting small and innocent in the green-painted equipment racks. Allison
stood up in the now-spacious carrier and looked at
Paul. "Are you satisfied?"

He nodded.

"Then it's smoke-test time." There was no humor
in her voice. She turned a switch. Nothing smoked;
displays flickered to life. Wili gave a whoop. The rest
of the interfacing was software. It would take unaided programmers weeks. Hopefully, Paul and Wili
could do it while they were on the move.

Allison, Paul, and Wili took one carrier. Mike—under
protest—took the other. There was plenty of room for
everyone and all the equipment in just one of the
vehicles. "They expect to see rovers in pairs, Mike. I
know it."

"Yes," said Allison. "Just follow my lead, Mike; I
won't do anything fancy."

The two vehicles moved slowly out of the parking
area, cautiously negotiating the field of mirrored tomb-
stones. The whine of their engines drowned the sound
of aircraft and occasional explosions that came from
far beyond the ridgeline. As they neared the crest, the
fog thinned and morning blue was visible. They were
far enough from the parking area that—even without
their electronics working—they might be mistaken
for Peacers.

Then they were starting downward, past the last of
the outer defenses. Soon they would know about the
inner ones, and know if Allison's news now fifty years
old, was still the key to the destruction of the Peace.

36

Della Lu caught up on the situation reports as she ate breakfast. She wore a fresh jumpsuit, and her straight hair gleamed clean and black in the bright fluorescent lights of the command center. One might think she had just returned from a two-week vacation—not from a night spent running all over the hills, trying to pin down guerrilla positions.

The effect was calculated. The morning watch had just come on. They were for the most part rested, and had none of the harried impatience of the team that had been down here all night. If she were going to exercise command—or even influence—upon them, she must appear cool, analytical. And inside, Della almost was. She had taken time to clean up, time even for a short nap. Physically, things had been much worse in Mongolia. Mentally? Mentally, she was beginning, for the first time in her life, to feel outclassed.

Della looked across the ranked consoles. This was

329

the heart of the Livermore command, which itself was the heart of operations worldwide. Before this morning she had never been in this room. In fact, she and most of the occupants didn't know quite where it was. One thing was sure: it was far underground, proof against nukes and gas and such old-fashioned things. Almost equally sure: it was within a few dozen meters of the Livermore bobble generator and its fusion power source. On some of the displays she could see command language for directing and triggering that generator. There was no point in having such control any more or less secure than the generator itself. They would both be in the deepest, most secret hole available.

A situation board covered most of the front wall. Right now it showed a composite interpretation of the land around Livermore, based on satellite reconnaissance. Apparently, the driving programs were not designed for other inputs. Reports from the men on the ground were entered on the display by computer clerks working at terminals connected to the command database. So far this morning, the board did not show any conflicts between the two sources of information. Enemy contact had been about zip for the last hour.

The situation was different elsewhere in the world: there had been no Authority presence in Europe or Africa for days. In Asia, events much like those in North America had taken place. Old Kim Tioulang was nearly as clever as Hamilton Avery, and he had some of the same blind spots. His bobble generator was just north of Beijing. The smaller displays showed the status of the conflict around it. The Chinese Tinkers hadn't built as many bobblers as their American cousins, and they hadn't penetrated as close to the heart of the Beijing complex. But it was late night there, and an attack was under way. The enemy had surprised K.T. just as it had the Livermore forces. The two bobble generators that were the backbone of Peacer power were both under attack, a simultaneous attack that seemed purposefully coordinated. The Tinkers had communications at least as good as the Authority's. At least.

According to the main display, sunrise was due in fifteen minutes, and a heavy fog covered most of the Valley. There were several possible enemy locations, but for now the Peace was holding off. The Tinker bobblers were extremely effective at close range; during the night, the Authority had lost more than twenty percent of its tank force. Better to wait till they had more information on the enemy. Better to wait till Avery let them use the big bobbler. Then they could take them on by the dozens, and at any range.

Lu finished breakfast, sat sipping coffee. Her eyes wandered about the room, half-consciously memorizing faces, displays, exits. The people in this brightly lit, quiet, air-conditioned bunker were living in a fantasy world. And none of them knew it. This was the end receptacle for megabytes of intelligence streaming in to the Peace from all over the world. Before that data arrived, it was already interpreted and winnowed by remote processors. Here it was finally integrated and put on the displays for the highest commanders to pass upon. These people thought their cute displays gave them some ultimate grip on reality. Lu knew that had never been true—and after last night she was sure the system was riddled with lies.

A door hissed open, and Hamilton Avery entered the command bunker. Behind him came Peace General Bertram Maitland, the chief military seat-warmer in the American Directorate. Somehow she had to get past him and convince Avery to junk remote sensing and fight this one with people.

Maitland and Avery strode to an upper rank of terminals. Avery glanced down at Lu and motioned her to join them.

When she arrived, the general was already busy at a terminal, a large-screen model in a flashy red cabinet. He didn't look up. "Intelligence predicts they'll resume the attack shortly after sunrise. You can see indications of thermal activity on the situation board already. It's barely detectable, since they don't have powered vehicles. This time, though, we'll be ready for them." He punched a final command into the terminal, and a faint buzzing penetrated the walls of the bunker. Maitland gestured to the situation board. "There. We just put every one of the suspected enemy concentrations into stasis."

Avery smiled his controlled smile. Every day he seemed a little paler, a little more drawn. He dressed as nattily as always and spoke as coolly as always, but she could see that he was coming near the end of his strength. "That's good. Excellent. I knew if we waited for a full charge we could make up our losses. How many can we do?"

General Maitland considered. "It depends on the size you want. But we can make several thousand at least, with generation rates as high as one per second. I have it under program control now: satellite recon and even our field commanders can report an enemy location and automatically get an embobblement." The almost subsonic buzz punctuated his words.

"No!" The two old men looked up at her, more surprised than angry. "No." Della repeated more quietly. "It's bad enough to trust these remote sensors for information. If they actually control our bobbling, we could very well use all our reserves and get nothing." *Or worse, bobble our own people.* That thought had not occurred to her before.

Maitland's expression clouded. His antagonist was young, female, and had been promoted with unseemly speed past his favorites. If it weren't for Hamilton Avery, she would be out there on some battalion staff—and that only as reward for her apparent success in Asia. Lu turned her attention to Avery. "Please, Director. I know it's fantastic to suspect enemy interference in our satellite communications. But you yourself have said that nothing is beyond this Hoehler, and that whatever is the most fantastic is what he is most likely to do."

She had pushed the right button. Avery flinched, and his eyes turned to the situation board. Apparently the enemy attack predicted by Maitland had begun. Tiny red dots representing Tinker guerrillas were moving into the Valley. Already the Authority bobbler had acted several more times under automatic control. *And what if this is fraudulent, or even partly so?* There might be Tinkers in the Valley, moving through the deep ravines that netted the landscape, moving closer and closer. Now that the possibility was tied to Paul Hoehler, she could see that it had become almost a certainty in his mind.

"And you were the person who predicted he would attack us here," Avery said almost to himself and then turned to the officer. "General Maitland, abort the programmed reponse. I want a team of your people monitoring our ground forces—*no satellite relays*. They will determine when and what to em-bobble."

Maitland slapped the table. "Sir! That will slow reponse time to the point where some of them may get onto the inner grounds."

For an instant, Avery's face went slack, as if the conflicting threats had finally driven him over the edge. But when he responded, his voice was even, determined. "So? They still have no idea where our generator is. And we have enough conventional force to destroy such infiltrators ten times over. My order stands."

The officer glared at him for a moment. But Maitland had always been a person who followed orders. Avery would have replaced him decades before if that were not the case. He turned back to the terminal, canceled the program, and then talked through it to his analysts at the front of the room, relaying Avery's directive. The intermittent buzzing from beyond the walls ceased.

The Director motioned Lu to follow him. "Anything else?" he asked quietly, when they were out of Maitland's earshot.

Della didn't hesitate. "Yes. Ignore all automated remote intelligence. In the Livermore area, use line-of-sight communications—no relays. We have plenty of people on the ground, and plenty of aircraft. We'll lose some equipment doing it, but we can set up a physical reconnaissance that will catch almost any-one moving around out there. For places further away, Asia especially, we're stuck with the satellites, but at least we should use them for voice and video commu-nication only—no processed data." She barely stopped for breath.

"Okay, I'll do as you recommend. I want you to stay up here, but don't give orders to Maitland."

It took nearly twenty minutes, but in the end Maitland and his analysts had a jury-rigged system of aircraft sweeps that produced something like complete coverage of the Valley every thirty minutes. Unfortunately, most of the aircraft were not equipped with sophisticated sensors. In some cases, the reports were off eyeballs only. Without infrared and side-looking radar, almost anything could remain hidden in the deeper ravines. It made Maitland and his people very unhappy. During the twenties, they had let the old ground-based system slide into oblivion. Instead, enormous resources had been put into the satellite system, one they thought gave them even finer protection, and worldwide. Now that system was being ignored; they might as well be refighting World War II.

Maitland pointed to the status board, which his men were painfully updating with the field reports that were coming in. "See? The people on the ground have missed almost all the concentrations we identified from orbit. The enemy is well-camouflaged. Without good sensors, we're just not going to see him."

"They have spotted several small teams, though."

Maitland shrugged. "Yes, sir. I take it we have permission to bobble them?"

There was a glint in Avery's eyes as he responded to the question. However Lu's theories turned out, Maitland's days with this job were numbered. "Immediately."

A small voice sounded from the general's terminal. "Sir, I'm having some trouble with the update of the Mission Pass area. Uh, two A-five-elevens have overflown the Pass. . . . They both say the bobble there is gone."

Their eyes snapped up to the situation board. The map was constructed with photographic precision. The Mission Pass bobble, the Tinker bobble that had nearly killed her the night before, glinted silver and serene on that board. The satellite system still saw it—or reported seeing it.

Gone. Avery went even paler. Maitland sucked his breath back between his teeth. Here was direct, incontrovertible evidence. They had been taken, fooled. And now they had only the vaguest idea where the enemy might really be and what he might do. "My God. She was right! She was right all along."

Della was not listening. There was no triumph in her. She had been fooled, too. She had believed the techs' smug assurance that ten years was the theoretical minimum for the duration of a bobble. How could she have missed this? *Last night I had them, I'll bet. I had Hoehler and Wili and Mike and everyone who counts. . . . And I let them escape through time to today.* Her mind racing frantically through the implications. If twenty-four-hour bobbles could be cast, then what about sixty-second bobbles—or one-second ones? What advantage could the other side gain from such? *Why, they could—*

"Ma'am?" Someone touched her elbow. Her attention returned to the brightly lit command room. It was Maitland's aide. The general had spoken to her. Della's eyes focused on the two old men.

"I'm sorry. What did you say?"

The general's voice was flat but not hostile. Even surprise was leached from him now. Everything he depended on had failed him. "We just got a call on the satellite network. Max priority and max encryption." That could only be a Director—and the only other surviving director was K.T. in China. "Caller demands to talk to you. Says his name is Miguel Rosas."

37

Mike drove. Fifty meters ahead, almost swallowed up in the fog, he could see the other crawler. Inside it were Paul and Wili and Allison, with Allison driving. It was easy to keep up until Allison trucked off the broad roadway into the hills. He came down a hill-side a little fast, and nearly lost control.

"You okay?" Paul's voice sounded anxiously in his ear. He'd established the laser link just seconds before.

Mike twitched the controls tentatively. "Yeah. But why come straight down that hill?"

"Sorry, Mike." It was Jill—no, Allison. "Sideways would have been worse; might have slipped treads."

Then they were moving through open country. The ring of periscopes was not as good as a wraparound holo, but it did give the sensation that his head was in the open. The keening of the engine covered any natural morning sounds. Except for their crawlers, and a crow flickering past in the mist, nothing moved. The grass was sere and golden, the dirt beneath white

338

and gravelly. An occasional dwarf oak loomed out of the fog and forced Allison and then Mike to detour. He should be able to smell morning dew on the grass, but the only smells were of diesel fuel and paint.

And now the morning fog began to part. Blue filtered through from above. Then the blue became sky. Mike felt like a swimmer come to the surface of a misty sea, looking across the waters at far hills.

There was the war, and it was more fantastic than any old-time movie:

Silver balls floated by the dozens through the sky. Far away, Peacer jets were dark bugs trailing grimy vapor. They swooped and climbed. Their dives ended in flares of color as they strafed Tinker infiltrators on the far side of the Valley. Bombs and napalm burned orange and black through the sea of fog. He saw one diving aircraft replaced by a silvery sphere—which continued the plane's trajectory into the earth. The pilot might wake decades from now—as Allison Parker had done—and wonder what had become of his world. That was a lucky shot. Mike knew the Tinker bobblers were small, not even as powerful as the one Wili brought to LA. Their range with accuracy was only a hundred meters, and the largest bobble they could cast was five or ten meters across. On the other hand, they could be used defensively. The last Mike had heard, the Bay Area Tinkers had got the minimum duration down to fifteen seconds; just a little better and "flicker" tactics would be possible.

Here and there, peeping out of the mist, were bobbles set in the ground: Peacer armor bobbled during the night fighting or Tinkers caught by the monster in the valley. The only difference was size.

The nose of the crawler dipped steeply, and Mike

grunted in surprise, his attention back on his driving. He took the little valley much more slowly than the last one. The forward crawler was almost up the other side when he reached the bottom. His carrier moved quickly through a small stream, and then he was almost laid on his back as it climbed the far side. He pushed the throttle far forward. Power screamed through the treads. The crawler came over the lip of the embankment fast, nose high and fell with a crash.

"The trees ahead. We'll stop there for a couple of minutes." It was Wili's voice. Mike followed the other crawler into an open stand of twisted oaks. Far across the Livermore Valley, two dark gnats peeled off from the general swarm that hovered above the Tinker insurgents and flew toward them. That must be the reason Wili wanted to get under cover. Mike looked up through the scrawny branches and wondered what sort of protection the trees really gave. Even the most primitive thermal sensor should be able to see them sitting here with hot engines.

The jets roared by a couple thousand meters to the west. Their thunder dwindled to nothing. Mike looked again across Livermore Valley.

Where the fighting was heaviest, new bobbles shone almost once a second. With the engines idling, Mike thought he could hear the thunder and thump of more conventional weapons. Two jets dived upon a hidden target and the mists were crisscrossed with their laser fire. The target tried something new: a haze of bobbles—too small to distinguish at this distance—appeared between aircraft and ground. There was a flash of sudden red stars within that haze as the energy beams reflected again and again from the multiple mirrors. It was hard to tell if it made an effective shield. Then he noticed the jets staggering out of their drive. One exploded. The other trailed smoke and flame in a long arc toward the ground. Mike suddenly wondered what would happen to a jet engine if it sucked in a dozen two-centimeter bobbles.

Wili's voice came again. "Mike. The Peacers are going to discover that we have been faking their satellite reception."

"When?" asked Mike.

"Any second. They are changing to aircraft reconnaissance."

Mike looked around him, wishing suddenly that he were on foot. It would be so much easier to hide a human-sized target than a crawler. "So we can't depend on being 'invisible' anymore."

"No. *We* can. I am also speaking with Peacer control on the direct line-of-sight." These last words were spoken by a deep, male voice. Mike started, then realized he was not talking directly to Wili. The fake had a perfect Oregon accent, though the syntax was still Wili's; hopefully that would go unnoticed in the rush of battle. He tried to imagine the manifold images Wili must be projecting to allies and enemies. "They think we're Peacer recon. They have fourteen other crawlers moving around their inner area. As long as we follow their directions, we won't be attacked . . . . And they want us to move closer in."

Closer in. If Wili could get just another five thousand meters closer, he could bobble the Peacer generator.

"Okay. Just tell us which way to go."

"I will, Mike. But there's something else I want you to do first."

"Sure."

"I'm going to give you a satellite connection to Authority High Command. Call them. Insist to speak with Della Lu. Tell her everything you know about our tricks—"

Mike's hands tightened on the drive sticks. "No!"

"—except that we control these two crawlers."

"But *why*?"

"Do it, Mike. If you call now, you'll be able to give away our satellite trick before they have proof. Maybe they will think you're still loyal. It will distract them, anyway. Give away anything you want. I'll listen, too. I'll learn more what's passing at their center. Please, Mike."

Mike gritted his teeth. "Okay, Wili. Put 'em on."

Allison Parker grinned savagely to herself. She hadn't driven a crawler in almost three years—fifty-three if you counted years like the rest of the universe. At the time, she'd thought it a silly waste of taxpayer's money to have recon specialists take a tour with a base security outfit. The idea had been that anyone who collected intelligence should be familiar with the groundside problems of security and deception. Becoming a tank driver had been fun, but she never expected to see the inside of one of these things again.

Yet here she was. Allison gunned the engines, and the little armored carrier almost flew out of the thicket of scrub oak where they'd been hiding. She recognized these hills, even with the hovering spheres and napalm bursting in the distance. Time didn't change some things. Their path ran parallel to a series of cairnlike concrete structures, the ruins of the power lines that had stretched across the Valley. Why, she and . . . Paul . . . had hiked along precisely this way . . . so long ago.

She tried to shake free of the painful double images. The sun was fast burning off the morning fog. Soon the concealment the Tinkers were using to such advantage would be gone. If they couldn't win by then, they never would.

In her earphone, she heard a strange voice reporting their position to the Peacer command center. It was eerie: she knew the message came ultimately from Wili. But he was sitting right behind her and had not spoken a word. The last time she looked, he seemed asleep.

The deception was working. They were doing what Peacer control said, but they were also coming closer and closer to the edge of the inner security area.

"Paul, what I saw from orbit is only about six thousand meters north of here. We'll be closest in another couple of minutes. Is that close enough?"

Paul touched his scalp connector, seemed to think. "No. We'd have to be motionless for almost an hour to bobble from that range. The best trade-off is still four thousand meters. I—Wili—has a spot in mind; he and Jill are doing prelim computations on the assumption we can reach it. Even so, he'll need about thirty seconds once we get there."

After a moment Paul added, "In a couple minutes, we'll break our cover. Wili will stop transmitting and you'll drive like hell straight for their bobbler."

Allison looked through the periscoped hull. The crawler was so close to the security perimeter, the towers and domes of the Enclave blocked her view to the north. The Enclave was a city, and their final dash would take them well inside its boundaries. "We'll be sitting ducks." Her sentence was punctuated by the swelling roar of a stub-winged jet that swept almost directly over them. She hadn't seen or heard it till that instant. But the aircraft wasn't strafing. It was loafing along at less than one hundred meters per second, a low-level recon.

"We have a good chance." Wili's voice came suddenly in her earphone. "We won't make our run until the patrol planes are in good position. We should be in their blind spot for almost five minutes."

"And they'll have other things to worry about," said Paul. "I've been talking to the Tinkers coming in on foot. They all know the site of the Peacer generator now. Some of them have gotten pretty close, closer than we. They don't have our equipment—but the Authority can't know that for sure. When Wili gives the signal, they'll come out of hiding and make their own dash inwards."

The war went far beyond their crawlers, beyond even the Livermore Valley. Paul said a similar battle was being played out in China.

Even so, victory or defeat seemed to depend on what happened to this one crawler in the next few minutes.

38

Della slipped on the earpiece and adjusted the microphone to her throat. She had the undivided attention of Avery, Maitland, and everyone else in earshot. None of them except Hamilton Avery had heard of one Miguel Rosas, but they all knew he had no business on a maximum security channel. "Mike?"

A familiar voice came from the earpiece and the speaker on the terminal. "Hello, Della. I've got some news for you."

"Just calling on this line is news enough. So your people have cracked our comm and recon system."

"Right the first time."

"Where are you calling from?"

"The ridgeline southwest of you. I don't want to say more—I still don't trust your friends. . . . It's just that I trust mine even less." This last was spoken low, almost muttered. "Look. There are other things you don't know. The Tinkers know exactly where your bobbler is hidden."

"What?" Avery turned abruptly to the situation board and motioned for Maitland to check it out.

"How can they know? You have spies? Carry-in bugs?"

Mike's forced chuckle echoed from the speaker. "It's a long story, Della. You would be amused. The old US Air Force had it spotted—just too late to save the world from you. The Tinkers stumbled on the secret only a few weeks ago."

Della glanced questioningly at the Director, but Avery was looking over Maitland's shoulder, at the terminal. The general's people were frantically typing queries, posting results. The general looked up at the Director. "It's possible, sir. Most of the infiltrators are north and west of the Enclave. But the ones closest to the inner zone boundary are also the closest to the generator; they seem to have a preference for that sector."

"It could be an artifact of our increased surveillance in that area."

"Yes, sir." But now Maitland did not sound complacent. Avery nodded to himself. He hadn't believed his own explanation. "Very well. Concentrate tactical air there. I see you have two armored vehicles already tracking along the boundary. Keep them there. Bring in more. I want what infantry we have moved there, too."

"Right. Once we locate them, they're no threat. We have all the firepower."

Della spoke again to Mike. "Where is Paul Hoehler—the man you call Naismith?" Avery stiffened at the question, and his attention returned to her, an almost physical force.

"Look, I really don't know. They have me working

a pointer relay; some of our people don't have their own satellite receivers."

Della cut the connection and said to Avery, "I think he's lying, Director. Our only lever on Mike Rosas is his hatred for certain Tinker potentials, in particular bioscience. He'll resist hurting his personal friends."

"He *knows* Hoehler?" Avery seemed astounded to find someone so close to the ultimate antagonist. "If he knows where Hoehler is . . ." The Director's eyes unfocused. "You've got to squeeze that out of him, Della. Take this conversation off the speaker and talk to him. Promise him anything, tell him anything, but find Hoehler." With a visible effort he turned back to Maitland. "Get me Tioulang in Beijing. I know, I know. Nothing is secure." He smiled, an almost skeletal grimace. "But I don't care if they know what I tell him."

Della resumed the link with Mike. Now that the speaker was off, his voice would sound in her ear only. And with the throat mike, her side of the conversation would be inaudible to those around her. "This is just you and me now, Mike. The brass thinks they got everything they can out of you."

"Oh yeah? And what do you think?"

"I think some large but unknown percentage of what you are telling me is bullshit."

"I guessed that. But you're still talking."

"I think we're both betting we can learn more than the other from talking. Besides—" Her eyes fixed on the Renaissance trigger box sitting on the table before Hamilton Avery. With a small part of her attention she followed what Avery was saying to his counterpart in Beijing. "Besides, I don't think you know what you're up against."

"Enlighten me."

"The Tinker goal is to bobble the Livermore generator. Similarly for the attack on Beijing. You don't realize that if we consider the Peace truly endangered, we will embobble *ourselves*, and continue the struggle decades in the future."

"Hmm. Like the trick we played on you at Mission Pass."

"But on a much larger scale."

"Well, it won't help you. Some of us will wait— and we'll know where to wait. Besides, the Authority's power isn't just in Livermore and Beijing. You need your heavy industry, too."

Della smiled to herself. Mike's phrasing was tacit admission he was still a Tinker. There were deceptions here—deceptions she could penetrate given a little time—but neither of them was pretending loyalties they did not have. Time to give away a little information, information that would do them no good now: "There are a few things you don't know. The Peace has more than two bobble generators."

There was a moment of silence in her ear. "I don't believe you—How many?"

Della laughed quietly. Maitland glanced up at her, then turned back to his terminal. "That is a secret. We've been working on them ever since we suspected Tinker infiltration—spies, we thought. Only a few people know, and we never spoke of it on our comm net. More important than the number is the location; you won't know about them till they come out at you."

There was a longer silence. She had made a point.

"And what other things make 'Peace' unbeatable?" There was sarcasm and something else in his words.

In the middle of the sentence, his voice seemed to catch—as if he had just lifted something. As was usual with a high-crypto channel, there were no background sounds. But the data massaging left enough in the voice to recognize tones and sublinguistical things like this sudden exhalation. The sound, almost a grunt, had not been repeated. If she could just get him to talk a little more.

There was a secret that might do it. Renaissance. Besides, it was something she owed him, perhaps owed all the enemy. "You should know that if you force this on us, we'll not let you grow strong during our absence. The Authority"—for once calling it "the Peace" stuck in her throat—"has planted nukes in the Valley. And we have such bombs on rockets. If we bobble up ... if we bobble up, your pretty Tinker culture gets bombed back to the Stone Age, and we'll build anew when we come out."

Still a longer silence. *Is he talking to someone else? Has he broken the connection?* "Mike?"

"Della, why are you on their side?"

He'd asked her that once before. She bit her lip. "I—I didn't dream up Renaissance, Mike. I think we can win without it. The world has had decades now more peaceful than any in human history. When we took over, the race was at the edge of the precipice. You know that. The nation states were bad enough; they would have destroyed civilization if left to themselves. But even worse, their weapons had become so cheap that small groups—some reasonable, some monstrous—would have had them. If the world could barely tolerate a dozen killer nations, how could it survive thousands of psychotics with rad bombs and war plagues?

"I know you understand what I'm saying. You felt

that way about bioscience. *There are other things as bad, Mike.*" She stopped abruptly, wondering who was manipulating whom. And suddenly she realized that Mike, the enemy, was one of the few people she could ever talk to, one of the few people who could understand the ... things ... she had done. And perhaps he was the only person—outside of herself—whose disapproval could move her.

"I understand," came Mike's voice. "Maybe history will say the Authority gave the human race time to save itself, to come up with new institutions. You've had fifty years; it hasn't been all bad. . . . But no matter what either of us wants, it's ending now. And this 'Renaissance' will destroy whatever good you've done." His voice caught again.

"Don't worry. We'll win fair and square and there'll be no Renaissance." She was watching the main display. One of the crawlers had turned almost directly inward, toward the heart of the Enclave. Della cut audio and got the attention of Maitland's aide. She nodded questioningly at the crawler symbol on the display.

The colonel leaned across from his chair and said quietly, "They saw Tinkers within the perimeter. They're chasing."

The symbol moved in little jerks, updated by the nearly manual control they had been reduced to. Suddenly the crawler symbol disappeared from the board. Avery sucked in his breath. An analyst looked at his displays and said almost immediately, "We lost laser comm. They may have been bobbled ... or may be out of sight."

Possible. The ground was rough, even inside the Enclave boundary. Riding a crawler over that would be an exciting thing. . . . And then Della understood the mystery in Mike's speech. *"Mr. Director."* Her shout cut across all other voices. "That crawler isn't looking for the enemy. It *is* the enemy!"

39

While they drove parallel to the perimeter fence, the ground was not too rough. When they turned inward, it would be a different story. There was a system of ditches running along the fence.

Beyond that was the interior of the Enclave. Allison risked a glance every now and then. It was like the future she had always imagined: spires, tall buildings, wide swaths of green. Paul said Authority ground troops were moving into the area, but right now all was peaceful, abandoned.

Wait. Three men came running out of the ditches. They paused at the fence and then were somehow through. Two of them carried heavy backpacks. These were their Tinker allies. One waved to their crawler, and then they disappeared among the buildings.

"Turn here. Follow them inward," said Paul. "Wili's told the Peacer command we're in hot pursuit."

Allison pushed/pulled on the control sticks. The armored vehicle spun on its treads, one reversed, the other still pulling forward. Through the side periscope she saw Mike's crawler, moving off to the north. No doubt Wili had told him not to turn.

They shot forward at top speed, the engines an eerie screaming all around them. Beside Allison, Paul was gasping. Thirty kph across open terrain was rough as any air maneuver. Then they were falling, and the view ahead was filled with concrete. They flew over the edge of the ditch and crashed downward onto the floor. The restraint webbing couldn't entirely absorb the shock. For a moment Allison was in a daze, her hands freezing the controls into fast forward. The crawler ran up the steep far wall and teetered there an instant, as if unsure whether to proceed upward or fall on its back.

Then they slammed down on the other side, collapsing the fence. Whatever automatic defenses lived here must be temporarily disabled.

She ground clear of the concrete-and-steel rubble, then risked a glance at Paul. "Oh, my God." He was slumped forward, a wash of red spread down his face. Red was smeared on the wall in front of him. Somehow he had not tied down properly.

Allison slowed the crawler. She twisted in her seat, saw that the boy remained comatose. "Wili! Paul's hurt!"

A woman's voice shrieked in her ear, *"You dumb bitch!"*

Wili twisted, his face agonized, like someone trying to waken from a dream.

But if he woke, if his dream died, then all their dreams would die. "Drive, Allison. Please drive." Wili's synthetic voice came cool from her earpiece. "Paul ... Paul wants this more than anything." Behind her, the boy's real voice was softly moaning. And Paul moved not at all.

Allison closed out everything but her job: they were on a surfaced street. She rammed the throttle forward, took the crawler up to seventy kph. She had only vague impressions of the buildings on either side of them. It looked like residential housing, though more opulent than in her time. All was deserted. Coming up on a T-intersection. Over the roofs of the multistory residences, the towers at the center of the Enclave seemed no nearer.

Wili's voice continued. "Right at the intersection. Then left and left. Foot soldiers are coming from the east. So far they think we're one of them, but I'm breaking laser contact . . . *now*"—Allison whipped into the turn—"and they should guess what we are very soon."

They continued so for several minutes. It was like dealing with an ordinary voice program: turn right. Turn left. Slow down. Keep to the edge of the street.

"Five hundred meters. Take the service alley here. They're onto us. Gunships coming. They can't locate us precisely enough to bobble. Whoever sees us is to shoot." He was silent again as Allison negotiated the alley. Still no sign of life from Paul.

"He still lives, Allison. I can still . . . hear . . . him a little."

Through the front periscope she had a glimpse of something dark and fast cross the narrow band of sky between the houses.

"Pull under that overhang. Stop. Throttle up to charge the cells. Thirty seconds for local conditions and I'll be ready to fire."

The moment they were stopped, Allison was out of

her harness and bending over Paul. "Now leave me. I need to think. Take Paul. Save Paul."

She looked at the boy. He still hadn't opened his eyes. He was further off than she had ever seen him.

"But, Wili—"

His body twitched, and the synthetic voice was suddenly angry in her ear. "I need time to think, and I don't have it. Their planes are on the way. Get out. *Get out!*"

Allison unbuckled Paul and removed the scalp connector. He was breathing, but his face remained slack. She cranked at the rear doors, praying that nothing had been warped by their fall into the ditch. The doors popped open and cool morning air drifted in, along with the increased keening of the engines.

She ripped off her headset and struggled to get the old man's body over her shoulder. As she staggered past Wili, she noticed his lips were moving. She bent down awkwardly to listen. The boy was mumbling, "Run, run, run, run. . . ."

Allison did her best.

40

No one understood the conflict as Wili did. Even when he was linked with Jill, Paul had only a second-hand view. And after Paul, there was no one who saw more than fragments of the picture. It was Wili who ran the Tinker side of the show—and to some extent the Peacer side, too. Without his directions in Paul's voice, the thousands of separate operations going on all over the Earth would be so scattered in time and effect that the Authority would have little trouble keeping its own control system going.

But Wili knew his time would end very, very soon.

From the crawler's recon camera, he watched Paul and Allison moving away into the managerial residences. Their footsteps came fainter in his exterior microphones. Would he ever know if Paul survived?

Through the narrow gap between the sides of the alley a Peacer satellite floated beyond the blue sky. One reason he had chosen this parking spot was to have that line of sight. In ninety seconds, the radio star would slide behind carven wooden eaves. He would lose it, and thus its relay to synchronous altitude, and thus his control of things worldwide. He would be deaf, dumb, and blind. But ninety seconds from now, it wouldn't matter; he and all the other Tinkers would win or lose in sixty.

The whole system had spasmed when Paul was knocked out. Jill had stopped responding. For several minutes, Wili had struggled with all the high-level computations. Now Jill was coming back on line; she was almost finished with the local state computations. The capacitors would be fully charged seconds after that. Wili surveyed the world one last time.

From orbit he saw golden morning spread across Northern California. Livermore Valley sparkled with a false dew that was really dozens—hundreds—of bobbles. Unaided humans would need many versions of this picture to understand what Wili saw at once.

There were ground troops a couple of thousand meters east of him. They had fanned out, obviously didn't know where he was. The tricky course he had given Allison would keep him safe from them for at least five minutes.

Jets had been diverted from the north side of the Valley. He watched them crawl across the landscape at nearly four hundred meters per second. They were the real threat. They could see him before the capacitors were charged. There was no way to divert them or to trick them. The pilots had been instructed to use their own eyes, to find the crawler, and to destroy it. Even if they failed in the last, they would report an accurate position—and the Livermore bobbler would get him.

He burst-transmitted a last message to the Tinker teams in the Valley: Paul's voice announced the im-

minent bobbling and assigned new missions. Because
of Wili's deceptions, their casualties had been light;
that might change now. He told them what he had
learned about Renaissance and redirected them
against the missile sites he had detected. He wondered
fleetingly how many would feel betrayed to learn of
Renaissance, would wish that he—Paul—would stop
the assault. But if Paul were really here, if Paul could
think as fast as Wili, he'd've done the same.

He must end the Peace so quickly that Renaissance
died, too.

Wili passed from one satellite to another, till he
was looking down on Beijing at midnight. Without
Wili's close supervision, the fighting had been bloodier:
there were bobbles scattered through the ruins of
the old city, but there were bodies, too, bodies that
would not live again. The Chinese Tinkers had to get
in very close; they did not have a powerful bobbler
or the Wili/Jill processor. Even so, they might win.
Wili had guided three teams to less than one thousand meters of the Beijing bobbler. He sent his last
advice, showing them a transient gap in the defense.

Messages sent or automatically sending. Now there
was only his own mission. The mission all else depended on.

From high above, Wili saw an aircraft sweep south
over the alley. (Its boom crashed around the carrier,
but Wili's own senses were locked out and he barely
felt it.) The pilot *must* have seen him. How long till
the follow-up bomb run?

The Authority's great bobbler was four thousand
meters north of him. He and Jill had made a deadly
minimax decision in deciding on that range. He
"looked at" the capacitors. They were still ten seconds from the overcharge he needed. Ten seconds?

The charge rate was declining as charge approached the necessary level. Their haywired interface to the crawler's electrical generator was failing. Extrapolation along the failure curve: thirty seconds to charge.

The other aircraft had been alerted. Wili saw courses change. More extrapolation: it would be very, very close. He could save himself by self-bobbling, the simplest of all generations. He could save himself and lose the war.

Wili watched in an omniscient daze, watched from above as death crept down on the tiny crawler.

Something itched. Something demanded attention. He relaxed his hold, let resources be diverted . . . and Jill's image floated up.

Wili! Go! You can still go! Jill flooded him with a last burst of data, showing that all processes would proceed automatically to completion. Then she cut him off.

And Wili was alone in the crawler. He looked around, vision blurred, suddenly aware of sweat and diesel fuel and turbine noise. He groped for his harness release, then rolled off onto the floor. He barely felt the scalp connector tear free. He came to his feet and blundered out the rear doors into the sunlight.

He didn't hear the jets' approach.

Paul moaned. Allison couldn't tell if he was trying to say something or was simply responding to the rough handling. She got under his weight and stagger-ran across the alley toward a stone-walled patio. The gate was open; there was no lock. Allison kicked aside a child's tricycle and laid Paul down behind the waist-high wall. Should be safe from shrapnel here, except—she glanced over her shoulder at the glass wall that stretched across the interior side of the patio. Beyond was carpeting, elegant furniture. That glass could come showering down if the building got hit. She started to pull Paul behind the marble table that dominated the patio.

"No! Wili. Did he make it?" He struggled weakly against her hands.

The sky to the north showed patches of smoke, smudged exhaust trails, a vagrant floating bobble where someone had missed a target—but that was all. Wili had not acted; the crawler sat motionless, its engines screaming. Somewhere else she heard treads.

The boom was like a wall of sound smashing over them. Windows on both sides of the street flew inward. Allision had a flickering impression of the aircraft as it swept over the street. Her attention jerked back to the sky, scanned. A dark gnat hung there, surrounded by the dirty aureole of its exhaust. There was no sound from this follow-up craft; it was coming straight in. The length of the street—and the crawler—would be visible to it. She watched it a moment, then dived to the tiled patio deck next to Paul.

Scarcely time to swear, and the ground smashed up into them.

Allison didn't lose consciousness, but for a long moment she didn't really know where she was. A girl in a gingham dress leaned over an old man, seeing red spread across a beautiful tile floor.

A million garbage cans dropped and rattled around her.

Allison touched her face, felt dust and untorn skin. The blood wasn't hers.

How bad was he hurt?

The old man looked up at her. He brushed her hands away with some last manic strength. "Allison.

Did we win ... please? After all these years, to get that bastard Avery." His speech slurred into mumbling.

Allison came to her knees and looked over the wall. The street was in ruins, riddled with flying debris. The crawler had been hit, its front end destroyed. Fire spread crackling from what was left of its fuel. Under the treads something else burned green and violent. And the sky to the north ...

... was as empty as before. No bobble stood where she knew the Peace generator was hidden. The battle might yet go on for hours, but Allison knew that they had lost. She looked down at the old man and tried to smile. "It's there, Paul. You won."

41

"We got one of them, sir. Ground troops have brought in three survivors. They're—"

"From the nearer one? Where is that second crawler?" Hamilton Avery leaned over the console, his hands pale against the base of the keyboard.

"We don't know, sir. We have three thousand men on foot in that area. We'll have it in a matter of minutes, even if tac air doesn't get it first. About the three we picked—"

Avery angrily cut the connection. He sat down abruptly, chewed at his lip. "He's getting closer, I know it. Everything we do seems a victory, but is really a defeat." He clenched his fists, and Della could imagine him screaming to himself: *What can we do?* She had seen administrators go over the edge in Mongolia, frozen into inaction or suicidal overreaction. The difference was that *she* had been the boss in Mongolia Here . . .

Avery opened his fists with visible effort. "Very

well. What is the status of Beijing? Is the enemy any closer than before?"

General Maitland spoke to his terminal. He looked at the response in silence. Then, "Director, we have lost comm with them. The recon birds show the Beijing generator has been bobbled. . . ." He paused as though waiting for some explosion from his boss. But Avery was composed again. Only the faint glassiness of his stare admitted his terror.

"—and of course that could be faked, too," Avery said quietly. "Try for direct radio confirmation . . . from someone known to us." Maitland nodded, started to turn away. "And, General. Begin the computations to bobble us up." He absently caressed the Renaissance trigger that sat on the table before him. "I can tell you the coordinates."

Maitland relayed the order to try for shortwave communication with Beijing. But he personally entered the coordinates as Avery spoke them. As Maitland set up the rest of the program, Della eased into a chair behind the Director. "Sir, there is no need for this."

Hamilton Avery smiled his old, genteel smile, but he wasn't listening to her. "Perhaps not, my dear. That is why we are checking for confirmation from Beijing." He flipped open the Renaissance box, revealing a key pad. A red light began blinking on the top. Avery fiddled with a second cover, which protected some kind of button. "Strange. When I was a child, people talked about 'pushing the button' as though there was a magic red button that could bring nuclear war. I doubt if ever power was just so concentrated. . . . But here I have almost exactly that, Della. One big red button. We've worked hard these last few months to make it effective. You know, we really didn't have that many nukes before. We never saw how they might be necessary to preserve the Peace. But if Beijing is really gone, this will be the only way."

He looked into Della's eyes. "It won't be so bad, my dear. We've been very selective. We know the areas where our enemy is concentrated; making them uninhabitable won't have any lasting effect on the race."

To her left, Maitland had completed his preparations. The display showed the standard menu she had seen in his earlier operations. Even by Authority standards, it looked old-fashioned. Quite likely the control software was unchanged from the first years of the Authority.

Maitland had overridden all the fail-safes. At the bottom of the display, outsized capitals blinked:

WARNING! THE ABOVE TARGETS ARE FRIENDLY. CONTlNUE?

A simple "yes<CR>" would bobble the industrial core of the Authority into the next century.

"We have shortwave communication with Peace forces at Beijing, Director." The voice came unseen, but it was recognizably Maitland's chief aide. "These are troops originally from the Vancouver franchise. Several of them are known to people here. At least we can verify these are really our men."

"And?" Avery asked quietly.

"The center of the Beijing Enclave is bobbled, sir. They can see it from where they're positioned. The fighting has pretty much ended. Apparently the enemy is lying low, waiting for our reaction. Your instructions are requested."

"In a minute," Avery smiled. "General, you may proceed as planned." That minute would be more than fifty years in the future.

"yes<CR>," the general typed. The familiar buzzing hum sounded irregularly, and one after another the locations on the list were marked as bobbled: Los Angeles Enclave, Brasilia Enclave, Redoubt 001 . . . . It was quickly done, what no enemy could ever do. All other activity in the room ceased; they all knew. The Authority was now committed. In fact, most of the Authority was gone from the world by that act. All that remained was this one generator, this one command center—and the hundreds of nuclear bombs that Avery's little red button would rain upon the Earth.

Maitland set up the last target, and the console showed:

FINAL WARNING! PROJECTION WILL SELF-ENCLOSE. CONTINUE?

Now Hamilton Avery was punching an elaborate pass-code into his red trigger box. In seconds, he would issue the command that would poison sections of continents. Then Maitland could bobble them into a future made safe for the "Peace."

The shock in Della's face must finally have registered on him. "I am not a monster, Miss Lu. I have never used more than the absolute minimum force necessary to preserve the Peace. After I launch Renaissance, we will bobble up, and then we will be in a future where the Peace can be reestablished. And though it will be an instant to us, I assure you I will always feel the guilt for the price that had to be paid."

He gestured at his trigger box. "It is a responsibility I take solely upon myself."

That's damned magnanimous of you. She wondered fleetingly if hard-boiled types like Della Lu and Hamilton Avery always ended up like this—rationalizing the destruction of all they claimed to protect.

Maybe not. Her decision had been building for weeks, ever since she had learned of Renaissance. It had dominated everything after her talk with Mike. Della glanced around the room, wished she had her sidearm: she would need it during the next few minutes. She touched her throat and said clearly, "See you later, Mike."

There was quick understanding on Avery's face, but he didn't have a chance. With her right hand she flicked the red box down the table, out of Avery's reach. Almost simultaneously, she smashed Maitland's throat with the edge of her left. Turning, she leaned over the general's collapsing form—and typed:

"yes<CR>"

42

Wili moped across the lawn, his hands stuck deep in his pockets, his face turned downward. He kicked up little puffs of dust where the grass was brownest. The new tenants were lazy about watering, or else maybe the irrigation pipes were busted.

This part of Livermore had been untouched by the fighting; the losers had departed peaceably enough, once they saw bobbles sprout over their most important resources. Except for the dying grass, it was beautiful here, the buildings as luxurious as Wili could imagine. When they turned on full electric power, it made the Jonque palaces in LA look like hovels. And most anything here—the aircraft, the automobiles, the mansions—could be his.

Just my luck. I get everything I ever wanted, and then I lose the people that are more important. Paul had decided to drop out. It made sense and Wili was not angry about it, but it hurt anyway. Wili thought back to their meeting, just half an hour before. He had guessed the moment he'd seen Paul's face. Wili had tried to ignore it, had rushed into the subject he'd thought they were to talk about: "I just talked to those doctors we flew in from France, Paul. They say my insides are as normal as anything. They measured me every way"—he had undergone dozens of painful tests, massive indignities compared to what had been done to him at Scripps, and yet much less powerful. The French doctors were not bioscientists, but simply the best medical staff the European director would tolerate—"and they say I'm using my food, that I'm growing fast." He grinned. "Bet I will be more than one meter seventy."

Paul leaned back in his chair and returned the smile. The old man was looking good himself. He'd had a bad concussion during the battle, and for while the doctors weren't sure he would survive. "I'll bet, too. It's exactly what I'd been hoping. You're going to be around for a long time, and the world's going to be a better place for it. And . . ." His voice trailed off, and he didn't meet the boy's look. Wili held his breath, praying *Dio* his guess wouldn't be correct. They sat in silence for an awkward moment. Wili looked around, trying to pretend that nothing of import was to be said. Naismith had appropriated the office of some Peacer bigwig. It had a beautiful view of the hills to the south, yet it was plainer than most, almost as if it had been designed for the old man all along. The walls were unadorned, though there was a darker rectangle of paint on the wall facing Paul's desk. A picture had hung there once. Wili wondered about that.

Finally Naismith spoke. "Strange. I think I've done penance for blindly giving them the bobble in the first place. I have accomplished everything I dreamed of all these years since the Authority destroyed the world. . . . And yet—Wili, I'm going to drop out, fifty years at least."

"Paul! Why?" It was said now, and Wili couldn't keep the pain from his voice.

"Many reasons. Many good reasons." Naismith leaned forward intently. "I'm very old, Wili. I think you'll see many from my generation go. We know the bioscience people in stasis at Scripps have ways of helping us."

"But there are others. They can't be the only ones with the secret."

"Maybe. The bioscience types are surfacing very slowly. They can't be sure if humanity will accept them, even though the plagues are decades passed."

"Well, *stay.* Wait and see." Wili cast wildly about, came up with a reason that might be strong enough. "Paul, if you go, you may never see Allison again. I thought—"

"You thought I loved Allison, that I hated the Authority on her account as much as any." His voice went low. "You are right, Wili, *and don't you ever tell her that!* The fact that she lives, that she is just as I always remembered her, is a miracle that goes beyond all my dreams. But she is another reason I must leave, and soon. It hurts every day to see her; she likes me, but almost as a stranger. The man she knew has died, and I see pity in her more than anything else. I must escape from that."

He stopped. "There's something else too. . . . Wili, I wonder about Jill. Did I lose the only one I ever really had? I have the craziest dreams from when I was knocked out. She was trying like hell to bring me back. She seemed as real as anyone . . . and more caring. But there's no way that program could have been sentient; we're nowhere near systems that powerful. No *person* sacrificed her life for us." The look in his eyes made the sentence a question.

It was a question that had hovered in Wili's mind ever since Jill had driven him out of the crawler. He thought back. He had known Jill ... used the Jill program ... for almost nine months. Her projection had been there when he was sick; she had helped him learn symbiotic programming. Something inside him had always thought her one of his best friends. He tried not to guess how much stronger Paul's feelings must be. Wili remembered Jill's hysterical reaction when Paul had been hurt; she had disappeared from the net for minutes, only coming back at the last second to try to save Wili. And Jill was complex, complex enough that any attempt at duplication would fail; part of her "identity" came from the exact pattern of processor interconnection that had developed during her first years with Paul.

Yet Wili had been inside the program; he had seen the limitations, the inflexibilities. He shook his head. "Yes, Paul. The Jill program was not a person. Maybe someday we'll have systems big enough, but ... Jill was j-just a s-simulation." And Wili believed what he was saying. So why were they sitting here with tears in their eyes?

The silence stretched into a minute as two people remembered a love and a sacrifice that couldn't really exist. Finally, Wili forced the weirdness away and looked at the old man. If Paul had been alone before, what now?

"I could go with you, Paul," and Wili didn't know if he was begging or offering.

Naismith shook himself and seemed to come back to the present. "I can't stop you, but I hope you don't." He smiled. "Don't worry about me. I didn't last this long by being a sentimental fool *all* the time.

"Your time is now, Wili. There is a lot for you to do."

"Yes. I guess. There's still Mike. He needs . . ." Wili stopped, seeing the look on Paul's face. "*No!* Not Mike too?"

"Yes. But not for several months. Mike is not very popular just now. Oh, he came through in the end; I don't think we'd've won without him. But the Tinkers know what he did in La Jolla. And he knows; he's having trouble living with it."

"So he's going to run away." *Too.*

"No. At least that's not the whole story. Mike has some things to do. The first is Jeremy. From the logs here at Livermore, I can figure to within a few days when the boy will come out of stasis. It's about fifty years from now. Mike is going to come out a year or so before that. Remember, Jeremy is standing near the sea entrance. He could very likely be killed by falling rock when the bobble finally bursts. Mike is going to make sure that doesn't happen.

"A couple years after that, the bobble around the Peacer generator here in Livermore will burst. Mike will be here for that. Among other things, he's going to try to save Della Lu. You know, we would have lost without her. The Peacers had *won*, yet they were going ahead with that crazy world-wrecker scheme. Both Mike and I agree she must have bobbled their projector. Things are going to be mighty dangerous for her the first few minutes after they come out of stasis."

Wili nodded without looking up. He still didn't understand Della Lu. She was tougher and meaner, in some ways, than anyone he had known in LA. But in others—well, he knew why Mike cared for her, even after everything she had done. He hoped Mike could save her.

"And that's about the time I'm coming back, Wili. A lot of people don't realize it, but the war isn't over. The enemy has lost a major battle, but has escaped forward through time. We've identified most of their bobbled refuges, but Mike thinks there are some secret ones underground. Maybe they'll come out the same time as the Livermore generator, maybe a lot later. This is a danger that goes into the foreseeable future. Someone has to be around to fight those battles, just in case the locals don't believe in the threat."

"And that will be you?"

"I'll be there. At least through Round Two."

So that was that. Paul was right, Wili knew. But it still felt like the losses of the past: Uncle Sly, the trek to La Jolla without Paul. "Wili, you can do it. You don't *need* me. When I am forgotten, you will still be remembered—for what you will do as much as for what you already did." Naismith looked intently at the boy.

Wili forced a smile and stood. "You will be proud to hear of me when you return." He turned. He must leave with those words.

Paul stopped him, smiled. "It's not just yet, Wili. I'll be here for another two or three weeks, at least."

And Wili turned again, ran around the desk, and hugged Paul Naismith as hard as he dared.

Screeching tires and, *"Hey!* You wanna get killed?"

Wili looked up in startled shock as the half-tonne truck swerved around him and accelerated down the street. It wasn't the first time in the last ten days he'd nearly daydreamed himself into a collision. These automobiles were so fast, they were on top of you before you knew it. Wili trotted back to the curb and looked around. He had wandered a thousand meters from Paul's office. He recognized the area. This part of the Enclave contained the Authority's archives and automatic logging devices. The Tinkers were taking the place apart. Somehow, it had been missed in the last frantic bobbling, and Allison was determined to learn every Peacer secret that existed outside of Stasis. Wili sheepishly realized where his feet had been leading him: to visit all his friends, to find out if *any*one thought the present was worth staying in.

"Are you okay, Mr. Wáchendon?" Two workers came running up, attracted by the sounds of near calamity. Wili had gotten over being recognized everywhere (after all, he did have an unusual appearance for hereabouts), but the obvious respect he received was harder to accept. "Damn Peacer drivers," one of them said. "I wonder if some of 'em don't know they lost the war."

"Sí. Fine," answered Wili, wishing he hadn't made such a fool of himself. "Is Allison Parker here?"

They led him into a nearby building. The air-conditioning was running full blast. It was downright chilly by Wili's standards. But Allison was there, dressed in vaguely military-looking shirt and pants, directing some sort of packing operation. Her men were filling large cartons with plastic disks—old-world memory devices, Wili suspected. Allison was concentrating on the job, smiling and intent. For an instant Wili had that old double vision, was seeing his other friend with this body ... the one who never really existed. The mortal had outlived the ghost.

Then the worker beside him said diffidently, "Captain Parker?" and the spell was broken.

Allison looked up and grinned broadly. "Hey, Wili!" She walked over and draped an arm across his shoulders. "I've been so busy this last week, I haven't seen any of my old friends. What's happening?" She led him toward an interior doorway, paused there and said over her shoulder, "Finish Series E. I'll be back in a few minutes." Wili smiled to himself. From the day of victory, Allison had made it clear she wouldn't tolerate second-class citizenship. Considering the fact that she was their only expert on twentieth-century military intelligence, the Tinkers had little choice but to accept her attitude.

As they walked down a narrow hall, neither spoke. Allison's office was a bit warmer than the outer room, and free of fan noises. Her desk was covered with printouts. A Peacer display device sat at its center. She waved him to a seat and patted the display. "I know, everything they have here is childish by Tinker standards. But it works and at least I understand it."

"Allison, a-are you going to drop out, too?" Wili blurted out.

The question brought her up short. "Drop out? You mean bobble up? Not on your life, kiddo. I just came back, remember? I have a lot to do." Then she saw how seriously he meant the question. "Oh, Wili. I'm sorry. You know about Mike and Paul, don't you?" She stopped, frowned at some sadness of her own. "I think it makes sense for them to go, Wili. Really.

"But *not* for me." The enthusiasm was back in her voice. "Paul talks about this battle being just Round One of some 'war through time.' Well, he's wrong about one thing. The first round was fifty years ago. I don't know if those Peacer bastards are responsible for the plagues, but I do know they destroyed the world we had. They did destroy the United States of America." Her lips settled into a thin line.

"I'm going back over their records. I'm going to identify every single bobble they cast during the takeover. I'll bet there are more than a hundred thousand of my people out there in stasis. They're all coming back into normal time during the next few years. Paul has a program that uses the Peacer logs to compute exactly when. Apparently, all the projections were for fifty/sixty years, with the smallest bursting first. There's still Vandenberg and Langley and dozens more. That's a pitiful fraction of the millions we once were, but I'm going to be there and I'm going to save all I can."

"Save?"

She shrugged. "The environment around the bobbles can be dangerous the first few seconds. I was nearly killed coming out. They'll be disoriented as hell. They have nukes in there; I don't want those fired off in a panic. And I don't know if your plagues are really dead. Was I just lucky? I'm going to have to dig up some bioscience people."

"Yes," said Wili, and told her about the wreckage Jeremy had shown him back on the Kaladze farm. Somewhere, high in the air within the Vandenberg stasis, was *part* of a jet aircraft. The pilot might still be alive, but how could he survive the first instants of normal time?

Allison nodded as he spoke, and made some notes. "Yes. That's the sort of thing I mean. We'll have a hard time saving that fellow, but we'll try."

She leaned back in her chair. "That's only half of what I must do. Wili, the Tinkers are so bright in many ways, but in others . . . well, 'naive' is the only word that springs to mind. It's not their fault, I know. For generations they've had no say in what happens outside their own villages. The Authority didn't tolerate governments—at least as they were known in the twentieth century. A few places were permitted small republics; most were lucky to get feudalism, like in Aztlán.

"With the Authority gone, most of America—outside of the Southwest—has no government at all. It's fallen back into anarchy. Power is in the hands of private police forces like Mike worked for. It's peaceful just now, because the people in these protection rackets don't realize the vacuum the Authority's departure has created. But when they do, there'll be bloody chaos."

She smiled. "I see I'm not getting through. I can't blame you; you don't have anything to refer to. The Tinker society has been a very peaceful one. But that's the problem. They're like sheep—and they're going to get massacred if they don't change. Just look at what's happened here:

"For a few weeks we had something like an army. But now the sheep have broken down into their little interest groups, their families, their businesses. They've divided up the territory, and God help me if some of them aren't selling it, selling the weapons, selling the vehicles—and to whomever has the gold! It's suicide!"

And Wili saw that she might be right. Earlier that week he had run into Roberto Richardson, the Jonque bastard who'd beaten him at La Jolla. Richardson had been one of the hostages, but he had escaped before the LA rescue. The fat slob was the type who could always land on his feet, and running. He was up here at Livermore, dripping gAu. And he was buying everything that moved: autos, tanks, crawlers, aircraft.

The man was a strange one. He'd made a big show of being friendly, and Wili was cool enough now to take advantage. Wili asked the Jonque what he was going to do with his loot. Richardson had been vague, but said he wasn't returning to Aztlán. "I like the freedom here, Wáchendon. No rules. Think I may move north. It could be very profitable." And he'd had some advice for Wili, advice that just now seemed without ulterior motive: "Don't go back to LA, Wáchendon. The Alcalde loves you—at least for the moment. But the Ndelante has figured out who you are, and old Ebenezer doesn't care how big a hero you are up here at Livermore."

Wili looked back at Allison. "What can you do to stop it?"

"The things I've already said for a start. A hundred thousand new people, most with my attitudes, should help the education process. And when the dust has settled, I'm hoping we'll have something like a decent government. It won't be in Aztlán. Those guys are straight out of the sixteenth century; wouldn't be surprised if they're the biggest of the new land grabbers. And it won't be the ungoverned lands that most of the US has become. In all of North America, there seems to only one representative democracy left—the Republic of New Mexico. It's pretty pitiful geographically, doesn't control much more than old New Mexico. But they seem to have the ideals we need. I think a lot of my old friends will think the same.

"And that's just the beginning, Wili. That's just housekeeping. The last fifty years have been a dark age in some ways. But technology has progressed. Your electronics is as far advanced as I imagined it would be.

"Wili, the human race was on the edge of something great. Given another few years, we would have colonized the inner solar system. That dream is still close to people's consciousness—I've seen how popular Celest is. We can have that dream for real now, and easier than we twentieth-century types could have done it. I'll bet that, hiding away in the theory of bobbles, there are ideas that will make it trivial."

They talked for a long while, probably longer than the busy Allison had imagined they would. When he left, Wili was as much in a daze as when he arrived—only now his mind was in the clouds. He was going to learn some physics. Math was the heart of everything, but you had to have something to apply it to. With his own mind and the tools he had learned to use, he would make those things Allison dreamed of. And if Allison's fears about the next few years turned out to be true, he would be around to help out on that, too.

Here is an excerpt from Between the Strokes of Night *by Charles Sheffield, coming in July 1985 from Baen Books:* `

Pentecost—A.D. 27698

The last shivering swimmer had emerged from the underground river, and now it would be possible to assemble the final results. Peron Turco pulled the warm cape closer about his shoulders and looked back and forth along the line.

There they stood. Four months of preliminary selection had winnowed them down to a bare hundred, from the many thousands who had entered the original trials. And in the next twenty minutes it would be reduced again, to a jubilant twenty-five.

Everyone was muddied, grimy, and bone-weary. The final trial had been murderous, pushing minds and bodies to the limit. The four-mile underwater swim in total darkness, fighting chilling currents through a labyrinth of connecting caves, had been physically demanding. But the mental pressure, knowing that the oxygen supply would last only for five hours, had been much worse. Most of the contestants were slumped now on the stone flags, warming themselves in the bright sunlight, rubbing sore muscles and sipping sugar drinks. It would be a little while before the scores could be tallied, but already their attention was turning from the noisy crowds to the huge display that formed one outer wall in the coliseum.

Peron shielded his eyes against Cassay's morning brilliance and studied each face in turn along the long line. By now he knew where the real competition lay, and from their expressions he sought to gauge his own chances. Lum was at the far end, squatting cross-legged. He was eating fruit, but he looked bored and sweaty.

Ten days ago Peron had met him and dismissed Lum as soft and overweight, a crudely-built and oafish youth who had reached the final hundred contestants by a freakish accident. Now he knew better. Peron had revised his assessment three times, each one upwards. Now he felt sure that Lum would be somewhere high in the final twenty-five.

And so would the girl Elissa, three positions to the left. Peron had marked her early as formidable competition. She had started ten minutes ahead of him in the first trial, when they made the night journey through the middle of Villasylvia, the most difficult and dangerous forest on the surface of Pentecost.

Now Elissa turned to look at him while he was still staring along the line at her. She grinned, and he quickly averted his eyes. If Elissa didn't finish among the winners that would be bad news for Peron, too, because he was convinced that wherever they placed she would rank somewhere above him.

He looked back at the board. The markers were going up on the great display, showing the names of the remaining contestants. Peron counted them as they were posted. Only seventy-two. The last round of trials had been fiercely difficult, enough to eliminate over a quarter of the finalists completely.

Peron wished he could feel more confidence. He was sure (wasn't he?) that he was in the top thirty. He *hoped* he was in the top twenty, and in his dreams he saw himself as high as fourth or fifth. But with contestants drawn from the whole planet, and the competition of such high caliber . . .

The crowd roared. At last! The scores were finally appearing. The displays were assembled slowly and painstakingly. The judges conferred in great secrecy, knowing that the results would be propagated instantly over the entire planet, and that a mistake would ruin their reputations. Everything was checked and rechecked before it went onto the board.

Peron had watched recordings of recent Planetfests, over and over, but this one was different and more elaborate. Trials were held every four years. Usually the prizes were high positions in the government of Pentecost, and maybe a chance to see the Fifty Worlds. But the twenty-year games, like this one, had a whole new level of significance. There were still the usual prizes, certainly. But they were not the real reward. There was that rumored bigger prize: a possible opportunity to meet and work with the Immortals.

And what did *that* mean? No one could say. No one Peron knew had ever seen one, ever met one. They were the ultimate mystery figures, the ones who lived forever, the ones who came back every generation to bring knowledge from the stars. Stars that they were said to reach in a few days—in conflict with everything that the scientists of Pentecost believed about the laws of the Universe.

Peron was still musing on that when the roar of the crowd, separated from the contestants by a substantial barricade of rows of armed guards, brought him to full attention. The first winner, in twenty-fifth place, had just been announced. It was a girl, Rosanne. Peron remembered her from the Long Walk across Talimantor Desert, when the two of them had formed a temporary alliance to search for underground water. She was a cheerful tireless girl, just over the minimum age limit of sixteen, and now she was holding her hand to her chest, pretending to stagger and faint with relief because she had just made the cutoff.

All the other contestants now looked at the board with a new intensity. The method of announcement was well established by custom, but there was not a trial participant who did not wish it could be done differently. From the crowd's point of view, it was very satisfying to announce the winners in ascending order, so that the name of the final top contestant was given last of all. But during the trials, every competitor formed a rough idea of his or her chances by direct comparison with the opposition. it was easy to be wrong by five places, but errors larger than that were unlikely. Deep inside, a competitor knew if he was down in ninetieth place. Even so, hope always remained. But as the names gradually were announced, and twenty-fourth, twenty-third, and twenty-second position was taken, most contestants were filled with an increasing gloom, panic, or wild surmise. Could they possibly have placed so high? Or, more likely, were they already eliminated?

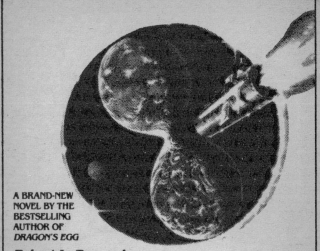

A BRAND-NEW
NOVEL BY THE
BESTSELLING
AUTHOR OF
DRAGON'S EGG

Robert L. Forward

THE FLIGHT OF THE DRAGONFLY

384 pp. • $3.50

The future is NOW!